T. A. BARRON

W9-ATY-101

Atlantis Rising

PUFFIN BOOKS
An Imprint of Penguin Group (USA)

The MAGICAL LAND of
Ellegandia
LAND of LOST DREAMS,
HOME of CREATURES MOST BIZARRE
& PORTAL to the SPIRIT REALM
Sheer cliffs
Beware the Smelldrude
Beware the crocodiles
MYSTERY BAY
Lakes of Dreams
(Strange magic in these waters)
C·o·a·s·t of D·r·a·g·o·n·s
INDRAGRASS MEADOWS
Ancient spirits walk these hills
Vale of Surprises
ATLANTIC OCEAN
E·U·R·O·P·E
Ellegandia
A·F·R·I·C·A

CITY of GREAT POWERS
(Excellent pastries found here)
Deadly Rapids
Bridge to Nowhere
Wind Horses?
Divine Monk's Temple
Rumors tell of Secret Entrance to Ekh Raku Dungeon
THE GREAT FOREST
Faerie Glens
DEG BOESI RIVER
Waterfall of the Giants
Pathways of Mystery
Moss Island (Home of Mist Maidens)
Woods of Endless Wonders
SWAMP
Highmage Hill
Hidden Cavern of Shirazzz
Enchanted Baobab Grove
Passage of Death
Ell Shango
Lakes of the Stars
Grukarr's Lair
HIGH PEAKS
UNKHMEINI
(Here light and dark are one)
The fabled nest of Erolien
PLAINS of ABUYA
Wyverns Lairs
TAB ~ 2012

To Larkin,

Whose spirit glows like a starstone

PUFFIN BOOKS
Published by the Penguin Group
Penguin Group (USA) LLC
375 Hudson Street
New York, New York 10014

USA * Canada * UK * Ireland * Australia
New Zealand * India * South Africa * China

penguin.com
A Penguin Random House Company

First published in the United States of America by Philomel Books,
an imprint of Penguin Young Readers Group, 2013
Published by Puffin Books, an imprint of Penguin Young Readers Group, 2014

Text copyright © 2013 by Thomas A. Barron
Map illustration copyright © 2013 by Thomas A. Barron

Penguin supports copyright. Copyright fuels creativity, encourages diverse voices, promotes free speech, and creates a vibrant culture. Thank you for buying an authorized edition of this book and for complying with copyright laws by not reproducing, scanning, or distributing any part of it in any form without permission. You are supporting writers and allowing Penguin to continue to publish books for every reader.

THE LIBRARY OF CONGRESS HAS CATALOGED THE PHILOMEL BOOKS EDITION AS FOLLOWS:
Barron, T. A. Atlantis rising / T. A. Barron. pages cm
Summary: The young thief Promi and the forest girl Atlanta battle
evil and in the process bring about the creation of Atlantis.
ISBN 978-0-399-25757-5 (hardcover)
[1. Fantasy. 2. Atlantis (Legendary place)—Fiction.] I. Title.
PZ7.B27567At 2013 [Fic]—dc23 2012044037

Puffin Books ISBN 978-0-14-751221-5

Printed in the United States of America

1 3 5 7 9 10 8 6 4 2

Contents

First of All . . . A Confession

Atlantis—a name, a place, and a mystery, all in one. Like you, I've always wondered about this mythic isle . . . and dreamed of boarding a magical sailboat to go there, explore its secrets, and discover what was lost for all time. The mysteries of Atlantis have called to many people over the centuries—ranging from Plato to Isaac Newton, J. R. R. Tolkien to Doris Lessing, Leo Tolstoy to Jules Verne. Distinguished company, for sure, but on this boat there is room for all of us.

Ever since Plato first described the horrendous cataclysm that destroyed the island in "a terrible day and night of destruction," this place has inspired countless stories, poems, songs, and musings. Take, for example, the words of Arthur C. Clarke, who said that Atlantis "will always be an ideal—a dream of perfection—a goal to inspire men for all ages to come."

Yet despite everything that's been written about Atlantis, we know very little. Why? Because those stories always focus on the island's violent end. Its destruction. Its disappearance from the known world.

But what about its *birth*? How was this magical place actually created? What people helped it happen—or tried desperately to stop it? What was it like originally, in its earliest days, before it became a celebrated legend? What secret forces gave Atlantis such remarkable—maybe even miraculous—power?

For years, I confess, these questions have gnawed at me, in

thoughts by day and dreams by night. The time has come to do something about that.

So come with me, then, as we sail away to Atlantis. We will explore the creation of a place—and a legend. And we will witness the birth of this wondrous isle. When that moment arrives, it will be a time of great triumph . . . although it will also hold the seeds of equally great tragedy to come.

On the way, we'll find a few surprises. As well as the dangerous mixture of magic, greed, passion, hope, and faith that caused the island to be born . . . and ultimately, to die.

Strange as it may seem, the story begins with a certain young vagabond—a knife thrower who almost never missed his target.

Almost.

T. A. B.

CHAPTER 1

A Distant Melody

That morning, you had no idea of all the momentous changes to come. Very soon, you learned. And then you traded your life and everything you ever loved for that little bit of magic—a truly terrible price.

And I am to blame for it.

—An entry in her journal

The only thing still with him from childhood was not a thing at all.

It wasn't a knife, a bracelet, or a stitch of clothing. All Promi had from those days, the only thing that had survived his years on the streets of the holy City, was the barest hint of a song.

Promi leaned back against the mud-brick wall, just off the crowded street, his whole body hidden by shadow. Ignoring the mad bustle of people, wooden carts, and goatherds on the cobblestones, he tried to listen—not with his ears, but with some inner sense that reached back to the time before memory. At first, he heard only silence, a hard, cold silence that surrounded him as completely as a block of ice.

Then came a lone, quivering note . . . followed by another. And another. And another.

He felt warmer, freer, with every note. They swelled inside him, filling him with a distant, haunting melody. He grinned, feeling renewed.

Gone! The small scrap of song vanished. But it left him, as always, with a sense that he'd first heard it long ago. And with a vague, lingering feeling of comfort that he couldn't begin to describe.

Did the song also come with the hazy memory of a mother's embrace? Her warm touch on his cheek? He shook his head, unsure, swishing his long black hair against his shoulders.

"Clear out! Move aside, all of you!"

The command from a temple guard rang in the street. People and goats scurried to get out of the way, as did a pair of geese who had only just landed on the cobblestones. Villagers poured into alleyways or pressed themselves against mud-brick walls—anything to avoid the approaching troop of guards.

Despite all the commotion, Promi merely raised his head. Casually, he surveyed the troop of six temple guards, all of whom wore perilous curved swords and fearsome expressions. But his gaze moved right past the guards to the priest who walked behind them.

Wearing a gold-embroidered shirt and billowy pants made of the finest white silk, the priest strode purposefully, almost regally. Upon his head sat a white turban, long a sign of authority in this country. His brown eyes scanned the villagers with obvious disdain. With one hand resting on his jeweled belt buckle and the other fingering his necklace of golden beads, he looked even more imperious than his guards.

Grukarr, thought Promi. *The Deputy High Priest himself. Time we met, don't you agree?*

Without taking his eyes off the priest, Promi shifted, planting his feet in an experienced knife-thrower's stance. Still hidden by shadow, he lowered his left hand and drew his dagger from its sheath. He willed his heartbeat to slow down, as he'd done so many times before. Every part of his body felt under control, like a perfectly synchronized clock.

Except for one. The skin on his chest started to prickle, growing hotter by the second. That happened only on his toughest days as a thief—when he felt sure his own life was on the line. In other words, when he was afraid.

And why, after hundreds of perfect throws of his knife—and as many successful thefts—should he feel afraid right now? *Maybe,* he answered himself, *it has something to do with Grukarr's love of cutting off people's hands or tongues—or gouging out their eyes as he did last week to that young boy Galmy.*

He ground his teeth, recalling poor Galmy's crime—forgetting to bow his head when Grukarr and his superior, the High Priestess Araggna, had walked by. It was the boy's horrid screams, echoing across the market square, that had made Promi decide to do something rash to teach Grukarr some manners.

Without getting caught, Promi thought anxiously.

While his whole chest felt hot, one place in particular burned like fire coals: the strange black mark over his heart. He'd often wondered what had caused it—and why it looked so much like a bird in flight. Just as he'd often wondered about other things . . . such as who his parents were. How he'd come to the City ten years ago at the age of four or five. And so much more.

But alas . . . the only clue he had to all those mysteries was the half-remembered song.

Stop thinking, you bone-brained bag of blather, he told himself sternly. *Focus!*

He waited, twisting his boots on the stones, as the troop of guards came closer. Grukarr, who was a full head taller than the guards even without his turban, scowled continually. Yet Promi wasn't watching his face. All the young man's attention went to the priest's jeweled belt buckle, its sapphires flashing bluer than summer sky.

Carefully, Promi raised the dagger. Ignoring the burning of the mark on his chest, he drew a slow breath. He watched as the entourage came closer, step by step.

This plan will work, he assured himself. *All I need to do is hit that buckle!*

Grukarr wouldn't be hurt—not in body, at least. But his sense of security would be shattered. The priest and his guards would erupt in panic, sure this was an attempted murder. Grukarr would finally feel some of the fear he'd brought to the people of the City, making him search for assassins day and night. And so, in the end, Promi would lose a knife. But Grukarr would lose his feeling of safety, his confidence, and his ability to sleep through the night—and never get them back.

Promi swallowed. *At least . . . that's the plan.*

Gripping the dagger, he cocked his arm. Pausing just long enough for the priest to come one step closer, he threw.

Just as Promi released the dagger, an alley cat raced past, brushing against his leg. He flinched, twisted ever so slightly—and the blade flew wide. Instead of hitting the jeweled buckle, it struck a burly guard's breastplate and fell onto the stones.

"Attack!" roared the guard.

Another pointed at Promi's shadowed form against the wall. "There he is!"

"Get him, you fools!" shouted Grukarr, his normally pallid face now red with rage. "Don't let him escape!"

Promi darted away from the wall, barely dodged one guard's

slashing sword, then rolled behind an abandoned cart to avoid a hurled spear. When all six guards rushed the cart, he did what they least expected: He grabbed the spear, leaped onto the cart, and used the spear as a pole to vault over all their heads.

He landed in the middle of the street—face-to-face with Grukarr. The enraged priest waved his arms and roared at his guards, "Get him, I command you!"

The guards spun around and converged on Promi. Curved swords raised, they charged the young vagabond who had dared attack their master. Their shared goal was clear—to slice Promi to pieces as swiftly and brutally as possible, so that Grukarr's anger wouldn't be turned against them.

Promi, however, had a goal of his own. While his first plan had failed, he still longed to humiliate Grukarr. He glanced over his shoulder at the oncoming guards, then locked gazes with the priest.

"Greetings to you, great lord," he said mockingly.

Quickly, Promi plucked his dagger off the cobblestone street. In a flash of rapid movements, he thrust the blade at Grukarr—and sliced cleanly through the priest's belt. Grukarr's precious buckle flew aside, clattering on the stones.

Promi rolled away just as two curved swords sliced through the air where he'd stood a split second before. Though he dropped his knife in that maneuver, he deftly grabbed the belt buckle. Pausing just long enough to grin at Grukarr, he dashed down the street.

"Wuhhh—why you . . . blubbaroarrr!" was all the priest could say.

Grukarr's face contorted with rage. Finally regaining his words, he screamed at the guards, "Get him, you idiots! And kill him! Or I'll skin the lot of you alive!"

The guards ran off, pounding after Promi.

Still seething, Grukarr watched the young thief turn down an alley and disappear, hotly pursued by the guards. "Whoever you are," he growled, "you will pay dearly for this crime."

He rose to his full height and placed his hands on his hips. "No one dares show such insolence to the mighty Grukarr. No one!"

Only then did he realize that, without his belt, his pants had fallen down.

CHAPTER 2

Flight from Danger

Running came so easily to you. But seeking? Not at all.

—Another entry in her journal

Down the alley dashed Promi, followed by all six vengeful guards. The young man veered onto a side street, vaulted over a wide gutter full of excrement and food scraps, and darted down another alley.

Right behind him came the guards, their boots pounding on the cobblestones. Desire for revenge twisted their faces. This was about more than just catching a street vagabond, a petty thief who'd stolen their master's jeweled belt buckle. No, it was also about saving their own skins. For if they didn't return with the young man's head, Grukarr would make certain they'd lose their own.

Promi's boots, by contrast, didn't pound.

Virtually silent, the light boots barely seemed to touch the stones before pushing off again. And that was the least of their special qualities. These boots were made from magical leather, with the power to grow as Promi's feet grew. They had fit him snugly ever since the day he'd stolen them five years earlier from the Divine Monk's traveling wardrobe. And in those years, they'd helped him outrun many pursuers and scale many of the City's mud-brick walls and tile roofs.

But his pursuers had rarely been as numerous—or as motivated—as these guards. He glanced back over his shoulder. The guard whose breastplate had deflected the knife was only ten paces behind, curved sword raised. And gaining.

Even so, Promi couldn't resist taunting him. "Come get me, you mush-minded moron! Or are you as slow as you are stupid?"

The guard charged all the faster, seething with rage.

Promi dashed down a narrow street lined with dozens of houses. Laundry lines stretched from one doorway to another, often obstructing the street. He leaped over several ropes, ducked under others, and kept running.

The guards weren't so careful. They merely plowed right through, bursting laundry lines and scattering fresh-washed clothing everywhere. One guard's legs got tangled, and he fell, skidding into the mud-brick wall. But the others ran on unimpeded.

Pounding boots echoed in the street. The first guard was now close—so close his sword could almost slash Promi's legs. And the rest of the guards weren't far behind.

How do I lose them? thought Promi desperately. Beneath his tunic, the strange mark in the shape of a bird was burning hotter than ever.

He burst out of the street—and into the City's central market square. People and carts crowded everywhere: fruit vendors setting up their stands, craftsmen displaying handwoven rugs and carved jewelry, and people offering to paint ancient designs on faces and hands. Monks wandered through the crowd, trying to sell strings of silver leaves that had been inscribed with prayers, to sing sacred chants, or to pound on their blessing drums—all to raise money to repair shrines and temple bells. Blacksmiths hammered, forging tools. A circle of women danced to the music of a bone flute. People led camels and herded animals as diverse as goats, boars, ducks, and pink flamingos.

Thinking fast, Promi rolled under one cart full of orange squashes, then zipped ahead of a woman leading a camel to a saddle maker, trying to put some space between himself and his pursuers. At first, it worked. But the lead guard thought equally fast.

Roughly, the guard grabbed the camel's reins. "Give me your beast!" he commanded. "In the name of Deputy High Priest Grukarr."

The woman, surprised and fearful, released the reins. Immediately, the guard mounted the camel and charged after Promi, knocking people and carts aside.

Seeing this, Promi knew he was in more danger than ever. He gazed around the market, searching for some way to escape. But what could that be? The camel seemed unstoppable.

If only I still had my knife, he thought. *Then maybe I could—*

He halted abruptly, seeing a knife on a blacksmith's bench. Promi lunged for it, planted his feet, took quick aim—then threw the blade.

Snap! The knife pierced the camel's reins, yanking them out of the guard's hands. The frightened animal reared back, kicking her legs.

Thrown off balance, the guard toppled off the camel's back. He landed right in a pen full of ducks. The birds panicked and flapped wildly, scattering feathers everywhere. The commotion scared a large herd of goats, who ran wild, stampeding through the market.

Promi chuckled, watching the guard try to keep himself from being pecked to death by angry ducks. But that moment of triumph didn't last long. The other four guards were pushing through the crowd, waving their swords. In a few seconds, they would be on top of him.

He dashed off—but suddenly stopped when a small girl, her orange hair tied in two braids, screamed just a few paces away. Several goats were running straight at her, about to trample her under their hooves.

Promi swerved, ran to the girl, and snatched her out of the path of the goats—just as the herd stampeded past. He didn't pause to say anything, but their eyes met, and she looked at him thankfully. He placed her gently on the rim of a cart loaded with carrots the same color as her hair.

Off he ran, hotly pursued by the remaining guards. They chased him across the market square, knocking over people and crashing into carts. One guard tripped and fell into a table of magical fruits from the Great Forest, shaking a crate of singing pears so hard the pears started wailing loudly.

Promi leaped over lines of prayer leaves, hurdled barrels of country ale, and dived under another camel. Still the guards kept up the chase.

Spying a wooden cage filled with color-shifting pigeons, Promi veered, grabbed it, and hurled it straight at the closest guard. The cage smashed at the guard's feet, sending up a furious cloud of scarlet, blue, and yellow wings. Meanwhile, the pigeons' owner, an elderly woman, started angrily beating the guard with her cane.

Promi ran off, but three guards still pursued him. More wrathful than ever, they hurled spears as well as curses. If they ever caught him, he knew, his remaining seconds alive would be very brief. And very painful.

Turning into an alley at the edge of the square, Promi sprinted down the cobblestones. Then stopped. The alley was blocked! A massive load of mud bricks lay just ahead. It was twice his height—and so unstable it looked ready to fall over at any moment.

Sizing up the precarious pile, he hesitated. If he tried to climb over it, the tottering mass could easily come crashing down on top of him.

All at once, his three pursuers came pounding down the alley. Seeing their prey trapped at last, they stopped. Eyes bright with victory, the trio formed a line to seal off the alley, eliminating any chance for escape. As one, they held out their swords and marched toward Promi, pressing him back against the pile of bricks.

Just as the swords came almost within reach, Promi did something wholly unexpected. He turned and started scrambling up the unstable pile. Aided by his supple boots, he climbed higher than the guards' heads before the pile started to tumble down. Just then, with a powerful leap, he jumped over his pursuers.

In the instant he flew over their heads, Promi spied a big gold earring on one of the guards. Never one to miss the chance to pinch something valuable, he deftly grabbed it and pulled it off the surprised guard's ear. Even as Promi landed, he put the gold ring on his own ear.

The guards spun around. More enraged than ever, they glowered at Promi with unbridled hatred. Unfortunately for them, in turning their backs on the pile of mud bricks, they didn't see it fall. Two of the guards were completely crushed, while the third barely escaped by rolling aside.

That lone remaining guard instantly bounced to his feet. Sword firmly in hand, he roared and lunged for Promi. The young man dodged the blade. Then, rather than go back into the marketplace where he might run right into the other guards, Promi chose a different escape route—one he hoped would leave this foe behind.

He grabbed an awning, then swung himself up to the alley wall. Swiftly, he climbed the wall to a roof covered with red tiles, each of which bore the design of a gold turban with a large ruby on it—the symbol of the Divine Monk. All at once, he realized that this roof was connected to the Divine Monk's temple, a mass of buildings, archways, and domes that culminated in an enormous bell tower.

Safe at last, he thought with relief. *Nobody can follow me up here.* He fingered his new gold earring. *And I managed to give Grukarr and his guards a very bad day.*

Suddenly the remaining guard's head appeared above the roofline. With surprising agility, he pulled himself onto the roof, not two paces away from Promi. The guard's eyes sizzled with desire for revenge.

Promi turned and dashed. He sprinted across the tiled rooftops of the temple, leaping over the gaps between buildings. But the guard kept up with him, swinging the deadly sword. None of Promi's maneuvers could shake this pursuer.

Deciding to try something bold, Promi ran to the very edge of one building and took a mighty leap—all the way to the bell tower. He landed, barely clinging to the tower's gutter. Then, aided by his special boots, he started to scale the vertical structure. At last, he managed to pull himself up to the base of the copper dome that shielded the bell itself. A pair of frightened doves flew away, shrieking.

The highest point in the City, he thought, amazed to find himself above everything he'd known all his years on the streets. *Probably the highest place I'll ever see.*

He scanned the remarkable vista. Below him sprawled the temple buildings and, beyond them, the entire City of Great Powers. Just outside the temple gates, people were gathering to celebrate the annual holiday feast of Ho Kranahrum—one of Promi's favorite events, since it offered plenty of food that was both tasty and easy to steal. There was even a special holiday pastry made with honeyed filo dough and almonds, so good that he always grabbed several.

He could also see, at the City's southern edge, the deep canyon of the Deg Boesi River, filled with mist rising from the rapids far below. And there—the dilapidated bridge that reached only halfway across the canyon, with silver prayer leaves strung from every post and plank. Even from so far away, he could see the prayer leaves flapping in the wind. Farther away, beyond the canyon, he could make out the dark line of green that had to be the edge of the legendary Great Forest.

Slam! The whole tower shook as the determined guard leaped onto it. Just as Promi had done, he scaled the wall with help from the gutter.

A bolt of fear shot through Promi. The guard would reach him in seconds. And from the top of this tower, there was no way to escape.

Except one.

Promi knew what he needed to do, though he'd never tried anything like it before. But now, with the guard fast approaching, there was no alternative.

Grabbing hold of the base of the copper dome, Promi planted his feet against the bell itself, a huge iron instrument whose loud bongs had called people to prayers for centuries. He pushed off, vaulting himself onto the dome.

The force of his push tilted the bell just enough that its clapper struck the side. A single, resonant *bonnnggg* rang out, echoing across the City.

Far below, people gathering for the holiday feast looked up. Gasps of astonishment came when they saw, against all odds, the figure of a young man climbing to the top of the bell tower, somehow clinging to the dome. Another round of gasps soon followed, for now the villagers could see an armed guard climbing right behind. The whole crowd hushed.

Teetering unsteadily, Promi stood at the very top of the dome. The only thing higher than himself was the pole with the temple flag—and beyond that, nothing but sky.

The guard, almost within reach, grinned up at him

malevolently. "You shan't escape now, you mis'rable thief." He cackled with satisfaction. "No way down from here, 'cept through my sword."

Promi looked down at him. "Wrong."

He reached for the temple flag, a deep green sheet of silk with dozens of golden stars on it, one for each Divine Monk who had led Ellegandia since the country's founding thousands of years before. Grabbing hold of the flag, he tugged hard, ripping it off the pole.

The guard, meanwhile, clambered up to face him. Sword raised, he swung with all his might at Promi's chest—but struck nothing but air.

Promi had leaped off the dome. The guard's jaw dropped. Like the people far below, he watched as the young man plunged to his death.

CHAPTER 3

Definitely Not Virtuous

The mark of a good pastry chef is that he can change his recipe on a sudden whim—and still make something edible.

—From Promi's journal

Wind rushed past Promi, shrieking in his ears, as he hurtled downward. The crowd below, like the astonished guard on the bell tower, gaped to see him plummeting to a gruesome death.

With all his strength, Promi spread his arms wide. Just before leaping off the copper dome, he'd grabbed two corners of the silk flag with his hands and stuffed a third corner into his mouth.

Hope this works . . . or I'm deader than donkey dung.

Whoosh! The flag suddenly filled with air, slowing his fall.

Seeing this, the crowd outside the temple gates gasped in unison. Then, as the parachute carried Promi safely down, several people cheered. Up on the bell tower, though, the temple guard could only swear angrily. Even in this land where cursing was a longstanding tradition, there weren't enough curses to convey the fullness of his rage.

Promi floated down to the City, drifting toward a maze of side streets near the river canyon. Still grasping the flag tightly with both hands and teeth, he thought proudly, *Not bad for a miserable thief.*

Spotting a wide intersection below, he tugged on one side of the flag to steer himself there. Down he floated into the jumble of mud-brick buildings. Below, the street was empty, a good place to land.

Just then he caught one of his favorite smells—the sweet aroma of pastries coming out of the oven. *Mmmmm . . . honey glaze. Roasted almonds. And maybe fresh raspberry syrup.*

Distracted by the whiff of sweetness, he drifted too close to the side of one building. Suddenly the flag caught on the spout of a gutter. *Rrrrippp!* The silk tore apart.

Promi plunged straight down. Luckily, he tumbled onto an awning, then rolled off before it snapped under his weight. Thanks to his boots that always seemed to help put his feet in the right place, he landed with a thud in the middle of the street.

Tossing aside the torn flag, Promi drew a satisfied breath. "Not too graceful," he muttered. "But still, on the whole . . . miraculous."

He grinned, stroking his newly acquired gold earring. Quite pleased with himself, he felt the bulge of Grukarr's belt buckle in his tunic pocket, right next to his journal. "The only thing I could have done better was to—"

Strong arms grabbed his shoulders from behind. "Got you!" boomed an angry voice. "You rascally thief!"

No, thought Promi, his heart pounding. *Not that guard again.*

Roughly, the arms spun him around. He found himself facing a wrathful man—not the temple guard but a burly baker. The fellow's apron, covering his ample belly, was splotched with fruit stains, flecks of dough, and sprinklings of flour.

Scowling at Promi, the baker growled, "You're the rascal who stole a whole tray o' my best huckleberry tarts last week. Aren't you?"

"Well, I guess so." Promi smacked his lips at the memory. "They were awfully good, I promise you. A fine recipe."

"I don't care a cursed clump o' crab claws what you think o' my recipe!" Keeping his hands firmly on Promi's shoulders, the baker nodded toward his pastry shop beneath the awning. "You robbed me!"

"I did. And . . . I'm sorry."

"Don't you have an honest trade, rascal?"

Promi nodded. "Yes."

The baker peered at him. "What is it?"

"I'm a thief."

The baker shook him hard. "That's no trade!" Glowering, he demanded, "An' now you dare to come back to steal somethin' more?"

"No, no, that's not why I'm here."

Skeptically, the baker waited to hear an explanation.

Promi felt sure the truth—that he'd been escaping from another, much more brazen theft—wouldn't improve the baker's mood. So he declared, "I came back . . . um, well, to pay you for those tarts."

The baker scowled even more fiercely. Squeezing Promi with his powerful hands, he snarled, "I'll show you how to pay."

Grabbing hold of the young man's neck with one hand, he clenched the other into a massive fist. "I'll pound you like a lump o' dough. That'll teach you not to steal from me!"

He drew back to slam Promi's jaw. Hard as he tried, Promi couldn't wriggle free. Beneath his tunic, the mysterious mark burned hot.

"Wait!"

A young girl rushed out from the pastry shop. Though her hair was sprinkled with white flour, there could be no mistaking the carrot color of her twin braids. "Papa, wait!"

"Back inside, child," the baker commanded, without turning from the young rascal he intended to strike. "I got some punishin' to do here."

Undeterred, his daughter clamped her arms around his apron. So wide was her father's body that she could only reach a small way around his waist. But she squeezed hard and begged, "Don't hurt him, Papa."

"An' why not? He's a thief, bad as a rotten egg."

"Because," she explained breathlessly, "he's the one who saved my life!"

The baker caught his breath. "From them tramplin' goats? In the market?"

"Yes, Papa."

Turning to her with disbelief, he asked, "Are you sure, child?"

"Totally sure." She nodded, making her braids bounce up and down. "He's the one! Snatched me out o' harm's way, jest in time."

The baker sighed, then released Promi. "Lucky for you, thief."

Rubbing his sore neck, Promi nodded. He looked down at the girl, and their eyes met for the second time that day. "Right you are," he agreed. "Lucky for me."

The girl giggled, blushing beneath the flour on her cheeks. "My name is Shangri."

"Thank you, Shangri. My name's Promi."

Raising his gaze to the baker, Promi said, "I promise you this. I'll never steal from your pastry shop again."

For a long moment, the baker scrutinized him. Though still

scowling, he said, "Fer all your mischief, lad . . . I'm guessin' you really are a virtuous sort."

"Me?" sputtered Promi, surprised. "No, no. I'm definitely *not* virtuous."

"You love pastries, don't you?" asked the baker, a new twinkle in his eye. "There's virtue in that."

"I surely do," Promi replied, licking his lips. "The sweeter the better."

Shangri giggled again. "Then maybe you should go to the spirit world up in the clouds. They say it's full o' sweet things everywhere, in sugary streams an' honey trees an'—"

"Quiet, child." The baker's severe tone cut her off. "You know that travel between the worlds is strictly forbidden! Even talkin' about it can get you punished by them angry priests, Araggna an' Grukarr."

"But Papa—"

"Hush, I said."

The baker scowled down at her. Now, young as she was, Shangri might have felt only her father's reprimand. But Promi could see the fellow's real concern for her safety. And he was sure the baker's vehemence sprang from love rather than any religious dogma. Despite how they'd met moments before, Promi decided he genuinely liked this burly, flour-covered fellow.

Shangri nodded to her father. "All right, Papa."

He tousled her hair, sending up a puff of flour. "Good girl."

She turned and ran into the pastry shop. Barely five seconds later, she ran back out again, this time holding a steaming hot cinnamon bun. With a smile that revealed several missing teeth, she offered it to Promi.

The smell of cinnamon tickled his nostrils as he took the pastry. "Why, thanks, Shangri."

"You're welcome."

Promi started to take a big bite of the cinnamon bun, but then stopped abruptly. Lowering it, he looked questioningly at the baker. "Is this . . . um, all right with you?"

The baker grinned. "It's all right, lad. You've earned that pastry."

Promi took his first bite, savoring the sweetness as he chewed. He swallowed, then said, "Still, I want to pay you for this one."

"Not necessary." The baker patted his belly. "'Tis payment enough to see how much you're enjoyin' it."

Promi shook his head. "No, I insist. Let me pay you as you deserve."

The baker shrugged. "All right, lad, seein' as you're insistin'."

Casually, Promi reached into his tunic pocket and pulled out the jeweled belt buckle. He tossed it to the baker, who stared at it in utter astonishment.

"That should cover the cinnamon bun," said Promi dryly. "As well as those huckleberry tarts."

The stunned baker peered at him. "But, lad—"

Promi held up his hand. "No haggling for a higher price, now," he said with a grin. Then, more seriously, he added, "But I'd suggest, if you ever need money, don't try to sell the whole buckle. Too easily recognized. Just sell those sapphires one at a time."

The baker pinched his lips. "You stole this?"

"Not from anyone who deserves to own it." Promi gave him a wink. "Now it's where it really belongs."

Taking another bite of the cinnamon bun, Promi spun around and walked down the cobblestone street. Seconds later, he turned a corner and disappeared.

In front of the pastry shop, Shangri peered at the glittering object in her father's hand. She'd never seen anything like it before. "Papa," she asked, "does that really pay for the cinnamon bun?"

"Aye," he whispered. "It does."

CHAPTER 4

Spicy Sausage

My favorite meals are freshly made, freshly spiced . . . and freshly stolen.

—From Promi's journal

Promi stole through the twisting, narrow streets, always keeping in the shadows. That was, by now, a habit: The fewer people who saw him, the better. Why make his life as a thief any tougher than it already was?

Besides, he now had a new acquaintance named Grukarr to watch out for. Not to mention some very angry temple guards . . . if, that is, the priest had allowed them to live.

No need to worry about Grukarr, he assured himself, passing a flower bed that overflowed with blue lilies. He paused a moment to savor their sweet smell, then moved on. *He's probably still trying to put his pants back on.*

Yet even as he thought that, he knew it wasn't true. He'd humiliated the priest, that was certain. And Grukarr wouldn't spare any effort to respond. The man was deeply

vengeful, jealous of his power, and extremely cruel—someone who enjoyed inflicting harsh punishments on commoners.

Especially a commoner who had dared to make him look like a fool in public.

Slipping around a corner into an alley, Promi couldn't resist a grin. Already, he felt sure, stories must be circulating about the brave young vagabond who'd stolen Grukarr's belt—and, in the process, his dignity. Just as there would be stories about the mysterious person (surely someone different from the vagabond) who had brazenly leaped off the top of the bell tower to escape a temple guard and then floated unharmed back down to the City.

He tapped the golden earring, his new prize. All in all, it had been a good day. *And now,* he told himself confidently, *it's about to get even better.*

For today, the feast holiday of Ho Kranahrum, he was going to attempt his most difficult—and most satisfying—job ever. Something he'd been planning for a full year. It wouldn't happen out on the street, but deep inside the Divine Monk's temple. Yes, right before the eyes of the Divine Monk himself, as well as his chief adviser, High Priestess Araggna. And maybe also her deputy—a certain priest by the name of Grukarr.

Running his hand over his empty sheath, Promi reminded himself, *First, though, I'll need a knife.*

He turned left, wending his way to the market square. As soon as he arrived, he almost bumped into a man selling snakes. The man wore them coiled around his arms, ankles—and even his head, wearing a cobra like a living turban. Promi could tell right away that the chaos he'd caused by his mad dash through the market had been replaced by the usual bustle of tradesmen, vendors, and common folks. Even the stampeding goats now stood calmly inside a makeshift pen. Only the splintered remains of a smashed cage sprinkled with brightly colored feathers showed any sign of what had happened earlier. That, and a faint humming that came from a table of magical fruit.

A moment later, he spotted a woodworker whose specialty was carving bowls, mugs, and the handles of knives. With practiced ease, Promi plucked a simple knife off the carver's bench, leaving several more valuable blades behind. Quietly, the young man blended back into the crowd.

This knife, he thought as he tapped his sheath, *will be used for a good cause.* He nodded. *A very good cause.*

Promi slipped out of the market square and turned down a small street, passing a stable of horses so silently that they didn't even bother to turn their heads in his direction. A moment later, he came to the area outside the temple gates. Hundreds of people thronged this place—the same people who had, not long before, witnessed his daring leap from the bell tower.

He glanced up at the copper dome glittering in the sun. That had been a good escape, one of his best. But the one he was planning for later today would be even better. *Assuming,* he reminded himself, *I don't get caught.*

As lightly as a breath of wind, he drifted into the crowd. Eager to celebrate Ho Kranahrum on the temple's main courtyard, many of these people had started gathering the night before. In their arms, slings, and wagons, they carried prayer leaves inscribed with the names of loved ones, blankets, and flasks of fresh water and home-brewed ale. As well as hundreds of sacks and baskets bulging with food. For this particular holiday offered more than a reason to pray: It was a good excuse to eat like hungry goats.

Ho Kranahrum was Ellegandia's only religious holiday that was celebrated not just by monks and priestesses in the temple but by virtually everyone, even in the smallest villages far away from the City of Great Powers. Why? Because this holiday was all about giving thanks for Ellegandia's vast bounty of foods provided by nature. And what better way to give thanks than to eat and drink your fill and then eat and drink some more?

As he slid through the crowd, Promi casually reached into someone's basket and took a honeycomb dripping with fresh clover honey. Then, having swallowed that, he grabbed a couple of filo dough pastries. And then a large homemade sausage spiced with cayenne pepper. He took a bite of the sausage, liking how the pepper blazed in his mouth.

Not bad, he thought, taking another bite of the sausage. *But I still prefer sweets.*

Just then, a pair of kindly-looking monks opened the temple gates. Like a river whose dam had burst, the villagers poured into the main courtyard. Paved with wide slabs of green marble, the courtyard offered plenty of space for people to sit down, stretch out their blankets, say prayers of gratitude to the spirits—and, above all, eat.

Chewing thoughtfully, Promi walked across the courtyard and borrowed a flask of cold water from a devoted family who had just bowed their heads in prayer. *That's what they get,* he said to himself, *for not paying attention.*

He crossed into the shaded archway at the far side of the courtyard and paused to study the nearest building. Ornately crafted with gilded beams, turquoise-blue tiles on the walls, at least a dozen balconies, many statues of immortal spirits, and tile mosaics featuring the images of gold turbans, the building could not be mistaken. Here was the Divine Monk's personal residence—the place where, in about two hours, the Divine Monk himself would feast on his own grand meal to celebrate the holiday.

Promi nodded. *He'll have one more guest than he expects.*

Looking over at the faithful people who teemed in the courtyard, praying and chanting and eating and drinking, he shook his head, mystified. Enjoying all their good food he could certainly understand. Just as he could understand their gratitude for

Ellegandia's fabulous bounty of fruits and grains, meats and spices. But worshipping some invisible spirits who supposedly lived somewhere up in the sky or inhabited the Great Forest? That was impossible to comprehend.

He took the last bite of his sausage and chewed slowly. *No, the only things I believe in are solid enough to be touched with my hand. Or,* he added with a pat of his sheath, *stuck with my knife.*

Turning back to the Divine Monk's residence, he scrutinized the façade, especially one particular balcony just below the corner of the roof. Behind it hung a bloodred curtain. That color made him think about what would happen if he made even the slightest mistake.

He rubbed his tunic over the strange mark on his chest, which was starting to prickle with heat. Then, to calm his nerves, he did something he'd done many times before. He reached into the tunic's inner pocket and pulled out a tattered old book—his journal.

Appropriately, the journal had originally been a book of recipes for making desserts. He had taken it from a shelf in a baker's kitchen years before. By now, almost every available margin and blank spot had been filled with his scrawled entries.

He pulled a worn charcoal pencil out of the book's spine and flipped through the pages, looking for a spot for this morning's entry. There! He found one, fittingly enough, at the top of a page with a recipe for cinnamon buns.

Hastily, he jotted some notes about his encounter with Grukarr, the priest's belt and buckle (and the pants they once held up), the rather unusual escape, and the baker's orange-haired daughter. Just as he'd hoped, the simple act of writing served to quiet his jitters. Why, he couldn't explain—just as he couldn't explain how he'd learned to read and write as a child. Perhaps he'd gained those skills from the same person who had sung that half-remembered song so long ago.

None of that mattered now, though. All Promi knew was that something about scribbling in this journal made him feel, well . . . *better.* Almost like it gave him some company—as if he were writing to a long-lost friend whose face he couldn't recall.

Truth was, the journal *itself* had become a friend. More than his threadbare clothing or even his perfectly fitting boots, this old recipe book felt like a faithful companion he'd never want to live without. Maybe that was because it held, by now, his most important experiences . . . and most secret thoughts.

Having finished the entry, he closed the journal and slid it back into his pocket. He licked his lips, recalling the sweet taste of those pastries. And licked them again, knowing that, with luck, he'd soon taste something even sweeter.

A theft he'd long contemplated.

He glanced again at the palatial residence, plotting the best route to that corner balcony. Then, in the blink of an eye, he disappeared into the shadows.

CHAPTER 5

The Target

If you were as big as your desire for sweets—then you, Promi, would be bigger than a giant. And if I were as big as my desire to see you again—then I would be bigger than you by far.

—From her journal, on a page so crumpled and torn you'd think she had started to rip it out

---

Soon afterward, hidden behind the bloodred curtain inside the balcony, Promi heard the group approach. Coming with them, he felt sure, would be his target.

A target he was determined not to miss.

A perfect throw, he vowed silently. *I'll have one chance, and only one.*

He drew a deep breath and willed himself to stay calm. Slowly, carefully, he drew his dagger from its sheath and clasped it in his left hand. Meanwhile, he tried to slow the galloping beat of his heart.

A bead of perspiration rolled down his brow, then onto the bridge of his nose, then into his eye. It stung, making him blink. But he didn't dare wipe his eye for fear of disturbing the curtain.

The mark above his heart was feeling warm again. Like a wind-blown fire coal, it grew hotter by the second. Yet he resisted making any movement to touch it.

Hardest of all to resist, though, were the smells. For he was hiding at the back of the Divine Monk's private dining room, where the monk would soon arrive with his entourage to eat the most sumptuous meal of the entire year. In fitting tribute to the holiday of feasting, the dining room table was already laden with mounds of grapes, freshly baked salt bread, tea leaf salad, squash and ginger soup, whipped avocado pastries, and—as of just a few seconds ago—a steaming platter of roast duckling with honeyed cherry sauce. Not to mention several flasks of rich red wine from the faraway vineyards of the Indragrass Meadows.

Promi could see none of this, of course, from behind the curtain. Tempting as it was to look, he refused to risk taking a peek. But he didn't need to see the table to know what it held. For he could smell every morsel of this feast, right down to the last drop of honeyed cherry sauce.

He could also tell, by the absence of a certain aroma, that the dessert hadn't yet arrived. Rumors said that, of all the special preparations that went into the Divine Monk's feast of Ho Kranahrum, of all the rare ingredients his chefs obtained from across Ellegandia, the most effort and skill went into preparing dessert. For this wasn't just any dessert—it was a pie made from a special kind of fruit so sweet that it could be grown, by ancient law, only within the temple's sacred garden.

Smackberries.

So prized were those berries, and so richly sweet their flavor, the temple garden was heavily guarded day and night all year round to prevent thievery. Promi swallowed, recalling the report he'd heard of a monk who had dared to pick a single smackberry.

The poor fellow's punishment, ordered by High Priestess Araggna and carried out by Grukarr, included losing his job . . . as well as his tongue.

Not only were smackberries grown nowhere else, they could be eaten by only one person: the Divine Monk. For the law proclaimed that no other mortal's heart could possibly be pure enough, and so close to the immortal realm, to deserve to taste such divine sweetness.

Clearly, thought Promi, *that rule was invented by a Divine Monk to keep all those berries to himself.*

Suddenly Promi caught a whiff of something warm and bubbling with nectarlike juices within a flaky, buttery crust. And sweet—so intensely sweet he'd never experienced anything like it before.

Smackberry pie.

The aroma tickled Promi's nostrils. He felt strangely lightheaded, almost intoxicated. Unable to resist any longer, he reached up with the tip of his knife and parted the curtain ever so slightly, just in time to see two monks bringing the pie on a mahogany platter. They set it down on the dining table, all the while looking longingly at the steaming hot dessert. After lighting several tall candles arrayed around the table, they promptly left the room.

At that instant, the Divine Monk himself arrived. He entered the doorway first with his belly, which protruded so far out front that his scarlet robe seemed to be covering three people instead of one. Upon his head sat the traditional gold turban, studded with diamonds and an enormous ruby in its center. He walked with a swagger, a stride befitting the supreme leader of Ellegandia, making his flabby chins bounce with every step. From his uppermost chin sprouted a scraggly white beard, decorated with precious jewels that jostled against his belly.

What struck Promi most, though, were the Divine Monk's eyes. He wasn't surprised by what they were—small, beady, and brown—but what they were not. Everyone in this country knew that green eyes signified natural magic, whether the ability to communicate with animals in the market or the power to hear the distant whispers of immortals on the wind. Green eyes were rare; most people, like Promi, had brown. Even so, while he already knew that no one in the Divine Monk's entourage had green eyes, he'd expected to find that the leader of the country's religion as well as its government would be different. But no, this portly fellow had not even a fleck of green in his pupils.

Right behind the Divine Monk came three old monks, so thin they didn't have any trouble walking side by side through the door. All of them wore identical tan robes that fell to their leather sandals. Yet each sported a different color sash—bone white, copper, and ebony—to represent the wide range of skin colors of Ellegandia's people.

The monk on the left carried an ancient drum whose skin was covered with sacred symbols designed to spread blessings every time it was struck. Beating the blessing drum with a silver mallet, the monk marched slowly into the room. By his side, the monk in the center held a flag (much smaller than the one Promi had used to escape from the bell tower). Embroidered with gold thread, the flag showed an eternally blooming golden flower, the symbol of Ellegandia. And the monk on the right carried a pole with a brass incense shaker. He shook it vigorously as he walked, releasing thick clouds of pungent incense.

But no amount of that incense could diminish the sweet smell of the pie. The smackberries' aroma continued to fill the room, making Promi salivate. Gazing longingly at the pie, he watched a thin stream of purple juice bubble over the edge of its sugary crust and roll down to the platter.

The Divine Monk's sense of smell was not as keen, though. He turned and barked at the incense bearer, "Stop shaking that wretched thing, will you? It hides the smell, my favorite in the whole mortal realm."

The incense bearer froze, and his face turned as white as his robe. For several seconds, no one spoke; the only sound in the room was the continued beating of the blessing drum. Finally mustering the courage to reply, the monk said, "But, Holy Wondrous Eternally Blessed Master . . . it is traditional to bring incense to the feast of Ho—"

"I said *stop*!" The Divine Monk bellowed so loud the dining table shook, rattling the silver plates, cups, spoons, and knives arrayed there.

Then he scowled angrily at the monk beating the drum. "You stop, too!" he snapped. "That incessant pounding of yours is giving me a headache."

The monks exchanged fearful glances. Then, in unison, they declared, "Whatever you command, He Who Has Been Kissed by the Wisdom of Immortal Spirits."

"The correct response," declared a thin, raspy voice at the doorway.

Recognizing that voice, Promi stiffened behind the curtain. For he knew that it belonged to High Priestess Araggna. Under his tunic, the skin on Promi's chest felt a new burst of heat.

The ancient, white-haired priestess entered the room. Wearing a dark brown robe, she shambled slowly, more like a walking corpse than a powerful figure in Ellegandia's government. Her skin was as pale as a sun-bleached prayer flag, her bony hands as brittle as pottery. Only her coal-black eyes, which gleamed with ruthless intelligence, seemed fully alive.

As always, she wore a most unusual bracelet—a deadly snake wrapped around her right forearm. An orange-striped boa constrictor, it slithered closer to her elbow as she passed through the doorway. The mere sight of the priestess's snake caused people to tremble with fright, for she often used it as a means of torture, commanding it to squeeze people's necks or crawl inside their clothes. It was said that if Araggna's snake hissed at you, then death would befall you that very day.

With a sharp look at the incense bearer, Araggna rasped, "Whatever the Divine Monk desires, that is your command. Never question him again!"

The old fellow shuddered with fear, trying his best not to shake loose any more incense.

The Divine Monk, by contrast, beamed, which made his multiple chins curl upward in unison. "Thank you, High Priestess. That was most helpful."

She bowed her head. "Anything to serve you, my master."

The Divine Monk rubbed his chubby hands together. "Oh, I do so love hearing you say that!" His beady eyes turned toward the pie, still steaming invitingly. "Almost as much as I love smackberry pie."

"Befitting the purity and sweetness of your nature," observed Araggna in a flattering tone that was not quite convincing.

But the Divine Monk didn't notice. He tugged excitedly on his jeweled beard. "In fact, I intend to start a new tradition, as of this day, and begin my holy meal with that very pie! Better to eat it while it's still hot—as testimony, of course, to my faith in the immortal spirits who guide our lives."

"How wise of you," said Araggna, her voice as thin as a dying breath.

Promi, however, knew that the old priestess was very much alive. And also very much feared throughout the land. For good reason: he'd seen her proclaim punishments in the market square, sometimes even worse than what she had ordered for the young boy Galmy who had forgotten to bow—a punishment that Grukarr had carried out with cruel zest. Araggna's victims, whose crime might have been stealing a peach or inadvertently using a forbidden word in a curse, could easily lose a hand or an eye. And those were the lucky ones, villagers who'd been brought before her when she was feeling uncommonly lenient. The less lucky ones often lost their heads, their families, or both.

Just then Promi noticed something unusual. Under the collar of Araggna's robe, an object glowed strangely, almost like a miniature lantern. What could it be? Probably just a trick of the light from the candles, he guessed. Yet . . . he couldn't be sure.

Keep your focus, he chided himself. *This is no time to lose your concentration!*

"Well, now," said the Divine Monk, patting his belly. "Are we all here and ready for the prayer?" In a quieter voice, he muttered, "The sooner we deal with that, the sooner I can eat some pie."

"Almost ready, my master," rasped Araggna. She snapped her withered fingers. "Grukarr! Enter now, you fool!"

Instantly, Grukarr appeared in the doorway. His expression was just as arrogant as when Promi had encountered him a few hours earlier, but his garb was different. He had changed to a flowing purple robe that needed no belt.

Noticing the change of clothing, Promi allowed himself a small grin.

Grukarr entered the dining room. He gave a cursory bow to the Divine Monk, then glowered at Araggna.

"Move along," she snarled impatiently.

As if to emphasize her command, the snake on her arm waved its tail menacingly.

"Move, Grukarr," she repeated. "You are keeping the Divine Monk waiting! There is no excuse for your tardiness—except for your stupidity."

Grukarr's cheeks flushed deep red. But he contained his anger and replied in a level tone, "You told me to wait outside the door for your command, High Priestess."

Araggna shot him a threatening glare. "Hold your impudence.

Right now the Divine Monk needs us all assembled so he can recite the ceremonial prayer."

You mean, thought Promi, *so he can eat that pie.*

"Let us proceed with our important work," declared the Divine Monk, eyeing the pie.

And I will take care of my important work, thought Promi, gripping his dagger.

Dutifully, Araggna and Grukarr walked to the table and stood beside each other. Behind them, the wooden wall, painted with scenes of past Divine Monks' glorious revelations and magnificent deeds, glistened in the candlelight.

The Divine Monk bowed his head (no easy feat with all his multiple chins) and intoned, "Now let us turn our thoughts away from lowly mortal concerns. Send them, instead, to the sky above, where our radiant guiding spirits reside. I bid you all to take the hand of the person beside you, that your divine thoughts may be joined."

Reluctantly, Grukarr and Araggna went through the motion of joining hands. In reality, though, only their sleeves touched. Fortunately for Grukarr, he wasn't standing next to the arm that held her snake. Nearby, the trio of monks fumbled with their ceremonial objects, setting them down so they could clasp hands.

Eager to proceed, the Divine Monk started to recite the traditional prayer. "O great immortal spirits," he began, then paused to lick his lips.

Meanwhile, unseen by any of them, Promi concentrated on his target. Gently, he parted the curtain and raised his knife, pausing to judge the precise trajectory. *Steady, steady,* he told himself.

All at once, he snapped his arm and released the blade.

Slam! The knife pierced the sleeves of both Araggna and Grukarr exactly where the fabrics touched, then buried itself deeply in the wall.

Thrown backward by the force of the blade, the two of them fell over each other in surprise. But the blade pinned them firmly to the wall. They cursed and clawed and kicked wildly. The snake hissed furiously.

"Attack!" shrieked one of the old monks, picking up his incense shaker to use as a weapon.

Just then, one of Grukarr's kicks smacked the incense bearer's shin. The old fellow howled in pain, toppled into the other two monks, and threw the shaker onto the floor. It exploded, sending clouds of incense into the air. People coughed and shrieked, their eyes burning.

Coughing wildly, the Divine Monk staggered into the table, tripped on himself, and fell face-first into the ceremonial feast. Cherry sauce, smashed grapes, and flasks of wine flew everywhere. The table buckled under his great weight, tossing more food to the floor. Candles broke, falling onto the tablecloth, which erupted in flames.

In all the commotion, nobody noticed that when the platter for the precious pie hit the floor, the pie itself did not. Promi had caught it. Firmly clutching his prize, he darted back to the balcony.

As the dust and smoke began to clear, Araggna glared at the dagger that still pinned her to the wall. "Help me, you fools!" she shouted. "Curse this day with everlasting plagues!"

"No," commanded the Divine Monk, "help me first!" He had landed belly up on the floor and lay there, squirming like a huge turtle on its back. No matter how hard he tried, he couldn't roll over, let alone stand. A huge glob of cherry sauce covered his turban's ruby.

Grukarr, for his part, remained silent and still. His gaze was fixed on the red curtain by the balcony, where he'd just watched a young man escape. A young man he clearly recognized.

Grukarr clenched his fists tightly. "You will pay for your crimes," he growled under his breath. "Whoever you are, you will pay."

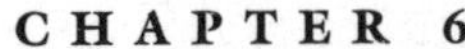

CHAPTER 6

Punishment

The only thing worse than a bitter pastry is a bitter pastry chef.

—From Promi's journal

"You *what*?" rasped Araggna, pacing angrily across her dimly lit chamber. Her dark eyes smoldered with fury. "You actually saw the attacker—and even recognized him—but did nothing at all to stop him?"

Grukarr growled, baring his teeth. "I did not see him, as I told you, until *after* he attacked us."

"That makes no difference!" she shrieked, shoving him backward into her marble washbasin. "You are an incompetent fool! I should have your eyes put out and your mouth sewed shut for all your stupidity!"

The boa constrictor on her arm coiled itself tighter. Then, its orange eyes on Grukarr, it hissed loudly.

Seething with rage, Grukarr barely

restrained himself from striking the priestess. But he couldn't ignore the barbed spear points of the four temple guards who were standing at the doorway, watching him suspiciously.

He drew himself up to his full, commanding height, made even greater by his white turban. Menacingly, he looked down at her—this wrathful old priestess who had the nerve to berate him. "I will find him," he vowed, "and kill him."

"Not too quickly," she countered, raking her fingernails against Grukarr's chest. "I want him to *suffer.*"

"Don't worry. I know exactly what to do with him."

"You had better succeed," snarled the High Priestess, her white hair still flecked with incense powder and duckling sauce from the attack. "For if you don't . . . it will be you who will suffer."

For an instant, Grukarr almost lost control again. But he held back his rage, clenching his jaw. *There will be another time,* he promised himself.

Then he spied, under the collar of her robe, a mysterious glow. It came from something she was wearing around her neck. *Yes,* he added vengefully, *and when that time comes . . . you will have no more need for that little treasure.*

He turned to leave.

"Wait," she rasped. As soon as he turned back, she peered straight at him and taunted, "Prove to me, for once, that you are not a complete imbecile."

His eyes narrowed, but he said nothing.

"By the way," she added, "I heard about that episode this morning in the market square. Through your carelessness and poor commands, you allowed some street beggar to escape—and, in the process, you turned six of our highly trained temple guards into laughingstocks! They should be respected, like all of us who wield authority." Araggna paused to pull a gooey mass of duckling sauce out of her hair. "Your sheer incompetence shames us all. It makes even the Divine Monk seem foolish."

"He needs no help from us to do that," grumbled Grukarr.

Instead of rising to her superior's defense, Araggna merely smirked. "You are right about that. He is unalterably a fool. But as long as I am here to, er . . . *guide* him, as well as keep the buffoonery of this country in line, we shall continue to thrive." She glared at her deputy. "Just to make certain you do no more damage to the reputation of the temple guards, I hereby strip you of your right to have them as your security detail."

Grukarr caught his breath. "No temple guards? What if I am—"

"Attacked? Spat upon? Jeered?" She savored the thought. "Well then, I suppose you will just have to deal with it yourself. You and that filthy bird who sometimes rides on your shoulder."

"Huntwing? He is a loyal, intelligent, well-trained servant."

"Better than you, then." She practically spat the words. "From now on, if you are to have any guards, you must find them yourself. I am retaining the entire corps of temple guards for my own protection." In an unmistakably threatening tone, she added, "We all need protection, you know."

Furious, Grukarr clenched his jaw. He glanced at the guards standing by the doorway. *Right you are,* he thought viciously. *We all need protection.*

He spun around and stormed out of her chamber.

"Don't forget," she called after him, "you have some punishments to carry out this afternoon before you leave the temple."

He halted, but didn't turn to face her. "I thought the top priority was to find the attacker."

"You *thought*?" she ridiculed. "Don't flatter yourself, Grukarr. Just follow my orders, that is all! I want at least something in this temple to happen as planned today. So go now to the prisoners and deliver all the punishments I promised."

"As you command." In a darker tone, he added, "All those who deserve it shall be punished."

CHAPTER 7

A Fine Day's Work

Thought you were so clever, didn't you? Typical! Just the way you were before . . . well, before that cursed prophecy changed everything.

—From her journal, beneath a sketch of something that looks surprisingly like the mark on Promi's chest

Purple juice dribbled down Promi's chin, seeping under the collar of his tunic. He wiped his neck with a tattered sleeve, folded his legs tighter beneath him, and retrieved a flake of crust that had fallen onto his boot—all while taking more bites of the sweetest pie he'd ever tasted. His own personal holiday feast.

"Not bad," he said with satisfaction, pausing to lick each of his purple-tinted fingers and finishing with a loud *smack*. "Now I know how these berries got their name."

Seated on a grassy knoll just outside the City's outer wall, under the shade of an old cedar, Promi sighed gratefully. Here he was with his hard-earned prize, savoring its sweetness . . . and also, for a change, relaxing on the warm grass with nobody chasing him, cursing him, or trying to kill him. It wouldn't last long, he knew—these moments never did—but that made it all the more precious.

He lay back on his elbows, keeping the still-warm pie on his lap. Sure, he'd lost another good throwing knife in grabbing it. But it was a most worthy cause! So he'd just have to find himself another knife, as he'd done many times before. This very afternoon, in fact, he could easily fetch one from an unsuspecting peddler in the market square.

Of course, he'd need to be extra cautious after his busy day. After all, he had not only stolen Grukarr's belt buckle and humiliated the priest in public, he had also left a trail of extremely angry temple guards around the City. And that was just the beginning!

Now he'd also stolen the Divine Monk's precious pie. In doing so, he'd violated at least a dozen laws, defiled the sacred temple, committed sacrilege on a high holiday, and—oh yes—totally destroyed the Divine Monk's dining room. Not to mention outraged the two most vengeful and dangerous people in the country, Grukarr and High Priestess Araggna.

He grinned. *A fine day's work.*

Gazing at the City wall, he felt satisfied that he was, indeed, all alone. From this spot, he could see from one end of the settlement to the other—though not as far beyond its borders as he'd seen from atop the bell tower. Still, if any guards tried to pursue him, he'd notice them in plenty of time to escape.

For centuries, this community at the edge of the Deg Boesi River had been the country's capital. In fact, it had long been called Ellegandia City. Then the current Divine Monk, in his typically humble way, had renamed it the City of Great Powers. (Whether he'd done that to honor the powerful spirits of the immortal realm, or to honor himself and his entourage, who were such great powers among mortals, nobody was certain.)

Yet despite its grandiose name, this place still felt a lot like a village. Sure, it was by far the largest settlement in the country, the site of the Divine Monk's temple, and the seat of government. But its life and people and rhythms were still much like those of any other village in Ellegandia.

Of course, Promi reminded himself as he chewed on a buttery edge of crust, that wasn't to say that Ellegandia was like anywhere else in the world. All the stories about Ellegandia celebrated the country's uniqueness. Its very name originally meant "a land alone" or "a place apart." Of course, nobody could be sure those stories were true, since no one from Ellegandia had ever traveled to other lands and returned to describe them. But Promi felt a strong instinct that his country was, in fact, very special. Maybe even, as the legends said, unique among all the other places on Earth.

Now, some of that specialness stemmed from simple geography—from being so utterly remote. Shielded on three sides by stormy seas and sheer cliffs, and on the fourth side by an impassable mountain range that separated Ellegandia from the rest of the continent—the land mass some people called Africa—it was a lonely, forgotten place. A kind of island, though one that was still attached to land.

On top of that, Divine Monks had decreed since the beginning of history that nobody could ever leave the country, on pain of eternal torment by the Great Powers. The reason? So that no one outside this realm would ever hear about Ellegandia's riches . . . and be tempted to try to steal them. For the most ancient prophets had warned the Divine Monks that Ellegandia held treasures found nowhere else on Earth.

Those treasures were, indeed, vast. Yet they didn't come just in the form of shiny jewels, colorful cloths, and precious metals. Such things existed here, but they were the very least of the country's riches. What really made Ellegandia special, what really made it so blessed by the Great Powers, was the abundance of something else.

Magic.

So much natural magic that it was said to flow in the very streams of the Great Forest, producing luminous flowers, talking trees, and sentient stones. And that wasn't all. In addition to magical creatures of every description, Ellegandia's forest was said to be the only place in existence that held creatures from everywhere else on Earth. So the Great Forest was not only a home for magical beings, but also an oasis for mortals of all kinds—a spectacular array of animals and trees, insects and birds.

That was, at least, the forest's reputation. Having never set foot there, Promi couldn't be sure how much of that was true. But those woods had certainly inspired plenty of stories from travelers and food gatherers. Growing up on the streets of the City, he'd heard plenty of those tales, some more believable than others.

What nobody could doubt, though, were the amazing fruits, nuts, herbs, spices, and seeds that people had brought out of the forest for centuries. As well as the silver leaves of the sacred muliahma tree, leaves the monks covered with intricate prayers. Plus all the bizarre and wondrous creatures brought to market from the forest, like those color-shifting pigeons he'd seen today—and thrown in the face of the guard.

Savoring the sweet taste in his mouth, Promi thought of one more example. The smackberries he was now enjoying, which had been grown in the Divine Monk's garden, originally came from the Great Forest. As he took another bite of pie, he thought, *I could almost believe these berries have been touched by a breeze from the spirit world.*

All this was why every old myth about this land sprang from the same two ideas. First, Ellegandia's magic was profoundly valuable, an eternal gift to every person, every creature, and every tree in the realm. No wonder the people's favorite blessing, saved for the most special occasions, was *I bless your eternal qualities.*

The second idea was a kind of responsibility. The Great Powers asked only one thing in return for all this magic—that Ellegandia's people do everything possible to protect its riches from the greed of others, whether humans or immortals. Promi didn't see how immortals could ever be a problem, since the mortal world and the spirit world were completely separate. And that separation was inviolable. But in any case, the myths always reminded people to safeguard their homeland's natural magic.

He shrugged his shoulders. That bit about immortals didn't really make sense. Maybe that was why he didn't like listening to the old legends. Or, for that matter, to any of the far-fetched tales about immortals—whether they lived up in the clouds of the spirit realm or in Ellegandia's forest groves. *If you believe in such things,* he told himself, *you've got to carry them around with you everywhere, like a satchel filled with rocks. And I like to carry as little as possible.*

He took another bite, savoring every ingredient from the sweet syrup to the sugary crust. All at once, he realized that he had company—not people, but several creatures who'd been drawn to the pie's alluring aroma.

Seated around him on the grassy slope were a mountain squirrel who waved his tail like a flag, a pure white kitten whose whiskers were as long as her legs, and a long-nosed anteater with a baby clinging to her back. A broad-winged butterfly with pink-and-black-striped wings floated over and landed on a mustard flower. Then up in the branches of the old cedar, he caught a flash of something deep blue. Feathers?

He peered into the branches, furrowing his brow. Could it be one of those rare hi-marnia birds? They were so elusive that almost nobody ever saw them. But he'd heard that their nests were sometimes found in the boughs of blue cedars in the Great Forest.

The kitten mewed plaintively. Promi shook his head and said sternly, "No way, you beggar. I earned this pie, every bite."

But the kitten merely stared at him. She opened her eyes to their widest, never blinking.

Promi sighed. "Oh, all right. Just this once."

Pinching a small piece of crust that oozed with smackberry syrup, he tossed it to the kitten. She pounced on it eagerly. Then, seeing the looks of great longing on the faces of the anteater and the squirrel, he threw each of them a scrap.

The butterfly landed on his wrist, wings trembling with anticipation. Promi shook his head, knowing he was beaten. Gently, he smeared a bit of sweet juice on a mustard flower. Instantly the butterfly glided over and began to dine.

Just about to get back to his own eating, he thought of something else. For the sake of fairness, he broke off one more chunk of pie crust and tossed it straight up into the cedar's branches. Though he heard a scurrying sound, he didn't see any more flashes of blue up there. But the crust didn't fall back to the ground.

Taking another bite for himself, he glanced again at the City's outer wall. As he chewed, he heard the distant chiming of a bell—not the big one in the bell tower that he himself had rung that morning, but one somewhere else in the temple complex. He also heard some muffled shouting from the market square, the ring of a blacksmith's hammer, and the gentle bleating of goats. The only other sounds he could hear came from his new neighbors, who were loudly chomping and licking their paws, as well as some more scurrying in the branches above his head.

"Welcome to my dining room," he announced. "The finest eating place in all of Ellegandia." With a chuckle, he added, "And it's certainly a lot nicer than the Divine Monk's dining room right now."

He waved his arms, gesturing to the assembled creatures, but they ignored him. They were too engrossed in devouring their treats. Only the butterfly gave any indication of having heard him, pausing briefly to flutter its wings before continuing to eat.

Promi thought back to his successful theft of the pie and chuckled again, spurting some purple syrup onto his leggings. The hardest part of the whole operation had turned out to be something he hadn't expected—trying not to fall over laughing when the incense shaker exploded, the Divine Monk crashed into the table, and the whole place erupted in chaos.

Best of all, he thought with satisfaction, *was that look of utter shock on Grukarr's face. A look I'm starting to enjoy.*

He licked his purple-stained fingers. *And Araggna's face was a good match. Why, she looked even angrier than usual, which is hard to imagine.*

Hearing something stir in the branches overhead, he glanced up. But he saw nothing through the mesh of blue needles . . . except a hint of rust color. Part of the hi-marnia bird? But no, they were supposedly all blue. So another kind of bird, then?

Only one piece of pie remained. Turning his attention to that, he lifted it and took a huge bite. The animals around him whimpered with disappointment, while the butterfly's antennae drooped.

"Oh, well," he said with a shrug. Then he broke off a lump of crust and divided it among them. Immediately they went back to the happy task of eating.

As he watched them, Promi couldn't help but think about the diversity of this land's creatures. He'd seen only a small sampling of them, of course—the ones people had captured and brought to market, or the rare ones brave enough to approach him as these had done. But that small sampling had been amazingly varied . . . and sometimes quite beautiful.

There really could be some truth to the old stories about this land's wondrously varied creatures. And that wasn't even counting the immortal beings who, it was said, had actually chosen to live in Ellegandia's deep woods rather than in the spirit realm on high.

That can't be true, thought Promi skeptically. *Why would any immortals choose to live on Earth rather than up in the sky with the rest of their kind? Ellegandia may be special . . . but let's not get carried away.*

His thoughts turned to another question. Where had Ellegandia's people come from originally? With all those barriers of ocean cliffs and impassable mountains, it couldn't have been easy. Some believed those first people had sailed here from a faraway land called Greece, and that a terrible storm at sea had hurled their boats over the tops of the cliffs. Others claimed that Ellegandians came from people called Berbers from the continent of Africa—and that those people had discovered some way to cross the high peaks.

Still others believed the first people of this land had been chosen by the immortals to live here. This theory held that men, women, and children from places all around the world had been plucked away from their old homes and magically brought to Ellegandia. Outlandish as this theory was, it did at least explain the great diversity of Ellegandia's people, whose skin color ranged from deepest black to palest white and all shades in between.

Promi chuckled. *I like that theory . . . for originality, at least.*

He sank his teeth into the last bite of pie. Frankly, he didn't care what the old legends said. Like the other stories spread around by monks and priestesses, they didn't concern him at all. No, the only things that mattered—the only things he could count on—were solid reality.

Such as, he concluded, *a tasty piece of pie.*

A heavy net suddenly dropped on top of him. Several men rushed over and roughly pinned him to the ground. Then he heard a voice that made his skin prickle with heat—a voice he'd never expected to hear again today.

"Well, well," declared Grukarr as he strode out from behind the tree. "What a perfect place you chose to eat your stolen pie." Lowering his voice to a growl, he added, "And to end your days."

Promi struggled to free himself from the net, trying with all his strength to throw off his captors. But a couple of sharp kicks to his head and ribs put a quick end to that. He groaned painfully.

"Indigestion?" asked Grukarr with mock sympathy. "That's what happens when you eat too fast. Or eat too well for your lowly place in society."

Striding closer, the priest planted a heavy boot on his prisoner's chest. Though the weight made it hard to breathe, Promi didn't struggle or moan. He didn't want to give this scoundrel any more satisfaction.

And Grukarr already felt plenty. He beamed down at the captive under the net and started to whistle jauntily, savoring his moment of triumph—a moment that was, for him, even tastier than smackberry pie. Then he released a different sort of whistle—a single, shrill call.

From the branches above came an answering call. Wings flapped, and a big, rust-colored bird with huge talons glided down and landed on his shoulder. The bird's savage eyes, rimmed in scarlet, studied the helpless prisoner.

"Introductions?" asked Grukarr in a tone both playful and poisonous. "Or do you need to rush off to steal something else?"

Hearing nothing but labored breathing from Promi, the priest went on, "This is Huntwing, my loyal servant. It was he who found you, relaxing after your day of criminal mischief."

The bird clacked his beak proudly. His large, vicious talons gripped Grukarr's shoulder.

"And these," continued the priest with a wave at the men who had jumped on Promi, "are my faithful minions. They will do absolutely anything that I command."

A few men grumbled at this. But one sharp look from Grukarr silenced them.

"At least," he went on, "they had better do so." Stroking Huntwing's talon, he explained, "You see, only a short while ago they sat in chains, convicted of terrible crimes. Their punishments, ordered by the High Priestess, would have left them without a limb—or a life."

Several of the men stirred uneasily. Grukarr paused a moment, enjoying their palpable fear, as well as his power over them.

"But in the name of kindness," he continued, "I took it upon myself to set them free. Now, they may not be as well trained as temple guards—but they will do whatever I tell them without question."

With a chortle, he added, "Or else . . . the punishments Araggna had ordered for them will be *mild* compared to what I will do." He tapped the bird's talon. "Isn't that right, my Huntwing?"

The bird clacked his beak savagely.

Ignoring the men's shudders, Grukarr said to Promi, "And now, you worthless vagabond, I have something special planned for you." Leaning hard on his captive's chest, Grukarr barked to one of his men, "Club him so he won't cause any more trouble."

Grukarr started whistling merrily again—then something struck Promi's head. He slumped to the grass. The last thing he heard before losing consciousness was the faint echo of that whistle, so very different from the half-remembered song that had given him such comfort during his short life.

CHAPTER 8

Eternal Qualities

The most important moment in creating a pastry doesn't happen in the oven, or even in the kitchen. No, it takes place long before, when a special stalk of grain emerges from the soil.

—A scrap from Promi's journal

Deep in a forest grove a few days' walk to the South, the wind suddenly fell silent.

Branches stopped clattering; leaves ceased their restless rustle. High in the trees, bright-feathered birds grew still, their voices no longer echoing. Insects quieted. Even the noisy squirrels fell mute.

Then, from deep in the grove, a young woman's voice lifted in song.

The seed holds the life of a tree;
A tree carries wonders untold.
The forest holds deep mystery:

A magic both newborn and old.
Leaf and droplet,
every part—
Form the Whole
and fill my heart.
Bless eternal
qualities—
Grace my soul
and all the trees.

Branches stirred again, rustling. Leaves brushed against each other; shaggy mosses started to sway. But they were not moving with any wind. No . . . they were dancing to the rhythm of the young woman's song.

She stood beneath a towering yew whose crown lifted higher than any of the surrounding trees. Her blue-green eyes shone as she sang. And in time, the yew's dark red berries, high in the branches, began to glow subtly.

A fern in the forest is slight;
A pebble is small by the shore.
Yet each holds a magical light:
Each morsel of magic brings more.
Sunlight and shadow grow stronger,
The day and the night are true kin.
Lives may be brief or still briefer,
Yet magic lies always within.
Leaf and droplet,
every part—
Form the Whole
and fill my heart.
Bless eternal
qualities—

Grace my soul
and all the trees.

The young woman continued to sing, tilting her head back as she looked up into the yew's branches so that her curly brown hair played on her shoulders. Gently, she lifted her left hand and placed her palm on the massive trunk. She worked her fingers into the contours of bark, as if she were stroking the face of an old friend.

Atlanta she was called, both by those who knew her well and by those who had heard about her unusually powerful gift of natural magic. Her name, which meant "voice for all" in the Ellegandian Old Tongue, might have been a burden for some. But not for her. She simply was who she was, someone who wandered the forest paths, helping others find their magic.

More than twenty of these people surrounded Atlanta now, standing in the shade of the ancient yew. Women and girls, men and boys, they looked as varied as the oaks, yews, acacias, banyans, blue cedars, elms, redwoods, and thorn trees around them.

People from the cavern lands wore sashes of mountain bear fur decorated with wyvern claws, while those from the Lakes of Dreams had plumed hats with bright yellow sunbird feathers. Others, who had walked here from the Indragrass Meadows, wore iridescent robes that smelled like fresh mint, along with vests of supple willow shoots. A few, who had come all the way from the western shores, perhaps even from Mystery Bay, stood in sandals made from the rutted skin of crocodiles. They hummed quietly to themselves all the time, as was their custom. And one sturdy fellow had trekked from the Waterfall of the Giants, within sight of the country's highest peak, Ell Shangro. His hat still smelled of waterfall lilies.

In addition, there were three priestesses and one monk from the City. The most senior priestess, a spry-looking elder, wore a traditional deep green robe, while her younger companions had chosen the tan-colored robes favored by those who resided in the temple. And their host, Atlanta, wore clothing that evoked the Great Forest—a simple purple gown of woven lilac vines.

As varied as these people were, they all shared a passion for natural magic . . . and a yearning to know more of its secrets. Which is why so many of them had traveled great distances to experience the Great Forest and learn from Atlanta.

On top of that, they shared one common physical trait—sparkling green eyes. Whether their irises showed just a few green flecks, looked as green as sunlit meadows, or combined shades of green and blue, they showed the unmistakable color of magic. In most parts of the country, such eyes marked someone as a valued healer; in others, as a person to be feared. But here in the Great Forest, the very heart of Ellegandia's natural magic, all these people felt fully welcome.

Air that is breathed by us all,
Winds that support every wing—
Rise over mountains so tall,
Carry the magic of spring.
All branches and roots interlink,
A web that embraces the Whole.
Upon it are words without ink:
Deep magic on natural scroll.
Leaf and droplet,
every part—
Form the Whole
and fill my heart.
Bless eternal
qualities—
Grace my soul
and all the trees.

As Atlanta's song ended, the ancient yew's branches fell still. In the quiet that followed, the elder priestess with the deep green robe spoke. "Thank you, young one. You bring beauty to this forest, and blessings to us all."

Modestly, Atlanta shook her head. "This forest holds blessings beyond any of us."

"True," the old priestess replied. "But too many people of this time—including some who wear the robes of priestesses and monks, who should know better—have forgotten that the immortals we worship are also present right here in the mortal realm, in this wondrous forest. Yes, just as much as they are alive in the spirit realm on high!"

From around the group came many murmurs of approval. The fellow with the hat that smelled of waterfall lilies gave a slight bow to Atlanta.

Feeling a new tingling in her hand that was touching the yew tree's trunk, Atlanta lifted her gaze to the branches. An expectant hush filled the grove, and several people traded glances.

All at once, a pair of long vines with golden leaves uncoiled themselves from the tree's upper limbs. Gracefully, like sinuous rivers, the vines flowed down the trunk. The first one to reach Atlanta curled lightly around her left hand. The other wrapped around her right hand and forearm. As the vines touched her skin, their golden leaves quivered.

"Now," she said softly, gazing up into the tree, "my old friend here will reveal its most magical language. Come, Master Yew, show these good people the speech of the vines."

Up and down the vines, golden leaves trembled and twirled. Those nearest Atlanta's hands moved most vigorously—and then started to change color. Beginning at the stems, streams of purple and blue, orange and white, flowed into the leaves, spreading out in complex patterns. Spirals and curls of color wrote themselves on the surfaces, while the leaves' serrated edges bent and waved in a slow, mysterious dance.

For a timeless instant, they held all their complex designs. Then, in unison, their colors drained away. The vines shrugged, giving Atlanta's hands a gentle squeeze.

"What did they say?" cried a small girl who wore a garland of blue irises in her hair.

"They welcome us all to this place." With a hint of a smile, Atlanta added, "And they bless our eternal qualities."

More nods and murmurs of approval moved through the crowd. At the same time, branches in the yew as well as neighboring trees started swishing and slapping. Atlanta gazed up into the living forest canopy, her face content as she listened to this gathering wind of words.

The swishing stopped—as if the entire grove suddenly held its breath. Atlanta's brow furrowed, more in surprise than concern. Meanwhile, the vines tightened around her hands. The leaves shook and changed colors, shifting from pale gold to deeper shades of red and black.

"Tell us," urged the girl with the irises in her hair. "What are they saying now?"

"Yes," called the old priestess. "Do tell us."

Atlanta's blue-green eyes widened as she stared at the leaves in disbelief. The vines shook her arms insistently, while the darker colors spread.

"They say . . ." she whispered hoarsely, too stunned to finish. Then, regaining her strength, she cried out the vines' message:

"Leave now! Hide yourselves!"

CHAPTER 9

True Religion

Sometimes a handsome pastry, dusted with sugar, can be just plain rotten inside.

—From Promi's journal, written in unusually bold scrawl

The warning came too late. Even as Atlanta shouted the message of the vines, a band of people swept into the grove.

Unlike those who had gathered under the ancient yew, whose garb was so colorful and diverse, the new arrivals wore only rough brown tunics, ragged leggings, and old leather boots. Many also carried weapons, whether a rusted sword or a plowman's staff. Several held unlit torches whose oily smell clashed with the fragrance of the grove.

Only one of the newcomers dressed differently. Taller than anyone else, he wore a robe of pure white silk, adorned only with a necklace of golden beads. On his head sat a white turban, stained at the bottom from his sweaty brow. Though he held no weapon, he conveyed an unmistakable air of authority.

Seeing him approach, the elder priestess gasped. The two younger priestesses by her side froze. And the monk accompanying them rubbed his hands together nervously.

"I am Grukarr," declared the tall man as he reached the center of the grove. He curled his lips into an almost pleasant smile. "For those of you who do not know me, I am a humble priest of the True Religion."

Atlanta's eyes narrowed suspiciously. Several people who had come here to learn about natural magic started muttering in anger or fear. Meanwhile, Grukarr's men pressed closer. One of them lifted an ax with a notched blade.

But Grukarr, still smiling, raised his hand. A large ruby gleamed from his oversized ring. "Now, now, dear people. I come here in peace. So do my followers."

He nodded sharply at the ax, then waited until it was lowered. "You see," he went on, "we love the forest just as much as you do. We value its resources, its creatures, and most of all, its magic."

With that, he gave a shrill whistle. Right away, a rust-colored bird descended and landed on his shoulder. The bird's talons, still bloody from a recent kill, gripped Grukarr firmly.

"A blood falcon," said Atlanta. "One of the few creatures who kill more than they need to eat." Anxiously, she squeezed the vines draped across her hands.

"The common name," agreed Grukarr, keeping his voice calm. "To those of us who know the true ways of the forest, however, he is a Royal Huntwing."

The young woman, her gaze no less piercing than the bird's, shook her curls. "My name is Atlanta, and I can tell you this: If you are part of something called the True Religion, that means you think any other form of worship is false. Including devotion to nature spirits. Which means you really know nothing of the ways of this forest."

Grukarr's smile vanished. His brown eyes peered at the young woman who had dared to contradict him. A storm seemed to gather under his brow, and his pale cheeks flushed.

Before he could speak, the elder priestess stepped over to join Atlanta. "She is right, you know. The spirits of the forest are just as worthy of devotion as the ones we pray to at the temple."

Scowling, Grukarr glared at the old woman. "Shame on you! As you should know by now, the True Religion honors the immortals who live on high, in the sky above us, and nowhere else. You certainly won't find them out here in the wild woods."

Drawing herself up straight, the elder replied, "Only if you have no eyes to see and no ears to listen."

Still holding the vines, Atlanta said to Grukarr, "We could teach you, if only you are willing to learn."

The priest scowled at this impudence. He started to answer harshly, but caught himself. Trying to stay calm, he said, "No doubt you could teach me many things. Which is fortunate, Atlanta, because it will encourage me to be . . . gentle with you."

His eyes glinted greedily. "You see, I have some uses, important uses, for your knowledge of this forest."

The elder priestess gasped.

Frowning, Atlanta replied, "What I could teach you about this forest is not about *uses.* No, it's about a deeper way of seeing. Breathing. Living."

Dropping any pretense of friendliness, Grukarr growled, "If that is your attitude, then it is you who must learn from me."

As if agreeing, the bird on his shoulder rustled both wings.

"You must understand," Grukarr declared confidently, "the righteousness of my cause." He shot a withering glance at the old priestess. "The True Religion, can *save* you—yes, even if you have strayed from the Truth. It is, in fact, the only path to salvation. The path out of the darkness and into the light."

He paused to stroke Huntwing's tail feathers. "But if you do not agree, here and now, to cast away your heathen ways, to end all your old-fashioned witchery and dark magic . . ."

His voice hardened. "Then I shall be forced to *educate* you."

The people whose eyes sparkled with green all tensed. Some glanced furtively at the forest, looking for a way to escape. Others turned anxious faces toward Atlanta, while the small girl with the garland of blue irises scurried to her side. Still others, such as the sturdy fellow from the land of waterfall lilies, clenched their fists, ready to fight.

Atlanta, for her part, stared down at the golden-leafed vines she was touching. Quickly releasing one hand, she tapped and stroked the vine that now dangled freely, communicating some sort of message. She continued as Grukarr straightened his turban, preparing to speak again.

"Do I hear no reply?" he demanded. "Is no one here willing to repent and follow my guidance?"

"Never," declared the elder priestess.

"No," answered several others.

"Impossible," said the girl with blue irises in her hair, her voice quiet but firm.

Malice written on his face, Grukarr declared, "Then I must take you to—"

He stopped abruptly as the free vine suddenly whipped toward him and struck him squarely on the forehead. He cried out in pain and tumbled over backward, losing his turban as he landed on the broken branches and dry leaves of the forest floor. Huntwing shrieked with rage and pounced on the vine, but only succeeded in battering the priest's face with his wings.

Blood streaming from his head wound, Grukarr rolled in the

leaves, trying in vain to bat away the bird. "No, you foolish beast! Get away!"

Atlanta, meanwhile, shouted to her followers, "Flee, all of you! Trust in the forest!"

She locked gazes with the old priestess. "Help them," she said hurriedly, "however you can."

"I will, Atlanta. But will you be safe? He has something terrible in mind for you, that's clear."

Atlanta nodded. "As long as this forest survives, so will I."

As the priestess hurried off, Atlanta pulled the small girl closer. Wrapping one arm tightly around the girl's waist, Atlanta gave a sharp tug to the vine still wrapped around her other forearm. Instantly, the vine retracted, pulling both of them up into the tree's highest branches. As they vanished, petals of blue iris drifted down to the ground.

Grukarr, finally free of his bird, forced himself to stand. Blood still oozed from the cut on his forehead, spattering his white robe. Dry leaves and needles stuck to his ears and eyebrows. Shakily, he bent to pick up his battered turban.

Most of his men rushed forward and tried to steady him, but he shoved them away. Angrily, he glared at all the heathens who were swiftly disappearing into the forest.

"Kill them!" he shouted, eyes ablaze. "Kill them all—except for that young woman. Find her and bring her to me alive!"

He donned the turban, brushed off his silk robe, and stomped out of the grove. Catching the arm of one of his torch bearers, he pointed at the old yew and commanded, "And burn that cursed tree to the ground."

Shouts and screams erupted in the once-peaceful grove. Dense smoke filled the air, blotting out everything else.

CHAPTER 10

Shadows

You didn't understand the essence of light, Promi—that it makes not only bright visions, but also dark shadows. Things you can see . . . and things you cannot.

—A passage from her journal

At last you understand! But now, I fear, it's too late.

—Also from her journal, added later

The pain in Promi's head woke him up. Not the throbbing ache from the clubbing, just above his right temple, though that seemed to swell as soon as he opened his eyes. No, this was a sharper pain in the back of his head.

A rock! He rolled aside, moving off the pointed stone that had been under his skull for however long. Hours? Days?

Then he felt another sort of pain, this one in his stomach. Hunger! How long had it been since he'd eaten that smackberry pie on the hillside? *Too long, that's for sure. I'm so hungry I could eat a wagon-load of goats.*

He reached to grab the rock and throw it away. But he stopped abruptly. Not because he'd changed his mind about throwing it, but because his arm simply couldn't budge.

What's this? Suddenly he realized that both his wrists were tightly bound together. And that rope also wrapped around his waist, leaving his hands dangling useless atop his belly. Just to make sure he couldn't go anywhere, the rope's longer end was tied to an iron ring in the stone wall beside him.

"Sizzling snakes, seeping sores, and skulking scourges!" he swore, so angry that he didn't even bother to finish the curse. "Tied up like a bundle of firewood! And I'm in . . ."

He paused, squinting into the darkness. As his eyes adjusted, he scanned the shadows between the few sputtering torches affixed to the stone walls. Huddled within those shadows were bodies—dead or alive, he couldn't tell.

A sound like a muffled groan came from somewhere down a distant corridor. And he could also hear something dripping on the stone floor. Otherwise, no sound but his own ragged breathing.

Dead as a tomb. That's how this place seemed. Where was he?

Except for the flickering light of the torches, he saw no movement anywhere. Then he noticed something large—a rat?—near the opposite wall. It was gnawing on something that looked suspiciously like a detached finger. The rat's black eyes glistened while it nibbled on a hunk of flesh attached to a fingernail.

"A dungeon," Promi said in a stunned whisper. "I'm in a dungeon."

He sighed miserably. Continuing to look around, he noticed, for the first time, that the stones of the walls and floor shone red in the wavering torchlight. At once, he remembered the gory legend of a dungeon that lay hidden, long ago, beneath the City's outer wall. A place so frightful and poisoned from centuries of torture and death that it had turned the color of blood.

Ekh Raku, he recalled. The dungeon's name meant "stones of blood." And it was rarely spoken, saved for only the most anguished curses.

So it's real. The dungeon's reputation was so thoroughly evil that some Divine Monk ages ago had decreed that it should be abandoned. Sealed up forever. Today, most people believed that it no longer existed. And some insisted that it had never existed in the first place—that it was just another scary story, like so many tales about wrathful immortals, invented to keep people in line.

Yet here it was.

And here, thought Promi grimly, *am I.*

He shook his head in disgust—then ceased, feeling a new explosion of pain. His head was so sore that even the gentle tap of his gold earring against his jaw sent painful tremors through his whole skull.

Wriggling closer to the wall, he slouched against the cold, dank stones. Again he wrestled with the rope around his wrists. Nothing loosened. He tried again, pulling and tugging with all his strength. But he still couldn't budge.

"Where is my knife when I need it?" he grumbled aloud, his voice echoing around the walls. Across from him, the rat paused for a second, then went back to gnawing flesh.

Promi winced at the putrid smell of rotting bodies that filled the dungeon. His stomach tightened, but he resisted the urge to vomit. Meanwhile, a stream of questions poured into his mind. Did the Divine Monk even know that this dungeon was still being used? Or was this a secret Grukarr and Araggna kept to themselves? Something they saved for their least favorite prisoners?

He grimaced, his head pounding like one of the monk's sacred drums. How could he have been so stupid to eat that precious pie out in the open, on top of the hill, where Grukarr's bird could easily spot him? And how could he have set aside all his usual caution when he most needed it?

The pounding in his head worsened. He wished he could reach his hand high enough to rub his sore skull. But he couldn't do it. Why, he couldn't do *anything*. Ever again. For he'd been cast into a dungeon—*the* dungeon.

Listening to the *drip-drip-drip* on the floor, he felt hopelessly trapped. He needed to do something to revive his spirits, to keep from giving up completely.

The song, he realized. *That will help.*

Quieting his mind, he opened himself to the distant memory of that melody, just as he'd done so many times before. He waited . . . and waited some more. Nothing came to him. Not even a single note.

Was the relentless dripping sound getting in the way of his memory? Or was it the oppressive darkness? The blood-soaked stones?

Whatever the reason, he couldn't hear the song. It had abandoned him—for the first time in his life. Had he lost it forever? The mark over his heart began to throb with heat.

"Nnnooooo," groaned a voice nearby.

Promi started. It came from one of the bodies in the shadows! He scanned the huddled forms, trying to see which of them was still alive.

Suddenly a leg kicked. The body, wearing a frayed brown robe that might have belonged to a wandering monk, rolled over and wriggled weakly, trying to get away from something.

As the body moved into the torchlight, Promi could see that it belonged to an elderly man. His head, topped by a mass of white curls, lay on the stone floor. Since he, like Promi, was roped to the wall, he couldn't move any farther from whatever he was trying to escape. So he just lay there, moaning and kicking helplessly.

Promi peered into the darkness, trying to see what could be tormenting the old fellow. Something moved by the man's foot.

A rat! Promi winced, watching it try to gnaw on one of the old man's toes.

"Nnnooooo," the elder groaned again, this time more weakly.

But the rat just ignored him. Curling its back, it hunched over its prey and sank sharp teeth into the flesh of the man's big toe.

"Stop!" cried Promi. "Get away from there!"

His voice echoed loudly within the stone walls, but the rat barely even noticed. It merely glanced up at Promi to satisfy itself that the young man couldn't do any harm. Then it went right back to gnawing—with a gleam in its eyes from the certainty that this new prisoner would supply many future meals.

"I said stop!"

This time, the rat didn't even bother to look up. It merely kept chewing contentedly at the toe. Not even the old man's futile twitching disturbed its dining pleasure.

Promi growled in frustration. Ferociously, he tore at his bonds, trying harder than ever to free his hands. But the rope held fast.

"Eeaaaah," moaned the elder, clearly in anguish. Unable to do anything else, he lifted his head and hit it against the floor, again and again. "Nooooo, please . . ."

The rat continued to tear at the bloody sinews.

Promi's heart pumped with rage. He wrestled with the rope, ignoring the way its coarse surface scraped his skin.

The old man moaned piteously. "Great Powers . . . save me, please . . ."

Free! Promi wrenched one hand from the bonds. Rolling to the side, he grabbed the rock that had been under his head. With the skilled, fluid motion of a knife thrower, he hurled it straight at the rat.

A perfect shot! The rock struck the rat's head so hard that the beast shrieked and fell over backward. A broken tooth flew from its mouth, skidding across the stones. Seeing Promi start to crawl closer, it shrieked again and scurried into the shadows.

Kneeling by the man's side, Promi whispered. "It's all right, old fellow. You're safe now."

Even as he spoke those words, however, he realized their folly. Safe? How could anyone be safe down here in the dungeon of Ekh Raku?

Nevertheless, he tore a strip of cloth from the bottom of his tunic and wrapped it around the man's bloody toe. Gently, he squeezed the toe, hoping to stop the bleeding. No bones had yet been severed, but muscles and skin were brutally torn. And blood kept pouring from the wound.

The white-haired man gazed up at him, blinking as if he were dazed. "You came . . ." he whispered, "from the Great Powers? The spirit realm?"

"No," answered Promi. "I just came from over there." He waved at the dungeon's opposite wall. "I'm a prisoner, like you."

The old fellow shook his head. "No, no. By all the years I've toiled as a monk . . . I'm certain! You have something . . . special . . . about you."

Promi shook his head. Removing the blood-soaked bandage, he tore off some more cloth and wrapped the toe again. "Sorry to disappoint you, but the only thing special about me is my ability to throw a knife. Or sometimes a rock."

He glanced around the corridor, looking past the flickering torches into the darkest shadows. No sign of that rat. Grimly, he turned back to the monk.

"Let's get you untied." He quickly loosened the rope from the elder's emaciated wrists. Carefully, he moved the old fellow over to the wall so that he could sit up.

The monk's wrinkled face shimmered in the torchlight as he

stared at Promi. "You may not know it, my good lad, but you truly have the grace of the spirits."

"Right," scoffed Promi. "Well, grace might be nice, but I'd much rather have something *useful* from the spirits—like wings. They can fly, can't they? At least in all the stories. Then maybe I could fly us out of here." Wistfully, he added, "And get us some food." He licked his lips, hoping to catch even the slightest hint of those smackberries. But he tasted nothing except sweat and grime. "I'm awfully hungry."

The monk nodded. "Yes, lad, so am I." He lifted his weathered hand and placed it on the young man's shoulder. "My name is Bonlo. And yours?"

"Promi."

"Well then, Promi . . ." The old fellow smiled so genuinely that no one, seeing his face, could have guessed the painful experience he'd just endured. "I thank you."

Even in the flickering light, it was easy to see Promi's blush. "So," he asked, "how did a monk like you ever end up down here?"

"I wasn't just any old monk, my good lad. The Divine One himself promoted me, after many years, to Priest Sage."

Promi cocked his head quizzically. "No idea what that is. A high rank?"

"The highest." The monk sighed. "Or at least it was. Until recently."

He gazed at Promi. "The Priest Sage is a kind of teacher, a mentor to younger monks and priestesses across the country. Someone who helps them deepen their bonds with the Great Powers—both those who dwell in the spirit realm above and those who live in the mortal world."

His jaw tightened. "And more. For thousands of years, the Priest Sage has also been a valued adviser to the Divine Monk. But alas . . . that, too, has changed."

Promi glanced at the bloody bandage. Moving closer to the old man, he asked, "What happened, Bonlo? How did you get thrown into this pit?"

The monk lowered his gaze. "Well . . . it comes down to this. Certain people in the priesthood started to listen less to the wisdom of the spirits and more to their own ambitions. They traded humility for arrogance, generosity for greed. Why, they even changed our religion's name from the Faith of All Spirits to . . ." He almost choked, saying the new name. "The True Religion."

"Hmmm," said Promi. "That sure has a ring of humility."

"Yes," Bonlo agreed bitterly.

"So you spoke your mind to somebody powerful—and wound up in the dungeon?"

"You see . . ." A new light, not quite humor and not quite sorrow, came into the elder's eyes. "I couldn't stop myself from trying to teach that person. Even when he was my superior. Alas, he had a temper that erupted like the volcano Ell Shangro."

Liking this fellow more by the minute, Promi nodded. "I've met a few bakers like that."

Bonlo managed a grin. "Good lad. I wish I could have been your teacher."

Promi grinned back. "Well, if I had been *your* teacher, I could have shown you some really important things. Like how to steal cinnamon buns."

The elder peered at him. "And more, I'm sure."

"Maybe. Anyway, who was this superior with the bad temper?"

"He was, long ago, my student. Both his parents died from a terrible disease when he was very young, so I took him in. Raised him for many years, almost as a son. But . . ." He winced at a memory more painful than his mangled toe. "I failed him, Promi. Failed to teach him how to rise above his desire to control everything and everyone around him, to gain that power he never had as a child."

Bonlo looked up at the ceiling. "I prayed to the Powers on high to help him—especially to Sammelvar, the great spirit of wisdom, and to fair Escholia, the spirit of grace. But it did no good! Even the spirits cannot help someone who doesn't want to help himself."

"What was his name?"

"Grukarr."

Promi shuddered. "That madman? He's horrible!"

"So . . . you've met him?"

Promi rubbed his sore temple. "Once or twice." He grimaced. "And I can tell you, it wasn't your fault he didn't respond to your teaching. That man is like a moldy, rotten fruit—all bad, through and through."

The old monk shook his head. "No one is all bad. I never gave up trying to help him."

"What happened in the end?"

Bonlo sighed. "When he became the Deputy High Priest and showed himself willing to do anything desired by Araggna, who is just as lustful for power as he is—I confronted him. Told him how far he had strayed from the core of our faith. Explained what a tragic mistake it was to exclude from worship all the nature spirits who live right here in our world."

"And," asked Promi, "he didn't take it well?"

"You could say that. He condemned me to die."

"Just for speaking honestly?"

"Yes, lad. He asked Araggna to order me killed—beheaded—in the market square. She gladly complied, for she had always seen me as a threat to her influence over the Divine Monk."

"That's horrible!"

"True, but I was fortunate. Because of all my years of faithful service, the Divine Monk mercifully intervened on my behalf . . . and sent me to this dungeon instead."

"Where," said Promi, "you would die anyway."

The old monk bit his lip, then spoke again, trying his best to sound grateful. "The Divine Monk did what he thought was best.

And besides, if I hadn't been sent here, I wouldn't have met you. And I must tell you, Promi . . . it is truly a blessing to die in such good company."

The young man shook his head. "Don't talk like that. Now that our ropes are untied—"

"There is no escape, my good lad. No one ever leaves Ekh Raku alive."

Promi scowled, sensing the truth in the monk's words—yet not wanting to admit it. "We might still surprise Grukarr."

Bonlo's expression darkened. "You may be right about him, lad. I suspect that not even Narkazan, the wicked warlord of the spirit realm, is more arrogant and vengeful. Yet they are both out there, free to move in their worlds . . . while we are stuck in here." He paused, then added a single word:

"Forever."

CHAPTER 11

Starstone and Prophecy

New ideas can be tasty, maybe even satisfying. But what I really want to taste is a nice big tray of pastries, warm and sweet, right out of the oven.

—From Promi's journal

Promi checked the monk's wounded toe again. The bandage, soaked with blood, looked even redder than the dungeon stones. Blood continued to drip onto the floor.

Feeling bad for the old fellow, Promi tried to change the subject to something other than their imprisonment. "When you taught scriptures and things like that," he asked, "did you have a favorite subject?"

"Oh, I liked just about everything." The monk's eyes, gray with flecks of green, brightened. "Though I did, I suppose, have a specialty."

"What was that?"

"History." Bonlo gazed at the nearest torch, watching its shadows dance on the stones. "Especially the War of Horrors . . . and the wonderful outpouring of magic that came afterward."

Promi scratched his chin. "That war—it was thousands of years ago, right? Something about an attack by immortals?"

"Only *some* immortals," corrected the monk. His face took on the expression of a teacher ready to guide a new student. "Led by Narkazan, the warrior spirit, a band of them attacked the Earth. That's right—our world! They hoped to conquer and enslave all mortal creatures, as well as the nature spirits who have made this their home. Why? To capture all the Earth's magic and use it to increase their own power. For that is what Narkazan craves most of all—power."

Promi sighed, not very interested. This was, after all, ancient history. "But they lost, right? So the war turned out all right in the end."

"Not if your village was destroyed, your body maimed, your family killed, or your river poisoned," answered Bonlo sternly. "It truly deserved the name Horrors! And remember this, my good lad: *Narkazan almost won.* He lost only because of the good beings from the spirit realm who fought against him—Sammelvar, O Halro, Escholia, and others. And the many brave mortals who joined them. As well as the most powerful nature spirits from this realm—the ones who still live today in places like the Great Forest."

Doubtfully, Promi asked, "The beings some people call river gods and tree spirits? They joined the battle?"

"Yes, lad."

"And helped humans beat back the invasion?" He frowned skeptically. "You're saying that these characters out of the old myths actually fought against Narkazan and still are here now?"

"That's exactly what I'm saying." Bonlo's tone became grave.

"Without that great alliance among spirits and mortals, the invaders would have surely prevailed. And our world would be very, very different today." Sadly, the monk shook his head. "Many of those mortals, people from all walks of life as well as creatures from the forests and birds from the sky, lost their lives to protect our world."

He sighed. "Some groups—such as the Listeners, gifted people who actually knew how to tap into the magic of the Great Powers—suffered far more than their share. Why, even though the strongest Listeners could produce enough power to change the course of a river or cause a thunderstorm on a sunny day, they were no match for the invaders. And so, in trying to save us, the Listeners lost so many people, they vanished entirely from the world."

Promi swallowed. "I, um . . . never knew that."

"Of course not. People have stopped talking about it, even right here in the city named for the Great Powers. But as soon as people forget their history . . . they are likely to repeat it."

"Those good immortals—the ones who fought against Narkazan—did they have anything to do with the special magic of Ellegandia? The gift I keep hearing about in the old myths?"

"Well, well," said Bonlo, amused. "Seems like you want to know more of the story! I understand, of course. *Every* good story needs an ending."

"All right," the young man admitted. "Maybe I *am* a little curious."

"Being curious is the first step to becoming a good student, you know."

Promi grinned. "So tell me, then, my good teacher . . . what gave Ellegandia so much magic?"

Bonlo ran a hand through his white curls. "Remember, now, the Earth has always possessed a healthy amount of magic. From the very beginning, you could find it in forests and oceans, marshes and mountains, all around the world. Anywhere the spirits of nature could flourish. So you could also find magic in Ellegandia—but no more than in many other places."

He tapped his brow, as if saying a silent prayer of thanks. "The immortals who fought Narkazan didn't do that because they wanted the Earth's magic for themselves. Quite the opposite. Those spirits understood something fundamental—the moral imperative of keeping the two worlds separate. Forever apart."

"But why?"

"Ah," replied Bonlo. "You ask an excellent question. And the answer is clear. Only if the two worlds are kept apart can mortal men and women choose the future of their world! Through their own free will. Yes, even if they make many grievous errors along the way. Free will, you see, is both very valuable and very fragile."

Promi raised his eyebrows. "So there can be no contact at all between the mortal and immortal realms?"

"There can be no *movement* between the worlds, no visitations to Earth from the spirits who live on high. But there can still be some forms of contact—especially prayer." The old man's expression clouded. "I have learned some helpful things—and some worrisome things—from prayer."

Interested, Promi bent closer. "Such as?"

"Such as there is a new war going on right now among the spirits on high. Narkazan is trying to dominate the whole spirit realm. So far, Sammelvar and Escholia have been able to contain him—but Narkazan is gaining rapidly. And there is also a Prophecy . . ." He caught himself and declared, "First things first, good student! I haven't even told you about the last war yet. And we are about to get to the best part."

"Which is?"

"What happened right after the War of Horrors ended."

Drawing a deep breath, Bonlo continued, "As a way of expressing deep gratitude for all those mortals and nature spirits who had done so much to win the war and preserve the independence of both worlds, Sammelvar and the other immortals gave the Earth a gift. A most precious gift."

"What?" asked Promi, intrigued.

"The Starstone." As he spoke the word, the monk's voice hushed. "Crafted by the immortals' most skilled magic makers, it is quite small—no bigger than a hawk's egg—but infinitely powerful."

"All right, but what *is* it?"

Bonlo grinned. "A special kind of crystal, capable of magnifying whatever magic is around it. Just as a magnifying glass makes things look bigger and closer, or just as a prism takes in colorless light and puts out all the brilliant colors of the rainbow—the Starstone takes in simple magic and puts out amazingly rich, complex, and enhanced magic. *Its very presence* makes the magic around it more powerful. And that makes everything more beautiful."

Promi's eyes widened. "That sounds precious, all right. So . . . where on Earth is this Starstone?"

"No one knows for certain. But many, including myself, believe it's hidden right here in our own little country."

Promi gasped. "Which would explain—"

"Ellegandia's special magic."

"Could it be," Promi wondered aloud, "somewhere in the Great Forest?"

"What better place to hide something so valuable?" The old man chuckled softly. "In an uncharted, magical forest deep in Ellegandia—a place unknown to the outside world."

"Which is why," Promi reasoned, "the Divine Monks have long decreed that nobody could leave the country. So the word of our magic—and this treasure—wouldn't spread."

"Correct, my good lad. For such tales would cause only temptation—and trouble. That is also why the immortal spirits built up the sheer cliffs that surround our peninsula on three sides—and the high peaks of Ell Shangro on the fourth."

Amazed, Promi stared at him. "The immortals did that? All to protect the Starstone?"

"Yes, and all the natural magic that now thrives here." For a moment, Bonlo watched the torchlight tremble on the dungeon wall. Then he added, "They did something else, too. The immortals placed a special magic on the Great Forest, the power to repel any invasion—whether it came, once again, from the spirit realm, or from forces right here on Earth. They called that power the *pancharm*. And it has protected the forest to this very day."

Promi's eyes widened. "So nobody could invade us to steal the Starstone?"

"Nobody. As long as the Great Forest survives, so will the pancharm."

For a moment, Promi didn't speak, trying to decide how much of this to believe. "This isn't just another myth, right? You're sure all this is real?"

Bonlo nodded. "As real as the holiday of Ho Byneri."

"The high summer holiday? What does that have to do with any of this?"

"Ah, good lad, you show genuine curiosity." He winked at Promi. "I warn you, though. Once you know a little of the truth, you will want to know more. And then you'll want to know the ending! As I said before, *every* good story needs one."

"Sure, sure. But what were you saying about Ho Byneri? It's a month away." Promi glanced grimly around the dungeon. In the distance, along with the sound of water dripping, he heard the unmistakable scurrying of a rat. "Not that either of us will live to see it."

Bonlo shifted his legs and bumped his wounded toe against the floor. He winced painfully. Then, as his thoughts returned to

Ellegandia's history, he relaxed again. "The holiday is actually just two weeks away. And contrary to what most people think, it wasn't created to celebrate the long days of summer."

"So why, then, was it created?"

"To mark the day the War of Horrors finally ended. The very day Sammelvar gave the Starstone to the mortal world."

Promi raised an eyebrow, still not sure how much of this to believe.

"More than that," the old monk went on, "Ho Byneri also marks something else. Something important . . . as well as dangerous. *It is the day each year when the veil between the worlds is thinnest.*"

Seeing the doubt on his companion's face, Bonlo continued, "Magic, you see, moves like a tide. It ebbs and flows—in and out, in and out, year after year—touching shores both mortal and immortal."

He drew a deep breath. "Magical events on a grand scale can shape that tide, affecting its flow. Now, just think about how much happened at the end of the War of Horrors! The movement of vast numbers of spirits between the worlds. The gift of the Starstone—possibly the most powerful magical object in the universe. And the pancharm to ward off invaders. Even the building up of Ellegandia's sea cliffs and mountains. *All on the same day.*"

Again, he shifted his weight. "As a result, the tide of magic, already near its low point, ebbed even more. And so . . . as we approach Ho Byneri, the veil that divides our world from the spirit world grows increasingly thin. On the day itself, at sunrise, it is so thin that it's barely there at all."

Promi blinked in surprise. "Immortals could pass into our world on that day?"

"That's right."

"Really?" Then a new idea struck him. "And so . . . on that day, mortals could also go to the spirit realm?"

"Well, perhaps." Now it was Bonlo's turn to look skeptical.

"Such a thing has never happened before. At least . . . not that anyone knows."

"But," insisted Promi, "it's possible."

"Highly unlikely, lad. Even the stories about wind lions, those spirit creatures who carry our prayers between the worlds, never say anything about carrying *people*."

"I know, I know," said Promi. "It's just that . . . well, what a great adventure that would be! Do you think the stories are true about all the sweet things up there? Rivers full of honey and desserts that grow on trees?" He smacked his lips. Suddenly he remembered his glorious feast of the pie—and how very hungry he was now. Especially since that pie had probably been his last meal ever. Glumly, he said, "Not that I like eating sweets."

The old man gazed at him with compassion. "I share your hunger, good lad. And your discouragement." He bit his lip. "I have many worries, and they are growing."

"Like . . . will we survive?"

Bonlo's expression darkened. "That is the least of my worries."

Puzzled, Promi cocked his head. "The least? What could be a bigger worry than that?"

"Not whether you and I will survive—but *whether Ellegandia and our world will survive*."

"What? You just told me all about this land's uniqueness, its special magic—as well as the Starstone and the pancharm that will keep us safe."

"Yes," said the elder gravely. "But I haven't told you about the Prophecy."

"Then tell me now."

"Well . . . not much is known, frankly. And much of that is just idle speculation. Besides, prophecies are famously ambiguous, so their meanings are uncertain. What I do know, though, from prayer, is the wording of this one. And believe me, lad, it's not encouraging. Do you really want to hear it?"

"Try me," answered Promi. "Though I should tell you, I don't believe in things like prophecies." He winked at Bonlo. "But you've got me curious. Like a good student."

The old man's eyes twinkled. "I only wish I could teach you about something happier. You will see why this prophecy is on my mind as we approach the holiday of Ho Byneri."

He recited:

The end of all magic:
A day light and dark.
First light Ho Byneri,
The Starstone's bright spark.
New power can poison,
Great forces can rend
Worlds highmost and low:
The ultimate end.

For a long moment, neither of them spoke. The only sounds in the dungeon were the occasional scurrying of rats and the steady *drip-drip-drip* of water on the stone floor. At last, Promi repeated the Prophecy's opening line.

"*The end of all magic.* What does that mean, Bonlo?"

"The same as that final phrase, I suspect: *The ultimate end.*"

Promi ran a hand through his sooty hair. "Sorry, but none of this makes much sense to me. Anyway, I can't get too concerned about it—or any other myth about worlds changing and magic ending." He shrugged. "Truth is, Bonlo, you got me wrong. I'm nothing special. I'm just a thief who throws a good knife, keeps a journal, and doesn't care about anything besides where to grab my next meal. So long as there are pies and pastries to steal, I really don't care about the rest of the world."

Bonlo peered at him closely. "You must have lost quite a lot, good lad, to speak that way."

Promi swallowed.

"And I don't believe a word of it," the monk went on. "No, I didn't get you wrong. In fact, I'd wager to say that—"

A scream erupted, cutting him off. Full of pain, it swept through the dungeon.

CHAPTER 12

A Blessing

Sure, I expected you to be completely foolhardy. You are, after all, Promi. But I never expected it to be so painful for you. And for that . . . I am truly sorry.

—From her journal, above a sketch of dark shadows gathered around a huddled form

The scream echoed down the dimly lit corridors. It came, Promi felt certain, from a woman—a woman in anguish. As her scream faded, other sounds took its place: the crack of a whip, another shriek of pain, then someone's cruel laughter.

Promi glanced at Bonlo. "I'll be back."

Looking fearful, the old monk nodded. "Be careful, lad."

"Will you be all right?"

"Yes, yes. I'm not going anywhere with this wretched foot. But if that hungry rat attacks me again . . . well, don't worry. I'll be fine."

Promi looked at him doubtfully.

Another scream echoed.

Promi slipped away, keeping to the darkest shadows. Pressed against the wall, he moved with the stealth of a practiced thief, slipping down one corridor and then another. Just beyond the flickering light from one torch, he paused to listen.

Right around the next bend, he could hear the woman's anguished breathing. Her tormentor laughed again and cracked a whip. She had grown so weak that this time she didn't scream, but only moaned miserably.

Creeping to the corner, Promi peered into the shadowy corridor. There stood a hulking guard who carried a whip. On the floor at his feet lay a woman clothed in rags, her long white hair spread across the red stones.

The guard, whose back was to Promi, raised his boot and kicked the woman in the back. She moaned again and mustered enough strength to crawl feebly away.

"Where you goin', witch?" The guard started to swing his whip. "No escape fer you, not never."

Craaaaack! The whip snapped, slashing the back of her neck. She stopped crawling, moaned once more, then fell silent.

Promi scowled. *Curse the sky and sea and everything in between! How can I stop him?*

Meanwhile, the guard glowered at the helpless woman. He grunted, deciding where to kick her next. Slowly, he raised his boot.

Frantically, Promi looked for something to throw. *One more kick like that could kill her.*

Seeing nothing he could use, he threw the only thing he could—himself. He sprinted across the stones and plowed into the guard from behind. Caught by surprise, the burly man slammed headfirst into the stone wall, so hard that a ceiling beam snapped and chunks of mud and mortar rained down on the dungeon floor.

The guard rolled over, dazed. Promi punched him in the jaw,

throwing all his weight into the swing. The big man crumpled to the floor, unconscious.

Dodging the chunks of mortar, Promi ran over to the woman. Dark welts covered one of her arms, and blood ran down her neck. She didn't stir when he touched her shoulder. Gently, he rolled her over.

Her eyes remained open but unseeing. Completely lifeless, her deep green irises stared up at him.

"Don't die, now." Promi gave her a shake. Still no response. He bent closer to check her breathing, but there wasn't even a hint of breath.

Dead! I'm too late.

A shadow dimmed the torchlight. As Promi turned, a heavy fist smashed into the side of his head. He reeled and fell against the wall. Barely able to stand, he could only watch as the wrathful guard strode toward him.

"You slimy beast," the guard spat. His massive arms and shoulders flexed as he clenched both fists.

Promi tried to move away, but didn't have enough strength. Nor could he stop his mind from spinning. Tasting something bitter on his tongue, he swallowed. Around the mark over his heart, the skin burned.

The burly man advanced and roared with rage. He kicked Promi in the ribs, sending the young man sprawling. "I'll break your bones, ev'ry last one."

Waves of pain coursed through Promi's body, but he still tried to sit up. That ended abruptly when a heavy boot stepped on his chest, pinning him to the floor.

Can't move! Can't breathe!

Squeezing the handle of his whip, the guard growled, "Then I'll wrap this around your scrawny neck and strangle you dead."

He raised a huge fist. "But first, boy, your face needs to change shape."

At that instant, the torch right behind him suddenly crackled and flamed brighter. The guard spun around—just as the torch's wooden pole swung forcefully and slammed into his head. Sparks exploded in the air, sizzling as they flew across the dungeon.

The guard staggered, then fell in a heap. Above him, still holding the torch, stood Bonlo.

The old monk swayed unsteadily. He dropped the torch, which hit the floor with a spray of sparks. He looked at Promi with an unmistakable gleam of satisfaction—then collapsed.

Despite the pain that surged through his chest, Promi crawled over to his friend's side. "Bonlo! You saved my life."

The monk blinked up at him. He drew a frail breath. "Yes, my good lad. And also . . ." He struggled to take another breath. "I managed . . . to end mine . . . with dignity."

"No, no," Promi insisted. "You're not going to die!"

Anxiously, he glanced at the old man's bloody foot. The severed toe now hung barely by a sinew; it was bleeding profusely. A trail of blood on the stone floor marked Bonlo's arduous journey through the dungeon.

Promi cradled the elder's head, meshing his fingers in the white curls. "Please," he begged, "don't die."

Weakly, Bonlo whispered, "Every good story . . . needs an ending."

For a long moment, they held each other's gaze. Then the old monk added, so softly it was almost inaudible, "It is truly a blessing . . . to die . . . in such good company."

His eyes closed.

Gently, Promi lowered the monk's head. "Wish I could bury you, old friend. Or burn you in great honor, the way they do Divine Monks."

Feeling another kind of pain, worse than the physical kind, Promi bit his lip. He tried to pull off his tunic in order to place it over the old man's face. But just that small movement caused his ribs to hurt so badly that he nearly fainted.

He sank back to the floor. His chest throbbed; his mind darkened. Turning his head toward Bonlo, he moaned, "Good thing you died first. That way . . . you thought . . . you really saved me."

Certain that he, too, would soon die in this dungeon, Promi moaned. He'd never taste another sweet treat—let alone one as fabulous as smackberry pie. He'd never move freely in the world again, choosing how and when to steal his next meal. And worst of all, he'd never even get to find out if he might actually do something meaningful with his life—the life Bonlo had tried so hard to save.

He cringed, knowing the hard truth: He wasn't the least bit special, despite what the old monk had believed. Why, he couldn't be more different from all those brave people Bonlo had described! They had given everything to protect their world—to make it safe for the Starstone.

"And what have I done?" he asked bitterly, his words echoing among the dank walls. "Nothing but steal . . . pies and cinnamon buns."

"Well," said someone nearby, "at least that's a start."

Promi gasped. With all his strength, he forced himself to lift his head. And he saw, gazing down at him, the white-haired woman.

He stared at her in disbelief. "Alive?" he sputtered. "You . . . you're *alive*?"

She merely watched him, toying with a single strand of her hair.

He shook his head, sending a blast of pain through his skull. How could she still be alive after the guard's brutal beating? She looked impossibly strong and healthy, with no welts on her arm, as if nothing had happened.

No, he realized with astonishment. *She looks even better than that.*

Sure enough, her face seemed younger somehow. Her skin was more ruddy and not so wrinkled. Her long hair, while still white, was thicker than before, sweeping gracefully around the contours of her face. Most striking of all, though, were her eyes. Radiant green, they gleamed with new light, like a forest at dawn.

CHAPTER 13

Listen One, Listen All

It wasn't easy, Promi. But it certainly got your attention.

—From her journal

"I thought . . ." A new wave of pain crashed through Promi's head and ribs, making him stop. "Thought you . . . were dead."

The woman peered down at him and almost smiled. "Perhaps I was."

She knelt beside him on the dungeon floor. Gently, she placed a hand on his chest. "Now, though, I am feeling very much alive."

"That's better . . . than I'm feeling." He tried to sit up but groaned and fell back, hitting his head against the stone floor. "Uhhh," he moaned. "That oaf broke one of my ribs."

The woman's fingers played lightly over his chest. "Five, actually." Her voice was quiet, barely louder than the sputtering torches on the wall. After a few seconds, she scowled. "But that's not the worst of it."

"How?" He tensed, waiting for another wave of pain to pass. "How . . . do you know?"

"Shhhhh," she commanded. "Be quiet so I can concentrate."

She tilted her head, as if she were listening for a distant sound. Her brow furrowed. Meanwhile, her fingers moved to a spot below his heart, tapped lightly, then stopped.

Seconds passed. Promi's whole chest seemed to shout in pain, convulsing with every breath. His mind spun, making it difficult to focus, but he couldn't miss her deepening frown. When, at last, she spoke, her tone was grave.

"Beneath the broken ribs, you have a punctured lung. Even now, it's filling fast with blood. Your kidney is torn and bleeding. And worse, your heart is also badly damaged—right under that mark of the bird on your chest."

He blinked in surprise. "That mark—it's under my tunic! How . . . do you know it's there?"

"Never mind," she replied. "But I can hear it clearly, just as I can hear your injuries."

"Hear?" He didn't understand why she had used that word. But he did, alas, understand her message. "Am I . . ." He swallowed a new wave of pain, then tried again. "Am I . . . dying?"

Grimly, she looked at him. "Yes. You are dying."

Promi drew a shallow breath, trying to ignore the swelling agony inside him. "Is there any . . . way to escape? To get help?"

She sighed, shaking her head. "You have only a few seconds to live." Sorrowfully, she stroked her long white locks. "Such a pity."

"A pity!" He coughed several times, each spasm worse than before. Blood coated his tongue; dizziness overwhelmed his mind. "It's worse . . . than that."

"Perhaps," she said calmly. "But it is truly inconvenient."

"Incon . . . venient?" He grimaced. "We're talking about . . . my life!"

"Yes. And more importantly, about my hair."

Great, he thought darkly. *She's completely crazy!*

The woman gazed at him, her green eyes alight. Even through the haze that was clouding his vision, Promi couldn't dispel the feeling that she looked almost—in some way he couldn't explain—like a different person. Truly changed from when he'd first found her. Meanwhile, she spread her fingers on his chest and spoke a single phrase.

"Listen one, listen all."

A sweeping, swishing sound, like a distant wind, flowed through the dungeon. Yet no real wind buffeted any of the torches.

No more than a few seconds had passed. But Promi could tell, beyond any doubt, that two things had changed.

He felt suddenly better! No more pain, no more coughs, no more dizziness. *Am I healed?* he wondered in disbelief. He sat up, thumping his chest.

Then he noticed the second change: the woman's white hair had completely disappeared. She gazed down at him, her hairless scalp glowing in the torchlight.

"Why do you look so surprised?" she asked. "I *told* you it was a pity."

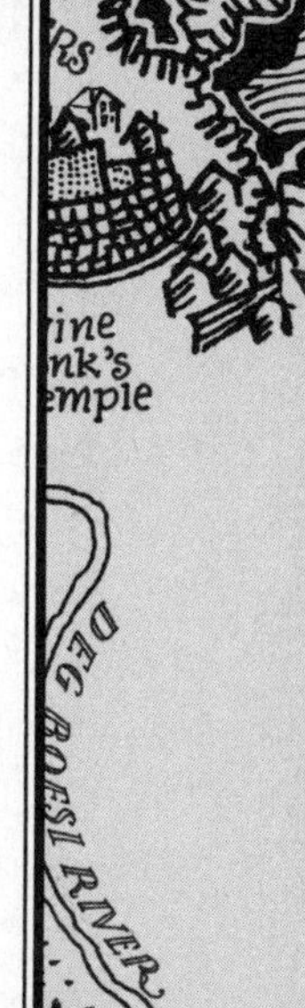

CHAPTER 14

To Hear the Unheard

I told you a lot, right then. More than I had planned. About the magic, the price, and the threat to our world. But there was one thing I couldn't bring myself to tell you.

The most important thing of all.

—From her journal

Promi sat up on the dungeon floor. He patted the ribs that had, only seconds before, been broken—and that now felt fully healed. Bewildered, he shook himself, his hair brushing his shoulders. Even the awful headache had disappeared.

"H-how . . . ?" he sputtered, peering at the hairless woman kneeling beside him. "How did you—well, do whatever you . . . um, did? And your hair?"

She rubbed the bare skin of her scalp. As if

trying to convince herself, she said, "So much trouble to wash hair like that."

"B-but . . . how? Yes, and . . . *how*?"

"Articulate, isn't he?" said a gruff little voice nearby.

Promi spun his head, searching for its source. The words hadn't come from the woman, who continued to watch him in silence. Nor from the guard, who was still unconscious; nor Bonlo, whose lifeless body lay on the stone floor.

"And he's not too observant, either." This time the little voice finished with a throaty chuckle.

The woman grinned. "Give him time, Kermi. He's still absorbing all this."

"Sure," replied the voice. "But he's about as absorbent as an old boot! Even that senseless guard lying over there could think faster than this young—"

"Hush, Kermi." She glanced up at the nearest torch, its flame dancing in her eyes. "Give him a chance."

Following her gaze, Promi finally saw who had spoken—a small, monkeylike creature hanging upside down by his surprisingly long tail, which he'd wrapped around the base of the torch. Deep blue, with patches of silver, the creature's fur seemed to vibrate in the wavering light. His large blue eyes looked much too big for his head—but even bigger were his round, furry ears, which swiveled constantly.

Smirking, the furry blue fellow gazed down at Promi. Then he did something completely unexpected: he blew a large, blue-tinted bubble, which floated up to the ceiling and popped when it struck a beam.

Turning to the woman, the creature grumbled, "Why should I give him a chance? He had one already—and completely botched it."

Promi's face flushed with anger. "Now, hold on! Because of me—"

"We all nearly died," said Kermi flatly. "But to be fair, when you were staggering around, you did at least manage to avoid falling on top of the old monk."

At the mention of Bonlo, Promi suddenly had an idea. He grabbed the woman's arm. "Can you save him too? If anyone deserves to live, he does."

Sadly, she shook her head. "Alas, I cannot heal the dead. Only the living."

"Too bad," said Kermi dryly. He blew a new pair of blue-tinted bubbles. "If you ask me, you saved the wrong one."

Leaping to his feet, Promi started to take a swipe at the sassy creature. Just before he swung his arm, the woman jumped up and grabbed his tunic sleeve. "Stop it," she commanded. "Both of you!"

She glared at the little beast dangling from the torch. "I mean it, now. Introduce yourself."

"I never introduce myself to strangers." Kermi shut his big blue eyes. "Besides, he's gone now."

Promi turned to the woman. "Who are you two? And how did you heal me?" He pointed at her arm and neck, no longer streaked with blood. "As well as yourself?" He studied her suspiciously. "And how come you look so much *younger*?"

"Oh," she said casually. "Must be my new hairstyle." She pretended to stroke her flowing locks. "It has that effect on people."

"And another thing. How did you—"

"Later," she declared, cutting him off. Flicking her hand toward the torch, she said, "That is my companion, a rare blue kermuncle. They are known for their sassy wit, their ability to blow bubbles, and their—"

"High intelligence," finished the creature proudly. He turned his gaze toward Promi and added, "Unlike some people."

The woman barely kept herself from laughing. She rubbed the side of her now-bald head and added. "But kermuncles are *not* known for their polite conversation."

Kermi snorted. "How about this? I absolutely *love* your new look! So . . . bald."

"Enough," she replied, narrowing her eyes at him. "Or I'll be forced to send you back to . . ." She caught herself. "To where you came from."

"Really?" he asked hopefully, his blue eyes wider than ever. "You'd let me go back?"

"No," she answered firmly. "I shouldn't have said that. You can't go back until—"

"I keep my promise," he said glumly. "I know, I know. But I never should have made it! He's so much stupider than—"

"You promised, Kermi! Don't forget that. Do I need to remind you what happens to kermuncles if they break a promise?"

The furry creature sighed. "I'd shrivel up and die! Which means that I could *never* go back home. Honestly, I can't understand why we kermuncles are made that way. Amidst such perfection, a true design flaw!" He glared at Promi, whose expression looked more confused than ever. "And what do I get for making that promise in a moment of weakness? The great joy of associating with someone who makes an acorn look smart."

Though he bristled at the kermuncle's insults, Promi kept his gaze focused on the woman. "You still haven't told me who *you* are. Or how you healed me. By the way, my name is Promi."

She bowed her head. "I am Jaladay." Cautiously, she glanced around the dungeon, then added, "And . . . *I am the last of the Listeners.*"

"Listeners? I thought they all died ages ago."

Frowning, she replied, "Almost true. We lost vast numbers of our faith in the War of Horrors. Then more died in the centuries that followed, killed by ignorant folk who feared them, calling them witches and goblins."

Promi pointed at the unconscious guard. "Folk like him."

"Yes," said Jaladay grimly. "But a few of us, very few, survived."

She nudged the guard's boot with her bare foot. "When that fellow found her—er, I mean *me*—he was certain I was a witch. Just as he'd been taught by those hateful and intolerant religious leaders he serves."

Promi glanced over at the body of his friend Bonlo. *Not all of them are hateful and intolerant,* he thought. *Some of them are truly good and loving.*

Unsure whether or not to believe Jaladay, he said, "Look, I've heard a few tales about the Listeners. How they could whip up a storm anytime they wanted. How they could read people's minds, predict the future, and more. You're telling me all that stuff is true?"

She nodded.

"That's hard to swallow."

Her gaze bored into him. "Harder than being magically healed of wounds that should have killed you?"

Instinctively, he patted his ribs. "No."

"Well, then," she said sternly, "don't forget how little you really know."

He chewed his lip. "I'm reminded of that every day."

"Good," declared Jaladay. "Then you're already walking on the path to wisdom."

Kermi chuckled, swaying from the torch. "Get ready for a very long walk."

Jaladay scowled at the kermuncle, then turned back to Promi. "Not all the legends you've heard are true, by the way. Only the greatest master Listeners could call up a storm—or do anything to influence the elements of nature. That takes the highest levels of magical power. And no one with that sort of power has walked in this world for many centuries."

She stepped closer, practically pressing her nose against his. "Though nobody except a master could call up a storm, any Listener of reasonable skill could *predict* the coming of a storm. Or, for that matter, read the secrets of someone's mind. That's how most of the legends got started."

She sighed. "And that's also how the fear of Listeners got started. Why villagers started to persecute my people—and why the Divine Monks, who felt threatened by this older faith, did everything they could to extinguish our ancient flame."

Promi swallowed. "How about healing someone's body? Is that something all Listeners could do?"

"Not all, but some. Although . . . something that difficult is a bit more, shall we say, *costly.*"

"Well, however you did it, I'm grateful to you for saving my life. But . . . I still have trouble believing all that Listener stuff. Why, even the crazy things I write in my journal aren't as wild as what you're saying."

Unexpectedly, Jaladay smiled. For an instant, she seemed to have lost some more years, as if she were really no older than Promi herself. "You keep a journal?"

"Sometimes." He tapped the tunic pocket that held his book full of scribbles in the margins. "Now and then. Just to remember things."

"What kinds of things?"

He shifted uncomfortably. "Oh, just . . . memories. Like a good meal, which hasn't happened in a while. Or dreams—especially the peaceful ones, though they come less often than scary ones. Or sometimes, good ideas for stories."

"You know," she said, "that shows intelligence and imagination."

From the torch above them came a rude snort.

Jaladay ignored it and said earnestly, "Imagination is precious. Why, it was that very quality in humans that inspired immortals to give them Listener magic."

Promi started. "This power of yours came from the spirit realm?"

"Long ago, yes. It was a gift from some spirits who enjoyed

visiting the mortal realms—before the War of Horrors led to a strict ban against any immortals coming to Earth."

She looked suddenly older. "But the truth is, this power isn't so much a gift as a burden. A responsibility."

Placing her hand on his shoulder, she explained, "That's why Listeners have sometimes given away their power—and why, Promi, I would like to give my power to *you*."

"Me?" He stared at her, astonished.

"That's right. And I want to do this now. You see, even though I've, well, revived enough to heal you . . . my time to live is almost gone."

"But," he objected, "how do you know that?"

"The same way I knew about your wounds. Or, for that matter, about the mark over your heart. By Listener magic." She sighed. "And since I am the last one of my kind, when I die . . . the magic will die with me. Disappear forever from the world. Unless I give it to someone else."

"Why me, though? Why would you give such powerful magic to me?"

"Harrumph," said Kermi. "Could be you're the only living person down here at this moment! Other than the guard, of course . . . but he doesn't look too interested. So don't think you're anything *special*."

Hearing that word again, Promi thought of Bonlo—and the old fellow's persistent belief in him. Promi looked over at the corpse, knowing just what he'd say if the monk were alive: *I still think you were wrong, my friend.*

Jaladay's expression hardened. "You have a choice. This magic could allow you to tap into the Great Powers, to draw strength from the spirits of both worlds, to do amazing feats. Yet this same magic could also bring you great pain. The loss of something you love. Or worse. For every use of this magic comes with a cost—sometimes a truly terrible cost."

She squeezed his shoulder. "Now you must decide, Promi. Do you want it or not?"

Torchlight flickered across his face as he considered her words. *Power. Pain. Magic.* And, last of all, *cost.*

Not just any cost. *A truly terrible cost.*

And yet . . . power like that would be useful. Very useful. For starters, he could use it to get food—and to make sure he never, ever felt hungry again.

That notion was especially appealing. Why, if he could predict a thunderstorm, then he shouldn't have any problem predicting when a truly tasty pie was about to emerge from someone's oven. Or how to escape unharmed, no matter how brazen the thievery. *Ah, the things I could do!*

Again, his gaze strayed to the old monk. Bonlo's face looked quite peaceful, full of kindness and trust. The very same qualities he'd shown to Promi.

And who knows, old fellow? Maybe I might find some way to use this new power that could actually justify your faith in me.

Resolved, Promi nodded. "Show me this magic."

The kermuncle, dangling from his perch, shuddered. "You are definitely going to regret this, Jaladay! Even worse, I have a feeling that *I'm* going to regret this."

"Hush, now." She glanced cautiously over her shoulder, then placed her hands over Promi's ears. As she peered at him with total concentration, her fingers vibrated ever so slightly. Finally, she lowered her hands.

"The magic is yours," she announced.

"Really?" He shook himself. "I don't feel any different."

"You will in time. The more you use the magic, the more you will be aware of it."

"But—"

"Above all," she declared, interrupting him, "you must

understand this: Listener magic does not take anything away from the world. Nor does it force anything new upon the world. Rather, *it simply listens to the underlying truth of the world.*"

The young man shook his head. "You'll have to do better than that if you want me to understand."

"Told you he's hopeless," groused Kermi.

"Let me put it this way," said Jaladay, cupping her hand to her ear as if she were trying to hear some faraway sound. "This magic allows you to hear not with your ears—but with your heart. With every particle of magic that lives in you—and also in the world around you."

"Is that why," he asked, "before you healed me, you said *Listen one, listen all*?"

"Right," she said approvingly. "Listener magic gives you the power to call upon the sources of magic, wherever they exist. To open yourself to the power of the spirits—whether they live in our world right here or in the spirit realm on high. To discover the deepest truths. To hear the unheard."

"*To hear the unheard*," repeated Promi. "You mean . . . like the real path of a storm. Or the real motives of a person."

"Or," she added, "the original condition of bones and muscles and organs . . . so that they can return to health."

Now it was Promi's face that suddenly looked grim. "What was that you said about a cost?"

"It's simple," she said with a sigh. "Every time you use this power to hear the deepest vibrations of the world . . . you must make a sacrifice."

"Like what?"

"For something easy, like reading someone's thoughts or seeing a hidden object like a sword behind a curtain, your sacrifice could be small. But for something more difficult, like healing someone's broken body, the price would be higher."

He eyed her with gratitude. “Like giving up all your hair.”

Tenderly, she rubbed her bare scalp. “Yes, I suppose that’s right. But as I said, it was always so troublesome. I’m glad to be rid of it.”

“Liar,” said Kermi, peering down at her.

She sighed. “The point is, your sacrifice must be in *proportion* to what you are seeking. The more important the goal, the greater the cost.”

In a voice tinged with compassion, she warned, “Just remember, if you ever choose to do something very large—then your sacrifice will also need to be very large.” Quietly, she added, “There are other things about how to use this power that you will have to discover for yourself. But soon enough, you will learn.”

“Harrumph,” said the little creature hanging from the torch. “That assumes he *can* learn.” He blew a wobbly blue bubble that floated slowly upward. “Within his lifetime.”

“Oh, he can learn,” insisted Jaladay. With genuine fondness, she ran a finger across Promi’s cheek. “Much depends on it.”

She looked at him so piercingly that Promi shifted with unease. It felt as if she could see right through him, to secrets he didn’t even know he held within himself. “You have no time to spare. Do you hear me? *No time.* For when the sun rises on the high summer holiday of Ho Byneri, just two weeks from now—”

“Ho Byneri?” he interrupted. Glancing down at the old monk, he recalled Bonlo’s words. “When the veil between the worlds grows thin?”

“Perilously thin. That is when the Prophecy will—”

Suddenly they heard footsteps clumping down a nearby corridor. Another guard! Coming closer with every step.

Promi started. “We’ve got to escape!” he whispered urgently.

But Jaladay shook her head. “There is no escape. Unless . . . you use your new power.”

His eyes widened. “B-but . . . I don’t know how.”

“Then learn how,” she commanded. “Use it now!”

The footsteps grew louder, echoing in the dungeon. "Jobo," called the approaching guard. "Where are you?"

With a quick glance at the unconscious guard beside them, Promi thought fast. What had she told him to do? *Make a sacrifice. Then say those words.*

Quickly, he chose to give up his gold earring, acquired so recently from the temple guard. Closing his eyes, he concentrated on the earring, thinking about its golden sheen and its weight on his earlobe.

With great determination, he whispered, "Listen one, listen all."

Nothing happened.

He opened his eyes, puzzled. Hearing the footsteps steadily approaching, he looked pleadingly at Jaladay. "Help me!"

She merely crossed her arms and said nothing.

Mind racing, Promi wondered what he'd done wrong. *Maybe I need to get rid of the earring, to prove this is really a sacrifice.*

He pulled it off and threw it away. The earring clinked and rolled down the torchlit corridor.

"Jobo," called the other guard. "Talk to me, you big oaf! Where are you?"

Again Promi whispered, "Listen one, listen all."

Still nothing happened.

Frantically, he thought, *Try something bigger! That's the answer.*

He pulled open his tunic, revealing the mysterious scar. In the flickering torchlight, the bird's black wings seemed to beat, as if flying. As soon as she saw this, Jaladay caught her breath.

"I'll sacrifice this scar," said Promi. "I'd be just as happy without it, anyway."

Jaladay didn't respond. She just continued to stare at the strangely beating wings on his chest.

Hurriedly, he said the Listener's chant.

Seconds passed. The guard's footsteps grew ever louder. He was close now—just around the corner.

Nothing! No magic at all.

Growling with frustration, Promi said to Jaladay, "What do I do? You've got to tell me!"

She shook her head. "That I cannot do. What remains for you to learn, you must find out yourself."

"But the guard—"

Abruptly, the footsteps stopped. Looking straight at them from the other end of the corridor was the guard just as brawny as his companion slumped on the floor.

"Jobo!" he cried, enraged. Drawing his broadsword, he raced headlong toward Promi and the others.

"Now," said Kermi dryly, "would be a good time to learn how the magic works."

"I can't!" Promi shouted, staring fearfully at the oncoming guard.

Jaladay sighed. "All right, then. I've saved just enough magic to do this. So now . . . I will make my final sacrifice."

Something about the way she said *final* rang ominously, but Promi didn't have time to think about it. Desperately, he looked around the dungeon for a weapon—anything he could use to shield them from the deadly sword. But he couldn't find anything.

With the guard only a few paces away, Jaladay glanced at the blue kermuncle. "Remember your promise."

Kermi nodded grudgingly.

"And also," she added, "keep yourself hidden."

Again, he nodded.

"Listen one," she declared, "listen all."

A sudden whooshing sound, like a distant wind, swept through the dungeon. Promi heard the wind—then only silence.

CHAPTER 15

The Bridge to Nowhere

If only I had known what was really there! Then again, maybe that was more than any person—any mortal, at least—should know.

—From Promi's journal

Promi opened his eyes, though it didn't make much difference. Everything was dark. So dark that his first thought was, *No! I'm still in the dungeon.*

As before, he was lying on his back. And as before, there was something pointed pressing into the back of his head. He sat up, reached for the offending object—then realized that his hands could move freely.

He wasn't bound. And he wasn't in the dungeon! He grabbed the object, a rock as before, and hurled it into the blackness. It clattered, rolling along what sounded like a lumpy, hard surface.

A street, he realized. As his eyes adjusted to the dark, he could make out the bumpy rows of cobblestones, abandoned mud-brick houses on both sides, and what looked like some sort of structure beyond. *All right, so I'm on a lonely side street in the middle of the night. But where exactly? And how did I get here?*

He scratched his head and pulled a clump of mud out of his long hair. All at once, the memories flooded back to him. Jaladay, mysterious but kind, neither young nor old. Dear old Bonlo, who had believed in him without any reason. The horrible dungeon of Ekh Raku. That brutal guard, the broken ribs. That annoying blue beast who wouldn't stop insulting him. And strangest of all . . . Listener magic.

Had it all been a dream? That made the most sense. After all, the whole experience had an improbable, dreamlike quality. Even the sounds of those scurrying rats, the flickering torches, and the relentless dripping seemed unreal.

What a dream! Next time I write in my journal, I'll try to describe it—if that's even possible.

Thinking back, the last thing that seemed absolutely real was stealing the Divine Monk's prize smackberry pie. And gobbling down every juicy, delectable bite as he sat on the hillside. Maybe he'd just eaten so much pie so fast that he fell into a deep but troubled sleep? And dreamed that whole terrible time in the dungeon?

Yes, he thought, more and more convinced. *Next time I eat a whole pie, I'll go more slowly.* He felt a powerful pang of hunger. High time to find another meal! A big one. All that wild dreaming had made him ravenous.

He looked around for any landmarks he might recognize. *If I just figure out where I am, then I'll know a nearby bakery.*

Staring into the darkness beyond the street, he realized that the structure he'd noticed seemed to be . . . well, *moving.* Wavering somehow, like a dark flame. Although the night was moonless, a few stars had begun to appear, shining dimly on whatever was out there. And in that light, it really looked like it was moving. Almost . . . alive.

He picked himself up, patted his tunic to make sure his journal was still in its pocket, started to walk down the cobblestones to get a closer look. Suddenly he stopped, recognizing the wavering structure.

It's that bridge! That old, half-finished one with all those prayer leaves. Indeed, it was the fluttering of those leaves in the night breeze that made the bridge seem to be constantly moving.

He studied the unfinished bridge. It stretched part of the way across the canyon of the Deg Boesi River, many man heights above the endlessly crashing rapids. Now, in early summer, that river constantly surged with melted snow from Ellegandia's highest mountains, sending up huge clouds of mist from its roiling waters. Promi knew that the rapids had claimed more than a few lives of people foolish enough to try to swim across it—including some who had decided to explore this very bridge, crawled out too far, and disappeared forever into the thick mist that always swirled around the unfinished end.

That explained all the prayer leaves, rows and rows of them, each inscribed with a prayer and affixed by the stem to a line of string. Placed on the bridge by the families and friends of those who had fallen off or who had otherwise perished in the river's deadly rapids, the silver leaves were more than memorials to loved ones. Like all prayer leaves that flew from treetops, bridges, hillsides, windows, and temple roofs across Ellegandia, these leaves were a form of communication with the spirit realm. For every time the wind blew over them, people believed, the prayers on the leaves were spoken again. Like an endless song to the heavens, their words continued to reach beyond the mortal world.

Of course, he thought with a smirk, *that's all nonsense.*

He remembered the young priestess he'd met very near this spot a couple of years before. He'd been sitting by himself at the edge of the gorge, feet dangling over the cliff, eating a stolen loaf of pumpkin bread, when she walked by. She wore her hair in the longest braid he'd ever seen, long enough to wrap around her waist like a belt. Her eyes seemed so kind, her manner so gentle, that he did something that surprised himself: he offered her a piece of bread. They sat together for a while, listening to the roar of the rapids, watching the fluttering prayer leaves. And she told him the legend of wind lions—magical creatures who continuously lope from this world to the spirit realm, carrying all those prayers.

He'd listened intently, intrigued by her description. But of course, he didn't believe a single word of it.

Now, in the dim light, Promi watched the silver leaves tied to the dilapidated bridge. Trying to imagine all the tiny, invisible lions that would be needed to carry so many prayers, he gave a snort of disbelief. *Poetic idea, I'll admit. But still nonsense.*

Gazing at the structure, he felt more sure than ever that the only things that moved on the bridge were the lines of leaves. And that the only place the bridge could lead was nowhere.

He chuckled to himself. *The Bridge to Nowhere.* Maybe that was why nobody lived at this end of the City. Too many invisible lions running past all the time! *Or,* he thought more grimly, *too many ghosts of people who fell off that rickety old thing and died.*

Time for that meal! He could feel his empty stomach churning.

He turned and started to walk away from the bridge. Just then he felt something bulky inside his boot—not down in the bottom, but in the wide rim around his calf. As always, the magical boot had shaped itself to fit perfectly. But this time, it had expanded to hold something he didn't need. Probably a rock or a clump of mud.

"Poverty and pestilence!" he cursed. "What's in my boot?"

Leaning against the wall, he yanked off his boot and shook it upside down. But nothing fell out. Nothing at all. Puzzled, he brought it close to his face and peered inside.

Two bright blue eyes blinked at him from inside the rim. "Took you long enough, you fool! Do you think it's comfortable riding in your smelly old boot?"

Promi shouted in surprise and dropped the boot on the cobblestones. His heart pounded, while the truth burned in his brain.

Real. It was all real!

CHAPTER 16

Thievery

You couldn't possibly have known what would happen next, Promi. If you had, everything would have changed.

—From her journal

I couldn't possibly have known what would happen next. But even if I had, nothing would have changed.

—From Promi's journal

Promi opened his mouth, closed it, opened it again, and closed it again—all the while staring into his boot. Right back at him stared those bright blue eyes below two round, swiveling ears.

Still not willing to believe what he was seeing, he stammered, "Y-y-you? Kermi?" he said at last.

"Right, you fool." The little creature pulled up his long tail and, with its tip, calmly scratched the tip of his nose. "And in case you're confused—more than usual, I mean—that name is short for kermuncle, not curmudgeon. Which wouldn't fit me anyway, since that term applies to somebody who is always grumpy and criticizing. Totally unlike me."

"Oh, yes," said Promi mockingly. "You're just about the sunniest creature I've ever met."

The kermuncle snorted rudely. "Anyway, you can't call me Kermi. Only *she* was allowed to call me that."

"I'll call you whatever I want," snapped the young man. But the mention of the kermuncle's former companion softened his mood. "Jaladay," he said quietly, thinking about her generosity . . . as well as her mysterious ways. "Where is she now?"

The blue eyes blinked slowly. "I'd rather not discuss that." In a harsher voice, he added, "Certainly not with you."

"Great, then. We feel the same way about each other." He tried to shake the little beast out of his boot. "Go on, now. Run off and find someone else to torture."

But Kermi held tight to the inside of the boot, his small claws digging into the leather rim. "I'll do no such thing, much as I'd like to go."

Promi raised an eyebrow. "Why not?"

"Because, you idiot, she asked me to stay with you. And in a moment of weakness, I agreed."

"That promise, right?"

Kermi's whiskers twitched. "A big mistake. Now I'm stuck with you, for better or worse. And something tells me it's going to be a whole lot of worse."

Remembering their final few seconds with Jaladay, Promi asked, "Why did she tell you to stay hidden?"

"None of your business, manfool."

"Well, then," offered Promi, "I relieve you of your promise. Now, go! Get out of my boot and also my life."

The blue eyes narrowed. "Can't do that." His little blue face looked genuinely sad. "I made the promise to her, not you.

Only she could take it back. And, well . . . she's not around to do that."

Promi furrowed his brow. "What happened to her? Tell me."

Kermi folded his tiny paws on his chest. "I told you already. I'm not going to discuss that." As if to emphasize his point, he blew a big, wobbly bubble that floated up and popped on Promi's nose.

"Aaaak!" cried Promi in disgust, wiping off the oily residue. "Just go away, will you? I have enough on my mind without having to haul you around in my boot."

"Harrumph. That would imply, first, that you have a mind. And second, that it's in your foot." He scratched his blue cheek. "The second part, I suppose, could be true."

"Go away, I said. Now!"

Kermi shook his head. "Have you no decency, man? I cannot leave your imbecilic side!" Heaving a sigh of deep regret, he declared, "I am honor bound. And the honor of a kermuncle is worth—"

The rest of his words were muffled by the scrunching sound of Promi shoving the boot back onto his foot. "Fine, then," said the young man as he started to walk down the cobblestone street. "Hope you enjoy the ride."

Two small paws and a blue, furry head poked out from the rim. "I certainly won't enjoy the smell."

But Promi didn't hear the insult. He was already occupied with a far more important task—finding that next meal. The bigger and sweeter, the better. His stomach rumbled with anticipation.

Briskly, he strode through one darkened street after another, walking in the direction of people's homes . . . and, more to the point, their kitchens. It wouldn't be long, he knew from years of experience, before he smelled someone's early morning cooking. A nice big tray of corn muffins with raspberry jam? A honeyed filo dough pastry? A sweet cream and banana pie? It didn't matter, so long as he'd be eating soon.

Too bad he'd lost his knife back at the temple; having one always made his job easier. He'd need to find a new one soon. Maybe, with luck, someone would have left a knife along with his breakfast.

As he walked along, keeping as always to the darkest parts of the streets so he wouldn't be seen, he found himself wondering about Grukarr. Throwing Promi into the dungeon was cruel enough. But to put Bonlo, that loving old man, down there—that was beyond cruel. That was sheer malice combined with an insane thirst for power. Which sounded exactly like Grukarr.

Someday, he vowed angrily, *we'll meet again. And then I'll do more than steal your belt buckle.*

To calm himself, he tried to recall that haunting, half-remembered song that had so often comforted him. To his relief, the notes came to him right away this time, sounding louder and clearer than ever. As if someone was singing them right into his ear! Could the Listener magic be helping him hear his own thoughts better?

Turning a corner, he passed the first people he'd seen on the street—an elderly couple carrying a fresh loaf of darkseed bread. The smell of those seeds, so much like roasted almonds, along with the sweet molasses in the bread, made his nose tingle. He took a deep breath, but kept on walking. Tempting as it was to grab their loaf and run, he never stole from elders, children, or mothers with infants. Why, he wasn't really sure. Probably because it just seemed too easy. Besides, it was much more fun to take food away from wealthy merchants, grumpy bakers, overstuffed monks, or witless magistrates.

That whiff of freshly-baked bread, though, was a good sign. Maybe there was a bakery nearby? That would be fair game—as long as it wasn't the bakery of Shangri, with her carrot-colored braids and easy giggle, and her papa, the new owner of a lifetime supply of sapphires. *Those people,* he promised, *I'll never rob again.*

Besides, there were always plenty of bakeries to choose from. And at this time of day, there would be so many hot pastries coming out of the ovens at once, the bakers might not even notice if several of them mysteriously vanished. His mouth watered at the thought.

As if on cue, he entered a small square marked by a stone fountain—and, right behind the fountain, a bakery. The smells of wildflower honey, melted butter, cinnamon, roasted grains, and sugar glazing all filled the square . . . as well as his nostrils. He grinned, knowing that he'd soon be eating breakfast. That thought so inspired him that he even forgot, for the moment, the unwelcome passenger in his boot.

Though sunrise was still more than an hour away, women in thick shawls and men in heavy cloaks were already lining up for bread and pastries, squeezing loaves to test the crust, asking for samples, and paying for their purchases before hurrying home. So much activity was happening inside the shop that the hapless old fellow at the counter scurried around frantically, trying to deal with it all.

Perfect. For an instant, Promi wondered if he should try to take something by using Jaladay's gift of magic. If she'd been able to send him out of that dungeon all the way to the street by the bridge, why couldn't he simply send a tasty loaf of bread right into his arms?

He shook his head. The truth was, he didn't even know how to use the magic. If Jaladay hadn't sent him to safety just in time, he could never have done it himself. On top of that, didn't she make it quite clear that every use of Listener's magic required a price? A sacrifice of some kind? And the whole point of being a thief was to get things for free, not give them up.

"What are you waiting for?" asked a gruff voice from the rim of his boot. "Are you going to stand here in the shadows all day, or will you get us some breakfast?"

Promi scowled down at the little creature. "Who said anything about *us*?"

"Well, I'll be a buzzard's brother!" exclaimed Kermi. "Such rudeness. And after all the kindness and patience I've shown you."

Promi rolled his eyes. "Just keep out of sight," he growled. "And stay quiet."

Judging the right moment, Promi sauntered up to the bakery's open door. Casually, he slipped by other customers and up to the counter. Shelves of steaming hot pastries, stacked from the floor to the ceiling, filled the air with luscious smells.

He licked his lips, wondering what to choose. At that instant, the harried baker brought out an enormous tray of steaming hot sugar buns. To Promi's delight, the tray also held one more item—a fat lemon pie. It bulged within a butter crust thick enough to have been a meal itself. Lemon filling bubbled over the edges, scenting the air with a wondrous blend of tartness and sweetness.

Promi reached for the pie, ready to snatch it before anyone even realized what he'd done. His hand wrapped around the side of the pie's wooden plate. Meanwhile, his thumb brushed against the butter crust, which released a puff of lemony steam. He grasped the plate, slid it off the tray, and deftly hid it behind his back—all without the busy baker noticing.

With practiced ease, Promi slipped through the press of people and out to the street. Once his boots touched the cobblestones, he allowed himself a smile. The tangy smells of lemon, butter, and sugar filled every breath. His stomach, at long last, stopped churning with hunger and instead seemed to vibrate with sheer excitement.

"Not bad," piped up a voice from the rim of his boot. "You've done this sort of thing before?"

"Once or twice," Promi replied, striding down the cobblestones.

Now, he thought, *the only question left is where to eat this pie.*

He wasn't going to make the same mistake as last time and place himself where he could be seen. So where should he go?

This wasn't a sacred pie from the Divine Monk's table, of course, so there wouldn't be anyone actively searching for him. Yet he did have a few enemies to avoid. Especially Grukarr's band of men—"faithful minions," he'd called them. As newly freed prisoners, they didn't look as battle hardened as temple guards. But they seemed just as dangerous, maybe more so because of their debt to Grukarr. And then there was that blood falcon, the bird who had spotted him eating on the hillside.

Instinctively, Promi glanced upward. Between the roofs of mud-brick homes, he saw nothing but empty sky, touched by the first golden rays of dawn.

All clear. He strode down the street, looking for just the right spot to have his long-awaited meal. The pie, still steaming, felt warm in his hands.

He turned into an alley, completely empty except for a beggar slumped against the wall. Striding past, he noticed it was a young woman around his age. Oddly dressed, she wore a soiled purple gown made from some sort of plant. The robe, streaked with dirt and clumps of something sticky like tree sap, testified to an arduous journey. So did the young woman's bare feet, toughened by a great deal of walking.

Her brown curls looked as tangled as a thornbush. And her expression, deeply sad, couldn't be missed. Nor could her look of hunger when she caught a whiff of Promi's pie and lifted her head.

She watched him walk past, full of longing—but too proud or exhausted to call out. Yet what Promi noticed most was not her hungry, disheveled appearance, but something else.

Her eyes. A rich shade of blue-green, they seemed to combine the blue waters of a sunlit lake and the green leaves of a sapling in spring.

The eyes gazed at Promi. He started to think again about

where to eat his sumptuous meal. Then, so suddenly it surprised even himself, he turned on his heels and went back to the young woman.

Without really knowing why, he gave her the lemon pie. He simply slid it onto her lap as if it belonged to her.

She blinked up at him in astonishment. "For . . . me?"

"For you," he said brusquely, already feeling his hunger pangs returning.

He turned to go, forcing himself to think about where to find another bakery—and not about what a stupid thing he'd just done. But she grabbed the sleeve of his tunic. "Thank you," she said. "That's too kind of you."

"I know," he said grumpily, pulling away. "I only did it to keep you from dying of hunger right here on the street."

She raised an eyebrow.

"That's right," he declared. "Dead bodies always get in my way when I'm moving fast."

She watched him, clearly not believing a word.

"And don't expect this to happen again," he warned, "because it won't. Just eat that pie and go back to wherever you came from."

"I will," she said gratefully. "This will give me the strength I need to go back to the Great Forest."

He hesitated. "You live there? I didn't know any people actually did."

"My whole life. Until . . ." The sadness returned to her face. "Recently."

"Well," he said, "good luck. Try not to go around dying on the street anymore."

Her eyes sparkled. "I'll try. And . . . what's your name?"

"Promi."

"Well, Promi, I am Atlanta." She smiled for the first time, a beautiful smile that illuminated her face. "And I bless your eternal qualities."

Still feeling grumpy, he said, "Just bless that lemon pie and be on your way."

"Would you like some for yourself?"

"No," he lied. "Not really hungry. And besides . . . I never share food with anyone."

"Right," she answered. "Just like you never give away your food to anyone."

"Good-bye." He spun around, ready to go—just as a heavy net fell on top of them.

Men pounced on the net, holding down the prisoners, all the while cursing loudly. A blood falcon screeched from somewhere nearby. Finally came another sound, one Promi remembered all too well—the sound of someone's merry whistling.

CHAPTER 17

No Escape

When you taste something hot, you're bound to get burned.

—From Promi's journal, with a sketch of someone's angry face

"Well, well," said Grukarr, grinning maliciously as he straightened his turban. "What a delightful surprise."

He chortled, stroking the talons of the fierce bird on his shoulder. It had taken his men only a moment to tie up the prisoners and set them side by side against the wall of the alley. Now he stood over them, exuding triumph.

"The net, my dear Atlanta, was intended just for you. Since you so kindly placed yourself where my Huntwing could easily spot you, the rest was easy."

"A terrible, horrible mistake," she fumed, trying to wriggle free from the ropes that bound her hands and feet.

Promi sighed. "Happens to the best of us." He glanced at the telltale bulge in his boot, knowing exactly what Kermi was thinking: *Or the stupidest of us.*

"What I didn't expect, though," Grukarr continued, "was to catch you, too, pie stealer."

He strode up to Promi's side and kicked him hard in the abdomen. The young man groaned with pain, unable to breathe for several seconds. But he quickly regained his composure. Determined not to give the priest any more satisfaction, he merely glared at his captor.

Grukarr returned the glare. "How you managed to escape from Ekh Raku, I can't imagine. But it doesn't matter at all now. For I'm going to kill you right here in this alley, slowly and exquisitely, while I watch you writhe in pain."

His gaze swung back to Atlanta. "First, however, I have some unfinished business with this lovely young woman of the forest. She is going to help me."

Atlanta shot him a look that could have cracked a boulder into pieces. "Never!"

Grukarr toyed with his necklace of golden beads. "Not even if it's the only way to save your beloved forest?"

She caught her breath. "What does the forest have to do with this?"

"Everything, my dear." The priest whistled merrily. "You see, there are changes—big changes—about to happen. While I cannot reveal them to you, I can tell you this much: They are all part of my grand plan. They will bring great power to some people, especially the new ruler of this realm . . . and great misery to others."

He reached out his hand to stroke Atlanta's flowing curls, but she leaned away. "Don't touch me," she snarled.

Pulling back his hand, he smirked. "Soon enough, my dear, you will cooperate fully. Oh, yes! I need you to help me find the most magical places in the forest—places where I can get what I need as quickly as possible." His voice took on a more threatening tone. "You have already cost me several days, you see. Days I have spent searching for you instead of doing . . . what I need to do."

He ruffled Huntwing's tail feathers. "But we still have enough time, and some to spare. Now that I have you, at last, I will get what I need." His voice lowered menacingly. "I always do."

"You are a monster! I told you I'd never help you."

"Oh, but you will, Atlanta. You will. Otherwise, everything you care about will be lost forever." Chortling softly, he added, "And if you still resist . . . I will introduce you to my good friend over here."

Grukarr waved at the dark shadows under the wall behind him. Promi and Atlanta both peered at the spot. At first, neither of them saw anything unusual. Then, simultaneously, they noticed one place that seemed darker than all the rest, a shadow within the shadows.

All of a sudden, that shadow moved! It floated eerily away from the wall, a living blot of darkness. Quivering constantly, the dark being crackled with black sparks as it slid to Grukarr's side. Though only as high as the priest's waist, it seemed immensely dangerous.

Promi and Atlanta gasped, staring at the shadow being. Grukarr's men stood like statues, frozen with fear. Even Huntwing moved as far away as possible on his master's shoulder and shifted uneasily.

With a nod toward the crackling shadow by his leg, Grukarr said pleasantly, "You have never encountered a creature of this kind? Such a pity. Meet my friend, a mistwraith from the spirit realm."

Down in Promi's boot, Kermi shuddered. At the same time, the young man could feel the skin of his chest start to prickle.

"From the spirit realm?" he asked Grukarr. "I thought nobody could—"

Footsteps interrupted him. Turning into the alley came six

temple guards, heavily armed, marching in perfect unison. Right behind them strode an elderly woman whose spry movements belied her age—High Priestess Araggna, scowling as usual. Around her forearm, coiled tightly, rode her snake.

Grukarr stiffened, clearly surprised, while Huntwing clacked his beak viciously. The mistwraith instantly moved back to the shadows to avoid being seen by Araggna. Some of Grukarr's men also slunk away, hoping the High Priestess wouldn't recognize them. But a few others clenched their fists and muttered angry curses at the woman who had sentenced them to such cruel punishments.

Promi and Atlanta, meanwhile, could only watch the scene unfold. Both took this opportunity to struggle with their bonds, trying to loosen them; both failed completely. Atlanta wondered who this vile-looking woman could be—clearly someone of great power, judging from Grukarr's reaction. Promi, for his part, wondered whether Araggna would recognize him. After all, her vision had been obscured by thick clouds of incense at their last meeting in the Divine Monk's dining room.

The High Priestess's guards fanned out, surrounding Grukarr. Araggna strode up to him and said imperiously, "My spies told me you were here, wasting time as usual."

Grukarr's eyes blazed with fury, but he held his tongue. He glanced at the armed guards surrounding him, composed himself, then replied respectfully, "Always at your service, High Priestess."

"Bah! You don't know what service means! Just as you don't understand true loyalty . . . or, for that matter, intelligence."

She snickered, a raspy, guttural sound. "Which is why you were stripped of the right to have any temple guards—and have to rely on untrained riffraff instead."

Several of Grukarr's men grumbled angrily. But a few sharp looks from the temple guards, whose hands lay on their sword hilts, was all it took to silence them.

Araggna's gaze fell on the two young prisoners. "What do we have here? A pair of beggars, from the looks of them. More recruits for your riffraff guards?"

"No," declared her deputy proudly. "I have caught, at last, the thief who stole the Divine Monk's pie from the temple."

Araggna started, surprised. "But you told me yesterday that you'd done that."

"Well . . ." began Grukarr, clearly flustered.

"So you bungled that attempt! Either he escaped from you, or you arrested the wrong person." She scowled more deeply than ever. "Let me see if you got the right thief this time." She stepped toward Promi.

Meanwhile, Atlanta leaned over to Promi and whispered, "From the temple? That couldn't have been easy."

He glanced over at the remains of the lemon pie, trampled in their capture, and shrugged. "At least that pie I got to eat."

Araggna came to a stop beside Promi, glaring down at him. On her arm, the snake lifted its head and hissed angrily. The priestess nodded and declared, "Why, yes, I do believe you are the one."

The old priestess whirled around to face Grukarr. As she did so, Promi noticed for the second time the hint of something glowing beneath her robe. A mysterious light gleamed under the cloth. This time, he couldn't say it was just an illusion. So what was it?

"Well, you imbecile," snarled the High Priestess. "At long last, it seems, you have done something right."

Grukarr trembled with rage. His cheeks turned almost purple. Even so, well aware of the armed guards who would instantly cut him down if Araggna ordered, he contained his anger.

Araggna watched him, amused at his frustration. "And who is the other one?" She waved dismissively at Atlanta. "Another thief?"

"No," grumbled Grukarr. "She is someone who could be useful to me . . . in, well, another way."

The priestess spat on the cobblestones. "You are truly a

disgrace." She sighed. "Today, however, I shall overlook your many failings. For you have somehow managed to capture the thief from the temple."

With a scathing last look at Grukarr, she turned back to Promi. Bound tightly, he looked harmless, as well as filthy and half starved—the sort of prisoner who might have inspired mercy from a captor. But not Araggna.

"You are convicted of high crimes and the violation of sacred places," she rasped. "So I condemn you to die, here and now."

The boa constrictor slithered higher on her arm, hissing all the while.

Crossing her bony arms, Araggna added, "Contrary to my normal practice of not sullying myself with punishments, I plan to stay here and witness your execution. Just to enjoy it."

She snapped her fingers at a burly guard who carried a double-bladed ax. "Get over here and kill the beggar." She nodded at Grukarr. "Before my clumsy deputy can botch this again."

Promi, meanwhile, wrestled with the ropes. But he couldn't budge! Escape seemed utterly impossible. None of his old tricks could help him now. Even if he'd had a knife, he couldn't have thrown it.

Glumly, he traded glances with Atlanta. Her face showed just what he felt—despair.

Roughly, the guard kicked Promi over on his side so that the young man's head lay on the cobblestones. Then the guard grasped his heavy ax with both hands and started to raise it.

How can I possibly get out of here? Promi's mind raced. *I've got no movement. No knife. No anything! Except maybe . . .*

Magic. He clenched his jaw. *But I don't know how to use it!*

His thoughts whirled. Desperately, he recalled what Jaladay had told him in the dungeon. And how he'd done his best to use his Listener magic—but failed completely. What had he done wrong?

The ax lifted higher.

Jaladay said I must make a sacrifice. But how?

And higher.

Suddenly he remembered how she had described the magic itself. It could bring great power . . . but also great pain. *The loss,* she had warned, *of something you love.*

And higher.

Something I love, he told himself. Was that some sort of clue?

The guard grunted. His ax was fully raised, ready to fall.

Something I love, repeated Promi desperately. That was it! The other things he'd tried to sacrifice—his earring, his strange mark—he didn't really care for. So he needed to give up something precious. Valuable. Something he truly loved.

"Kill him," the priestess commanded.

Promi closed his eyes, focusing all his thoughts on what he was going to sacrifice.

The ax began to fall.

"Listen one," he whispered, "listen all."

The sound of rushing wind swept through the alley. Yet no one felt even the slightest breeze.

The guard's ax struck hard—but hit only the cobblestones. Sparks flew from the blade.

"No!" shouted Araggna and Grukarr in unison.

Promi and Atlanta had vanished completely, leaving only the knotted ropes that had bound them.

CHAPTER 18

Sacrifice

Must say, I was impressed by what you did on your very first try! I hate to admit it, but you actually knew what you were doing.

—From her journal

Never in my life have I felt so stupid. I had absolutely no idea what I was doing.

—From Promi's journal

An instant later, Promi and Atlanta found themselves sitting in a forest grove carpeted with sweetstalk fern. They gazed at each other in astonishment.

It worked! thought Promi triumphantly. Then, an instant later, he realized, *Now I have to deal with that sacrifice.*

Atlanta pinched herself to make sure this was real. "Are we . . . alive?"

"Seems that way," replied Promi. *Thanks to magic*, he told himself, still not believing it. *Magic that I actually just used.*

"We're free!" she shouted. "Free!" She

turned and gave Promi an exuberant hug—then suddenly feeling awkward, pulled away. She shook her head, bewildered. "But how?"

"Well," said Promi hesitantly, "I suppose . . . I did it."

"You? You really saved us?"

He nodded, still amazed. "Just a little magic I, well, picked up somewhere."

"Thank you!" she cried, instinctively hugging him again. Then, just as quickly, she drew back, her cheeks red with embarrassment.

Meanwhile, the sound of a breeze swelled swiftly, filling the forest, though no actual wind stirred the trees. Not so much as a single leaf quivered on the surrounding acacias, elms, and oaks. Then, just as swiftly, the sound ended, replaced by the ebullient singing of a meadowlark, its notes spiraling downward like a waterfall of song.

Atlanta cocked her head, listening to the meadowlark's melody. Then she leaned over to smell the nearest stalk of fern. Pressing her nose deep into its amber fronds, she drew a long breath. As she exhaled, she shook her head, making her curls bounce against her neck. "It *is* real," she said, her voice full of wonder. "Not a dream."

"Harrumph," grumbled a small voice from the rim of Promi's boot. "I wish it *were* just a dream. Then I could wake up."

Atlanta froze. "What's that? That voice?"

"Nothing," answered Promi. "Just a little menace who insists on riding in my boot. Like a wart on my toe. You really don't want to meet him, I promise."

"What?" She slid over to his side, pushed away the ferns, and stared in astonishment at the small, furry fellow with big blue eyes and even bigger ears who was peering up at her. "This beautiful creature? Why, I've never seen anything so adorable!"

The kermuncle's whiskers quivered in delight. Promi, meanwhile, shook his head in disgust.

Kermi blinked flirtatiously at Atlanta, then glanced at Promi.

"You should stay with this one, manfool. She's clearly a lot smarter than you."

"Oh, you really are amazing," cooed Atlanta. Gently, she stroked the blue fur on top of his head. "You are not only beautiful, you also have the power of speech."

"Actually," muttered Promi, "it's the poison of sarcasm."

"Jealousy," said the little fellow with a sigh. "Just ignore him. He's always like this. I have no idea why."

She swiveled in the ferns and placed a hand on Promi's arm. "Those two people, the priest and priestess . . ." She scowled. "They're *monsters.*"

"Monsters," he replied, "would be better company."

"Yes. And as bad as she is, I've seen enough of him to think he's even worse."

"So have I," said Promi, remembering poor Bonlo's tale of betrayal. "And she is so old, at least she'll probably die soon. But I fear we've only seen the beginning of evil from Grukarr."

Suddenly, all around the meadow, trees quaked violently. They shook their branches and dropped leaves like tears that spun slowly to the ground.

"Don't say his name again," warned Atlanta. "He marched into this forest a few days ago and left behind only misery. His name, among these magical trees, is the ultimate curse."

Promi nodded. "So we really are here? Your home, the Great Forest?" More quietly, he added, "That's where I hoped we'd go . . . but I couldn't be sure we'd get here."

She drew a slow, deeply pleasurable breath, taking in a world of aromas. Not far away, she could smell the moss growing on a mahogany trunk, the moist fur of a mother fox hurrying back to her den, the needles of an enormous cedar, and the luscious skin of a ripening pear.

"Yes," she said, exhaling slowly, "we're really here." All at once, her reverie ended. "Wait! Exactly how did you do that? With no trees around, my own magic was useless. But that didn't stop you!"

Before he could reply, she blurted out, "And how can you have magic, anyway? Your eyes are brown, as brown as walnut wood—not green at all."

Promi ran his hand over an amber stalk, trying to decide which question to answer first. And how to make those answers even slightly believable. "Look, I'm not really sure. This magic was . . . well, *given* to me. By someone I met—in a dungeon. Can't explain why she gave it to me, of all people. Probably by mistake. All I can say is . . . that's the first time I've ever used it."

"The first time?" Atlanta straightened her back in surprise. "That's powerful magic for anyone. Especially a beginner." She scanned the deep forest around them. "Believe me, I know a little about magic."

"Yes, well . . ." He shook himself, feeling more uncomfortable by the second.

"All right, you moron," said Kermi, tapping a paw on the edge of the boot. "Tell her what you *do* know about the magic."

Promi scowled. "As I said, not much. Except that it's called Listener magic."

She eyed him skeptically. "*You?* A Listener? Like the ones in the legends?"

He nodded shyly.

"A Listener who's hard of hearing, if you ask me," muttered Kermi. "Nearly stone-deaf, in fact."

Atlanta stared doubtfully at this young man she'd first thought was just a pie thief. "Listeners, if they still exist, are supposed to have vast power—the highest form of natural magic. So if what you say is true, why are you reduced to stealing from a bakery? Couldn't you get food in a million other ways?"

"That's how I've *always* gotten food. Ever since I can

remember." He swallowed, recalling the taste of freshly nabbed cinnamon rolls. His empty stomach twisted. Longingly, he thought, *Even just one bite of that lemon pie . . .*

"Why haven't you used your magic in all those years?"

He rubbed his belly, still thinking about the lemon pie. "The magic? I just got it last night."

"Last night? And you can already transport people anywhere you choose?"

He blushed. "Don't know how the magic works. Just like I don't know how the magic in these boots works." He lifted the one that didn't hold Kermi. "They fit my feet perfectly, grow with me, and even expand to take a passenger." With a frown, he added, "Even if the passenger is—"

"A true genius," finished Kermi. "Someone who deserves better." He blew a wobbly blue bubble that floated up toward the sky. Then, his voice wistful, he said, "I wish I were back at my favorite shore right now. Just Jaladay and me, watching the clouds. I would be dreaming of new—"

"Insults," said Promi, now his turn to interrupt. "That's your favorite thing to do, right?"

Kermi scowled. "Only with certain company. By the way, man-fool, you haven't told Atlanta the whole truth. You *do* know something else about Listener magic, don't you? Something you haven't mentioned."

"Because I haven't *wanted* to mention it, you wicked little beast!"

Atlanta leaned over the kermuncle and said sweetly, "Don't let him upset you, little one." She tousled the fur on top of his head. Then, facing Promi, she scolded, "You shouldn't talk to him like that! Such a darling little creature, it's a wonder he still wants to ride with you."

Kermi released a soft whimper—which was a bit hard to hear over Promi's growl of rage.

After stroking the tiny blue head a while longer, Atlanta turned back to Promi. "I still can't believe all this. But you did bring us here somehow. Couldn't you just tell me what else you know about the magic?"

He folded his arms. "I don't want to talk about it."

"Please?"

"No."

"*Please?*" She looked at him imploringly.

"Oh, all right." He felt thoroughly dejected. "Every time I use the magic, I need to . . . well, give something up. Make some sort of sacrifice."

Her eyebrows lifted. "Really? And the greater the magic you need, the bigger the sacrifice?"

"Something like that."

She touched his shoulder. "What did you give up to save us, Promi? Tell me."

He crossed his arms more tightly. "Honestly, I don't want to talk about it."

"I know, but . . ." She smiled fleetingly—a subtle, tentative smile, but lovely nonetheless, like the first ray of moonlight to touch the forest floor. "I'd really like to know."

He chewed his lip for a moment, then replied, "I gave up eating. Not just sweets like lemon pies or cinnamon buns, but *everything.*"

She gasped. "For how long?"

He growled again. "A long time."

"How long?"

"I told you, *a long time.*"

"Tell me, won't you? How long?"

He grimaced. "For the rest of this day! All the way to sundown. That doesn't sound so bad to you, maybe. But to me . . . I'm so hungry, it's going to feel like a month!"

A wave of sympathy washed over her. "Oh, my. That really is

awful!" She leaned closer. "I'm that hungry, too. Which is why, I think, you gave me that pie."

"A whole lot of good that did," he grumbled.

"My, my," exclaimed Kermi, "that really was a big sacrifice you made."

Promi perked up, surprised to hear what sounded like genuine compassion from his tormentor.

"Why," Kermi continued, "you might actually weaken so much you'll die. Or worse yet—you might just complain a whole lot until you get your next meal and then go on living."

If a glare could ignite a fire, the one Promi gave the kermuncle would have started a major blaze. "Wish I could have sacrificed *you*! But that wouldn't have worked, since it had to be something I care about."

"Oh, manfool, you cut me to the quick." Kermi's whiskers quivered as if from distress, which made Atlanta reach over again to stroke his head. He blinked at her in thanks, then went on. "Just to show you I have no hard feelings, I'll let you share in this."

Reaching down deeper in the boot, he pulled out the remains of a half-eaten cinnamon bun. "See? You're not the only one who can steal a pastry now and then. Especially when the bakery shelves are low enough I can grab it right from your boot."

Promi's eyes widened at the sight of such a delectable treat—then shut tight. Even more than hunger for the pastry, he felt sheer frustration that he couldn't eat it.

Seeing his look of agony, the kermuncle smirked. "Go on now, manfool. Eat it." He tossed the chewed bun to Promi.

The young man caught it, his eyes smoldering. "I told you I can't . . . eat . . . anything." He threw the bun back at Kermi.

"Oh, right. How silly of me to forget! Such a pity." He pouted his tiny cheeks. "But Atlanta, my dear, you're welcome to eat it. Even if he can't."

She brightened. "Thank you, little . . ."

"Kermi."

"Thank you so much, Kermi. What a generous being you are! But now that we are here in my forest home, I have plenty to eat."

"Unlike him." He waved a paw at Promi. "How terribly, terribly sad," he said, grinning broadly.

Promi's gaze bored into him. "Just you wait, you little menace. I'll find some way to chew on *your* buns."

"Harrumph," replied the kermuncle in a horrified tone. "How rude."

"Enough." Promi stood up in the ferns. He offered a hand to Atlanta, but she bounced to her feet without any help. Happy to be back in the forest, she pranced like an energetic faun.

By contrast, Promi swayed, feeling weak from hunger. "Wish I could eat even just a bite of something," he lamented. "But I have a feeling that if I broke my vow and ate before supper . . . something very bad would happen."

Atlanta nodded. "You'd lose the magic, that's certain. Maybe more."

"Besides," said Kermi from the rim of the boot, "I'd never let you hear the end of it." He licked the cinnamon glazing off his paws, smacking his lips with pleasure. "Such a pity you can't eat for all that time."

Promi ground his teeth. "What I *can* do is walk. Straight back to the City, so I can feed myself a decent supper. Or breakfast, if it takes me that long to get there."

"What?" Atlanta stared at him in surprise. "There's wonderful food right here! Why don't you stay in the forest for a while?"

He shook his head. "No, thanks. I prefer living where I know how to get food."

"Steal food, you mean," groused Kermi.

"Sure. It's not a bad way to live, really. All I have to do is watch out for G—"

Though he caught himself before saying the priest's name, tree branches nearby clacked and shook angrily.

At the same time, Atlanta shuddered. "So wicked, that man! I wish I knew exactly what he plans to do with the forest."

"He said he wanted your help to find its most magical places. To get whatever he needs."

"But what is that? And why does he need it?"

"No idea," said Promi. "All we know is that he needs it soon, for some reason. And that it's part of his *grand plan*—something that will empower whoever will be the next ruler of Ellegandia."

"Not just Ellegandia," corrected Atlanta. "He said, 'the new ruler of this realm.' And I got the distinct feeling he meant, by that, the whole mortal realm."

Promi's eyes widened. "You might be right. But how could that ever happen? The rest of the mortal world is separate from Ellegandia. We're sealed off by ocean cliffs and mountains all around."

"Who knows? One thing's certain, though." She stared worriedly at the trees surrounding them. "The person he called the next ruler—that means *him*."

Promi shifted uneasily, feeling renewed heat on his chest. "And how did he get that—that *thing* from the spirit realm?"

"A mistwraith," said Kermi ominously. His whiskers trembled, as if he knew more. But even if that was true, he wasn't about to elaborate.

"I thought there was a strict law against any spirits coming to the mortal world," said Promi. Recalling what Bonlo had taught him, he added, "Though we are getting close to Ho Byneri, when the veil grows thin, so maybe it's easier to break that law now."

Atlanta extended her arms wide. "There are plenty of spirits here already. Throughout this forest." Then, gazing at him, she asked, “Are you sure you don’t want to stay and maybe meet some of them?”

“I’m sure.” He rubbed his belly. “Supper’s waiting for me back in the City. Now, just tell me which way to walk, and I’ll be going.”

“But if you stay here, Promi . . . you could help.”

“With what?”

“With stopping that evil priest! He’s coming back, I’m sure—searching for me and whatever he needs for his plan.” Her expression hardened, as water turns to ice. “And I am going to fight him.”

CHAPTER 19

The Way

I really ought to know by now. One bite of a bad cookie spells trouble. The bite may be small, but the bellyache huge.

—From Promi's journal (scrawled in the recipe book chapter titled "Dangerous Cookies: Bake Them Right or Not at All")

"Fight him?" asked Promi, surprised. "I thought you'd do whatever it takes to avoid him! Are you crazy?"

"Maybe," Atlanta replied. "But I know that if I don't find some way to stop that madman, this whole forest—this whole world of magic and beauty—will suffer."

She spun in slow circles, her arms extended as she gazed up at all the trees ringing the meadow. As she twirled, branches quivered and stretched toward her, the greeting of trees leafy and needled, ancient and young. One particular tree, a graceful birch, stretched so far that it was nearly horizontal, until at last it brushed the tip of her finger with its uppermost leaf.

Atlanta stopped, her finger still touching the birch leaf. "This is more than my home. This is my family."

"Still crazy!" he declared. "How could you even start to fight him?"

Her blue-green eyes flashed with determination. "I've got to try."

"But you're just one person! Up against him and all his thugs. Not to mention that mistwraith."

Stooping, Atlanta picked up an acorn from among the ferns at her feet. She twirled it slowly in her fingers, then said, "See how small this is? There's simply no way to tell from its size what it could become. What magic it could hold."

She dropped the acorn. "So I must try."

He studied her for a long moment, then shook his head. "Then you'll try alone."

"But Promi—"

He looked down at the ferns by his feet, unwilling to meet her gaze. "I'm just a thief, Atlanta. A loner. Someone who survives by stealing pies and throwing a knife."

"Even after what we heard about Grukarr's plans?"

"Look," he declared, "I don't like him any more than you do. But at least I'm smart enough to stay out of his way! No, this battle for the forest is between you and him. It's not my fight. Can you understand that?"

Icily, she glared at him. "No, I can't."

For an instant, Promi was tempted to tell her about the other battles he'd heard about recently, battles that were also not for him. Or for anyone remotely sane. Like the ones Bonlo had described, involving a new war in the spirit realm, a frightful prophecy, and a dangerous thinning of the veil between the worlds.

Maybe that would convince her that some battles were just meant to be avoided—because they were too big, too dangerous, or just too unlikely to be real.

No, he thought with a sigh, *she'll never be convinced. Not when she still believes she can save her beloved forest.*

Atlanta looked at him pleadingly. Gesturing at the trees, she said, "This is your forest, too. Even if you don't live here."

"My home is the City."

"Sure, but where do you think the lemons for that pie you stole came from? And all the fresh vegetables, fruits, and nuts you see in the marketplace? The fuel you burn? The water you drink?"

She glanced up at the sky, shining blue between the branches. "Don't you see, Promi? All the magic in this country ties together. From the highest summit of Ell Shangro to the lowest beach of the western shore—the magic of every place is connected." Scanning the grove around them, she said quietly, "And this forest is the most magical place of all."

A squirrel with very large eyes and a shaggy tail, seated on the branch of a nearby acacia, chattered loudly in agreement.

Suddenly, Atlanta flinched. Her gaze fixed on a young fruit tree that looked strangely withered. Its frail trunk bent from the weight of its shriveled, pale orange fruit. Even to Promi's inexperienced eye, this tree seemed sickly. Now, one unhealthy tree wouldn't seem so unusual in most forests—but in this richly verdant place, it felt like a violation.

Atlanta rushed over to the sapling. Gently, as if taking the hand of a friend, she clasped its lowest bough. She shook her head, aghast. Then she whispered, "No! Not here."

She whirled around to face Promi. "You've got to join me! Now it's not just that horrible priest endangering this forest. It's the blight. And it's spreading fast! Last week, it was only in a few groves on the eastern reaches. And now it's here, deep in the interior."

He frowned, shifting uneasily. "Sorry. But as I said . . . this isn't my fight."

"You are really that selfish?"

"I just want to stay alive, that's all! And so, if you won't tell me which way to go, I'll just have to figure that out myself."

"Lovely," commented Kermi. "We're about to get lost forever."

The shaggy-tailed squirrel made a different sound this time, much more like a chuckle.

Even as Promi turned to go, Atlanta grabbed his sleeve. "Wait. What if . . . I offer you a gift before you go?"

He pulled free. "There's no gift from you I'd want."

"Not even supper?" Her eyes twinkled. "The most sumptuous supper you've ever had in your life?"

He froze, tempted. "In my life?"

She nodded.

"Will there be any dessert?"

"More than you can eat."

"That I doubt." He swallowed an imaginary bite of something wondrously sweet. "Will you also give me directions to the City?"

"Yes," she promised. "First thing in the morning."

He eyed her suspiciously. "Don't think for a second this is going to make me change my mind."

"Why would I ever think that?" she shot back. But she gave the squirrel a sly wink.

Though Promi didn't see the wink, he still felt suspicious. "How far away is this supper?"

"Not far," she promised. "I'll show you the way."

He patted his belly, yearning to eat. "Well, all right. But no tricks."

"No tricks." Reaching down, she plucked a frond of sweet-smelling fern and slid it through a hole at the collar of her gown of woven vines. "Now, follow me."

She turned, cast her gaze around the grove, and took the first step. But not the second one. With immense care, she placed her bare foot on a lush patch of moss, moving so slowly that a pair of green-backed beetles had plenty of time to scurry out of the way. Unhurriedly, she transferred more weight to that foot.

Holding that position, one foot in moss and the other in ferns, she almost seemed frozen in place. Her only movement came from her eyes, which slowly scanned the tracery of branches overhead, and from her nose, which sniffed several new aromas—a ripe bunch of grapes nearby, a bird just hatched from its shell, and a fragrant wild rose.

Surprised by her stillness, Promi asked, "Are you all right?"

Without turning, she replied, "Yes."

"So," he pressed, "will you show me?"

Again she replied, "Yes."

He cocked his head, confused. But before he could say anything more, Atlanta stirred and lifted her other foot. With the same graceful slowness, she took another step.

This time, her foot landed in the midst of some pink-spotted toadstools, so gently that several of them slipped right between her toes. They stood in those spaces like tiny parasols. Meanwhile, a butterfly with rich purple wings and antennae as long as its whole body landed delicately on her neck. Feeling the light brush of its wings upon her skin, she grinned.

But Promi wasn't pleased. "What's going on?" he demanded. "You said you'd show me the way!"

"This is it," she declared. "Come along."

"How?" he cried, exasperated. "You're just standing here, like one of these trees!"

"Thank you," she replied, as if he'd just paid her a high compliment. "But they're much better than me at being present."

"Present?" He shook his head, more confused than ever. "What does that mean?"

From his perch on the branch, the squirrel snickered loudly.

"Come walk with me, and you'll find out," said Atlanta. She took another leisurely step. This time, she set down her foot on a fallen twig, so gently that it didn't snap but merely sank into the soft soil.

"Oh, all right," he grumbled. "But only because I'm so hungry."

Following her example, he took three steps as slowly as he could. Even so, he moved much more quickly than she had done, his boots crunching on the ground. Seconds later, he'd caught up and stood by her side.

Bewildered, he said, "I don't understand, Atlanta! Where are we going?"

She drew a long, full breath, then answered, "Within."

Promi scowled at her. "Wherever you're taking me, we'll *never* get there like this."

More snickering came from the squirrel.

Atlanta, meanwhile, took another gentle step, this one into some needles that had fallen from a mighty spruce. As her toes lowered, the needles crackled quietly. The tangy scent of spruce rose into the air. Turning to Promi, she explained, "This part of our walk isn't about getting there. It's about being here."

"Curse you and all the crocodiles and cockles on the crashing coasts, Atlanta! Which is the way?"

"This is," she declared. "Walking is the way."

Ready to explode with frustration, Promi grabbed her shoulder and shook it, making the purple-winged butterfly take flight. "If you're not going to take me to supper, I'm just going to leave."

"Not a good idea, manfool." Kermi blew a stream of small, blue-tinted bubbles. "You're better off with her."

"Then why don't *you* just stay with her, bubblebrain?"

"Tempting," said the kermuncle. "But . . . a promise is a

promise. We're stuck together, you and I, like sap to bark." Under his breath, he added, "And I know who's the sap."

Again the squirrel snickered, waving his tail so hard he almost fell off the branch.

"All right," Atlanta said resignedly. "You're just impossible! I'd hoped that, as a Listener, you'd understand."

"All I want," he declared, "is that supper you promised."

"Then follow me."

She strode off, leading him out of the grove and into a wide meadow of lemongrass. The wispy blades brushed against her legs and Promi's boots, while lemony scent filled the air.

For Promi, this was a new form of torment. The smell of the grass reminded him of the lemon pie he'd never tasted, stoking the fires of his hunger. He raised his sleeve to his mouth and tried chewing on the tattered cloth. It tasted nothing like that pie—more like a rancid mixture of mud, soot, and sweat, with a dash of dungeon stones and rat fur.

He spat out the sleeve. *What can I do,* he wondered, *to keep from going crazy with hunger?*

At once, he knew. Even as he walked, he turned his thoughts inward, calling up the song from his childhood. The distant, quivering notes came quickly, filling his mind with their melody. And with them came that feeling of comfort he cherished.

Atlanta, meanwhile, was feeling her own hunger pangs. Though the afternoon light was beginning to grow dimmer, she spied a split oak she recognized and just beyond it, a cakefruit tree. Its boughs drooped low with succulent purple fruit shaped like little round cakes.

Veering toward the tree, she gracefully plucked one fruit without breaking stride. Though she felt a bit guilty to eat while Promi could not, the sweet fragrance of the fruit was just too much to resist. She took a bite, savoring every sensation. Her lips touched the fruit's tender skin, her teeth broke through with a soft *plissssshhh,* and her mouth filled with a sudden burst of flavor like sun-warmed clover honey.

Furtively, she glanced over her shoulder at Promi. He was so focused on hearing the haunting notes of his song, he hadn't even noticed that she was eating. So without hesitation, she took another bite, then another and another. Soon the cakefruit disappeared, right down to its seedy core. Tossing the core to a spot where one of the seeds might grow, she thought, *Now, that's my kind of pastry.*

As the light continued to dim, they kept walking. In time, they came to a clear stream flowing out of the depths of the forest. They followed it, listening to its constant splash, as the woods grew darker. Just when Promi started to have trouble seeing clearly, the waterway divided and then, a short distance later, came back together, forming an island in the middle. Moss, thick and soft as the richest wool, covered the island completely. Vapor from the embracing stream fell on its surface like a gentle rain, making it glisten in the dusky light.

The instant they stopped to look at the mossy island, both of them kneeled and plunged their faces into the water. After several swallows, Atlanta lifted her head and glanced over at Promi, who was gulping eagerly. Though she still felt angry at him, she was glad that his vow not to eat didn't prevent him from having a good drink of water.

And who knows? she thought hopefully. *He might still change his mind.*

Finally, he pulled his face out of the stream. Tiny rivulets ran down his cheeks as he said, "Excellent."

She nodded. "Just wait until you taste your supper. Which will be soon."

"Not soon enough." He shook his head, spraying her with

droplets. “I’m so hungry I tried to eat my tunic back there.” Looking down at the soiled cloth, he decided, “Time to wash it, I think.”

He pulled the tunic over his head and dunked it in the water. Thick clouds of brown and red filled the stream, then vanished. As he tossed the tunic onto the bank, he splashed some water onto his chest, under his arms, and behind his neck.

Suddenly Atlanta gasped. “What’s that?” Anxiously, she pointed at the black mark over his heart. “It looks like . . . some kind of bird. With wings, a beak, and even talons.”

“Oh, that?” He grabbed his wet tunic and pulled it back over his head. “Just a weird birthmark I’ve always had. Nothing special.”

She watched him, unconvinced. “A mark like that doesn’t just happen.”

“Well,” he confessed, “it only appears when I’m hungry. And the more hungry I get, the bigger it grows.”

Atlanta raised an eyebrow.

“Not really. The point is, this stupid mark doesn’t mean a thing.”

She shook her curls. “So you keep telling me. Say, Kermi has been awfully quiet recently.”

He tapped the bulge down in his boot. “As I said, these special boots adjust themselves to fit. And judging from how far down inside he is, I’d guess he decided to take a nap.”

“Poor little fellow,” she said with sympathy. “He must be exhausted.”

“Maybe,” mused Promi, “I should dump him into the stream?” Seeing her scowl, he added quickly, “Just to give him a drink, I mean.”

Her eyes narrowed. “If you weren’t so mean to him, he’d be nicer to you. He’s really very sweet.”

“Right. Sweet as poison hemlock.”

"Well," she said, "maybe I should add that to the menu for supper."

"No thanks. But speaking of supper—"

She clapped her hands. "Come, cross over the stream. There's no finer place to dine than Moss Island."

CHAPTER 20

A Whistle in the Woods

Have you learned yet, Promi, the paradox? Natural magic holds both joy and sorrow. There is nothing so beautiful as its flowering . . . and nothing so terrible as its end.

—From her journal

Grukarr stomped through the forest. Around him rose the glittering boughs of star cedars, a grove of massive trees whose every cupped needle held a drop of morning dew. On a sunny day like this, those dewdrops caught the light and sparkled, trembling with the slightest breeze, filling the grove with a rich yet subtle radiance. Travelers who passed through this place often felt as if they were walking through a galaxy of thousands and thousands of stars.

But not Grukarr. He didn't even notice the glittering cedars, the dewdrops, or the radiance. Just as he didn't see the rare clusters of spiraling moss that draped from the cedars' boughs or the orange eyes of three young owlets who watched him from their nest hidden inside a hollow burl. He barely even noticed the black shadow that hovered beside him, floating above the carpet of fallen needles.

"Curse those two young wretches! Curse their blood and bones, poison their next meals, and stifle their very last breaths!"

Grukarr growled the curse viciously for at least the hundredth time that morning. It happened to be one of his favorites, a balm that always soothed his mind and lifted his spirits in troubled times. Not today, however. Today things felt so bleak that not even a cherished curse could help.

Angrily, he marched ahead. One of his boots crushed a sprig of ripe boatberries, each one shaped like a tiny golden hull with a billowing sail. Indigo juice splattered his boot and the mud-stained hem of his robe—already so dirty from his trek through the forest that it looked more brown than white.

Hearing the squelch of the berries, he glanced down at his boot and cursed again. "Cut out my enemies' intestines, tie them in knots, and burn them to ashes! I hate this filthy forest. And all the magic wielders who hide here!"

He paused, vengefully smashing under his boot a family of yellow mushrooms with transparent stems. "How," he puzzled, "could those two criminals have vanished like that? What was the source of that magic? Not her, since we were deep in the City, much too far from the forest for her to use its magic. Yet . . . I can't believe it could have come from him, either—that ignorant pie thief. So how did they escape?"

Kicking the remains of one mushroom off the toe of his boot, he asked the mistwraith, "You didn't detect any other immortals nearby, did you?"

The shadow being quivered and brushed against his legs. Black sparks flew into the air, sizzling whenever they hit leaves or soil.

"So they don't have anyone from the spirit realm to help them." He ground his teeth angrily. "All the better. When I finally do catch them—I can crush them completely. After the forest girl helps me, that is."

The mistwraith crackled again, shooting more sparks.

"Yes, I'm sure she will do it! Or else she will see her precious forest wither away and die."

Malevolently, he grinned. "Killing those two will be lovely. But what I'm going to do to that old witch Araggna—that will be even better." He wiped his boot in some grass, eliminating any trace of the mushrooms. "Of course, I must choose the perfect time and place. She has too many spies . . . as well as those infernal temple guards always around her."

His grin twisted into a frown. "For now, I must continue to endure her insults. As if that escape from the alley was somehow my fault! Curse the Divine Monk's navel! I wish I could have strangled Araggna right there. But no, not yet."

The mistwraith writhed impatiently. It passed through the trunk of a young oak tree, killing it instantly.

"Not yet, I said." Grukarr growled like a wounded tiger. "Right now, our highest priority is to find those two. Especially her! The day, the dawn, draws near! So we will keep searching this cursed forest, while Huntwing and my minions scour the City. And while we are here, perhaps you can—"

A sudden, high-pitched crackle interrupted him. By his side, the shadow being turned a lighter shade.

Grukarr peered down at his immortal companion. "Nearby? Are you certain?"

More crackling.

"Well, well," said the priest with the faintest hint of satisfaction. "We won't rest until we find the forest girl, of course. But finding *that* would make this long day of slogging worthwhile. Take me there!"

The mistwraith surged ahead, floating out of the grove and into a grassy meadow. A family of field mice suddenly scattered as it approached, while a pair of mirror-winged butterflies took flight, the dark shadow reflected on their wings.

At last the mistwraith slowed. Near the edge of the meadow, where three streams converged, it stopped. Stealthily, it hovered just above the grass.

Grukarr hurried to catch up, almost stumbling on a fallen branch that held a parade of red-capped mushrooms. Halfway across the meadow, he too halted. For he saw what the mistwraith had found.

Faeries. Hundreds of them—a whole colony of these secretive creatures, each one no bigger than a man's thumb.

They were doing all the things faeries love to do most in their secret hideaways—zipping playfully through the air, drawing magical flowers that sprouted on the water, and telling stories to their bright-eyed children. They danced on the rapids. Dined on rose nectar. Used their magic to make sculptures out of honeycomb. Sang ethereal harmonies that flowed like streams of sound.

Grukarr's brown eyes opened wide. He fingered his necklace of golden beads eagerly, knowing that very few creatures held as much magic as faeries. Only baby dragons, unicorns, and mysterious beings called starsisters—whose power to make light was so great, it was said, that they could make sunbeams look like shadows—possessed as much magic as faeries.

And here were hundreds of them.

Turning toward the hovering mistwraith, Grukarr nodded. The shadowy immortal began to float silently toward the faery colony.

To avoid frightening their prey, the priest stood as still as a tree. He watched, noticing for the first time that most of the faeries wore some sort of garb. Many sported thin, translucent cloaks wrapped around their necks and the base of their wings. All but the youngest wore tiny shoes of hollowed-out red berries and amulets made from various seeds.

One faery, a mother, carried her honey-haired child in a backpack made from an acorn. Its smooth surface had been decorated with colorful paintings of clouds, trees, and summer flowers. As the child slept, the faery mother sang a soothing song to bring peaceful dreams.

Females tied their flowing hair with green or pink ribbons fashioned from flower petals or woven moss. Males wore rust-colored leggings and fluffy cotton hats with tiny holes to allow their antennae to protrude. Yet no clothing could match the beauty of the faeries' unadorned wings, whose shining blue surfaces glowed like crystals as delicate as the air itself.

Trash, thought Grukarr with a sneer. *Forest trash. How, by the Great Powers, such insignificant creatures ever gained such enormous magic, I will never understand.* His mouth twitched malevolently. *But that will soon change.*

At that instant, the mistwraith reached the streams. A few faeries suddenly noticed the intruder and shrieked in alarm. Dozens of them rose into the air, their wings buzzing as they started to fly away. The mother faery stopped singing to her child in the painted acorn, screamed in fright, and joined the escape.

Too late.

Even as the shrieks began, the mistwraith expanded. In the blink of an eye, it stretched into a deadly blanket that blocked the sun, while shooting out dark tendrils that surrounded the fleeing faeries. All across the shadowy blanket, black sparks exploded. With each spark, a single faery cried out—then fell into the water or onto the grass, its wings now drab and motionless, devoid of light.

The faeries were not dead. Not yet, at least. For now, they lay on the ground or floated helpless on the water, unable to fly or sing or conjure even the smallest spell. The mother lay stunned on the bank, unable to reach out and touch her child who had fallen out of the acorn and rolled down to the water's edge.

What had happened to them was, in fact, worse than death. They would gladly have died instantly to avoid this fate.

They had been robbed of their magic—and consequently, their ability to move or speak. All their magic had been devoured by the mistwraith. Its shadowy folds rippled with satisfaction, making a contented, swishing sound.

Victorious, Grukarr kissed his ruby ring. He started to whistle happily, then strolled over to the stream, kicking aside a pile of winged bodies.

For several seconds, he surveyed the scene to make absolutely sure that not a single glowing wing had escaped. All the while, he whistled. Finally satisfied, he turned to the mistwraith and watched as the shadowy being shrank back to its normal size.

"Excellent work, my friend. You have gathered more magic in this moment than in all the days we have been together. And the more magic we gather . . . the more we will have for the great moment of triumph."

The mistwraith shuddered with pleasure, releasing a shower of sparks.

Grukarr's expression hardened. "We have much more work to do, however. And very little time before dawn on Ho Byneri." He added in a commanding tone, "Which is why I am sending you back to the realm of immortals."

The mistwraith crackled in surprise and darkened like a thundercloud before a storm.

"Yes," continued Grukarr. "I need you to go back—and urge our master Narkazan to send more mistwraiths. Straight to my lair at the Passage of Death! I need them now, with no more delay."

Angrily, the shadow being crackled again.

"I *know* Narkazan needs every mistwraith he has right now for his battles on high! Do you think I don't know his plans?"

Grukarr bent lower, keeping one hand on his turban so it wouldn't fall off. "You must convince him that sending me more mistwraiths right now will *guarantee* him victory in those battles. For they will help me provide him with the ultimate weapon to defeat all his enemies."

The mistwraith, clearly anxious, floated backward on the grass. It crackled so fast that the sound was more like a hum punctuated with black sparks.

The priest shook his head. "No, he will not punish you for bringing this message. Show him how much magic you have inhaled in just one encounter with faeries. That should convince him. And tell him I will soon have more than a hundred times that much magic!"

Another burst of crackling.

"Of course I will find the forest girl! Watching you just now, I thought of the perfect way to trap her." He smirked with satisfaction. "And when I do . . . she will do all I ask. Or see her precious forest die from the blight. She will cooperate, believe me."

Silently, the mistwraith floated around Grukarr's legs. Then it crackled with more sparks.

"You still doubt me? Then remember the Prophecy! Its meaning could not be more clear."

Lowering his voice, Grukarr declared, "At dawn on Ho Byneri, when the veil is thinnest, I will deliver to Narkazan all the magic he needs to give the Starstone a whole new purpose—to make it the most powerful weapon in the universe."

He beamed. "That will spell *the end of all magic* in the mortal world. And the beginning of a whole new era." Puffing out his chest, the priest nodded confidently. "And for that service, he will give something to me: the world of mortals."

Agreeing at last, the mistwraith lightened a shade, though it still looked as dark as a moonless night. With a sharp crackle and a burst of sparks, the immortal vanished.

Once again, Grukarr scanned the remains of the faery colony. Seeing the small, helpless bodies lining the banks, hanging from the grass, and spinning in the stream's eddies, he sighed in satisfaction. He began to whistle again, even more cheerfully.

Maybe, he thought as he tapped his foot to the rhythm, *I will whistle something for the commoners at my coronation. Just to show that I am an emperor who is also a man of the people.*

Glancing over his shoulder at the forest, he remembered Atlanta. His whistling ceased. "I will find that wretched young woman," he muttered. "And soon!"

He turned to leave—then stopped. For there, in the shade of a rose bush by the farthest stream, he'd spotted a pair of luminous wings.

A faery! Grukarr's lip curled in rage. "How did you escape, you little beast?"

He glared at the tiny creature who cowered, wings trembling, under the rosebush. "I can't deal with you now, unfortunately. But your time will come very soon! Before Ho Byneri, I can promise you that."

Grukarr spun and started to march off. He knew that these three streams would lead him eventually to a path he knew well—one that he used often to visit his secret lair near the mountains. This time, however, he would not follow the path to the lair, but back to the City. For he had an important task to perform. A task he wanted to do before setting the trap for Atlanta.

A task, he thought as he walked, *for a future emperor.*

CHAPTER 21

Secrets

Any dessert, whatever its ingredients, can be a tasty treat or a rotten mess. All depends on how it's prepared.

—From Promi's journal

Grukarr walked stealthily down an alley at the City's edge. Keeping in the shadows, he moved almost as quietly as a mistwraith, as if he were floating over the cobblestones.

Still wearing his mud-streaked robe after his long trek through the forest and carrying his turban in the crook of his arm, he might have been mistaken for a beggar by anyone who happened to glimpse his shadowed form. But as far as he knew, no one had spotted him. And he was determined to keep it that way. Far too much was at stake.

If anything went wrong with his plans, there would be no one around to help him. His ally from the spirit realm was no longer at his side. Huntwing was as loyal as ever, but right now the bird was elsewhere. And

Narkazan? These days the spirit lord's attention was focused entirely on the battle to win control of the immortal realm.

Careful, now. Careful, Grukarr told himself as he moved closer to the end of the alley. Anxiously, he fingered his necklace of golden beads. *Must stay hidden from Araggna and her spies.*

Step by step, he slid through the dark passageway. At last, he reached the end, encountering a stone gutter that carried waste and rainwater down to the river. Opposite the gutter stood an old building, long ago abandoned, whose worn mud-brick walls had almost collapsed. A part of its roof had, in fact, fallen in. As Grukarr watched, a rat scurried out of the gutter and into a crack in the building's foundation.

Made it all the way here, he thought, *with no problems. But I haven't yet made it inside.*

Carefully, he surveyed the old building, then checked all the nearby streets. Everything looked clear. Feeling his racing heartbeat, he tried to remain calm. *What strange things I do to gain the power I deserve! Soon, if all goes well, there will be no more need for such miserable tasks.*

Once again, he checked the surrounding streets. No sign of spies—or temple guards. Jaw clenched, he stepped over the gutter and up to the building's door.

Abruptly, he kicked the door open. It slammed against the inside wall, so hard the whole building shook. Mud-bricks cracked and fell to the dirt floor.

Grukarr strode inside.

The first thing he saw were about fifteen men lounging by a large pile of rudimentary weapons—axes, shovels, wooden pikes, bows, and some rusty blades, mostly daggers along with one old broadsword. Caught completely by surprise, the men leaped to their feet. Only one didn't move: a gray-bearded fellow dozing soundly with an empty jug of ale under his arm.

"Halt!" shouted the nearest man as he jumped up. His broad

face showed a scar that ran from cheek to chin. He grabbed the sword and pointed it at Grukarr's chest, ready to attack. "One more step an' you die."

The priest's gaze locked onto the scowling man. But instead of scowling back, Grukarr merely chortled. "Easy now, Rending."

With a screech of recognition, Huntwing flapped over from his perch on a ceiling beam and settled on his master's shoulder. Grukarr stroked the bird's rust-colored wing.

"Oh!" exclaimed the man, dropping the sword. "It's you."

"That's right," growled Grukarr, replacing his turban on his head. "I came for a surprise inspection." He glanced around at the motley group. "And what I see does not please me."

Rending tensed. "But Master . . . we done searched the whole City fer that forest girl. Been doin' nothin' else since you released us from the temple jail. Jest like you commanded."

Wrathfully, Grukarr kicked at a shovel, sending it flying across the room. "And what did you minions find? Nothing."

Huntwing scraped his talons together, as if longing to use them to gouge someone's eyes out.

"Not yet, my Huntwing," said Grukarr soothingly. "These men still have one more chance to prove their worth. But if they fail . . . you shall have your way with them."

Several men went pale, while a few others backed away from the bird who glared at them so savagely.

"Or, if I choose," the priest continued in an even more malicious tone, "I will send every man in this room back to jail to receive the punishments already ordered by High Priestess Araggna."

A wave of shudders and grumbles passed through the men. Only when Huntwing clacked his beak did they fall silent.

"Now," growled Grukarr, "before I give you your new orders, I want to remind you that I will tolerate no more failure. And also no slackers!"

"No slackers among us," replied Rending nervously. "We is all eager to serve you."

"Is that so?" answered Grukarr. His gaze shifted to the man dozing on the floor. Striding over, he kicked away the man's jug of ale. But the man stayed asleep, snoring contentedly.

Grukarr's eyes narrowed. Grabbing a shovel, he raised it and slammed it hard against the fellow's head. The man shrieked and rolled over. He lay motionless on the dirt, blood streaming from his head wound.

Stunned by Grukarr's brutality, Rending winced. His scar reddened. None of the men dared to speak or move, not even to try to stop their companion's bleeding.

The priest scanned them icily. "Now, I believe, you understand. I have not worked so hard for so long—even going so far as to free you rabble from jail—to fail because of some lazy, witless drunkards."

His nostrils flared. "Here are your new orders. You will march in the direction of Ell Shangro and the other mountains, all the way to my secret lair."

Grukarr paused, stroking his bird's tail feathers. "Huntwing here will guide you to make sure no one gets lost. Or tries to turn back. And he will show you where to find the special masks I have made to protect you from . . . certain dangers. Do you understand?"

All the men nodded.

"Good. Then get out of my sight."

Immediately, the men grabbed their weapons and hurried out of the old building.

Grukarr peered into Huntwing's savage eyes. "Make sure they get to the lair as soon as possible. I have uses for them there."

Huntwing clacked his beak in assent and flew off. The priest watched him go, then muttered quietly, "Uses that will expand my power—the only true purpose of a commoner's life."

Straightening his turban, he thought, *That was something Bonlo, that sentimental old fool, never understood. He even dared to question my authority! May he rot forever in that dungeon.*

Grukarr walked to the door and peered cautiously outside. His men had all departed, leaving the area empty. Still, he paused to make sure there was no one in the surrounding streets who might see him. Just to be safe, he removed his turban and tucked it under his arm.

Convinced all was clear, he stepped over the gutter, crossed the street, and turned into a narrow alley. The passage was dark enough, layered with shadows, that he paused to let his eyes adjust. And he breathed a sigh of relief that his exit from the old building had gone so smoothly.

Now, he thought, *my time of triumph is near.*

He started to stride deeper into the alley—but heard a rustling sound. He froze, surveying the shadows.

Just then, six temple guards stepped into view, three ahead of him and three behind. Curved swords drawn, they surrounded him, blocking any possible escape. Grukarr jumped, then fumbled to put his turban back on his head.

"That won't help you now," rasped a voice behind him. Grukarr whirled around to face Araggna as she stepped out of the shadows. She faced him, the lines around her eyes etched more harshly than ever. On her forearm, the boa constrictor slithered menacingly.

"I charge you," she said coldly, "with willfully releasing prisoners from custody—prisoners I had ordered punished."

"But, High Priestess," protested Grukarr, "I was only—"

"Silence!" she commanded. "You were only doing what serves your own ambitions, as always. Do you think me such a fool? My spies have kept me well informed of your disobedience and incompetence. As if I needed any more evidence of that."

She scowled at him. Then she tapped the collar of her robe,

feeling the luminous object hidden underneath. Whatever it was sent light through the cloth as well as the gaps between her fingers.

"I know what you want," she rasped. "You want *this.*" Again she tapped her collar. "And all its power."

Her eyes gleamed. "The precious Starstone! Though I have tried to keep it secret since that monk found it in the forest and brought it to me weeks ago, I could tell that you recognized its magical light—light that fills its wearer with enormous strength."

Shifting her expression, she seemed almost compassionate. "You were right to want it, Grukarr. Every minute I wear it, I feel my power growing, my youthful strength returning. It is truly the treasure of legend, with the ability to magnify whatever magic it meets."

Unable to contain his overwhelming desire, the priest whispered, "It is magnificent."

Araggna's normal harsh expression returned. "And you shall never have it!"

Grukarr stiffened, though he still couldn't take his eyes off the glowing bulge beneath her robe.

Straightening her back, the High Priestess declared, "For crimes against the Divine Monk's holy order and the state of Ellegandia, I hereby sentence you to death."

The snake raised its head, glaring straight at Grukarr, and released a loud hiss.

Grukarr shuddered, anxiously looking around to see if he could somehow manage to escape.

"No more delay," rasped Araggna. "Guards! Cut him down right here in this alley."

Then Grukarr did something surprising. He clapped his hands and declared, "Now."

Instantly, the temple guard nearest to Araggna swung his sword and sliced off the head of her snake. The priestess shrieked as the boa's body slipped off her arm and fell to the ground.

The other guards, at the same time, moved to surround Araggna. Pointing their swords at her, they glared vengefully.

Too stunned to speak, Araggna looked back at them. Never one to pay much attention to the lowly people who served her, she rarely even glanced at the faces of her guards. But now she realized something was wrong.

These men were not the same ones who had been guarding her yesterday! In fact . . . she didn't remember them guarding her *ever*. Yet they did look vaguely familiar. But why?

She gasped, realizing the truth. "Criminals!" she rasped. "I sentenced you to die for your violations of the law."

"That's right," answered Grukarr pleasantly. He stepped between two of the guards. "And I released them. Now they are sworn to serve me."

"Outrage!" cried the priestess. "You are beneath scum, Grukarr."

He merely smirked. "It was you who gave me the idea, High Priestess. Yes, when you stripped me of my own guards."

Ready to explode with rage, Araggna couldn't stop shaking. "You will pay for this, Grukarr. The immortals on high will punish you!"

"Perhaps," he said casually. "But I doubt it."

He reached for her collar, grabbed the slender cord around her neck, and yanked hard. The cord snapped, allowing him to pull out from under her robe a luminous crystal whose every facet pulsed with light. Holding the Starstone in his hand, Grukarr grinned with deep satisfaction.

"You won't have any further need for this." He stuffed the glowing crystal into his pocket, then gazed at the priestess. "I should say it has been an honor and a pleasure to serve you." After a pause, he added, "But it has not."

Shaking with fury, Araggna couldn't speak. All she could do

was glare hatefully at Grukarr and silently curse the world that had betrayed her.

With a wave of his hand, Grukarr commanded the guards, "Now do to her what she wanted done to you."

He spun around and strode out of the alley. Behind him, Araggna screamed in agony. Feeling quite pleased, Grukarr started to whistle serenely.

CHAPTER 22

Feast of the Forest

When in doubt, put aside everything else and do what matters most. Eat.

—From Promi's journal, written
on the opening page of recipes

Moss Island, sparkling with vapor, gleamed in the last light of day. The stream that divided to form the island and hugged its edges splashed continuously, thrumming with tranquil tones. Aside from one old willow tree, nothing but moss grew there—so thick and soft it could have been a bed of green feathers.

Led by Atlanta, Promi waded across the stream to the island. Her bare feet sprang across the river stones, while he walked unsteadily in the current, barely keeping his balance. Yet while the water was fairly deep, none of it got inside his boots. For those magical boots, sensing water lapping at their rims, instantly grew a little bit taller. That kept any water from dousing his feet—as well as Kermi, who lay curled around one ankle, sound asleep.

Reaching the other side, they sat down on the lush carpet of moss. Promi's stomach rumbled, and he glanced around the island. "Er . . . beautiful place," he said. "But I don't see any signs of supper."

"You will," Atlanta promised.

"When?"

"Soon, Promi. But first I need to sing something."

He frowned, rubbing his belly. "I can't eat songs."

Ignoring him, she started to sing, so quietly her voice could barely be heard above the splashing stream:

Mist arises all around,
Forest deep I roam—
Music made from ev'ry sound
Fills the
Singing hills of home.
Creatures gather as I sing,
Seedlings spring from loam—
Music flies like birds awing
In the
Singing hills of home.
Endless magic touches life:
Muscle, flesh, and bone—
Music lift us out of strife!
Bless the
Singing hills of home.

As she sang, the first stars glowed through the gaps between the willow branches. Meanwhile, birds began to gather in those boughs. A woodland grouse with a puffy chest, a family of red-feathered sparrows, two small owlets, a rainbow-winged beecatcher, and a great hornbill with an enormous crown all settled in the willow. As soon as they landed, they ceased chirping or rustling so that Atlanta's voice could carry farther. One of the first to arrive, a young hawk with iridescent green bands on his wings, floated down to the island and perched right beside Promi on a broken branch in the moss.

Tap. Tap. Tap. A small woodpecker hit against a branch, keeping perfect rhythm to Atlanta's song.

The original blessing drum, thought Promi.

Meanwhile, more animals came. A monkey with yellow fur leaped onto the island from a forest vine, his tail clutching a bunch of plump pink berries. Gently, the monkey stretched out his tail and placed the berries on Atlanta's thigh. Without breaking the rhythm of her song, she gave him a grateful wink.

Before she'd finished the second verse, a butterfly floated over and landed on her shoulder. Even in the subtle starlight, its wings flashed rich shades of green. Its antennae bobbed with the music, as if they were keeping time.

A mountain gazelle with her newborn, still wobbly on his thin legs, crossed the water to stand beside Atlanta. A huge black crab clambered out of the stream and sat on the bank, watching with extended eyes. And a thin green snake, whose color precisely matched the moss, slithered out of the shadows to listen.

Then came a rare smelldrude, a creature resembling an oversized otter with vibrant blue eyes, who was almost never seen . . . but was occasionally smelled. Promi had never believed the tales he'd heard about smelldrudes, who supposedly showed their moods by producing smells. But just to be safe, he scooted a bit farther away. For while a happy smelldrude, like this one, smelled like fresh peaches or popping corn, an anxious one could make a whole meadow reek of dead fish. And a genuinely upset one could fill a forest grove with a fragrant mixture of rotten eggs, stale monkey brains, and curdled vomit. Hence the old saying *Beware a smelldrude in an ugly mood.*

Warily, Promi eyed the creature. The smelldrude, a female with wide, webbed feet, did the same to him. Her aroma took on the slightest hint of fish.

Even as Atlanta finished her song, more creatures arrived. Some, such as the family of iridescent beetles shaped like tiny crowns, came by air; others, such as the red-spotted turtle, by water. And many more came by land, trotting and scampering out of the forest.

The largest creature was a centaur whose white hooves glowed in the starlight. Not bothering to cross over to the island, he settled himself on the far side of the stream. While he nestled his lower body, shaped like a horse, in the grass, his upper body, shaped like a muscular man, leaned over the water to look closely at Promi.

Peering into the centaur's ebony eyes, the young man swallowed. "Pleased . . . to meet you," he said uneasily.

The centaur folded his arms across his chest and rumbled in a deep voice, "There is more, and less, to you than appears."

Surprised, Promi asked, "What does that mean?"

Atlanta, sitting beside him, chuckled. "Meet Haldor. He sees visions—usually dark ones."

Before Promi could reply, the centaur continued, "All of which will change after you die."

Now totally confused, Promi gazed at the harsh face looking down at him. "Well . . . thanks. That explains a lot."

Haldor studied him, unblinking. "Fear not. Your death will come soon and be terribly painful."

"How nice," muttered Promi. With a glance at Atlanta, he added, "This fellow could ruin anyone's appetite. Even mine."

Kermi poked his furry blue head out of the boot. He stretched his tiny arms, blew several bubbles, then turned to Promi. "Hello, manfool. Did I just hear something lovely? About someone's painful death?"

"No," the young man replied. "It wasn't about you."

Atlanta waved her hand at the centaur. "That's enough for now, Haldor. It's time for the meal I promised him."

The great beast nodded knowingly. "Enjoy it, for it shall be one of your last."

Promi just shook his head, more unsure than ever what to make of this dour supper companion.

"A feast!" proclaimed Atlanta. Facing the assembled creatures, she asked, "Would you help, my friends? Go quickly and return with the very best foods you can find."

With that, the birds took flight and the animals departed. Even the turtle slid back into the stream. Only one remained—the centaur. Too comfortable to move, he just stayed in the grass, staring glumly at Promi.

Meanwhile, Atlanta reached up and clasped a dangling bough of the willow. Gently, she tapped it, using three fingers. At the same time, she whispered in a strange language full of whooshes, swishes, and clacks of her tongue.

Seconds later, a slight breeze seemed to stir the tree's branches. Several of them started to sway, making their own whooshing and clacking sounds. The noise swelled, spreading to the trees across the stream. More trees made sounds—sycamores and elms, acacias and thornberries, cedars and banyans. One bodhi tree started to hum in deep, resonant tones. Before long, all the surrounding forest joined in the chorus that had started with a few taps of Atlanta's fingers.

Promi leaned back on the moss. "That's nice, Atlanta, but I really need some food. I'm feeling faint."

"Just watch," she said.

A luminous purple bird swooped down through the waving branches. In its slender beak, it carried a single raspberry. Though it circled to land on Atlanta's shoulder, she tilted her head toward Promi and whistled softly. The purple bird veered, its wings flashing in the light of the setting sun, then dropped the raspberry into the young man's lap before flying back to the forest.

Surprised, he glanced at Atlanta, then immediately popped the berry into his mouth. Sweet, fruity flavor exploded on his tongue, while juices slid down his throat. His whole body tingled from the sensation. *Food! I'd almost forgotten.*

"Just a small taste to give you strength," she explained.

"Strength to wait?"

"No. Strength to *eat.*"

She'd hardly spoken the words when a pair of bushy-tailed starlings floated through the trees, each bearing a sprig of wild mint. Along with them came a silver falcon whose talons clasped a large cabbage leaf. As soon as the falcon placed the leaf on the ground beside Promi, the starlings glided over and dropped their mint. The sprigs spun slowly downward, and by the time they landed on the leaf, several more birds had arrived. They brought with them a variety of edible flowers, along with spinach, parsley, chives, and baobab leaves—all of which they piled on the leaf.

"Might as well start on your salad," suggested Atlanta. "Just don't forget the dressing."

"Dressing? You're not serious."

At that instant, a large, bronze-hued squirrel hopped over some stones in the stream and scampered onto the island. Its dark eyes glinted, and its ears twitched constantly. In its forepaws, it held a strip of bark that had curled into itself, forming a shallow bowl. And within that bowl lay some thick, tan-colored cream sprinkled with nuts.

"What's wrong, Promi? Never seen hazelnut cream before?" She tried to sound disappointed. "Poor boy, you've only experienced human bakeries."

Taking the squirrel's gift, Promi dipped his finger in the cream.

White lather, along with a few bits of nut, clung to his skin. "Mmmmm," he said, licking the finger clean. "Wonderful."

"It's made from milkfruit, well shaken, with a squeeze of lemon juice," she explained with satisfaction. "And of course, only the best local hazelnuts."

All at once, more food arrived. From every direction came a feast from the forest. A hollow burl piled high with wild mushrooms, brought by a white ibex. A leaf full of raw grains soaked in meadowblossom honey, carried by a scarlet bird of paradise. A root filled to the brim with guava juice, delivered by the same yellow monkey who had been one of the first creatures to arrive. Curled in his tail, he also brought a bark bowl of baby plums—the sweetest ones Promi had ever tasted, even without the bits of honeycomb sprinkled on top.

Watching him devour the plums, Atlanta asked drily, "Like them, do you?"

Promi glanced at her, his mouth crammed full of fruit. "Wup ebah gabe you dat idea?"

She nodded. "Looks like you could just live on those plums. Or anything sweet."

"Right," he replied after a big swallow. "When it comes to food, the sweeter the better."

"Typical," said Kermi, who had climbed up to a willow branch. Hanging by his tail, he crinkled his furry blue snout. "That's all you think about, manfool. The next sweet! The only place you could ever get enough of them is the spirit realm."

"Perhaps," said the centaur in an unusually optimistic tone, "you will find your way there after your violent and brutal death."

Ignoring him, Promi mused, "A land of sweets is my kind of place."

"Then the spirit realm is for you," commented Atlanta. "I've heard stories that the rivers there flow with nectar, sugar cakes grow on trees, and all the flowers are sweeter than honey."

The green butterfly, who had perched again on her shoulder, shook its antennae with delight.

"Too bad it's impossible for mortals like you to get there," said Kermi with a vengeful grin.

Promi looked up at him. "Well, maybe I'll just have to find a way."

The kermuncle rolled his eyes. "I won't hold my breath."

"Good. If you held your breath too long, you might turn blue. And *nobody* with any sense wants to be blue."

"Harrumph. Better to be blue than *you,* manfool." For emphasis, he blew a stream of bubbles.

Promi went back to eating—not because he couldn't think of a few good curses, but because the meal had only just begun. Food was piling up fast all around him.

Animals and birds arrived in droves, bringing freshly picked watercress, the smallest (and juiciest) tomatoes Promi had ever eaten, an extremely tart apple, and a cinnamon root so potent that one bite popped his eyes wide open. Plus a bunch of rosehips sprinkled with nutmeg. A ripe persimmon that tasted surprisingly like vanilla. Three pears, so juicy they dribbled all over his tunic. And half a stalk of sugarcane, brought by the smelldrude. (What had happened to the other half, Promi didn't need to ask, since she smelled deliciously sweet.)

As if that weren't enough, animals delivered a bunch of miniature bananas, some golden almonds, and one fiery hot chili pepper. Along with a stack of fresh butterpetals, an enormous nut Atlanta called *coco de mer,* and some more sprigs of mint.

Every so often, Promi leaned over and drank from the freshwater stream. Then, without delay, he went right back to eating. On the rare occasions when he paused briefly, it was just to close his eyes and savor the smells around him. Which included the pleasing scent of fresh ginger, thanks to a young unicorn who emerged from the forest with a ginger root on the tip of his horn. Shyly, he dropped the gift by Atlanta's side and then trotted back into the forest, his golden mane sparkling.

At last, Promi couldn't possibly take another bite. Feeling fully satisfied, he turned to Atlanta. She was sitting in the moss, playing with a family of small golden birds who kept fluttering around her, landing on her nose and ears and curly hair. She laughed at their antics.

Turning to Promi, she said, "Well, well. Ready for more?"

He grinned. "Not a chance. Never thought I'd say this, but . . ." He patted his belly. "I'm completely full."

"Yes," agreed Kermi. "But the question is, full of *what*?"

"Was it worth all the wait?" asked Atlanta.

Promi considered the question, then shook his head. "No." He smacked his lips. "But what a way to end it!"

She smiled at him, still encircled by the playful birds. "So . . . any chance you might consider changing your mind? To help save this wondrous place?"

His grin melted away. "I already told you. That's, well . . . not my fight."

She glared at him. "Your meal. But not your fight."

Uncomfortably, he shifted. "Well, I—"

Atlanta's shout cut him off. "There!" she cried. "Look there!"

CHAPTER 23

A Story Whispered by the Wind

It's easy to be an idiot. Believe me, I know from experience. But to be a complete, total, hopeless idiot? Now, that takes constant practice.

—From Promi's journal

Atlanta was pointing at the stream. Seeing what had caught her attention, Promi froze. Even Kermi, dangling from the willow branch above their heads, watched in astonishment.

The water flowing around the island began to bubble and churn. Soon the stream was rising above its banks—not with more liquid, but with vapors that sparkled with starlight . . . as well as another kind of light that radiated from within.

Enthralled, they watched as luminous walls of mist rose out of the stream all around them. The walls climbed higher, reaching over the top of the willow tree. Somewhere above the highest branches, the walls of mist bent inward and closed together, forming a protective dome. Now it sheltered Atlanta, Promi, and all the creatures who had joined them (except for the centaur, who had glumly watched the rising vapors from the outer bank).

The gleaming walls of mist began to undulate. Promi caught his breath. Strange shapes, like living bodies, formed and then melted away, only to form anew and melt away again. There he saw an arm . . . a hip that curved into a waist . . . and a partial face with long, flowing, vaporous hair.

"What are they?" he asked Atlanta, without taking his eyes off the elusive shapes.

"Mist maidens," she answered quietly. "I've only seen them once before—years ago, the very first time I came to this island." Stroking the antennae of the luminous butterfly on her shoulder, she whispered, "They appear only at the request of the river god."

Promi started. "An immortal? Here?"

"Throughout this forest," she replied. "They almost never show themselves. But they are here nonetheless."

Watching the mist maidens, Promi was too amazed to speak again. He could only gaze at the vaporous beings who encircled them, moving with a graceful, dreamlike rhythm. *Their dance,* he thought in wonder. *This is their dance.*

In time, the wondrous beings ceased dancing and melted back into the vapors. The undulating walls of mist retracted, pulling back down into the stream. Seconds later, the whole magical display had vanished.

They sat in silence, watching the flowing water, for a long moment. Finally, Atlanta spoke again, her voice a mixture of awe at what they'd just witnessed and resentment at Promi for his unwillingness to help in her quest.

"Another example," she said, "of the magic of this place."

Knowing that anything he said would make her even more angry, he merely nodded. How could he ever explain that he simply wasn't made for battles as big as saving her beloved forest? Just as he couldn't bring himself to believe old Bonlo's wild tales of wars between immortals, magical crystals, and prophecies of doom—he couldn't imagine giving up the life he'd always known to help Atlanta. And now, having finally figured out how to use his Listener magic, he intended to save it for only the most dire emergencies, when his everyday skills weren't enough to do the job. Or to save his skin.

The fewer sacrifices I need to make, he told himself, *the better.*

Pulling his journal out of his tunic pocket, he drew a quick sketch of the mist maidens rising out of the water. Underneath, he scrawled, *Magical creatures everywhere in this forest. Plus amazing foods. Hope they all can survive whatever is to come.*

Slipping the charcoal pencil back into the recipe book's binding, he stiffened. For some reason he couldn't explain, writing that entry hadn't made him feel better, which writing had always done before, regardless of the situation. That was why he considered his journal to be his dearest possession—except, of course, for that thin sliver of a song from his childhood.

Puzzled, he replaced the book in his pocket. Instead of making him feel better, writing that particular entry had made him feel *worse.* How could that be?

The centaur, who had been morosely watching the vanishing mist maidens, shifted his gaze to Atlanta. He clacked his two white forehooves together and rumbled, "You should tell us a story."

She raised an eyebrow. "Now, Haldor?"

"Yes," the centaur answered. "Before something bad happens."

With a sharp glance at Promi, she grumbled, "It already has." Then, seeing the eager faces of the animals and birds surrounding her, she asked the group, "Would you like a story?"

All around her, wings fluttered, tails bounced, and creatures chattered and growled and piped their approval.

"All right, then. Just a short one." Atlanta drew a breath and announced, "This is a story whispered to me by the wind."

The great bird soared high overhead, its golden tail feathers flashing in the sun.

Far below, on the dry plains of Abuya, a lone boy watched its flight. He was a lowly shepherd, he knew, just one person sitting on a rock while a flock of sheep grazed on stubbly grass. To the winged bird on high, he was no more than a speck of dust, a meaningless shadow.

The boy's shoulders sagged beneath his ragged tunic. For he had nothing. No family. No honor of his own. Though he worked as a guardian for other people's sheep, he did not possess so much as a shepherd's staff. He even lacked a name and was called simply Boy by the people of his tribe.

Yet as he watched Erolien, the mighty golden bird, soaring among the clouds, he realized that there was one thing he surely did have. Something that belonged to him, and him alone.

A dream.

He wanted to do what no one from his tribe had ever done before: to find the secret nest of Erolien, high on the smoking summit of the mountain Ell Shangro. There he would meet the great bird, three times taller than even the biggest man. And he would take one of the bird's golden feathers—a treasure more precious than a chest full of jewels. Then he would return to his tribe, surprising everyone with his great prize, the golden feather.

He clucked his tongue in satisfaction. "Yes, they will treat me like a god. And if they want to worship me, I will let them. For that would be right."

The boy stood up and started walking toward the mountains, leaving behind the sheep and the tribe and the life he had known.

Whatever happened, he knew, he would never return without the golden feather.

Across the plains, he walked and walked and walked still more. Many days passed, melting into weeks. The terrain was mostly flat, though he crossed several parched riverbeds where only a trickle of water flowed. His legs ached and his bare feet stung. Worst of all, the distant mountains never seemed any closer.

Yet he continued to walk, eating only locusts and ants and the occasional worm. More days passed, more than he could bring himself to count. The mountains, at last, seemed closer. He could even see Ell Shangro, jutting up like a sword of stone—high, steep, and treacherous.

Then he came to a deep canyon that blocked his path. He gazed down, studying the sheer cliffs and the dark line of a river far below. Despite the dryness of his throat, he swallowed in fear. And for the first time in many weeks of walking, he looked back over his shoulder in the direction he had come.

"I will not give up," he declared. "Not after I have come so far."

So he climbed into the canyon, slowly working his way down the cliff. His hands and feet bled, while his leg muscles trembled from the strain. But somehow he held on.

Suddenly the ledge beneath him broke. He fell headlong down the cliff, smashing into rocks. With a splash, he landed in the river and weakly pulled himself ashore.

When he awoke, hours later, the river roared beside him, as if it were enraged that he had somehow escaped death. He coughed painfully and tried to crawl higher on the shore. But a sharp pain exploded in his ankle and he collapsed onto his back.

Beaten. He knew he was beaten. Even though he had somehow survived that fall, he still needed to climb out of this canyon and then go even farther if he hoped to realize his dream.

But there was no more hope. No more strength. He coughed again, racked with pain. He lay on his back, looking up at the sky.

A flash of gold flew above him, like a sun racing across the heavens. Yet this was no sun. It was Erolien, the great golden bird!

With a sudden burst of passion, he shouted to the sky: "Hear me, Golden One! Hear my plea! If you give me the strength to climb out of here and complete my quest . . . I will not keep your precious feather for myself. No, I will give it to my people! They will try to honor me for this magnificent gift. Yet I will refuse. For the gift came not from me—but from you."

All at once, he felt a new surge of strength. It flowed through his arms, his legs, even his injured ankle. And it had come, he knew, from Erolien.

Though he could not explain how, he climbed out of that canyon. And though his body was frail and broken, he limped onward, heading toward the mountains. All through that night he walked, guided by the light of the moon, over rising hills and through forests of spruce and fir.

Higher he climbed, and still higher. Rising above the last stand of twisted trees, he topped a ridge. Between the weathered rocks scattered across the ground, he saw a lone purple flower that trembled in the alpine breeze. Nodding, he said, "You, too, have survived."

Now, rising beyond the ridge, he could clearly see Ell Shangro. Its mighty shoulders lifted high above the surrounding peaks, while the jagged crater on its summit spewed enormous plumes of smoke into the sky. Snow and ice draped its upper slopes, a pure white robe that only centuries of winter could weave.

Onward he trudged, climbing through drifts of snow. He thought about the great golden bird, imagined its powerful wings soaring above the clouds. And he savored the vistas that he could now see, vistas that belonged to Erolien: endless mountains, rolling plains, and the sparkling waves of a faraway ocean.

He continued to climb, higher than any mortal man had climbed before. Soon his feet, frozen by the snow, lost all feeling.

Yet he pushed ahead. The snowfields grew deeper, making every step a challenge. Often he broke through and sank up to his waist. It took all his remaining strength to pull himself out and keep moving.

At long last, he spied a towering buttress that rose out of the snow. Like the head of a mighty bird, it lifted proudly skyward, shining bright in the sun. And at the very top of the buttress sat an enormous tangle of branches, glittering with golden feathers.

The nest!

He gasped in awe. Though his body was weak and frozen, his spirit soared. For he had found the nest of the great golden bird. He had seen what no other person had ever seen. And for the first time, he knew the truth of his quest.

Kneeling in the snow, he peered up at the luminous nest. "I need no golden feather!" he cried triumphantly, though only the wind and snow could hear his words. "I need only this moment."

He fell forward, his face in the snow, his arms spread wide as if they were wings. Sunlight played across his skin, touching it with gold.

Wind blew across his body, tousling his hair and rippling his torn tunic. But in all other ways, he lay perfectly still. He no longer breathed. He no longer dreamed.

Until . . . he took flight. His arms became powerful wings; his eyes saw the world beyond.

And the great bird soared high overhead, its golden tail feathers flashing in the sun.

CHAPTER 24

A Most Unlikely Vision

I love eating a rich new pastry. But I don't always love digesting it afterward.

—From Promi's journal

When Atlanta's story ended, silence enveloped Moss Island. No one stirred or made any sound louder than breathing; not a single wing rustled. Meanwhile, starlight touched the island and all the creatures there with a gentle radiance, softer than a candle's glow through a veil.

Promi turned to Atlanta, meeting her gaze. For a long moment, they looked at each other, neither one speaking. The story had disturbed Promi deeply, more than he could even start to explain. Anxiously, he rubbed the strange mark over his heart.

The centaur clacked his forehooves, breaking the silence. He seemed to be in a trance, gazing at something far away, beyond the island, beyond the forest. "Someday," he intoned, "this country will change. It will become an island, set completely apart from the rest of the world."

Now Promi and Atlanta exchanged puzzled glances. "An island?" whispered Promi. "Really?"

Atlanta shook her head and whispered back, "That's just Haldor's vision language. He doesn't mean it literally. Anyway, this country is so remote, it's already a kind of island."

"Yet even as an island," the centaur continued, still gazing into the distance, "this place will touch the wider world. But mark my words: its enduring power will spring not from its landscape, so rich in magic. Not from its towering buildings and great inventions of the future. And not from its magnificent creatures who are as varied as the world itself."

Haldor's voice dropped lower. "No, the lasting power of this place will come from its stories. People from every land will seek those stories, share them, and cherish them."

Still in a trance, he clacked his hooves again. "And when the island is no more, those stories will live on for the rest of the world."

Sounding even more somber than usual, he concluded, "Be warned, though. Our magical island will not survive! No, it shall be lost forever, sinking deep into the sea, after *a terrible day and night of destruction*."

The centaur's final words lingered in the air for a moment, echoing in the forest as well as the minds of everyone who heard them.

Kermi, dangling by his tail from the willow, stroked his whiskers. "Delightful fellow. I love to hear him speak in that triple-bass voice. Too bad nobody has any clue what he's saying."

"For once," said Promi, "I agree with you."

Kermi blew a large, wobbly bubble. "Then I must be wrong."

Promi's eyes narrowed. But before he could reply, Atlanta gasped and grabbed his wrist. Following her gaze, he, too, gasped.

Something new was emerging from the stream. It wasn't a sea animal. Or a mist maiden. Or anything Atlanta or Promi had ever expected to see lifting out of the water.

"A hand!" Promi blinked, astonished, as an enormous, watery hand rose higher. Water cascaded off its liquid fingers, flowed over its wrist, and swirled in a spiral down the arm beneath it.

Quickly, Promi glanced at the others. Atlanta was entranced, watching closely. All the animals and birds sat motionless and silent. Even Kermi was at a loss for words, his round ears quivering.

Promi cocked his head, now soaked with spray from this watery being. "What in the name of Ellegandia," he asked, "is that?"

"That," answered Atlanta, her voice full of awe, "is Bopaparruplio. The spirit of freshwater rivers and streams. I've never actually seen him before, just heard about him from the trees."

Hearing this, Kermi quickly climbed higher, where he'd be completely hidden by the willow's branches.

"The river god?" asked Promi. "Why would he show himself now?"

At that instant, something gleamed in the center of the river god's liquid palm. A tiny globe the size of a pearl took shape, hardening as they watched. A fluid form of light sparkled inside it, as if the moon's reflection on a river had been captured within a bubble.

With a flick of the spirit's wrist, the bubble of light flew into the air. It landed perfectly in Atlanta's hand, which lay open on her lap. She gasped, closing her fingers over the watery jewel.

"For me?" She stared at the radiant bubble and then at the liquid hand.

"Fffffor jussssst you," splashed the watery voice that rose out of the stream. "Sssssave it ffffor the time you need it mossssst."

"Bu-but . . ." she stammered. "What does it do?"

"You mussssst dissssscover that ffffor yourssssselfffff."

Before she could ask anything else, the hand twisted sharply and rubbed two watery fingers together. A shiny, pointed object appeared between the fingers. With another flick of the wrist, the object flew into the air—and landed, point down, in the moss beside Promi.

"A knife!" He wrapped his hand around the dagger's silver hilt and drew it out of the moss. Holding it high, he could see it shimmer with translucence, more like an icicle than any kind of metal.

He hefted the knife, gauging its weight and balance. Like ice, it was surprisingly cold to the touch. Yet it didn't slip at all in his grasp, resting securely upon his fingers. Then something else about it caught his attention—a thin line of dewdrops that dangled freely from the base of the hilt, gleaming like a silver string.

Curious, Promi reached out to touch the string. The instant his fingertip made contact, the string tensed, curled, and wrapped itself around the wrist of the hand holding the dagger. Meanwhile, the portion that now connected his wrist to the knife's hilt started to stretch and contract, again and again, as if it were magically breathing.

He grinned, guessing what its purpose might be. Pushing himself to his feet, he stood on the moss. With barely a glance across the stream at a dead spruce tree whose branches had long ago fallen to the ground, he lifted the dagger and snapped his wrist.

The dagger flew straight at the tree. With a *kthunk*, its blade plunged into the trunk.

Unable to resist a chance to annoy his companion, Kermi said from his hiding place in the branches, "Nice throw, manfool. Too bad now you have to go all the way over there to get your knife back."

"No, I don't." Promi winked at Atlanta. "Watch this."

He gave his wrist a sharp tug. The silver string, which had extended to the tree, suddenly tightened. It plucked the dagger out of the trunk and snapped back to Promi, whose waiting hand caught the hilt once more. When he touched the string with his free hand, it immediately untied from his wrist and dangled loose again, making it easy for him to slide the magical dagger into its sheath.

"Well, I—harrumph," sputtered the voice in the branches. "Never saw anything like that."

"Nor have I." Promi turned toward the immense hand of the river god. "You have given me a great gift. And I thank you."

"So do I," chimed in Atlanta, springing to her feet. She studied the luminous bubble for a few seconds, then slipped it securely under her sleeve. "Whatever it's for, I'm grateful."

"Jussssst remember thisssss." The fountainlike hand turned toward them, dousing them with spray. "Your gifffffftsssss are worthlesssss without courage, ffffortitude, and love."

The liquid fingers of Bopaparruplio curled, making a fist, then started to drop back into the stream. Just before the hand sank away completely, the splashing voice declared, "I give you thessssse treasssssuresssss ffffrom the water . . . but I cannot, alasssss, give you hope."

With barely a ripple, the hand of the river god vanished. Atlanta and Promi stared into the stream, hearing the watery echo of those words.

"No hope," said Atlanta solemnly. Turning to Promi, she asked, "Not even from you?"

He swallowed, then slowly shook his head. "I'm still going to leave in the morning."

She waved at the stream. "After all this?"

He said nothing.

Blue-green fire ignited in her eyes. Pointing at the knife from the river god, she cried, "Then you should give that back! That, and all the other things you've taken from this forest your whole life."

"I can't help, Atlanta. Not against so much—the priest, the blight, and whatever else."

"You mean you *won't* help," she shot back. "You think only about yourself! Do you even care if all these creatures survive?"

"Sure I do. But like I said before—"

"I know," she finished. "Not your fight."

His face hardened. "That's right."

She glared at him so fiercely that he backed away on the moss. On top of that, he couldn't miss the unhappy look of the monkey and the angry hiss of the snake. The young hawk on the broken branch raked his talons, chipping off some bark. And most frightening of all, the smelldrude's aroma was starting to carry a hint of rotten eggs.

"This," rumbled the centaur, "is the kind of behavior that precedes a violent death."

Meanwhile, the hawk screeched angrily. The monkey bared his teeth, growling. And the snake hissed louder.

"Wait." Atlanta held up her hands and spoke calmly. "No one will fight or die tonight." She shot Promi a disgusted look. "Even if it's deserved."

She lowered her hands. "No, let's all try to get some sleep." Whether to Promi or herself, she added, "If we can."

CHAPTER 25

The Wounded Heart

It's painful to wish you could learn something that's impossible to know. But there is one thing worse—to wish you could unlearn something that's impossible to forget.

—From Promi's journal

Hoping to find room enough to sleep along with all the other creatures on the island, Promi scanned the moss. Spying one open spot, he claimed it, though he was nearly touching the mother gazelle's hooves. For a while, he watched the stars, then closed his eyes.

Meanwhile, Atlanta found a spot at the edge of the island, right beside the stream, so she could hear only its constant splashing. Kermi curled up beside her, wrapping his tail around himself to keep warm. Across the stream, the centaur lay down completely and soon started to make a sound that was part whinny and part snore.

One by one, the other animals and birds dropped into sleep. Even the smelldrude settled into a lilac-scented slumber. And the radiant butterfly who had sat on Atlanta's shoulder found a willow leaf where it could close its wings and sleep safely.

Promi lay awake for some time. His mind kept returning to Atlanta's story about the boy who lost everything, even his life. He shifted positions, trying in vain to use his boots as a pillow. Several times, he checked to be sure the new magical knife was in its sheath. Finally, he drifted off to sleep.

But he did not sleep well.

He rolled and tossed. Sometimes the gazelle kicked in her sleep, striking his chest with her hooves. But far worse was the deeply disturbing dream that came to him. It came again and again, always the same. Yet each time, it felt more frightful than before.

He dreamed that he awoke on the mossy island. But now he was all alone. Atlanta wasn't there, nor were any of the animals and birds. Even the mist maidens were gone. He had no companions, and heard no sound except the beating of his heart.

Then, to his shock, he realized that his heart was not in his chest! No, it lay an arm's length away, there in the moss. Though it continued to beat, and he could see it pulsing, it was completely outside of himself.

Worse yet, his heart was badly wounded—bleeding and bruised. Its beats grew steadily weaker; its blood soaked the moss.

Dying! his mind screamed. *My heart is dying!*

Yet when he tried to move, to reach over and touch his heart, he couldn't budge. Completely paralyzed, he lay on his back, unable to do anything but watch.

My heart! My own heart. I must help it. Heal it. Save it.

But he couldn't do anything.

Even as the heart weakened, its beats grew louder, drumming in his ears. He tried with every morsel of strength to reach out and touch it. His useless body trembled with the strain; his mind reeled.

Always, right then, the whole scene vanished. Promi remained asleep, his mind a blank. Yet he tossed uneasily, as if he remembered what he'd just experienced. Or as if he knew somehow that the dream would return. Which it did, time after time.

Finally, after many repetitions, the dream ended—and this time, Promi woke up. The instant he opened his eyes and saw Atlanta kneeling over him, he shouted in surprise and rolled away. Grasping his chest, he felt his heart, still beating inside himself. Then, in a flash, he knew he was truly awake.

Rolling back over, he sat up and faced her. "I—I'm sorry. You, um, scared me there." Using his sleeve, he wiped the perspiration out of his eyes. "I had, well . . . a rough night."

"You certainly did." She studied him with genuine concern. "You weren't really asleep. It was more like . . . a trance. I couldn't wake you, no matter how hard I tried."

"Couldn't wake me?"

"Right." She brought her face closer to his. "And, Promi, you were in pain. Crying out. Something about . . . your heart."

Instinctively, he rubbed his chest, feeling the skin that bore the mysterious mark. With a swallow, he said, "I had a dream, that's all. Nothing to worry about."

"Want to tell me about it?"

"No," he said with finality. "I don't."

"All right," she replied gently. "At least it's over now. You're awake at last."

His gaze sharpened. "How long was I out?"

"Long enough," said a gruff little voice above his head, "that even I was starting to miss you."

Promi looked up to see Kermi, dangling upside down by his

tail. The long appendage was wrapped casually around a branch. Only then did the young man notice that all the other animals and birds had left the island. No sign of them remained. Haldor, the centaur, had also gone—no doubt to confound some new audience with his dark visions.

He peered up at the bright blue sky showing through the branches. "It's morning."

"Observant as ever, manfool," said Kermi dryly.

"Late morning," added Atlanta. "Almost noon."

Gracefully, she sat beside him on the moss. Because neither of them wanted to raise the sore subject of Promi's decision to go back to the City, they remained quiet. They simply listened to the splashing stream.

Finally, Promi said, "It was amazing to be so close to all those creatures last night."

Atlanta nodded, watching the water flow past. "Always good to gather here on Moss Island. Even without visits from mist maidens and the river god." Heavily, she sighed. "For the whole evening, I forgot about the blight and the rest."

He turned, looking at her as she watched the stream. *She really is beautiful,* he thought. *And she truly loves this place and everything in it.*

"What do you think," he asked quietly, "caused the blight to start?"

She shrugged sadly. "Nobody knows. Not even the wisest old trees. But I'm starting to wonder if it might have to do with the Starstone."

"The Starstone?" Bonlo's description came back to him in a flash. "The gift from the spirit realm? With the power to magnify magic?"

"That's right." She faced him. "Only those of us who live here know that it's been hidden right here in the Great Forest. For years beyond count."

"But the Starstone is such a *good* thing," he objected. "How could it have anything to do with the blight?"

Atlanta bit her lip, then said, "It's gone. Someone took it—maybe a traveler or a wandering monk—just a few weeks ago. And without its power, the forest might have been weakened, which made it vulnerable to a disease like the blight."

Promi frowned. "I can't believe it's gone."

"And the worst part is," she added glumly, "no one has any idea where the Starstone is now. So we can't even try to get it back."

An idea struck Promi with the force of a lightning bolt. "I do!"

She grabbed his arm. "You know where it is?"

"Yes. I saw it—twice, in fact."

"Where?"

"Around Araggna's neck."

The same realization struck Atlanta. "I saw it too! Glowing under her collar."

"Right." His elation swiftly faded. "But if that old priestess has a treasure of such power . . . it can't be good."

Atlanta blew a long breath. "You're right. Why, the only person worse would be Gr—" She caught herself before saying his name. Even so, the willow arching above them shuddered, dropping leaves on the moss.

Promi, too, shuddered. "What a terrible thought, to have something so beautiful and powerful in the hands of either of them!" He swallowed, then said under his breath, "Almost as terrible as that dream."

She gazed at him sympathetically. "Sure you don't want to talk about it?"

"Totally sure." Instinctively, he rubbed the skin over his heart. "Let's just say it was like a kind of blight. Except . . . instead of hurting the forest, it was hurting . . ."

"You."

He nodded gravely. "Like part of me was . . . well, *wounded.* Maybe even dying. And I couldn't do anything at all to heal it."

Her face creased with pain. "That's how I felt . . . when my parents died."

"How old were you?"

"Young. Too young."

Gently, he touched her wrist. "How did it happen?"

Atlanta turned back to the stream and didn't speak for a moment. At last, she said, "In the swamp—Unkhmeini Swamp, at the base of the high peaks." She frowned. "They had a theory about a place on the other side of the swamp and went to explore it. The swamp is not very big . . . but it's terribly dangerous, full of poisonous gases and worse. So they left me at our cottage on the southern side of the forest. Told me they'd be back in two or three days at the most."

Her voice dropped to a whisper. "They never came back."

"And you don't know what happened to them?"

She grimaced. "No, but I do know this: Of all the places in this country I may go in my life, I'll never go there. *Never.*"

"What was the place," asked Promi, "they wanted to explore? I'm just . . . curious." He realized, with a pang, that old Bonlo would have been pleased to hear him say that.

"The Passage of Death," she answered, wincing at the name.

"I've heard of that—in the legends people tell on the streets. The place where spirits of dead people supposedly go if they can't find their way to the immortal realm." He scratched his chin thoughtfully. "That never seemed like much of a passage to me—a place where spirits get stuck forever."

Morosely, she nodded. "That's what intrigued my parents. They couldn't believe it was so wrongly named. Even wondered if the name was given to that place just to keep people away, so that whatever is really there wouldn't get discovered."

"They were brave to go, Atlanta."

"Foolish, you mean. The swamp they needed to cross is the exact opposite of this forest, a place of horrors and death."

"So . . . who raised you?"

"Isn't it obvious?" She raised her arms. "The animals, the trees, the mist, the magic." She swallowed, then said, "I just wish I could have known them . . . a little longer."

Softly, he said, "I lost my parents, too. Only I don't remember how. Or what they were like. Or anything about them."

"So who raised *you*?"

"I raised myself. With some help from the knives I learned how to throw." He glanced down at the new blade in his sheath. "Except for this gift from the river god, every single thing I've ever owned—my journal, my boots, my knives, my clothes—I stole."

Atlanta leaned a bit closer. "You have nothing left from your childhood? Nothing at all?"

"Just . . . a song. Not even the whole song, really. A few notes I can remember hearing someone sing to me. That's all."

She shook her head, trying to imagine what Promi's life in the City must be like. After a while, she said, "Now I understand."

"Understand what?"

"You, Promi." She peered at him, her blue-green eyes alight. "No wonder you don't want to get too attached—whether to a person or a place like this forest. Every attachment you had as a child was torn away. Don't you see? You've lost everything once before, so you're afraid of losing whatever else you find."

"Nonsense," he scoffed. "That's not true at all! I just like my life as a thief. The freedom, the excitement, the—"

"Idiocy," grumbled Kermi from the branch. He blew a casual stream of bubbles. "And you've really mastered that part."

Despite himself, Promi grinned. "Got me there, bubblebrain."

The kermuncle's normally wide eyes narrowed to slivers. "Don't call me that."

"Tell you what," Promi offered. "I'll never call you that again if you won't ride inside my boots again." He reached over to the boots, which hadn't worked very well as a pillow, and pulled them on. "They may be magical enough to hold you, but they fit so much better without you."

"Harrumph. So you're telling me, manfool, we're about to go somewhere?"

Promi turned to face Atlanta, uncomfortably shifting his weight. "I should go back to the City."

She frowned and slid away on the moss. "Right," she said somberly. "And I promised to give you directions."

Just as somberly, he nodded. "You did." Fumbling for words, he said, "It's, um . . . been, well . . . good to meet you."

She didn't respond.

"But," he added, "no need for those directions."

Raising an eyebrow, she asked, "Why not?"

"Because, Atlanta . . . I'm coming with you."

CHAPTER 26

The Messenger

No melon ever tasted so good! Just remembering it makes my mouth water. How I wish I could have that again—not so much the melon as that brief, beautiful moment.

—From Promi's journal

"Yes!" shouted Atlanta.

She threw herself at Promi and hugged him. The force of her leap knocked him over backward. Together, they rolled on the soft moss of the island to the edge of the splashing stream.

As they fumbled to sit up, Promi spat out a clump of moss. "I guess," he said, "this means you're glad."

She shrugged nonchalantly. "Oh, maybe. What you're doing is just, um . . . a small thing." A corner of her mouth edged upward. "But I do appreciate small things."

Promi grinned. "Glad to hear it."

Kermi dangled lower on his branch,

hanging right in front of Promi's face. "Guess what? I, too, appreciate small things. Like your brain."

Promi's grin only broadened. "Pretty good insult, bubblebrain. You really can be clever sometimes."

Hearing this, Atlanta nodded. "Impressive, Promi."

But Kermi reacted differently—with something close to horror. "Did you actually just pay me a compliment?" He stared, aghast, at the young man. "I must be losing my mind."

"Can't lose what's already lost," replied Promi.

The kermuncle glared at him.

Atlanta sighed, then said, "Time to get moving. If we're going to stop Gr—I mean, that priest—we'd better get started." Quietly, she added, "And Promi . . . it sure feels good to say *we*."

"Right," he answered. "But where exactly do you suggest we start?"

She leaped to her feet with the ease of a deer. "Highmage Hill. It's the highest point in the whole forest. If we go there, we might see something that tells us what he is really planning."

Promi looked doubtful. "That's one possibility. But maybe, instead, we should go after the Starstone."

Atlanta shook her head. "I want to know what that priest is up to! If we can discover his plan, we can save this whole forest. That's our top priority, more important than anything else."

Seeing her determined expression, Promi set aside his doubts. "All right, then. Let's go."

"Not so fast, manfool." Kermi bounded down to the moss and slipped into Promi's boot. Magically, it expanded just enough to give the little fellow room to ride inside the rim.

"Those are amazing boots," Atlanta observed.

"Too amazing," the young man replied, looking at the bulging leather around Kermi.

With a nod of thanks to the willow tree and a last glance

around Moss Island, Atlanta stepped across the stream and into the forest. Promi followed close behind, impressed by how fast she could move when she wanted to cover ground quickly.

Speedily they walked, following unmarked trails and contours that Atlanta knew well. Without breaking stride, she often paused to stroke the branch of one tree or pat the trunk of another, as if she were greeting a friend on a busy street. A few times, as well, she waved to creatures including an ibex, a fox, and a mother owl in her nest. Only once did her pace falter—when she saw, across a marshy meadow, a sickly acacia tree. Promi didn't need to ask her to know that it had been stricken with the blight.

Finally, after a couple of hours, Atlanta veered toward an enormous honeymelon tree. They sat on its massive roots under branches that wrapped themselves around bright green melons. But as imposing as the tree itself was, most striking of all was the taste of that honey-sweet fruit. No melon Promi had ever tasted in the marketplace came close to this burst of flavors both sweet and tart.

"Never thought I'd eat so soon after that dinner last night," he said, melon juice dribbling down his chin. "But walking made me hungry again."

"And you used your new knife for the first time," Atlanta added. She glanced down at the small bulge under her sleeve where she'd placed her own gift from the river god. Even now, it glowed through the woven vines of her gown. *What,* she wondered, *is it for?*

Meanwhile, Promi took another big bite of melon, and said, "Dis mewon is so wunnafoo."

"Don't talk with your mouth full," admonished Kermi. He, too, sat on the tree roots, nibbling at a slice.

"Why nop?" answered Promi, more juice dribbling. "Dere is much mowah to eap, an' too liddle time."

"So articulate," grumped the kermuncle.

"Fank you, bubboobwain."

"Kindly don't call me that again," replied Kermi. "Or I'll pop you like one of my bubbles." He shook his head, then grumbled, "Why I ever let Jaladay convince me to endure your company, I'll never know."

"Who is Jaladay?" asked Atlanta. She reached over and gently touched one of Kermi's whiskers. "A friend?"

The creature's large blue eyes grew moist. "The best of friends. She was . . ." He stopped, regaining his usual crusty composure. "A whole lot smarter than master melonhead here."

Atlanta sensed this wasn't the time to ask more. But she resolved to find another chance. Reaching for a sprig of wild watercress, which grew among the roots, she considered the blue kermuncle. There was something more to him than met the eye, that was certain. He wasn't just unusual in the ways she could see . . . but in some other more mysterious ways, as well.

She swallowed another bite. "Time for us to go."

"Lovely," said Kermi. "I get to trade the smell of fresh melon for stinky boot."

"You can walk, if you'd rather," Promi suggested. "Did it ever occur to you to thank me for carrying you around?"

The kermuncle's big eyes grew even bigger. He looked genuinely puzzled. "Why would I ever do that?" He blew a long, thin bubble that hung in the air like a question mark.

Before Promi could reply, he heard a faint humming sound nearby. Atlanta, too, heard it and sat up straight. Her worried expression only deepened as she listened.

"What is it?" he asked.

She didn't answer, except to mutter, "But they never fly alone. Never."

A pair of luminous blue wings fluttered out of the forest, drawing nearer. Whatever sort of creature bore them seemed weak or injured, judging from how erratically it flew. At first, Promi thought it was some sort of butterfly or moth. Then, as it came close enough, he realized what it was.

"A faery!" he said in surprise. "I've never seen one before."

"I've seen many," replied Atlanta. "But not in this part of the forest, so far from their glens. And certainly not just one by himself."

Weakly, the faery approached, each beat of his radiant wings an effort. Seeing Atlanta, the little fellow flapped one last time and glided into her open hand. He lay on her palm, nearly motionless. But for the delicate antennae, which trembled constantly, it was hard to tell that he was still alive.

Along with Promi and the kermuncle, she gazed at the bedraggled faery. His cotton hat, now more gray than white, sat askew on his head. One of his hollowed-out berry shoes had fallen off somewhere; the other had lost its red sheen for all the scratches. His translucent cloak, dingy and tattered, now clung to him by a few threads. Even the glorious blue wings showed several rips around the edges.

"Something terrible has happened," groaned Atlanta. "This faery is almost dead! What caused this? Something tells me it's the work of—um . . . that horrible man."

"Can you ask the faery?"

"No," she answered glumly. "Faery language is just too different, too densely packed with magical symbols. I've never been able to figure it out. Not even a word! As far as I know, the only non-faeries who can speak it are a few elder unicorns."

Weakly, the faery's wings fluttered.

Atlanta frowned. "I'm sure he has something vital to say. If only we could hear it!"

"We can," declared Promi.

"How?"

"When you said the word *hear*, it reminded me of . . . a way of Listening."

"Harrumph," said Kermi. "Wondered when you'd figure that out."

Atlanta caught her breath. "But that means . . . a sacrifice."

Promi nodded grimly. "I'll sure miss them, but . . ." He closed his eyes, concentrating. Then he spoke the words, "Listen one, listen all."

The sound of rushing wind filled their ears. As always, though, no real wind stirred even a single leaf on the surrounding trees. As the sound died away, Promi peered down at the tiny, crumpled figure on Atlanta's palm. The faery's antennae trembled, more vigorously than before.

All at once, Promi rocked backward against the tree root. If he hadn't already been on the ground, he would have fallen down. A whirl of images and ideas slammed into his mind, crowding out every other thought, filling every one of his senses to the limit. He reeled, dizzy from the intensity of all the visions, suddenly aware that the magical mind of a faery held much more detail and richness than his own.

As quickly as the visions had flooded over him, they vanished. He was left there, sprawled against the root, panting from exertion.

"Promi!" cried Atlanta, grabbing his arm. "Are you all right?"

"He's fine." The kermuncle's whiskers quivered with amusement. "He just learned what it's like to have a real brain, that's all."

Groggily, Promi sat up straight again. He rubbed his forehead, which continued to throb from the onslaught of images. Slowly, his eyes came back into focus.

Turning to Atlanta, he explained what he'd seen—haltingly at first, stopping occasionally to shake his head at the horror of it all. Tears filled their eyes as he described the mistwraith's brutal attack on the colony, the wrenching theft of so much magic, the wasteland of stunned faeries. He struggled to explain, because the visions in his mind seemed so much more intense than any human words could possibly convey.

"But why?" asked Atlanta, shaking with a mixture of anger and sorrow.

"No idea." He pushed a hand through his hair. "But . . . the priest did say a few things."

"What?"

"It all came so fast . . . it's hard to remember."

"Try, Promi."

He closed his eyes for a moment, hoping to recall as much as possible.

"The Starstone," he announced gravely. "The priest—he has a plan to get it. And to change it into a terrible weapon! What he called *the most powerful weapon in the universe.*"

Atlanta stifled a shriek. "He can't! That's unthinkable!"

"Not to him."

Composing herself, she objected, "He doesn't have enough power to do something like that."

"He doesn't," replied Promi. "But Narkazan does."

At the mention of the warlord of the spirit realm, Kermi gasped. "What an evil alliance! The worst of both realms."

Grimly, Promi nodded. "The priest said he'll give Narkazan the magic needed to fuel the weapon—at dawn on Ho Byneri, when the veil is thinnest."

"Just ten days from now," said Kermi.

"And for that service," Promi continued, "Narkazan will make him the ruler of Ellegandia . . . and the rest of the mortal world."

Atlanta stomped her foot on a root of the honeymelon tree. "That wicked priest! That's why he wants my help. To collect magic for their weapon." Her eyes practically sizzled with rage. "But I'll never do it!"

Remembering something else, Promi grabbed her wrist. "He spoke about setting a trap for you. And said you'd definitely agree to help."

"Wrong. He'll never catch me, not with all my friends in this forest. And nothing he could possibly do would make me help him."

Gently, she stroked the faery's tattered wing. "He's done enough damage already."

Promi's brow furrowed. "There's more to his plan. He's called for more mistwraiths. Not just to capture magic, but to do something else."

"What?" asked Atlanta.

"I don't know. But he wants the mistwraiths sent right away to his lair."

She ran a hand through her brown curls. "His lair! Wherever that is—it's where we should go."

"But—"

"I'm sure of it," she declared. "Did you hear anything about where this lair might be?"

"Yes, but . . ."

"Well?" she demanded. "Where?"

"It's, well . . ."

"Tell me!"

Promi clenched his jaw, then said, "At the Passage of Death."

She froze. "Are you sure?"

Slowly, he nodded. "Which means . . . to get there, we need to cross—"

"The swamp," she whispered, aghast. "Why there? Of all places, why there?"

Peering into her eyes, he said, "Maybe we shouldn't go. Maybe there's another way to stop him."

"No," she answered, wincing as she spoke. "We must go, Promi. There's no other way."

"Are you sure? That swamp is so dangerous—you said so yourself. It's where your parents . . . um, disappeared."

She chewed her lip, then said, "Maybe I can finish what they started."

Touched by her bravery, Promi said nothing.

"At least," she said reassuringly, "the swamp isn't very big. Bad as it is, we can cross it in less than a day."

Kermi grumbled, "If we survive that day."

Atlanta touched Promi's forearm. "Thank you for what you did. Now, at least, we know what we need to do . . . to save everything we care about."

He rubbed his aching brow, still trying to sort through all the images that had electrified his brain.

"So . . . what did you sacrifice?" Atlanta raised an eyebrow. "Not food again?"

"No. Painful as that was, something told me I needed to make a bigger sacrifice this time. A permanent one."

"What?" she implored. "You don't have much to give up."

"That's true," he said glumly. "Especially now that I no longer own any . . ."

"Boots!" she exclaimed, suddenly noticing his bare feet. "That's terrible, Promi!" Kindly, she added, "But after your feet toughen, you'll really feel the forest under you."

"If I have any feeling left, that is." He gazed glumly at his toes, so much paler and more tender-looking than hers. "It was stupid, I know . . . but it was all I could think of to hear the faery's message."

She didn't say a word, though her look of gratitude was enough to make him feel a bit better. "At least," he said, trying to sound more upbeat than he felt, "I still have my journal."

"I wonder," said Atlanta darkly, "whether you'll want to write about what happens next . . . or just forget about it."

"For once," said the blue kermuncle, "I agree. This really is terrible." Facing Promi, he added, "I am genuinely sorry, manfool, that you had to make such a sacrifice."

Taken by surprise at such sympathy, Promi raised an eyebrow. *Well, well. He's actually concerned about my well-being.*

"Thanks," Promi replied gratefully. "But really, you don't need to—"

"Truly terrible," Kermi interrupted. "Now I'll have to ride on your shoulder, so much less comfortable."

Promi scowled. *So much for my well-being.*

"Let's go, then." The young man stood up, wincing at the twigs and poky bits of bark that seemed to impale his feet. He shot a glance at Kermi. "Climb on if you must. And try to stay quiet."

"Tut, tut, manfool. Have some respect."

"For a bubble-blowing demon like you?"

"For your superiors, whatever their form. You simply have no idea how lucky you are to share my company."

The kermuncle blew a string of big, wobbly bubbles. Then he scampered up to Promi's shoulder. Thumping his tail against the young man's back, he said, "What are you waiting for? Time to toughen up those tender feet of yours."

Promi sighed and said to Atlanta, "Ready when you are."

"Almost," she replied. Carefully, she placed the bedraggled faery in her only pocket, a small pouch on her hip. She stretched the lilac vines of the pocket to create a cozy space for him. And just to make sure he'd be comfortable, she slipped in a few sprigs of watercress and a wild raspberry.

Patting the outside of the pocket, she said softly, "There, now. You just rest quietly until you feel better. One day, you'll be strong enough to fly again."

"Are we going or not?" Kermi thumped his tail impatiently on Promi, as if he were urging an ox to get moving. "Normally, I don't like to watch someone suffer. But this will be an exception."

CHAPTER 27

Swamp Specters

What makes an excellent pastry? It's part ingredients, part oven, and part baker. And of those, the one that matters most is the baker.

—From Promi's journal

Deep into the forest they walked, through the rest of that day and the next. Atlanta led them through sunlit groves of cedar and birch, over hillside trails, and down fern-laden pathways favored by unicorns. Driven by the nearness of Ho Byneri, they moved fast—although Promi's tender feet slowed him down enough that Atlanta had to stop regularly so he could catch up.

"Can't you go any faster?" asked Kermi from his perch on Promi's shoulder.

"Maybe you should try to carry me," he replied testily. "Then you'll—ouch!—see what it's like to have your feet impaled every step."

"No thanks," gloated the kermuncle. "I'm enjoying this ride too much."

Gingerly stepping through a pine grove, where the floor was covered with the poky remains of countless cones, Promi grimaced. This pain in his feet was constant—much like the hunger he'd endured before the feast on Moss Island. Was this what the life of a Listener was destined to be like? Going from one sacrifice to the next, one form of agony to another?

Atlanta, meanwhile, was immersed in her own questions as she trekked. Did she really have the strength to follow the path that led to her parents' death? Had they died in the swamp . . . or at the Passage of Death? And would she be able to find Grukarr's lair without being discovered by his mistwraiths? Her stomach knotted with fear, growing tighter with every step.

Often, she would kneel by a stream, open her pocket, and offer the wounded faery a drink of water. By dipping her finger into the stream, she could give him a few drops without requiring him to move. He looked just as weak and bedraggled as ever, but each time she did that, she felt a small rush of gratitude that warmed her heart. And he gave her the same response whenever she picked him a leaf of fresh basil, always a favorite of faeries.

Once in the late afternoon, she stepped through a boggy patch near a lake. Something about the bog's smell reminded her of the swamp, and her stomach tightened. Without thinking much about it, she placed her hand over the pocket and said to the faery, "It's all right, little friend. The real swamp is still a long way from here."

Instantly, she felt a rush of warmth and reassurance. The fears seemed to fade, and the knot in her stomach loosened.

"Am I comforting you, little friend?" she asked with a grin. "Or are you comforting me?"

Midmorning on the third day, they passed a steep, rocky slope that rose swiftly above the forest floor. Highmage Hill. Though there wasn't time to climb it, Atlanta still wondered what the view from the top might tell her about the forest—and, in particular, about the spread of the blight. She had seen far too many ravaged trees on this trek.

It's bad enough, she thought as she padded across a meadow of flytrap flowers, *to see one tree in trouble. But to see the dying stands we've passed . . . that's almost too much to bear.*

"Come on," she called impatiently to Promi as he climbed a knoll to join her. "We've got to find that lair! And then do whatever it takes to save this forest!"

"I know, I know," he replied. His feet felt impossibly tender from constant abuse. "Why did I ever give up those boots? By the Divine Monk's hairy armpits, I wish I had them!"

"So do I," agreed Kermi, blowing a bubble that popped in Promi's ear. "The boots, I mean—not the armpits."

As they entered a stand of baobab trees, Atlanta suddenly changed directions. She led Promi to a hidden spring bubbling out from the baobab roots. Spying an unusual herb with leaves shaped like tiny green hands, she smiled.

"This herb," she explained while picking all the sprigs she could find, "is called sweetmint. My parents showed me where to find it . . . just in case I ever needed to enter the swamp."

"Really?" asked Promi, puffing as he joined her. "How does it help?"

Slipping the sprigs into her sleeve, she replied, "As long as you keep it in your mouth, the sweetmint stops the poisonous vapors in the swamp from harming you. Don't know how it works, but it does."

"Well," said Promi as he leaned against a baobab's smooth trunk and rubbed his sore foot, "with a name like *sweetmint,* I know I'll like it."

"What matters most," she reminded him, "is that it keeps those vapors away. And maybe even the swamp specters."

"Specters?" He stopped rubbing his foot. "Really?"

"Yes," she answered grimly. "Legends say they are angry spirits who feed on human misery. Or maybe they're the same spirits who are stuck at the Passage of Death."

Promi shuddered. "How far to the swamp from here?"

"Oh, we're still at least a day's walk away. The swamp is a long way past the headwaters of the Deg Boesi, which we'll cross at the eastern edge of this baobab grove."

He cocked his head, taking in the sounds and smells of the grove. "I think I can hear the headwaters flowing nearby."

"You really do have a Listener's ears," she commented. "I can't hear the river at all." Then, on second thought, she said, "But it could be a trick of these trees, you know. Some believe these baobabs are enchanted, full of their own schemes for travelers."

Promi raised an eyebrow, wondering. He pulled his journal from his pocket and scrawled (in the margins of a recipe for oatmeal molasses cookies) a description of the enchanted baobabs—their enormous trunks, the facelike burls that sprouted from their bases, their gray bark that seemed to pulse with life, and their gently rustling leaves. To finish off the entry, he drew a quick sketch of a baobab ringed with sweetmint.

Kermi thumped his tail on Promi's back. "What are you writing, manfool?"

"Oh, just listing all the ways I love you. It's very short."

Finished, he closed the journal and gave its cover a gentle stroke, just as he would the face of a friend. Then he replaced it in his tunic pocket.

"Ready?" asked Atlanta. "Once we cross the river, we keep going east for the rest of the day. By tomorrow afternoon, we'll get to . . ." She paused, as if something were caught in her throat. "The swamp."

Through the rustling baobabs they walked. Suddenly, Atlanta ran ahead—then stopped abruptly. She stood at the edge of a river channel that was more mud than water. And beyond it lay a vast swath of murky pools, twisted trees, and rising clouds of noxious fumes. Bog grass, yellowish brown, grew in sickly patches among the reeking pools. Dark vapors swirled everywhere.

"The swamp," said Atlanta, aghast. "It spread . . . all the way here."

Equally stunned, Promi and Kermi stared at the Unkhmeini Swamp. What few skeletal trees were still standing looked at the very edge of death. Some of the murky pools bubbled and frothed, spewing gases, while others held the carcasses of stricken animals and birds. Yet not a single vulture dared to go near those decaying bodies.

"How . . . ?" asked Promi.

"The blight has spread," answered Atlanta. "And with it, the swamp." She shook her head. "I had no idea."

"Is it possible," Promi wondered aloud, "that whatever evil work Grukarr is doing at his lair made this happen?"

All at once, the baobab trees started to moan and sway as if struck by a wicked wind. Branches twisted and creaked all around them, shaking off loose leaves, until finally the grove quieted again.

Promi winced. "Said his name, didn't I?"

"Yes," whispered Atlanta. "But I have a feeling these trees weren't just reacting to that." She locked gazes with him. "I think they were answering your question."

Nodding, he replied, "I'll take that as a yes."

Looking again at the swamp that stretched all the way to the hazy outlines of mountains in the distance, Atlanta frowned. "It smells putrid, doesn't it? Even from here."

Gently, she laid her hand over the pocket that held the wounded faery. "Don't worry, little friend. I'll keep you safe."

Even as she felt a wave of thanks from the tiny creature, she slid a sprig of sweetmint into the pocket. "Chew on this until we leave the swamp."

Offering another sprig each to Promi and the kermuncle on his shoulder, she reminded them, "This will keep you safe. But only as long as you keep it in your mouth."

"That won't be hard," replied Promi. "I love sweets and adore mint."

He popped the sprig into his mouth, chewed once—and promptly gagged. "Yeccchhh! This tastes like charcoal!"

"Well," she said with a shrug, "I guess whoever named it had a sense of humor."

"Or," he groaned, "a sense of torture."

Atlanta took his arm. "Listen, now. Bad as it tastes, it *works.* And each sprig should last a long time. Keep it in your mouth, and those fumes won't kill you."

Scowling, he gave a nod.

She swallowed nervously. "All right, then. The Passage of Death is all the way on the other side of the swamp, at the base of the high peaks."

"Lovely," grumbled Kermi. "Sounds like a journey to a vacation resort."

Taking a last breath of partially fresh air, Atlanta took her own bite of sweetmint and started to cross the muddy ravine. Promi followed, surprised at the coolness of the mud that swathed his feet and oozed between his toes. And more than anything, he felt a mounting sense of dread.

As they climbed onto the opposite bank, mud slurping at their feet, they suddenly found themselves staring into a boiling mud pit. Like a cauldron of poisons, it bubbled and churned, blacker than the darkest night. Rancid fumes belched into the air, darkening the sky.

"This way," said Atlanta, skirting the mud pit's edge.

Promi came right behind, doing his best to avoid the ghastly pit. When the rancid vapors drifted toward him, he chewed his sweetmint with new vigor.

Soon they came to another pit, this one not boiling. As they stepped past, Promi noticed something strange. The mud inside it seemed to be moving, even though there were no signs of heat and no cloud of fumes.

How could that be? he wondered, pausing at the edge to look more closely.

Snakes! He leaped backward, almost tumbling into a different pit. The skin around the mark on his chest burned with fear.

"Manfool!" cried Kermi, barely clinging to his neck. "What's wrong?"

In answer, Promi merely pointed as he crept closer to the pit. Within its depths, dozens of shiny black bodies slithered. Every so often, the snakes' orange eyes would gleam in the shadows.

Atlanta came over to see what had caught their attention. Seeing the snakes, she stiffened.

"Must be over fifty of them," said Promi.

"Let's not stay to count them, all right?" Kermi settled himself again on the young man's shoulder, then thumped with his tail. "Keep moving."

"Good advice," said Atlanta.

She went back to leading them, keeping a good distance away from any mud pits, whether hot or cold. Glancing over her shoulder, she said, "Bad as this is . . . it will be worse after dark. That's when the swamp specters—*aaahhh*!"

Shrieking, she slipped and fell into a pool of muck that dragged her deeper and deeper. Quicksand! Clawing at the edge of the pool, she tried desperately to pull herself out. But the quicksand sucked at her legs, drawing them irresistibly downward.

"Promi!" she cried, flailing wildly in the muck.

He dashed forward, almost sliding into the pool himself. He veered and grabbed a dead branch that lay on the ground. Kneeling at the edge, he stretched his arm with the branch as far as he could toward Atlanta.

"Take it!" he shouted. Ignoring the burning skin on his chest, he stretched farther over the quicksand.

"Can't reach it!" She lurched toward the branch, but every movement made her sink deeper. Now the quicksand covered her knees and would soon reach her thighs.

Promi spun his head, searching for any way to reach farther. But he saw nothing. Only more muck and deadly pools.

Suddenly an idea struck him. "Kermi!"

The kermuncle, clinging to Promi's neck, read his thought. "Let's do it."

Kermi jumped down and grabbed the end of the branch. At the same time, he placed his long tail in Promi's hand. "Go ahead, manfool, before I change my mind."

Taking the tail, Promi squeezed tight. The kermuncle crawled forward. Together, they pushed the branch toward Atlanta, stretching as far as they could.

She grabbed it! Bracing himself, Promi tugged with all his might. Atlanta waded closer, struggling against the quicksand. At last, she rolled onto the firmer ground by Promi's side. Seeing that she was safe, both her rescuers fell flat, exhausted.

Panting, she turned to Promi. "Thank you! I would have . . ."

He nodded. "Just glad this branch was here."

She gazed at him. "And I'm just glad *you* were here."

"Ahem." Kermi cleared his throat. "And what am I? A marsh marigold?"

She smiled at the little fellow. "Thank you, too, Kermi. You were heroic."

He blew a bubble, seeming to be embarrassed. "Well, not really."

"That's right," agreed Promi. "It was really his *tail* that was heroic."

Atlanta and Promi burst into laughter. Meanwhile, Kermi wiped some of the muck off his whiskers.

They pressed on, moving deeper into the swamp. Doing their best to avoid noxious fumes and deadly pits, quicksand and poisonous snakes, they advanced slowly. Though no more disasters struck, the light faded swiftly. Before long, they were trekking in twilight.

"No farther today," announced Atlanta. She pointed to a slight mound not far ahead. "That looks solid, a good place to spend the night."

As they settled on the mound, covered with scraggly grass, Promi said, "This is a lot different from Moss Island."

Atlanta sighed. "A lot."

Still chewing the herb she'd given him, he asked, "Will this sweetmint last until morning? What if I fall asleep and it falls out of my mouth?"

She glared at him sternly. "Don't let it."

"All right," he promised.

"I have enough to get us through," she explained. "But not any extra." Leaning closer, she added, "And the greatest danger at night is not the fumes." Hesitantly, she reached out her hand and clasped his. "It's the specters. That's how, I'm guessing, my parents died."

He squeezed her hand gently. "That's not how you will die, Atlanta. Or any of us."

Not quite believing him, she nodded. Then, with her other hand, she stroked the pocket that held the faery. "You'll survive this night, little friend. I promise."

A rush of gratitude filled her, and she stroked the pocket again. She could feel the trembling of tiny wings.

"I think," said Promi, "we should take turns keeping watch. I'll go first." He winked at Atlanta. "You've been working harder than any of us today. So you should get some sleep."

She gave him a grateful look. "All right. But when you start to get tired, or if you see any, um . . . visitors—wake me up."

"Fine." He cocked his head toward Kermi, already sound asleep on the grass. "He worked hard, too. At least . . . his tail did."

Atlanta lay down, her head on her arm. "Just keep . . . your sweetmint . . ." She finished the sentence in her sleep.

Sitting cross-legged, Promi peered into the deepening gloom. Darkness shrouded the swamp, except for the eerie glow from some of the fumes in the mud pits. Other than that, everything grew increasingly black. Shadows melted into shadows, twilight into night.

Then something changed. Pairs of gleaming lights, looking almost like fire coals, flickered in the distance. Promi stared at them, trying to make out their source. Meanwhile, he kept the sweetmint right on his tongue, just in case it helped to ward off more than poisonous fumes.

Closer the lights came, always in pairs, moving in a strange, rhythmic dance. Promi watched them intently. They weaved and swayed, illuminating the swamp, dancing in a free-flowing motion that was disarmingly pleasant. Almost . . . hypnotic.

Eyes, he thought dreamily. *They look like eyes. Dancing so beautifully.*

By now, he didn't care that the eyes were encircling him, drawing steadily closer. He didn't notice the long, curved claws that occasionally gleamed in the darkness. Just as he didn't notice that his jaw hung slack, his mouth wide open . . . or that his sweetmint had fallen to the ground.

As the eyes closed in around him, the claws lifted to strike. Yet Promi saw nothing but the serene, ongoing dance of lights. He sat there, utterly still, waiting for whatever would happen next.

The claws raised to the level of his neck. They paused, set to slice off the head of this mortal who had dared to enter their realm. Just as they struck—

"Promi!"

Atlanta threw herself at him, knocking him over on his side. He slammed his head onto the turf, regaining his senses—just in time to see Atlanta wave her remaining sprigs of sweetmint in the air.

Eerie shrieks echoed around the bogs. The claws withdrew; the gleaming eyes scattered. Within seconds, the swamp specters disappeared.

Awkwardly, Promi sat up. His head hurt, and he felt dizzy, but his gaze met Atlanta's. In the dim, wavering light from the fumes, he could see that she was both frightened and relieved. He started to speak, but before he could say a word, she popped a fresh sprig of sweetmint into his mouth.

"Try not to lose this one," she said sternly. Then, more softly, she added, "You said you wouldn't die."

"I won't tonight, thanks to you."

She almost grinned. "That makes us even."

"Good," he replied, rubbing his sore head. "But next time you save my life . . . try not to kill me in the process."

Quietly, she chuckled. "I'll think about it."

CHAPTER 28

The Passage of Death

A recipe you think you know well can still surprise you.

—From Promi's journal

At the first light of dawn, Promi and Atlanta set off again. Grimly aware of the dangers all around, they continued to trek east toward the mountains—and to Grukarr's lair. Though they walked together, their bare feet squelching in the mud, they rarely spoke. Even Kermi, riding on Promi's shoulder, stayed unusually quiet.

For Atlanta, the worst part of this trek wasn't the endless peril of quicksand, snake pits, or swamp specters. No, it was the painful awareness that her parents had died in this very place—maybe in the next pit or fumarole to come into view.

Why, she asked herself, *did they choose to*

explore the Passage of Death? The very name made her wince painfully. Frowning, she realized that crossing this murderous bog was itself a kind of passage of death. *Yet here I am, doing the same thing.*

Promi, for his part, worried about something else—something he liked even less than Unkhmeini Swamp. Their time was fast running out! Already Ho Byneri was only a week away. And the high peaks, where Grukarr's lair was hidden, still seemed very far away.

All through that day, they trudged onward. When night fell and they couldn't go any farther, they settled on a patch of grass that had somehow retained a hint of green color. But even that sign of life didn't revive their spirits.

That night, as Atlanta took her turn at keeping watch, the swamp seemed strangely calm. She scanned the desolate bog, knowing that this was truly the last place she'd wanted to see. And the last place her parents had ever seen. Yet she also knew that, to have any hope of saving the forest and all its creatures, she had to be here.

For several hours, she watched the glowing fumes and shifting shadows, puzzled why they seemed so calm—as if the whole swamp were holding its breath. Waiting for something. But for what?

Whenever she felt drowsy, she pinched her ears. All the while, she chewed her sweetmint. Through the rest of the night, she watched, always alert for trouble. To her relief, she saw no sign of the swamp specters.

Finally, dawn's first light started to filter through the fumes. Golden rays spread across the scene, making the swamp seem, at least for this moment, a bit less dreadful. The darkest shadows withdrew; light spread everywhere.

A pair of shapes suddenly caught her attention. Swathed in

vapors, they looked hazy, undefined. Yet . . . they seemed very much like human figures. And they were, without question, moving toward her.

She bit her lip. *Could it be . . . ?*

Blinking her eyes, she reminded herself, *It's not them. It can't possibly be them!*

Yet even as her intellect and experience told her this was folly, her deep longing told her otherwise. The figures drew nearer, striding toward her through the vapors.

She glanced over at Promi, fast asleep, his head upon his arm. Beside him, Kermi lay on the grass, sleeping just as soundly. *Won't disturb them,* she decided. *Not until I'm really sure.*

Turning back to the hazy figures, she caught her breath. They were holding hands! Helping each other across the bog. Just as her parents would surely be doing!

Her heart pounded with excitement. She leaped to her feet, trying to see clearly through the swirling vapors. The figures still looked blurry. But more and more, they resembled the two people she most wanted to see.

Without even watching where she was going, she stepped off the patch of grass and into the muck. As her feet sloshed ahead, one of the figures raised an arm and waved.

"Mama?" she asked, the name catching in her throat. "Papa? Is that you?"

Now both of them waved. Then they stopped and opened their arms to greet her, their brave daughter who had traveled so far and endured so much to find them.

Atlanta broke into a run. Heedless of the danger, she hurtled straight toward a deep, bubbling pit that belched poisonous fumes. Just as she was about to plunge into it—

Promi tackled her from behind. They rolled in the mud, finally stopping at the edge of the pit.

Shouting, Atlanta kicked and struggled to get up again, shoving Promi away. But when she looked for the alluring figures, they had vanished. Only shreds of vapor remained.

At once, she realized her terrible mistake—and just how close she'd come to death. She turned to Promi and started to explain, then suddenly burst into tears. Leaning her muddy head against his shoulder, she sobbed.

Gently, he wrapped his arm around her. He didn't try to say anything, sensing words couldn't help. They simply sat there, dripping with mud, while she cried.

When, at last, her tears ended, she lifted her head and said just one sentence: "They were my family."

Sadly, he nodded. "Even though I can't remember anything about my family, losing them still hurts."

She wiped one of her eyes, streaking her cheek with mud. "That's horrible. At least I still have some memories."

Lowering his gaze, he said, "The only memory I have, that little bit of song, I'm not even sure is real."

She reached over and took his hand in her own.

"Maybe," asked Promi hesitantly, "we can be . . . each other's family?"

Atlanta smiled. "I like that idea."

CHAPTER 29

Secret Work

Once in a while, I do something stupid. And then once in a while, I do something extremely, idiotically, unforgivably stupid. You can guess which I do more often.

—From Promi's journal

Together, Promi and Atlanta walked back to the patch of grass and woke up Kermi. As soon as the kermuncle opened his eyes, he exclaimed, "Look at you two! You're so filthy you might as well have actually gone and rolled in the mud!" Then, just to Promi, he added, "But even you, manfool, aren't that stupid."

Atlanta gave Promi a wink. "Really, you should keep out of the mud."

"I'll try harder," he said with a grin.

Grumbling about getting his fur more dirty than it already was, Kermi reluctantly climbed up to his customary perch on Promi's shoulder. Then, with no more delay, they set off, trekking toward the mountains again.

Now, though, the journey felt different to both Promi and Atlanta. While nothing about the swamp had changed—the terrain was no less dismal and the danger no less present—they felt somehow lighter than before. Their feet lifted a bit more easily; their legs moved a little more confidently. It was as if they were tied together with an invisible thread, pulled along by each other's strength.

At midday, Promi spotted a rare spring with freshwater, bubbling out of the ground near a pair of twisted orange trees. Gratefully, they stopped to drink. Although what remained of the trees' fruit had long since vanished and their only company was the twisted skeleton of a camel, the taste of clear water pushed suffering aside. No elixir from the spirit realm could have tasted better.

"Mmmmm," said Atlanta, lifting her head from the spring. She replaced her sprig of sweetmint in her mouth, and not even its burnt charcoal flavor could detract from the wonder of freshwater. "I'd almost forgotten how good this is!"

"Me too," replied Promi, water dripping from his cheeks and chin. "The only thing that would improve this would be a good big slice of lemon pie with honey crust."

She almost grinned. "Too bad you left that lemon pie back in the City."

Kermi lifted his small blue face from the spring and shook the droplets off his whiskers. "Don't you people ever think about anything besides food?" He rubbed the fur of his tummy. "Not that I'd turn down a meal about now."

"Why complain?" asked Promi. "You ate at least three moths yesterday. Plus one of the dried-up apples Atlanta found on that old tree."

"Harrumph. You have no taste at all, manfool. Except, of course, in your choice of companions."

Atlanta nudged Promi's shoulder. "He's got you there."

But Promi didn't feel like responding. Scanning their bleak

surroundings, his worries came flooding back. "We're never going to get there in time. Look how far the mountains are from here."

He pointed to the vague outline of the high peaks, only barely visible through the swirling clouds of gases. "It's at least another day's walk. If we can survive that long."

"Look at it this way, manfool." Kermi blew a thin, ragged bubble. "If the swamp doesn't kill us, we'll all die anyway after Ho Byneri."

Atlanta blinked. "My, that's encouraging."

"Unless," the kermuncle continued, "we can get to Grukarr's lair, figure out his plans, somehow save the forest, and—oh, yes—rescue the Starstone before Narkazan can turn it into a terrible weapon. Did I leave anything out?"

She blew a long sigh. "When you put it that way, it does sound a bit . . . difficult."

"Impossible," corrected Promi.

"Insane," offered the kermuncle. Then, seeing Promi slouch glumly against one of the orange trees, he added, "Why don't you do something to cheer yourself up, manfool? Like . . . write in your journal?"

The young man shook his head. "I only write down things I want to remember." He tapped his tunic pocket. "This journal has been right here with me in all the best times I've ever had."

Kermi nodded. "Like your times with me?"

Still not ready to find any humor in their situation, Promi didn't answer. He merely sat there, rolling his sweetmint on his tongue.

Atlanta bent again over the spring and filled the small flask she carried on the hip of her gown. Then, having closed the flask, she dipped her finger into the spring and offered some water to the faery in her pocket. Eagerly, he lapped at the droplets, his antennae quivering with pleasure. Though Atlanta couldn't be sure, the tiny creature's wings seemed a bit stronger and more shiny than before.

But she suspected that was only because of the strange light of the swamp.

"May you heal completely someday, little friend." Even as she said the words, a wave of hopefulness washed over her. For a brief moment, she actually believed that somehow, against all odds, she and her companions might prevail.

Just then, a subtly glowing shape caught her eye. Crawling along the edge of the nearest mud pit, the shape—about the size of her thumb—moved slowly toward her. She stood up and darted over to see what it was.

"A snail," she said in wonderment, seeing its glowing, iridescent shell. The snail radiated a soft lavender light, a stark contrast to the mud and smoke of the pit.

She bent down to pick it up. The snail slid slowly across her palm, its shell glowing like a sunlit amethyst jewel. *How beautiful,* she thought. *So there are some creatures besides poisonous snakes and marsh ghouls in the swamp!*

Bringing the snail closer to her face, she said aloud, "You remind me that even in this desolate place, something good can survive."

She decided to bring the snail over to Promi. *This will cheer him up,* she told herself.

Just then she heard him shout. She put down the snail, whirled around, and ran back to him.

Wide-eyed, he stood between the twisted trees. "Atlanta! I have an idea!"

"An idea?" she asked. "The way you shouted, I thought you were in trouble."

"We're *all* in trouble," grumbled Kermi, now hanging by his tail from one of the tree branches. "*Especially* if this buffoon has one of his ideas."

Ignoring the kermuncle, Promi said in a rush, "Our biggest problem right now is time, right?"

Kermi scoffed. "That's true if you don't count a deranged priest, a power-hungry immortal, a place called the Passage of Death, and an invincible weapon. Oh, right—and a swamp full of death traps."

"Hush," said Atlanta. "I want to hear his idea."

"At your own risk," grumped the little fellow, swinging from the branch.

"So," Promi continued, "if time is running out, ask yourself this: Is there any other way we could see what's really going on at the Passage of Death? Without actually trekking all the way there and losing however much more time?"

Confused, she shook her curls. "No! There isn't any other way."

He put his hand on her shoulder. "But there is." With a sad smile, he added, "I've pretty much filled every page already."

Suddenly realizing what he was about to do—and what he was going to sacrifice—she protested, "No, Promi. Not your journal!"

But he was already whispering, "Listen one, listen all."

The sound of wind rushed through the swamp, though none of the dark clouds of vapor were blown away. Inside Atlanta's pocket, the faery trembled, feeling the presence of powerful magic. But all Atlanta noticed was the sudden disappearance of the bulge in Promi's tunic that showed where he'd kept his journal.

Promi opened his arms wide. "Now show us," he implored, "what is happening with Grukarr and the Passage of Death."

A hazy figure appeared, striding toward them out of the swirling fumes. Grukarr! Atlanta gasped, afraid the priest himself had arrived. But no, she realized, this was only an image—a vision brought forth by Promi's magic.

Against the backdrop of swamp vapors, the image of Grukarr grew more clear. Judging from the building behind him, an ornately designed structure with a red tile roof and mosaics depicting gold turbans, he was standing in a courtyard inside the Divine

Monk's temple. Possibly the same courtyard where Promi had stood just before sneaking into the Divine Monk's dining room to steal a certain pie. On the priest's shoulder sat Huntwing, whose savage eyes gazed at his master.

Grukarr adjusted his white turban, clearly enjoying its symbol of power. Yet something in his expression made it clear he wanted to exchange it for a gold one. When he lowered his arms, something flashed under the collar of his robe. The Starstone!

"Huntwing," he commanded, "I need you to fly to the Passage of Death. See how many new allies have arrived. The time is near for them to strike! I need to know how many we have. Then fly back here to tell me."

The blood falcon clacked his beak and rustled his wings.

"Meanwhile," said the priest, "I must gather more minions to do the secret work at my lair." His expression hardened. "They die too easily! After all my efforts to free them from prison, the least they could do is to work longer before dying."

Huntwing lifted his wings to fly. At that moment, the image faded away.

Promi stared in astonishment at Atlanta. "He has the Starstone. I'm sure of it."

She nodded. "Which means he probably killed Araggna. She would never have parted with it willingly."

"Right." His brow creased. "What did Grukarr mean by *allies* at the Passage of Death? Getting ready to strike—on Ho Byneri, no doubt. Could he mean mistwraiths?"

At the mention of those immortals, the faery quaked in Atlanta's pocket. Gently, she touched her gown so the faery could feel the warmth of her hand. But this time, the gesture didn't calm him. He grew even more panicked, beating his wings furiously.

"And another thing," said Promi, still trying to make sense of what they'd heard. "What did he mean by *secret work* at his lair? Why does he need more men to do it—and why are they dying?"

All at once, a new vision began to form on the vapors. It looked like a view of the high peaks from the air. A view that could be seen by a bird—perhaps Huntwing—in flight.

The bird's-eye view shifted, swooping down closer to the snow-capped mountains. There, jutting up higher than all the rest, stood Ell Shangro, the great smoking volcano. Below it, on one of its lower ridges, was a gaping black hole, a tunnel that ran deep into the mountain—maybe all the way to the other side, opening onto the plains of Africa.

Then the image moved lower, revealing something even more startling. Just below the tunnel entrance, on the wide fields covering the plateau above the eastern edge of the swamp, many men were camped—so many it was difficult to count. Five thousand? Or more?

Swooping closer, the image showed clearly that the men were armed with weapons of all kinds. Swords, spears, bows and arrows, maces, and shields abounded. Many of the men wore breastplates and helmets. At least several hundred had brought camels to ride, as well as packs of armored wildebeests.

"An army!" exclaimed Promi, watching in horror. "Grukarr's allies are *soldiers*—an army of invaders!"

"Yes," said Atlanta, bewildered. "But how could they ever hope to prevail? Won't the pancharm that the spirits placed on the Great Forest keep them away?"

Promi shook his head, unsure what to think. Even as they watched the vision, more soldiers continued to stream out of the tunnel. "So the Passage of Death—"

"Is really a passage, after all," finished Atlanta. "A tunnel that pierces the border of Ellegandia and connects it to the rest of the continent!"

"Which is probably why," guessed Promi, "the ancient Divine Monks spread those stories about trapped spirits who'd kill anyone who came near."

Glancing over her shoulder at the brooding vapors of the swamp, Atlanta swallowed. "Maybe the stories were really true . . . as we've seen." In a softer voice, she added, "And as my parents discovered."

Promi sent her a compassionate glance.

Abruptly, the vision shifted again, showing a conical mound just below the army's encampment. All around its base, men were working—but it was impossible to see exactly what they were doing. What looked like bodies lay scattered on the ground. And throughout the area floated several dark, shadowy shapes that could only be one kind of being.

"Mistwraiths," growled Kermi. "My least favorite immortals."

At that instant, the vision clouded over and vanished. Atlanta and Promi stood there among the shifting vapors, pondering the meaning of all they had seen.

CHAPTER 30

Shirozzz

Fire can cook those pastries you love, Promi. Or fire can burn you badly.

—From her journal

After a long silence, Promi asked, "So what do we do next?"

Kermi dropped down to a lower branch on the twisted tree and hung by his tail. "I have a good idea."

"What?" asked both Atlanta and Promi.

"Eat." The kermuncle's blue eyes opened to their widest. "I am *sooooo* hungry."

"So am I," said Promi. "But I'm afraid eating will have to wait. We have a lot to do and very little time! Besides, there isn't much to eat in this forsaken place."

"Have it your way," sulked Kermi. He climbed up to the highest branch of the tree.

"More than ever," said Atlanta, "I'm convinced we need to go to Grukarr's lair—that cone-shaped mound below the Passage. If we could see what's really happening there, we'd know the key to all his plans."

Looking doubtful, Promi replied, "But there's a small matter of that huge army camped nearby. And at least a dozen mistwraiths floating around. Somebody would have to be completely crazy to go there!"

"That describes us," grumbled Kermi. "No doubt about it."

Atlanta placed her hands on her hips. "Now, wait a minute. The army won't see us because they're up on that plateau above the lair. And anyway, they're not our biggest problem—the forest's pancharm will take care of stopping them. The thing we really need to worry about is that evil priest and what he's trying to do with the Starstone."

Promi scratched his chin thoughtfully. "Maybe we should reconsider the idea of going back to the City to take back the Starstone." Warming to the idea, he added, "I know a pretty good thief who could snatch it from Grukarr! Before he and Narkazan can do any damage."

She peered at him skeptically. "Are you just wanting to get back to the City?"

"No! Well . . . yes, eventually." He shook his head vigorously. "But that's not why I suggested it."

"All right, I believe you." She gave him a friendly nudge. "But I had to check." Then, her tone more serious, she said, "Anyway, I don't like that idea. First of all, we've come too far in this swamp to turn back now. And second, if I come with you to find Grukarr, he might somehow capture me—which we know he wants to do so he can get more forest magic. Maybe that is even the trap he talked about."

"No," answered Promi. "I doubt—"

"People!" shouted Kermi from the highest branch. "I see something that may solve our biggest problem!"

"What?" asked Promi.

"Follow me." Kermi bounded down the twisted tree, dropped

to the ground, and scampered away. Trading uncertain glances, the others followed him.

He led them around one smoking mud pit, past another where several snakes hissed at them, over a thin patch of bog grass, and finally to a mass of thorn bushes. Atlanta and Promi hesitated, seeing the perilous, finger-length thorns, but Kermi plunged right in and vanished into the bushes.

Promi pursed his lips. "Are you game, Atlanta?"

"I am if you are."

Together, they pushed into the bushes, doing their best to avoid the nastiest thorns. Even so, sharp points scraped, poked, and tore at their clothes, as well as their skin.

To protect her little friend, Atlanta cupped her hand over her pocket, creating a shield so the faery wouldn't be stabbed. She felt the familiar rush of gratitude . . . along with a hint of warning. What about? She couldn't tell.

All at once, they broke through the barrier of bushes—and into the last kind of place they ever expected to find in this swamp. Bushes ringed them all around, protecting something truly unique.

"A garden!" said Atlanta, amazed.

"An oasis!" exclaimed Promi.

"A meal," corrected Kermi, who was devouring a bunch of purple grapes. He lay on his back beside a leafy head of lettuce, holding the grapes over himself with his tail. While lowering the succulent fruit into his mouth, he said, "Told you I solved our biggest problem! Finding food."

Tomatoes, radishes, zucchini, beans, chili peppers, carrots, and other vegetables covered the ground, while grape vines hung from a row of short poles. On one side of the garden, a patch of curly brown mushrooms sprouted, smelling as rich as any that grew in the forest. On another side, stalks of corn, oats, and sugar cane reached skyward. Like the dwarf cacao tree that grew nearby, laden with pods holding cocoa beans, none of those stalks grew any taller than the surrounding thorn bushes.

Filling out the garden were all sorts of herbs and spices—dill, cinnamon, mint, ginger, garlic, and more. Every available space, it seemed, was being used. And around the edges, someone had carefully planted an unbroken line of sweetmint.

Spying a basil plant, Atlanta picked a leaf and slid it into her pocket. "Enjoy this, little friend." She peeked inside the pocket, delighted to see the faery already nibbling avidly on the leaf.

Stooping to pick a luscious tomato, she told Promi, "You can put aside your sweetmint for now. What's growing here is enough to protect us from the fumes."

He needed no more encouragement. Stuffing a crescent fruit into his mouth, he savored its sweet, chocolate-like flavor. After swallowing the last of it, he asked, "Who planted all this?"

"A fine chef," proposed Kermi, sniffing a chunk of gingerroot before popping it into his mouth. "Or several fine chefs."

"Whoever they are," said Atlanta, enjoying a juicy bite of tomato, "I bless their eternal qualities."

"Look here," called Promi. He strode over to a circle of dirt where nothing had been planted. "This is the only spot in this whole garden that's empty."

Coming over to join him at the circle's edge, Atlanta wondered, "Why, though?"

Kermi bounded over and climbed onto the young man's shoulder. "Such a waste of space, when they could be growing some tasty melons right here."

"It doesn't make any sense," declared Promi.

Hoping to find a clue, he and Atlanta stepped onto the dirt. The instant their feet touched the spot, it opened like a trapdoor.

"*Aaaaahhh!*" screamed all three of them as they plunged downward.

Rolling and bouncing, they dropped underground, finally

slamming into a floor of packed dirt and twisted roots. Chunks of mud and broken branches rained down on top of them. Promi untangled his twisted limbs, then rubbed his tender feet. Gazing around the cavern, he noticed that the air reeked of something like smoke.

He looked over at Atlanta, who had landed on her shoulders and was slowly rolling over. "Are you all right?"

"Nothing broken," she replied, rubbing her neck. As soon as she sat up, she opened her pocket to check on the faery. "And he looks fine. No worse than he did, anyway."

"How about me?" grumbled the kermuncle, who lay sprawled across some roots. "Doesn't anyone care how I'm doing?"

"Sure we do," said Promi dryly. "Wouldn't want you to lose your happy disposition, would we?"

Just then, he noticed something odd. "Look," he said, pointing up at the dim shafts of light from the trapdoor they'd fallen through. "Hardly any light is reaching us from up there. Yet down here, it's bright as day."

"You're right." Bewildered, Atlanta studied her surroundings. "How can that be?" She crawled across the dirt floor toward a deep niche in one wall. "The light, I think, is coming from over here."

Just as she was about to look inside the niche, a glowing ball of fire shot out from it. She screamed and rolled away, barely avoiding the flaming missile. The whole cavern filled with bright orange light.

The fireball struck a wall, igniting an exposed root, then bounced down to the earthen floor. There it sat, burning intensely, directly opposite Atlanta, Promi, and Kermi. It seemed to be some sort of fire creature, shaped like a flaming hand with seven fingers. And it appeared to be studying them closely, deciding which of them to roast to death first.

The companions all huddled together, facing the fire creature. With their backs against a wall of dirt, they didn't have any room to maneuver if it should leap at them. All they could do was watch the brightly flaming hand.

Promi glanced over at Atlanta and saw that a few of her brown curls, just above her left ear, had been singed. Without saying anything, he put his arm around her shoulder. She didn't object.

As it considered the intruders who had fallen into its cavern, the fire creature sputtered and crackled like a burning branch. The incandescent fingers, all seven of them, waved in the air, sending ripples of orange light across the cavern walls. Finally, the flaming hand leaned toward them, as if reaching out its fingers to touch them—or incinerate them.

Atlanta and Promi backed up as far as they could, pressing themselves against the wall. Strangely, though, the blue kermuncle didn't move. Even when the fiery fingers reached almost close enough to singe his whiskers, he remained still.

Then Kermi did something even more strange. He spoke to the flaming hand.

"Hello, Shirozzz."

The fiery fingers shot straight up, stretching three times as high as before, crackling noisily.

"Don't worry, Shirozzz," the kermuncle said in a calm voice. "We won't spoil things for you." He waved his tail at Atlanta and Promi. "She is someone you can trust. And he . . . well, he's not smart enough to worry about." Lowering his voice, Kermi added, "As for me, you can trust me to keep your secret . . . if you will keep mine."

Atlanta leaned forward and asked, "What—I mean, who—is this, Kermi? How do you know him? And what's all this about secrets?"

The flaming hand stretched taller, towering above them. Its orange form burned almost as intensely as a star, too bright to look at directly. The cavern grew stiflingly hot.

Kermi's big ears swiveled as he thought about the best way to answer. After a few seconds, he turned to Atlanta. "As to my secret, I'm not telling anyone. Even you. That's because it's, well . . . secret."

She sighed. "And Shirozzz?"

"He is, you see, an *outcast.*"

The flames crackled so loudly they seemed about to explode. The cavern grew even hotter.

Keeping his voice calm, Kermi continued. "Shirozzz is, as you might have noticed, a firebeing. And there was a time when he used his impressive powers to cook. He was famous for his amazing meals—all, er, handmade."

He glanced at Promi, who was wiping sweat off his brow. "You would have liked those meals, manfool. Not the quality, since not everything was sweet, but the sheer quantity. So much food that even you couldn't eat it all."

Turning back to Atlanta, he continued, "Shirozzz became, it's fair to say, the greatest chef of his people. Crowds of admirers followed him everywhere, celebrating his culinary feats and hoping to learn some of his recipes."

Seeming to relax, Shirozzz flamed less intensely. The cavern grew noticeably cooler.

"This fellow was not satisfied, though. The ingredients he found in his, well, home country—they just weren't as varied as he liked. He started to search farther and farther afield, until, at last, he discovered the wonderful foods and spices of Ellegandia."

The fiery hand trembled vigorously. The companions couldn't tell, though, whether that came from good memories or bad.

Kermi's whiskers stiffened. "The trouble was . . . creatures of his kind were not allowed to come here. Too much danger—from fires and other things. But Shirozzz ignored the ban. He persisted in visiting again and again to find the ingredients he most wanted. Especially, if I recall correctly, a certain variety of mushrooms."

"Curly brown ones, I'll wager," said Atlanta. "Forest dwellers call them *monkey tails.* And I saw them growing up above."

Shirozzz crackled loudly.

"All this continued for many years," Kermi went on. "Until finally . . ."

The firebeing slumped over, curling his flaming fingers on top of himself. The light and heat diminished, until he seemed only a small remnant of the being they'd first encountered. Atlanta, compassionate as she was toward all creatures, felt tempted to hug him . . . but resisted, guessing that putting her arms around those flames probably wasn't a good idea.

"Finally," finished the kermuncle, his tone quite somber, "Shirozzz was banished forever. He was cast out from his homeland and told never to return." He gazed thoughtfully at the firebeing, blowing a bubble that reflected the orange flames. "You see . . . Shirozzz comes from the spirit realm." He nodded, popping the bubble. "He's an immortal."

CHAPTER 31

An Earful

Just what, I wonder, did you hear? And, Promi . . . did you also hear its deeper meaning?

—From her journal

"An immortal!" cried both Promi and Atlanta. Their voices echoed for several seconds in the underground cavern before finally fading away.

Both of them stared at the crumpled firebeing. Though he continued to burn, Shirozzz now looked more like a humble campfire than a towering hand of flame. Let alone a once-great chef with countless admirers.

"Even worse than being banished from the spirit realm," Kermi explained, "this poor fellow was exiled to the most inhospitable place of all—the Unkhmeini Swamp."

Shirozzz shrank down to a low, flickering flame.

"Although," Kermi noted with a hint of admiration, "it appears he has managed to sneak beyond the swamp's borders a few times to gather some tasty things for his garden. Including those mushrooms he loves so much."

The flame sputtered guiltily.

Atlanta glanced at the kermuncle and asked, "How do you know him? When did you meet before?"

The furry little fellow stroked his whiskers modestly. "Oh . . . we had a few adventures together. In search of some special cooking ingredients."

At that, the firebeing straightened up and brightened slightly. Now he looked again like a flaming hand, though considerably smaller than just a moment earlier.

"Relax, old friend," said Kermi with a rare note of compassion. "We won't reveal your hiding place to anyone. No one will ever come looking for you—not foolish folks who'd fear and despise you, and not greedy folks who'd want to use your power. You are safe."

"That's right," agreed Atlanta. "Safe."

The flaming hand reached a bit higher and waved gratefully. The orange light strengthened.

"Unless you don't cooperate," declared Promi, his tone harsh.

Shirozzz burst into a frenzy of flame, and sparks shot from his fingers. The cavern blazed with firelight.

"What are you saying?" demanded Atlanta. She stared at Promi, her eyes burning with their own kind of flame.

"Manfool!" spat Kermi. "You are even more stupid than I thought. As well as rude."

"Maybe so," answered the young man calmly. "But Shirozzz and I have something to discuss. Something important."

"Something idiotic, you mean. Harrumph."

Leaning forward, Promi peered straight at the firebeing. "In your time with the immortals, did you ever hear anything about the Prophecy? The one that talks about the Starstone and what's going to happen on Ho Byneri?"

Instantly, the firebeing shot up to its full height. The flaming fingers angrily raked the cavern walls.

"Hmmm," said Promi. "I thought so."

Atlanta's expression melted into amazement. Like Kermi, she gazed in surprise at Promi.

"And," he went on, "do you know the meaning of its opening line, *The end of all magic*?"

Shirozzz exploded like a miniature starburst, so bright the companions had to close their eyes. Heat filled the cavern—but not for long, since after a few seconds, the firebeing returned to his former size. He trembled with either great ferocity or great fear.

"As I suspected." Promi wiped some sweat off his brow. "Tell us what you know, then."

Orange sparks flew from the firebeing's fingertips, sizzling as they hit the cavern walls.

"Tell us," commanded Promi.

Shirozzz resisted, shaking vehemently from side to side.

"Tell us."

The firebeing merely kept shaking.

"If you tell us what you know . . . then we will not reveal your secret hiding place." Then, his expression stern, he added, "And if you don't—you will *never* be safe again."

The fiery hand waved uncertainly, then condensed down to a flaming fist. All at once, it sprang at Promi's face, so fast the young man had no chance to dodge. Just before they collided, though, Shirozzz veered to the side—and flew straight into his ear!

Promi shouted as the fireball plunged deep inside his skull. Atlanta shrieked. Half a second later, the firebeing flew out of Promi's other ear, having passed right through his brain.

Shirozzz landed back on the ground where he had been before.

His flaming fingers groped at the air, burning bright, as if nothing had changed. Promi, however, looked very different indeed. Eyes wide, he wobbled weakly, then fell back against the cavern wall.

Atlanta grabbed his arm and shook him. "Oh, Promi! Are you all right?"

Slowly, he blinked, trying to see through the orange flames that still danced before him. "Well . . . yes." He blinked again, gathering his wits. "Though I don't know how."

"That's easy to explain," said Kermi gruffly. "There's nothing at all between your ears to get burned."

Promi spun his head toward the kermuncle. The fires in his mind were receding, so he could see at least the outline of the furry blue creature. "That might be true, you little demon. But at least now . . ." He shot an urgent glance at Atlanta. "I know what we need to do."

Eagerly, she asked, "You do?"

He nodded, then focused on Shirozzz. "Your secret is safe."

The immortal blazed a little brighter, his fiery fingers dancing.

"What did you learn?" asked Atlanta. "And how did you guess that he'd know?"

Promi leaned back against the dirt wall. "As to your second question, maybe I just, well . . . Listened."

Atlanta grinned slightly. Meanwhile, Kermi's small face showed an expression that neither of them had seen before, an expression that came surprisingly close to approval. Or perhaps it was just a trick of the firelight.

"And as to your first question," said Promi, "I learned more than I asked for."

Kermi waved his paw at the firebeing. "That was dangerous, Shirozzz! You could have killed him."

The flames withered slightly.

"Alas, though," Kermi went on, "you didn't succeed." He blew three or four bubbles that floated up toward the trapdoor. Turning to Promi, he asked, "So what can you tell us?"

The young man swallowed, recalling the firebeing's visions, each of them edged in sizzling flames. Then he declared, "The Prophecy goes like this." And he recited:

The end of all magic:
A day light and dark.
First light Ho Byneri,
The Starstone's bright spark.
New power can poison,
Great forces can rend
Worlds highmost and low:
The ultimate end.

As the words echoed among the cavern walls, Atlanta asked, "So what does it all mean?"

"Even the good friend who taught me those two stanzas, a monk named Bonlo, couldn't say for sure." Promi smiled sadly, for merely saying Bonlo's name had rekindled his affection for the old fellow, just as blowing on hot coals will revive a flame.

"But," continued Promi, "you can bet the Prophecy is talking about Narkazan's plan to turn the Starstone into a terrible weapon. *The end of all magic*—that could be the death of magic in our world."

Her voice strained, Atlanta said, "And the death of so many mortal creatures, too."

"Don't forget about the immortal realm," said Kermi glumly. "*Worlds highmost and low* means both worlds are at risk."

The firebeing's fingers stretched higher, as if he wanted to reach through the cavern's ceiling and up into the sky, all the way to his former home in the spirit realm.

"That must be what the Prophecy calls *the ultimate end,*" said Atlanta somberly.

Shirozzz shrank back down, his flaming fingers crumpled on the dirt floor.

"That's not all," announced Promi. "Shirozzz just told me something new. Something important."

"What?" demanded Atlanta.

He drew a deep breath. "There is more to the Prophecy! A third stanza that Bonlo, and I suspect many others, never heard before."

Slowly, he said the words:

One alters the balance
Between light and dark:
The person who carries
The soaring bird's mark.

Atlanta gasped. "The mark on your chest! I knew it meant something."

"Exactly what," cautioned Kermi, "remains to be seen."

Without thinking, Promi rubbed the place on his chest. For an instant, he recalled that horrible dream from the island, where he'd seen his own wounded heart. It had been right there beside him, bleeding, and he couldn't reach it. Couldn't help it. Couldn't heal it.

Atlanta's tender voice snapped him back to reality. "Do you really think," she asked softly, "you might be the one who could change the balance?"

He shrugged. "I don't know. But maybe . . . I should find out."

"What are you going to do?"

"You mean," he corrected, "what are *we* going to do?" His gaze locked into hers. "I'm going to find Grukarr and steal the Starstone."

Slowly, she nodded. "And I'm going to trek the rest of the way to his lair and find out what's really happening there. I just can't shake the feeling it's crucial to stopping him—and saving the forest."

Promi frowned. "I was afraid you'd say that. After all we've been through, it won't be easy to be—"

"Separated." She took his hand. "I know."

He drew a deep breath. "Let's meet in, say, five days. At Moss Island. That should give us time to do what we need to do and still have a day or two to spare before Ho Byneri."

"All right, then. Moss Island." She chewed her lip, surprised at how awkward she felt. "I . . . hope you'll be careful."

"Oh, I will," he said, trying to sound more confident than he felt.

"Remember, now," she warned him, "as hard as your sacrifices have been so far, those might just be your easiest ones. Especially with the stakes so high. I've heard the old stories about Listeners who gave up—well, everything they had in tough times. Their hope, their sight, or even their minds."

"His mind you don't have to worry about," cracked Kermi. "Not much there to lose."

"So be smart about whatever you sacrifice next," pressed Atlanta. With a warm grin, she added, "I want to recognize you when all this is over."

Gently, Promi touched her cheek. "And I want to recognize you."

Gathering his courage, he said, "And also, Atlanta . . ." He paused, fumbling for words. "I want to, um . . . well, need to, um . . ."

She nodded reassuringly. "I know."

He sighed. "Right now, what we both need most of all . . . is good luck."

"Harrumph." The kermuncle frowned at both of them.

"You'll need a lot more than that! What you *really* want is a quiggleypottle."

"A quiggleypottle?" repeated Promi, not sure he'd heard right.

"What's that?" asked Atlanta.

Kermi shook his head, making his whiskers wobble. "Young people today know so little."

"What is this . . . quiggley, um, whatever?" she demanded.

"I am sorry, but I can't help you. If you don't know what a quiggleypottle is, you'll have to find out on your own."

She scowled at him. "Fine, then. Right now we have more important things to think about. Such as saving the universe. Which won't be easy."

"Especially," added Promi, "with no quiggleypottle."

CHAPTER 32

Sweets

You love those pastries, don't you? But nothing is as sweet as a friend.

—From her journal

The first golden rays of dawn were caressing the top of the temple bell when, three days later, Promi entered the City of Great Powers. As he'd done many times before, he slipped into a shadowed street and silently made his way toward the market square by the temple. But this time, his bare feet stepped on the cobblestones—a whole new experience. Sure, his feet had toughened during his barefoot trek through forest and swamp . . . but this felt completely different from wearing his magical boots.

And that was the least of what felt different. For starters, this morning he wasn't hoping to steal a freshly baked pie, a cinnamon bun, or some other pastry. No, he hoped to steal something far more precious—a crystal of miraculous power. Power that could be used to

magnify beauty and magic . . . or to destroy anything in its presence.

Grukarr isn't going to be easy to trick this time, he reminded himself. *This won't be so simple as nabbing his belt buckle.*

The two biggest differences of all, though, didn't involve bare feet or today's challenge. They weren't even physical. One was the new realization that the strange mark on his chest might truly mean something—whether terrible or triumphant, he couldn't say. Either way, it was startling to think that the black shape of a bird in flight marked not just his skin but, in fact, his *life.* Even thinking about it now made his chest prickle with heat.

The other crucial difference was, amazingly, the strangeness of being separated from Atlanta. His whole life as a loner, those years of living by his wits on the streets—all that had changed in the course of a week! How was that even possible? He'd never missed *anyone* before . . . except perhaps the person who'd sung that haunting song to him as a child. Now, though, he missed Atlanta all the time, with every step on the cobblestones.

When, he wondered, *will I see her again?* He swallowed. Would she survive her quest and make it safely to Moss Island? Would he?

And it's not just about whether we will survive, he reminded himself as he turned down a darkened alley. *It's about whether our whole world will survive.*

A familiar thump on his back jolted him back to the present. "Manfool," said Kermi from his perch on Promi's shoulder, "I can tell you're thinking. That always worries me." Again he thumped with his tail. "And I'd bet you're thinking about pastries."

"You'd lose the bet," the young man replied, skirting the edge of a square where several temple guards were drinking big mugs of cinnamon tea. "I'm actually thinking about—well, it's none of your business."

"Ah," said the kermuncle with a throaty chuckle. "So you're thinking about *her.*"

"And what if I am, bubblebrain?" Promi frowned, wishing the little beast weren't so perceptive. Muttering, he added, "I curse the Divine Monk's hairy bottom that you made that promise to Jaladay."

The kermuncle sighed. "So do I." Then, brightening, he said, "But I must say, you *are* entertaining. Especially when you're feeling lovesick."

Promi growled, then did what he'd done so often in his life when he wanted to be alone with his thoughts: he reached for his journal. But it wasn't there. His tunic pocket was empty.

He paused, leaning back against a mud-brick wall. As morning light touched the tops of the buildings around him, he closed his eyes and did the one thing that always comforted him—turned his inner ear to that half-remembered song. The notes came quickly, filling him with their soothing melody.

Feeling better, he opened his eyes. "Time for breakfast," he announced. "It's been a while since I've had a good, fresh-baked pastry."

On his shoulder, Kermi bobbed his head knowingly and blew a stream of small bubbles. "Go ahead and eat, manfool. It's not like we have anything important to do today."

"First things first," Promi replied. "The only question is, where to begin? Someone's morning pie cooling on a windowsill? A good sweet roll from a bakery? Some fresh fruit at the market?"

The answer suddenly presented itself. A rickety cart drawn by a pair of goats and guided by a boy in a straw hat turned out of an alley just in front of Promi. Loaded with several baskets of newly picked apples, the cart rattled over the cobblestones, its fruit bouncing.

Promi grinned, for he recognized those apples. Called "monk's favorite" by most people, they were the sweetest apples in all of Ellegandia.

Time, he told himself, *for a little nourishment.*

Casually, he drew the silver dagger from its sheath. It still felt as cold as ice from a river. He tapped its hilt, watching the magical string wind around his wrist. Then, with the relaxed air of an experienced knife thrower, he hefted the blade, judging its weight. Suddenly he snapped his left arm forward, giving his wrist a slight twist as he released the dagger.

The blade impaled a large, juicy apple, plunging in with a squirt of apple juice. At the same moment, Promi flicked his wrist, making the silver string suddenly contract. The apple flew off the cart, nearly knocking off the boy's straw hat as it whizzed past.

The boy, confused, stopped the goats and peered into the shadowy street behind him. He saw nothing strange. How odd, he thought, to have a single apple bounce off the cart that way! One of the wheels must have hit a loose stone. He'd need to watch his load more closely until he arrived at the marketplace.

While the boy puzzled, Promi was standing in the shadows, busily devouring the apple. "Mmmm, so sweet," he said, taking another big bite. The apple snapped crisply as his teeth sank into it.

"No problem," said Kermi sarcastically. "You don't need to offer me any." He blew a large, apple-shaped bubble. "Even if it is my favorite fruit."

Promi took another bite, chewed it pleasurably, then swallowed. "Didn't know you liked apples, bubblebrain." Using the back of his hand, he wiped some juice off his chin. "Here, just because you were so nice to Atlanta, you can have half."

Taking the apple in his tiny paws, Kermi started nibbling. "Why, thank you, manfool. I think a little of her good nature might have rubbed off on you."

"Maybe so," Promi said wistfully.

Just then, he saw a girl walking toward the market with a tray of cinnamon buns, still steaming hot from the oven. Surprisingly, though, it wasn't the pastries that most captured his attention. It was the person carrying them. Though white flour dusted the girl's twin braids, their carrot color couldn't be missed.

"Shangri!" he called.

She whirled around, almost scattering her cinnamon buns on the street. Seeing him, her freckled face lit up with delight. "Promi!"

He strode over to her while Kermi ducked behind his shoulder to remain unseen. "Careful now," Promi told her while pushing some buns back to the middle of her tray. "Don't want to lose these precious things."

Beaming, she asked, "How are you, Promi? All's well? You haven't been by Papa's pastry shop fer sev'ral days."

"True. I've been, er . . . busy."

"Not stealin' things, I hope?"

He winked at her. "Only belt buckles."

She giggled. "Papa's been wearin' it ever since you gave it to him. Under his apron, o' course." She nodded, bouncing her braids. "Want to stop by fer a hello? An' maybe a pastry or two?"

"Wish I could. But right now . . . I can't." Feeling a pang for the simplicity of his old life, he added, "Someday soon, I hope."

Young as she was, Shangri could see the sadness in his face. "What's troublin' you, Promi? Can I help?"

Though touched by her concern, he shook his head. "Thanks, Shangri, but there's nothing you can do."

"How 'bout this?" She grabbed one of the cinnamon buns and gave it to him. "Maybe this'll help some."

He smiled and took a big bite. Licking the sugar coating off his lips, he said, "These are the *best.*"

Merrily, she giggled. Lowering her voice to a whisper, she said, "Don't tell Papa . . . but I still think you should go to the spirit world! Jest to drink from their sugary streams an' sip their sweet honey all day."

He chuckled, finishing off the pastry. "Who needs to go there when we have your bakery right here?"

As she beamed at him, he tousled her carrot hair. "Better get yourself to the market, now. Before those cinnamon buns get cold."

"All right. But Promi . . ."

"Yes?"

"You be careful."

He nodded. "I will, Shangri. And *you* watch out for stampeding goats in the market."

Still hearing her giggle, Promi turned and started down an alley. Soon he'd come to the temple wall—not so easy to scale without his boots, but he'd do his best. Once inside the Divine Monk's temple, he had a hunch where he would find Grukarr: in the private quarters of the newly proclaimed High Priest.

He strode through the shadows. Though his heart still felt heavy, he could taste, for now, the sweetness of cinnamon on his tongue.

CHAPTER 33

Confidence

Can't you understand, Promi? Just like bread in an oven, a person either rises—or gets burned.

—From her journal

Hours passed as Promi waited, hidden behind one of the ornately carved columns in Grukarr's private quarters. Keeping his breathing shallow, in case one of the priest's lackeys was nearby, he could feel the prickle of heat on his chest. But he remained still, his left hand poised by his silvery dagger.

At last—footsteps. Coming closer! Leather shoes slapped against the polished wood floor. And with that sound came another: someone whistling.

Grukarr.

Carefully, Promi peeked out from behind the column as the priest entered, adjusting the collar of his purple cloak as he whistled pleasantly. Fortunately, no guards were with him, and Huntwing was nowhere in sight. Yet that didn't diminish the fiery heat on Promi's skin.

Now that he's High Priest, he's looking pretty confident—too confident. Promi swallowed. *I won't make the same mistake.*

Suddenly, Grukarr halted. His whistling ceased. Just one foot inside the room, he sensed something wasn't quite right. What, though?

The priest scanned the room. Was it the flickering flame from the candle on his bureau? That wrinkle on the curtain by the window? The hint of a strange smell, something like the fur of a monkey?

His brown eyes narrowed. Just then, he heard the faintest whisper of a sound. Someone's breath! Grukarr opened his mouth to shout for his guards—just as Promi stepped out from behind the column, dagger ready to throw.

"You!" spat the priest. "How did you ever get in here?"

"I have my ways," answered Promi. "Don't cry out. That is, if you'd like to live another instant."

Mouth agape, Grukarr kept silent. Rage burned in his eyes. How in the name of Narkazan could he have been outwitted by this worthless street beggar *again*?

Moving closer, Promi swaggered across the room, always pointing his dagger at the priest. Unnoticed was the bulge in the back of his tunic that showed where Kermi was hiding. Promi kicked aside Grukarr's fur-lined slippers and ran a hand across the gold-embroidered bed cover. All this was done to exude confidence . . . but the truth was quite different. He'd rather have crawled into a viper pit than stayed so long in Grukarr's quarters.

"I bring you greetings," said Promi, "from many places—including Ekh Raku dungeon." He stopped, peering hard at the man who dearly longed to rule over all mortals. "I met someone there who knew you well. Someone named Bonlo."

At the mention of his teacher, Grukarr winced. But only for an instant. Right away, his haughty expression returned, and he snarled, "What children's fables did that doddering old fool tell you?"

"Just one." Promi's gaze seemed sharper than the point of his knife. "That despite all the evil you have done, he still believed you could change."

Grukarr's skin color darkened to burgundy.

"Oh," added the young man casually, "and I should also mention that your plans for Ho Byneri are going to fail."

The priest stiffened.

"That's right. We know all about your schemes! The army of invaders at the Passage of Death. The secret work at your lair. And even the extra mistwraiths you've sent for."

Obviously taken aback, Grukarr scowled. Then, regaining his composure, he spat, "Vagabond! You know only a little! The fullness of my plans will dazzle you. And destroy you completely."

Waving his dagger before the priest's face, Promi asked, "Do you mean your idea for the Starstone? To make it a deadly weapon?"

Grukarr flinched. "How did you . . . ?"

"Never mind about that." Promi pressed the knife's point against the priest's chest. "Just give me the Starstone, and I might show you more mercy than you deserve."

"I don't have it," declared Grukarr.

"Don't lie to me."

"It's no lie, you fool! I don't have it."

Using the knife, Promi lifted the collar of the priest's cloak. Nothing there! "Tell me where you hid it."

Grukarr hesitated.

Raising his blade, Promi growled, "You have three seconds. Or I will gladly slice your throat."

The High Priest swallowed. "It isn't—"

Footsteps echoed in the hallway, interrupting him. Instinctively,

Promi glanced over Grukarr's shoulder to see who was coming. The priest slashed with his forearm, knocking away the blade. The silver dagger clattered on the floor.

Quickly, Promi tugged the magical thread. The dagger zipped back into his hand. But just as he clasped the handle, he felt another blade jab against his chest, right over his heart. Knowing he'd been outmaneuvered, he stealthily slid the dagger back into its sheath.

Grukarr, holding his own blade, which he'd drawn from under his cloak, glowered at Promi. The priest pushed on the blade, hard enough that its sharp point cut through Promi's tunic and pricked his skin. A trickle of blood flowed over the mark on his chest and seeped into his frayed garment.

"Guards!" shouted Grukarr. Immediately, the footsteps quickened and three men appeared at the doorway. Each carried a spear, which they instantly pointed at Promi.

Grukarr shot the temple guards a withering glance. "You imbeciles let an intruder into my quarters. I shall deal with you later, but rest assured, you will be punished."

All three men cringed. They knew Grukarr well enough to believe his vengeance wouldn't stop with them. Their families and their homes were also in danger. So they jabbed their spears against Promi, hoping to win a little mercy from their master. Meanwhile, the bulge under Promi's tunic slid sideways to avoid a spear point.

Grukarr smiled maliciously, then whistled a few jaunty notes. "Now," he declared, "you shall finally get what you have earned many times over."

Promi tried to look fearless, but his whole chest seemed on fire. *You worthless bag of boneless baboons!* he cursed silently. He knew that he had failed completely—failed his quest, his homeland, and somehow worst of all, Atlanta.

"You will not live to see my plans realized," snarled Grukarr. "Nor will you see my unchallenged reign as emperor."

"You mean," retorted Promi, "as Narkazan's bootlicker! What makes you think, once you've given him the prize he wants, that he'll have any more use for you?"

Surprisingly, Grukarr didn't get angry. He merely chortled to himself. "You speak of the Starstone? Well, I have some plans of my own."

"To get it back? That's not possible—not if it's in the spirit realm."

Smirking, the priest replied. "For you, vagabond, that would be true. Why, for you to get the Starstone now would require a leap off that bridge!"

He paused to chortle again. "For me, however, the situation is different. And since you are about to die and the truth will make you suffer even more, I will show you why."

Replacing his knife in its sheath, Grukarr opened a satchel under his cloak. Carefully, he pulled out a small copper disc with a white rim. Across its surface, magical symbols were painted, gleaming mysteriously. Holding the disc by the rim, he gazed at it with obvious pleasure.

"Do you know what this is?" he asked. Then, before Promi could speak, he said, "No, of course you don't. Only the most learned priests and priestesses could recognize it, so how could a mere commoner?"

Slowly, he twirled the disc in his hand. "A shonsée disc is a kind of magical magnet. And this is the *original* shonsée disc, made ages ago by Tanalo, the greatest craftsman among the immortals. With the proper incantations, it can be primed to bring any magical object instantly."

"And you have primed it to bring you the Starstone?" asked Promi aghast.

"Yes," Grukarr answered proudly. "Of course, for the magnet to work, the Starstone must be near enough to be within sight. But that time will come, I assure you. And when it does, all I need to do is tap it—just the right number of times, mind you, or I would perish. But I will do it perfectly. And then the Starstone, transformed by Narkazan into a weapon that even he will fear, will belong to me!"

Gloating, he slipped the disc back into his satchel. Then he faced his prisoner and scowled. "You have wasted far too much of my time, vagabond! I am already late to lead the monks in evening prayers."

He nodded to the guards. "Take him out to the square and kill him in the most violent way possible. Make an example of him, do you hear me? Slice off his head—but slowly enough that he will choke on his own blood. Then cut out his heart and any other organs you choose." Feigning sadness, he said to Promi, "I would have them do it right here, but I just can't have all that blood on my beautiful floor."

With his boot, Grukarr tapped the polished wood. Addressing the guards again, he commanded, "Then throw whatever is left of his body into the dungeon for the rats to feast upon. And, oh yes," he added with pleasure, "if you find an old prisoner down there named Bonlo . . . cut out his tongue for daring to speak to this criminal."

Someone shoved Promi from behind, and the guards started to hustle him away. But the shove made him stumble into Grukarr, so hard the priest almost lost his turban.

"Fools!" he barked. "Never again soil my clothes with the touch of a prisoner!"

Scowling, Grukarr watched them go. Yet they had only just left his private quarters when he felt a surge of delight and started whistling merrily.

Meanwhile, Promi trudged slowly along the passageways that led to the central square. In his hand, he clasped the magical disc he'd stolen from Grukarr's satchel when he'd bumped into him. As soon as they were well away, he slid the disc into the pocket that used to hold his journal.

Even such artful thievery didn't improve his mood, though. His mind spun with urgent questions. Did Grukarr really mean what he'd said about a bridge? Why? And which bridge? The half-finished one called the Bridge to Nowhere? Or one of the others that crossed the river lower down?

One more question vexed him as he walked, feeling the spear points digging into his skin. What sacrifice should he make to save his life . . . and maybe also his world? That sacrifice would need to be something big. Very big. But what?

He bit his lip, knowing the answer. It was truly dreadful to contemplate, but it should be enough to make the magic work. This would be, by far, the greatest sacrifice he'd ever made.

All right, he told himself, gathering his strength. *Just hope this works.*

The guards marched him down the stone stairs to the square, now darkening with nightfall. As soon as they arrived, they flexed their muscles, preparing to slice off the prisoner's head and cut out as many organs as possible to gain favor with their master. As one, they raised their spears and thrust—just as the young man whispered some sort of chant.

He vanished! Their blades pierced nothing but air.

A sudden sound of wind rushed over them, although it didn't move even a hair on their heads. Astonished at Promi's escape, the three guards stared at each other. In that moment, they knew two things. First, the young man had disappeared through some sort of magic. And second, they would never tell anyone. For if Grukarr ever heard that this prisoner had escaped, they would surely die as brutally as the priest had commanded. Only for them, there would be no magical escape.

Frightened, they slowly backed away from the spot, turned, and ran down the darkened streets. Behind them, the sound of wind faded and then vanished.

CHAPTER 34

Prayer Leaves

What would you have done, Promi, if I had been there beside you? Probably the same utterly foolish thing.

But at least I could have warned you.

—From her journal

Promi opened his eyes. The sound of rushing wind vanished and was replaced by the constant flapping of prayer leaves—and, far below him, the continuous rumbling of river rapids.

Right away, he recognized the bridge where he was sitting, though it seemed rather ghostly in the glimmer of the night's first stars. It looked just as dilapidated as when he'd first seen it a week ago, after his escape from the dungeon. Maybe even more dilapidated, since now he was close enough to see all the broken planks, collapsed rails, and tattered leaves of the unfinished bridge.

The Bridge to Nowhere.

Gingerly, he felt the sore spot on his chest

where Grukarr had pushed a knife point into his skin. Just a scratch, no more . . . yet it seemed to hurt more than it should. Had it somehow bruised his ribs? Or wounded, in some way he couldn't fathom, that mark of a soaring bird?

Rubbing his tunic, now stained with blood on the spot, he thought back to the final part of the Prophecy:

One alters the balance
Between light and dark:
The person who carries
The soaring bird's mark.

He bit his lip. *Is that really me?* All around him, prayer leaves rustled and flapped. *The one who could alter the balance?*

"Well, now," a gruff voice said directly into his ear. "You do pick some odd destinations, I must say."

Kermi's voice shook him back into the present moment. For a change, Promi actually felt relieved to hear the blue kermuncle's insult, since it felt good right now to have some company. Even perpetually grumpy company. Not that he'd ever say that to Kermi.

"So tell me," the kermuncle continued, wrapping his long tail around himself, "just what did you sacrifice to get here in one piece?"

Promi hesitated, feeling the ache of his loss—an ache that he knew would stay with him forever. It felt like a kind of hole deep inside himself that he'd never be able to fill.

"I'm not going to talk about it," he answered at last. "Certainly not to you."

"Aw, come on, Promi." The creature's fuzzy tail tickled his earlobe. "Tell me. I'm just curious."

"Not on your life."

"Please? As a gesture of kindness to me, your loyal friend?"

"No! All you'll do is torture me about it. And believe me, it feels bad enough already."

"Harrumph. Some friend you are."

Promi ignored the growling on his shoulder and rose to his feet. As always, he checked his sheath; his knife was still there. Grasping hold of the broken wood railing, he looked down into the steep gorge.

Crashing below him, many man heights beneath the bridge, ran the river Deg Boesi. Brimming with melted snow from the high peaks, perhaps even from the glaciers on the summit of Ell Shangro itself, the river frothed and churned, creamy white in the starlight. Great clouds of mist lifted from its waters, sometimes blocking the view, other times sweeping over the unfinished bridge. That was why the prayer leaves and the strings that held them all glistened with droplets of mist.

Down below, he could see two smaller bridges, made from ropes with thin planks, over the water. Could one of them be the bridge Grukarr had mentioned?

He hesitated, trying to remember the priest's exact words about the Starstone's location. To find it now, Grukarr had said, *would require a leap off that bridge.*

Something about those words made Promi feel that they referred to this rickety, half-built bridge. He might be wrong about that—and he really wished that were so. But he couldn't ignore what his instincts as a Listener told him.

Grukarr meant this one, he thought grimly.

He watched the prayer leaves around him flap and flutter. Looking more closely, he could see the intricately written prayers that monks had inscribed on each and every leaf. Often those words were accompanied by drawings of a loved one who had died or a particular immortal spirit to whom the prayer was directed.

Promi sighed with admiration—both for the monks' skill at

calligraphy and the people's faith in the power of these prayers. With each gust of wind, those people believed, the messages on prayer leaves would travel all the way to the spirit realm. Yes, and they would be carried on that journey by wind lions tiny enough to bear one message per lion.

How ridiculous! He shook his head, now so wet from misty vapors that he sprayed drops in all directions. Even if he could somehow accept the idea of all those little wind lions roaming between the worlds in vast, invisible prides—which was crazy enough—he'd never felt comfortable with the notion that immortal spirits actually cared about what happened to anyone on Earth. Why should they?

And yet . . .

After everything he'd seen recently, he found himself wondering about that very notion. Thanks to Bonlo, Atlanta, Grukarr's mistwraith, the river god, and Shirozzz . . . he'd encountered a lot of evidence that there wasn't so much separation as he'd thought between the mortal and immortal realms.

Studying the silver prayer leaves all around him, he felt sure about something else—the great devotion of the people who had so carefully placed them on this bridge. Whose enduring faith inspired so much work. And whose actions sprang from the purest of motives, to honor the memory of someone they loved who had perished in the raging river.

Many of those lost ones had died by accident, by a flipped boat or a step too close to the canyon's edge. But there were others, too, who believed the legends so wholeheartedly that they had willingly leaped off this bridge, hoping to land somewhere in the spirit realm.

Promi frowned. *How crazy can you get?* he asked himself, glancing down at the mighty rapids far below. *Who would even think about doing such an idiotic thing?*

His dark eyes narrowed. *You would, Promi.*

But why? Was it for Atlanta? The forest? The Prophecy? Or for something else, something he could only describe as *hope*?

He shuddered, peering down into the gorge and at the roaring river at its bottom. *There's no other way.*

Even if he survived this leap, he knew, it could be the least of his challenges. If, by some miracle, he landed in the spirit realm, he needed to find the Starstone quickly—before it was forever corrupted by Narkazan. Or else there would never be any chance to keep it from falling into evil hands, let alone return it to the Great Forest.

On top of that, if he ever needed to use Grukarr's magical disc, he'd have to be within sight of the Starstone. And he'd also have to figure out how the disc actually worked—or he would surely, to use Grukarr's word, *perish*.

He gulped. First things first. He had to make the leap.

Slowly, carefully, he started to move closer to the unfinished end of the bridge. With each footstep, the planks beneath him creaked and groaned as if warning him of his folly. Prayer leaves snapped and rustled, joining in the chorus, urging him to go back. To firm ground, to the mortal life he knew so well.

He kept walking. The end of the bridge, opening to darkness and certain death, drew nearer. Boards creaked, leaves fluttered. And still he kept walking.

"Are you sure you don't want to tell me what you sacrificed, Promi?" The kermuncle's voice was insistent. "That way I'll know before you leap off this bridge and die."

"Not on your life."

"Harrumph. You mean not on *your* life."

Promi bit his lip, glancing down over the end of the bridge into the churning waters. "What I need right now," he muttered, "is a miracle."

"Or at least," said Kermi darkly, "a quiggleypottle."

Grasping the end of the railing, Promi stood at the very edge.

His bare feet rested on the final plank. Each of his toes could feel the cold spray rising from the raging waters of the Deg Boesi River.

"All right," he said glumly, "it doesn't matter now anyway. So I'll tell you what I gave up."

Kermi's whiskers quivered with anticipation, brushing against the young man's neck. "Yes?"

Promi sighed. "I gave up sweets! Pies, cookies, fresh fruit, cakes, cinnamon buns, honey tarts—everything."

"All your most favorite things to eat?"

"Afraid so." Promi smacked his lips, trying to remember the taste of that apple he'd eaten just that afternoon, or the first sugary bite of Shangri's cinnamon bun. "But it couldn't be for just a day or even a year. No, to get us out of Grukarr's clutches, to live long enough to try to get the Starstone, I gave up sweets *forever*."

"Forever?"

"Right. Had to make sure the sacrifice would be big enough to work, since there wasn't any room for error."

"Well," said the kermuncle, sounding—for the first time—genuinely impressed. "That *was* a major sacrifice." Attempting to be helpful, perhaps, he added, "Life hardly seems worth living without any sweets! So, Promi . . . it really is a good thing you're going to die."

"Thanks a lot."

"Anytime, manfool."

Promi glanced behind him. Through the fluttering prayer leaves, he could see the mud and stone walls of the City and the temple towering behind. Would he ever see those cobblestone streets again? Or the Great Forest? Or a certain young woman who lived there?

He turned back to the end of the bridge and peered down at the sheer drop into the gorge. Vapors rose steadily from the tumultuous rapids, parting like elusive curtains, forming into strange shapes and wispy scenes. His skin felt burning hot. Yet he kept staring straight into the rapids.

Tighter than ever, he gripped the wooden rail. Just to feel the press of wet wood against his living hand.

Then he leaped.

CHAPTER 35

Crossing

The most perilous journey is not to someplace far away, but to someplace always near.

—From her journal,
written with unusually dark strokes

Atlanta trekked deeper into the swamp, trudging through murky pools and around the rims of quicksand pits. All around her stretched the desolate bog, broken only by the skeletons of dead trees and rotting carcasses. Noxious fumes, thicker than smoke, belched into the air.

She stumbled on a dead branch, but caught herself before falling. Even so, the action made her pant with exertion, as if she'd been running for an hour. Puzzled, she frowned. Why should she feel so tired?

Anxiously, she chewed her sprig of sweetmint, feeling grateful for its protective powers. For there was one thing even more bitter than its charcoal taste on her tongue—the knowledge of what this dreadful place had taken away from her. At least, she reminded herself, she wouldn't be fooled again by some deadly swamp illusion of her parents. But what comfort was that in the face of so much loss?

And, she added somberly, *so much fear?*

While Atlanta stood there thinking, a thick black snake slithered toward her from behind. Silently, it came closer, its orange eyes gleaming.

What if I'm wrong, she worried, *about Grukarr's lair?* What if she really should be back in the Great Forest, doing everything possible to protect it from harm? Or at Promi's side, facing Grukarr? Had she made her choice to go to the priest's lair out of wisdom . . . or out of a stubborn desire to prove she could do what her parents could not?

The snake advanced stealthily, flicking its tongue over its fangs. In seconds, it could strike at the back of her leg, paralyzing her with venom. Then it could easily strangle her, just as it had done so often to other creatures.

Deep inside her pocket, the faery stirred. Sensing some imminent danger, he fluttered one of his wings.

Abruptly, a gust of wind blew over the swamp. Vapors scattered, revealing for the first time in days a patch of blue sky overhead.

Encouraged by this sight, Atlanta shook herself and started walking again—just as the snake hissed and hurled itself at her. Hearing its attack, she jumped aside barely in time. She glanced back and saw its orange eyes glaring at her vengefully. That was enough to propel her ahead, practically running across the bog.

Finally, she paused, panting hard. Once more, she wondered why she was feeling so tired. Maybe the sweetmint wasn't doing its job? She spat out the sprig in her mouth and quickly replaced it with another.

Chewing harder than ever, she wondered if the problem was really this terrible, toxic air. Maybe even the strongest sweetmint couldn't shield her completely from all these noxious fumes. Such bad air was bound to make her feel a bit weak.

With determination, she vowed, *But I'm still plenty strong enough to get to Grukarr's lair.*

Continuing to tramp through the bog, she placed her hand over her pocket. Gently, she said to the faery, "I promise you this, little friend. We will make it back! To the forest, to the home we love."

The faery stirred, drumming against the pocket with his wings. A rush of gratitude filled Atlanta's heart, along with a feeling of renewed hope. Despite her tired and aching body, she felt suddenly more confident than she had at any time since parting with Promi.

She blew a long breath, thinning the vapors before her face. What was it about that young man she liked so much? Enough to feel his absence as she would a missing part of herself?

She scowled. He was, after all, truly a loner. A thief. And on top of that, a City dweller. Why, he'd never even set foot in the forest until . . .

Until he saved me. Her scowl melted a bit, even as she stepped over the rotting remains of a once-beautiful bird now buried in muck.

"I hope you're all right, Promi," she said aloud. "Wherever you are now . . . I hope you're safe."

Yet even as she spoke her wish, she knew it hadn't been granted. He was in grave danger, just as she was. This time, the reassuring wave of confidence from the faery was not enough to make her feel any better.

Then, seeing a glimpse of lavender light on a nearby mound of dead grass, her spirits lifted a bit. For she knew that the light came from one of the iridescent snails who lived in this swamp—and who, despite everything, continued to glow with beauty.

She strode faster. Pushing herself harder than ever, she trekked through the quagmire, never pausing, though she often felt out of breath.

Keep moving, Atlanta. She skirted a boiling cauldron of mud, blacker than a bottomless hole. Her eyes stung, her throat burned. And her legs seemed weighed down by stones.

Keep moving. Avoiding a quicksand pit, she lurched sideways. Mud sucked at her feet, trying to drag her down. But she pressed on.

Suddenly she slipped, lost her balance, and slid down the bank of a boiling mud pit. She shrieked, losing her sweetmint. Her foot hit a dead branch that lay halfway down the bank, barely keeping her from plunging into the frothing muck. She lay by the branch, covered with mud, coughing uncontrollably.

Eyes watering, she forced herself to stop coughing. Her head spun from the poisonous air; her vision swirled. But she was not defeated.

Clumsily, she placed a hand on the branch to support her weight—when suddenly it tightened into a coil and hissed at her.

A snake!

She rolled aside as the snake struck. Its deadly fangs gleamed as it bit the hem of her gown, just a hair's breadth from her leg. As it loosened its grip to bite again, she gave it a desperate kick.

The snake flew into the air, hissing angrily, and landed in the boiling mud. Weakly, Atlanta clawed her way back up the bank, coughing all the while. It took all her remaining strength to reach the rim.

Exhausted, she lay in the mud. Her coughs wouldn't cease, and her mind spun. Dizzily, she tried to sit up. But even that was more than she could do right now. *Must get . . . more sweetmint,* she told herself.

She reached for another sprig. But all her sweetmint was gone! And without it, she was at the mercy of this swamp. This foul air. And this terrible place that had killed her parents.

She fell back, weaker by the second. Tears welled in her blue-green eyes. No chance now she'd reach the lair and learn Grukarr's secrets. Just as there was no chance she'd survive and see her beloved forest—or Promi—again.

Slumping on the mud, her only movement now came from the spasms of coughing. Her legs curled into her chest; her head lay on her forearm. Darkness seeped into her mind, obscuring everything like a cloud of poisonous gas.

"I'm sorry," she whispered to the faery in her pocket. "So . . . sorry."

Her eyes closed. Her mind blackened. Her heartbeat slowed, ready to stop.

And then . . . something pricked the outermost edge of her thoughts, nudging her back to consciousness.

A hard lump pressed into her forehead. It was inside her sleeve. The gift from the river god!

New energy surged through her, flowing like a river. She opened her eyes. Pulling the tiny, radiant globe out of her sleeve, she watched it glow in her hand. A bubble of liquid light.

And she knew, at last, just what it was meant for.

Atlanta opened her mouth, placed the bubble on her tongue, and swallowed. Instantly her mind cleared and she stopped coughing. Her throat felt cleansed, as if she'd taken a cool drink of water from a mountain stream. A stream that renewed her strength, restored her balance, and revived her spirit.

Best of all, she could breathe again! She drew a deep breath, filling her lungs. Instead of the rancid fumes of the swamp, all she tasted now was the pure, misty air of a forest cascade.

"River god," she said gratefully, "I bless your eternal qualities."

Within her pocket, the faery's antennae quivered as he added his own blessing.

Slowly, she rose, though her legs still wobbled from weakness. Yet none of that troubled her now. She had only one thing on her mind—to find Grukarr's lair.

CHAPTER 36

The Leap

Which felt greater, I wonder? The lightness of plunging into the mist—or the heaviness of leaving so much behind?

—From her journal

The last thing Promi heard before he leaped off the Bridge to Nowhere was not the crashing rapids. Nor was it the inner voice of caution that screamed, *Stop, you idiot. Don't jump!*

Instead, it was a simple sound that drowned out all the rest: the flap of a fluttering prayer leaf.

That flap of a leaf that held a single prayer was not loud enough to be noticeable, let alone memorable. Not to most people, at least. Yet for some reason, that solitary flap seemed to explode inside Promi's mind. It echoed, reverberating, as if it wasn't just an instantaneous sound—but an entire assembly of sounds, like a chorus of voices.

Those voices carried the words of a prayer,

chanting them over and over again. They also carried all the hopes and longings that had first inspired that prayer. And they bore something else, as well, in a mysterious way.

Promi.

The flapping, the chanting, seemed to hold him. Support him. Lift him.

The instant he jumped, when his feet pushed off the broken plank at the end of the bridge, his senses switched off. He couldn't feel anything—not the rush of cold air against his face, not the wet vapors from the river far below. He didn't know if Kermi had stayed on his shoulder—or if, much more likely, the furry blue creature had scampered away just in time to stay alive.

The only sense that continued to work was his hearing. And all Promi could hear was the sound of that leaf, echoing, and the unending chant of its prayer.

Time froze, it seemed, while the chant rolled on. Then, rising above the other sounds, he heard something different—a familiar voice. It was Atlanta, telling the story from Moss Island, what she had called *a story whispered by the wind*. And he realized that, in the tale of that boy's great loss, there was also, perhaps, something gained.

Suddenly, Promi was falling! Through mist, wet and cold, he tumbled—plunging down, down, down. As he fell, the mist thickened until it was less like a cloud than a kind of billowing, shifting landscape.

All the sounds of flapping and chanting faded away. The only thing he heard, for a brief instant before it, too, ended, was a distant whooshing like the sound of great wings.

Then he landed, more gently than he could have ever expected. But he didn't land in the river that crashed below the bridge, nor on any sort of ground where he could stand. Indeed, he wasn't standing at all. He was sitting—astride a great creature that glowed like liquid silver.

A wind lion.

"Alive!" shouted Promi, astonished. "I'm alive!"

He stared at the magnificent creature whose full, silver-hued mane billowed before him. "And sitting on a lion!" *Not a tiny one, either,* he added to himself. *A huge, powerful lion much bigger than me.*

Slowly, the lion turned his head and regarded Promi with one of his great brown eyes. Though nothing was said, Promi got the distinct feeling the lion was telling him, *But of course, you fool! Don't believe everything you hear in those legends.*

Without warning, the lion reared back on his powerful hind legs. Promi grabbed hold of the mane to keep from falling off. The lion's huge forepaws swept through the mist, then all at once—the lionsteed bounded off, carrying Promi deeper into this new, vaporous realm.

They plunged into the cloudscape, Promi's heart pounding with excitement. *Wherever we're going,* he thought, *it's fast!* The lion's mane blew with the same moist breeze that also slapped Promi's face. And yet . . . this creature was not really running.

No, he was *flying*. Promi couldn't see any wings, no matter how hard he tried. But they certainly were vaulting through the mist as if they were airborne. And the rush of air, the constant *whooshhhhh* of motion—all this felt like flight.

He did detect, on both sides, a constant vibration in the mist. *Invisible wings?* he wondered. *Or a kind of magical wind?*

As the lion veered to one side, Promi leaned the other way to balance—a bit too far. He started to slide off! With a gasp of fright, he squeezed forcefully with his thighs, though the lion's furry sides were slippery with mist. Somehow, he managed to right himself just before he tumbled off. But now he clung even tighter to the shaggy mane.

"So," sneered a voice into his ear, "you're as good at riding as you are at walking."

"You!" He glanced at his shoulder to see the unmistakable wide blue eyes of the kermuncle. Kermi was staring at him, a sassy look on that little face. "I thought you had enough sense to stay back there on the bridge."

"Harrumph. So did I." Reaching up with his long tail, he punched Promi's earlobe. "But life with you is so entertaining, I just couldn't miss it."

Promi took a hand off the mane long enough to rub his tender earlobe. "Why didn't you stay with Atlanta? She actually enjoyed your company."

Kermi's small shoulders sagged. "Believe me, I considered that. But I made that promise to Jaladay." He shook his head, making his long whiskers wobble. "Which I've only regretted a few thousand times."

The mention of Jaladay made Promi fall silent. He recalled her deep green eyes, as bright as the dawn. Who was she, really? Why did she feel so sure she could trust him with Listener magic? Why had she been so glad to know that he kept a journal? And why did she have to die so soon, before he really got to know her?

All those questions rolled through his mind. Plus some more: Would she be surprised to know that, thanks to her gift of magic, he'd escaped death several times? That he'd found an unlikely friend in the Great Forest? Or, still more amazing, that he was right now riding on the back of a real wind lion, plunging into the mist, hoping to find the Starstone that could save his world?

He sighed. There was something even more astounding that had happened to him. Something no one, not even Jaladay, could have possibly guessed. No matter how much he longed to do it, he would never eat another sweet pastry.

The lionsteed released a low, rumbling laugh. Then, invisible wings shimmering like starlight, the creature spoke.

"You, young Promi, have much to learn."

"You know my name!" He was so startled that he let go of the mane and nearly fell off the lion's back. But as soon as he'd grabbed hold again, he felt comforted, as well as grateful, that this glorious being had recognized him.

"I do know your name," the lion declared in a voice that was as richly toned as it was wise. "And much else, besides. I can hear your thoughts, just as I can feel your fears . . . and your hopes."

Promi sat up straight. "You know all that? Well, then, great lion . . . will you take me all the way to the Starstone?"

The lion cocked his head. "My name is Theosor. And I have come to carry you as far as you need to go."

Promi swallowed, uncertain. "Even . . ."

"Yes," answered the wind lion. "Even to the innermost depths of the spirit realm."

CHAPTER 37

Riding the Wind

Sometimes, when you don't know where you are going, it is enough to know why you are going.

—From her journal

Deeper into the mist they plunged. Though he still held tight to the wind lion's mane, Promi found himself feeling more and more comfortable astride Theosor. He leaned forward, gazing past the powerful shoulders that glistened like moonlight on water, past the vibrations of invisible wings, and into the billowing mist.

Watching the ever-shifting clouds, Promi started to catch sight of shapes he could recognize. Mountains of mist rose steeply, towering above them, before swirling vapors swallowed them completely. Valleys, softly undulating, stretched farther than he could see one instant—and then, the next instant, disappeared. A silver sea came into view, and he could hear the distant roar of its wispy waves. Then the sea transformed into a canyon, opening wider than he'd ever imagined. Seconds later, the canyon bulged and billowed, forming itself into a mountain.

Amazing, thought Promi, awestruck. *I never thought any place like this existed.*

"Welcome to the spirit realm." Theosor's ringing voice sounded more cautious than welcoming. "Here you will find as many dangers as wonders."

Beneath the strange mark on his chest, Promi's heartbeat quickened. "What sort of dangers?"

"Dangers that wait only for you, young cub."

Kermi gave a rude snort. "Just try to stay on the wind lion's back, manfool." He lay on Promi's shoulder, wrapping his tail around the young man's neck. "And do let me know if you decide to jump."

"I'll do that, bubblebrain."

Right in his ear, Promi heard the pop of several bubbles.

"Hmmm," the young man puzzled aloud, "do I hear thunder in the distance? Or just an annoying little bug?"

This time he heard a small but unmistakable growl.

Promi watched the ever-shifting landscapes around them. Releasing the lion's mane briefly, he placed a hand on the creature's immense shoulders. "Can you tell me what you know about the Starstone? Where is it now?"

Theosor didn't answer, continuing to soar through the shifting mist. Around them, mountains rose and fell, seas appeared and then vanished, one vista melted into the next. Suddenly Promi noticed that, within each place that formed, there were glimpses of . . . what?

More places! He could see hints of mountains within oceans, canyons inside peaks, misty cities within wide valleys. And within those inner places, still more places lay hidden.

The spirit realm doesn't just change over time, he realized. *It changes within itself, all the time.*

Layer upon layer. Change after change. Mysteries within mysteries. *So this is the realm of immortals. Always evolving, always the same.*

The wind lion veered one way and then the next, sailed over one billowing mass of vapors and then under another, following a path that only he could detect. At last, he spoke again, his deep, rumbling voice rolling like windblown clouds.

"The Starstone, young cub, is now in the hands of Narkazan. And it is guarded most heavily."

"Narkazan? You're sure?" Promi sighed. "I was hoping that maybe he didn't have it yet."

Theosor growled angrily, a sound like swelling thunder. "He has it, yes. And he yearns to use it to conquer this realm as well as Earth—and all the other mortal realms, as well."

"There are more?"

"Many more," answered the wind lion, banking a turn. "But your world is the necessary first step to conquering the others."

"So . . . ," asked Promi, "has he corrupted the Starstone yet? Turned it into his ultimate weapon?"

The great lion flared his nostrils. "That, young cub, I do not know."

Promi frowned, sinking his hands deeper into the lion's mane.

The lionsteed turned, then suddenly leaped at a burgeoning hill of mist. But he didn't jump over it, as he had so many others. Instead, he plunged straight through it.

Swirling vapors surrounded them, pressing closer than before. Promi thought he saw a wispy forest of clouds. Then a sparkling tower that refracted light vibrantly, as if it were made of solid rainbows. Then a sea of faces: women and men, elders and children, birds and beasts of all kinds—including a turquoise-scaled dragon with bright, intelligent eyes.

For an instant, the dragon's gaze met Promi's. All at once, the young man felt a strong burst of emotions—fear for the spirit realm, grief for those who had been lost to Narkazan, and, at the end, a desperate plea for help.

The misty landscape suddenly changed into a new scene. Promi gasped, for it was a scene he had often dreamed of seeing: a river of golden honey, flowing slowly down a valley under verdant hills. As they soared above the valley, they passed over enormous falls of honey that tumbled into the river, sending up clouds of crystallized vapor that made the air as sweet as powdered sugar.

Yet . . . instead of feeling joyous, Promi felt a sharp jab of sorrow. For this was both a dream come true and a sacrifice made agonizingly clear. While he could taste and smell the sweetness in the air, he knew he could never drink from that river of honey—let alone dive right into it, as he would have gladly done just a short while ago. Or else, he felt sure, the Listener magic would desert him forever, and he'd never be able to use it to help his world . . . or Atlanta.

He grimaced. *I remember too much about sweets.* The crunch of cinnamon crust, the sweetness of honeycomb, the tang of fresh strawberries—all so sensuous and tempting. But he couldn't experience them ever again.

"In this realm," Theosor explained, eyeing a golden patch of sweetfern on the riverbank, "people dearly love to eat sugary things. Fortunately, there are many sweets to choose from. Why, in the higher provinces, fruit pies and nectar confections even grow on trees! There is even a meadow where—"

"No more!" cried Promi, cutting the wind lion short. "I gave up eating sweets. Forever."

Theosor shook his head, waving his shaggy mane. "How sad for you, young cub! From now on, I will do my best to avoid such places. But that will not be easy here in the spirit realm."

Feeling the lionsteed's compassion, Promi nodded. "Thanks. Even if—"

Flash! A sudden bolt of light shot out from a nearby cloud. The wind lion dived sharply to avoid being hit. Promi almost fell off, while Kermi shrieked and squeezed the young man's neck in a stranglehold.

The searing blast sailed just over their heads, barely missing them. It exploded on a second cloud, smashing with enormous force. Vapors scattered everywhere as the cloud sizzled from the impact.

Promi, able to breathe again after Kermi's grip loosened, held tight to the lion's mane. He gaped at the sizzling cloud. "What was *that*?"

Just then another blast of light erupted from the second cloud. It shot through the sky, slamming into the first cloud with a thunderous boom that echoed across the realm.

"Flashbolts," replied Theosor with a sweep of his massive paw. "They are a potent weapon in this war with Narkazan."

Veering, he flew under the battling clouds. As they passed beneath, Promi could hear angry shouts and cries of pain through the vapors. Another flashbolt erupted, sizzling across the sky.

"Theosor, I thought immortals couldn't be killed. So what good are those flashbolts?"

The wind lion rumbled grimly, "Immortals cannot be killed. But they can be stunned by such power—or made to suffer dearly."

Promi listened to the fading cries as they passed under the clouds.

"Of course," added the lionsteed, "any mortal struck by a flashbolt would instantly burn to nothingness. Not even ashes would remain."

Promi gulped. "How nice."

"Just try to stay clear of them," urged Kermi. "At least while I'm riding on you."

Just before they left the battle behind, Promi glimpsed the remains of a building poised on one cloud's edge. A fortress of some kind? Still smoking from the flashbolt, its silvery beams wobbled, then collapsed in a towering burst of vapors. More agonized shouts came from the scene.

Leaning forward, Promi asked the wind lion, "Who is winning this war? Can Narkazan be stopped?"

"We are trying, young cub. The rebellion is still alive, though our numbers are small. It helps that our leaders, Sammelvar and Escholia, have more virtue than a hundred Narkazans." Theosor shook his mighty head. "Alas, virtue alone cannot win a war. Our greatest strength is simply *why* we are fighting. Not just for power, as he is. No, we are fighting for something much more precious: freedom. For our world as well as yours."

The wind lion roared with passion. The sound reverberated among the clouds like an unending roll of thunder.

Finally, Promi spoke. "But you cannot defeat him if he corrupts the Starstone."

"That is true, young cub. If Narkazan does that to the Starstone, using his darkest powers—and if he can fill it with potent magic from your world—then all will be lost."

"So tell me," asked Promi as he watched the vibration of the invisible wings. "Where is Narkazan keeping the Starstone?"

Immediately, the wind lion veered to the left and soared through a shimmering wall of mist. New light shined on them, tinted with radiant blue. They were flying over a stormy sea of clouds, full of shadowy shapes that Promi couldn't even begin to describe. Then, without warning, they plunged straight down into the frothing blue waves.

Bitter cold pressed into Promi's skin, seeping into his bones. He shivered uncontrollably, even as he dug his hands deeper into the lion's mane. Theosor's breath made frosty clouds in the blue vapors; icicles formed on his whiskers.

Spray shot everywhere as they exploded out of the sea of clouds. Warm mist blanketed them, and the icicles melted instantly. Promi, no longer shivering, gazed around them at the swirling mists of the spirit realm, mists that reached farther than he could guess in all directions.

He shook his head, incredulous at the wonders of this place. Then, in a flash, his mood darkened. *Will I ever leave here alive?*

"That depends," rumbled the wind lion, who had heard his thoughts.

"On what?" asked Promi, still surprised by Theosor's telepathic ability.

"On whether you can capture the Starstone in time. If so, you just might survive."

"Where is it?"

The lion's deep voice lowered even further. "In Narkazan's cloud palace, Arcna Ruel. It is guarded not only by the warlord himself, but by his army of deathless warriors. Stealing it will not be easy. Some would say it's impossible."

Promi's expression hardened. "My specialty."

"Good, young cub. Because either you succeed or you die. There is no other option." The wind lion spun to the right, his wings whooshing. "Do you have a plan?"

"Harrumph," snorted Kermi. "That's like asking him if he has a brain. The answer is obvious."

"Well," Promi began, "I guess I'll just . . ." He ground his teeth. "All right, then. So I don't have a plan."

Without slowing his flight, Theosor turned his head to look back with a great round eye. Sensing the lionsteed's doubts, Promi reached a hand forward, so far that he could feel the creature's warm breath on his fingers.

"I don't know if I can do this," he confessed. "But I do know one thing. I must try."

Theosor peered at him a while longer, then blew a long breath on the young man's hand. "So be it, brave cub. But you must be careful."

Straightening his neck again, the wind lion explained, "Narkazan has been planning this for ages, ever since the advent of the Prophecy."

Promi glanced down at his chest, knowing that under his tunic lay the mysterious mark of the soaring bird. And here he was, right now, soaring through the endlessly evolving world of the spirits. Part of the Prophecy was surely true—the grave danger to his world, *the end of all magic*. But what about the other part, the part about him? Could that really be true, as well?

Closing his eyes, Promi called back the memory of that haunting melody from his childhood. The notes came quickly, and as always, filled him with an inexplicable feeling of comfort. Just as if the person who had sung that song to him so many years ago was still alive, still within reach.

He listened to the half-remembered song, drinking in the notes as if they were a magical potion. For in a way, they were. Even more important than the fact that those notes were the only thing he had left from his mysterious younger years, the notes invariably made him feel somehow stronger. Even at a time like this.

The wind lion swerved, knocking Promi out of his reverie. As they entered a dark tunnel of mist, Theosor asked, "Do you still wish to try, young cub?"

With his thighs, Promi squeezed firmly. "I do."

"Then we will need to get you inside Narkazan's castle. And if you can somehow capture the Starstone, we must also escape from his warriors—who can, I warn you, fly just as fast as any wind lion."

"Sure," the young man replied, stroking the side of Theosor's neck. "But you are not just any wind lion."

"Take no comfort from that, young cub. Evading them will be most difficult."

Promi grinned. "Some would say it's impossible."

The wind lion released a growl. "My specialty."

Nodding, Promi said, "That's all the plan we need. And we have several days until Ho Byneri to figure out the details."

"No, young cub." The wind lion swished his long tail. "Time moves differently in this realm than it does in yours. You have just one day left."

Surprised, Promi rocked back. "Ho Byneri is *tomorrow*?"

"Right. And we will arrive at the cloud palace in just a moment."

Theosor leaped upward, sailing over a purely purple rainbow. As they dropped down to the rainbow's far side, lit by its rich glow, he said, "You do, at least, have one advantage—surprise."

The young man drew a deep breath. "That could help."

"Yes. Narkazan will not expect an attack by just one person. Why, that's even more unlikely than the notion that the person from the Prophecy would turn out to be a young man from Earth instead of an immortal! He would never guess both of those are true."

A short while ago, thought Promi, *neither would I.*

Just then a veil of mist lifted, revealing a grand castle in the clouds. It was the most spectacular structure he'd ever seen—immense, imposing, and terrible all at once. Promi shivered as he looked at Arcna Ruel, the cloud palace of the warlord.

CHAPTER 38

The Cloud Palace

I wish I could have been right there with you, Promi! But maybe, in a way that would have surprised us both, I was.

—From her journal

Theosor swerved, gliding behind a huge spiral of mist to ensure they would not be seen by any of Narkazan's warriors. There he hovered, his invisible wings vibrating in the vapors. Through a thin opening, Theosor, Promi, and Kermi peered at the cloud palace floating just across the valley. Darker than a thundercloud, it seemed to glower back at them.

"It's enormous," said Promi, astonished. "What in the world—the spirit world, I mean—is it made of?"

"Vaporstone," the wind lion replied. "A supercondensed cloud with the strength of stone and the lightness of mist. It takes no small amount of magic to produce, especially in the quantity needed to build such a fortress. But that was Narkazan's goal—to show off his power."

"He succeeded." The young man stared at the imposing face of the palace. Six gigantic turrets towered over the battlements, while a great dome rose from the center. A massive gate attached to an encircling wall was patrolled by dozens of floating shadows. *Mistwraiths,* he realized. *And there are more inside, I'm sure.*

"Right, young cub." The great lionsteed bobbed his head. "They are to our world what the plague is to yours. They consume life and devour any magic they meet."

Promi frowned, watching the shadowy forms slide through the air like clouds of death. "What else is in there?"

"Hundreds more warriors. Some are in human form, others take more ghastly shapes—wrathful ogres and jagged-winged birds, faceless ghouls and poisonous serpents. And some may even stay invisible all the time."

"At least," Promi said with a glance at the small blue creature on his shoulder, "there aren't any kermuncles."

To his surprise, he heard what could only be a chuckle from Kermi. "Count your blessings, manfool."

The spiral of mist started to shift, transforming into a huge, luminous tree. On every branch, glowing fruit sprouted in bunches, like huge grapes made from both light and vapor. Its great knobby roots stretched outward, clasping the cloudlike terrain.

To stay hidden, Theosor slid over to a rippling curtain of rising mist. Once again, he hovered so Promi could take a closer look. After several seconds, the young man finally spoke—and his tone was decidedly grim.

"No windows, Theosor. No windows at all! How am I supposed to get in there—through that gate?"

"Look again, my impatient cub. At the turrets."

Promi studied the tall structures, from their domed roofs down to where they joined the wall. All were solid vaporstone, without a hint of an opening. Suddenly, at the very top of one, he saw a tiny dot of darkness. Just a shadow on the turret? Or a darker patch of stone?

He leaned forward, peering closely, his hands resting on the mighty lion's shoulders. He caught his breath. It was, indeed, a window!

"The only one," announced Theosor. "It leads, I would guess, to Narkazan's private chamber. In his arrogance, he allowed himself the only view from inside the palace."

"And created," said Promi, "the palace's only weakness."

"Yes." The wind lion pawed the air vigorously, as if striking something harder than mist. "But remember this. Getting in will be much easier than getting out alive."

Promi nodded. "Let's go."

Theosor reared back and sprang upward, placing them behind a wavering cloud that was blowing toward the palace. Promi held his breath as they glided closer and closer. Soon, beneath them, he spied the outer wall. The heavily guarded gate. A turret, then another . . . but not the right one.

There! Below them rose the turret, jabbing at the clouds like an enormous spear.

Instantly, the wind lion dived out of the sky. He swooped toward the turret while Promi lifted himself to a crouch on his back. Like a sudden gust of wind, Theosor sailed past the window, slowing just enough for his rider to . . .

Leap! Promi dived into the air and plunged through the window.

CHAPTER 39

The Glow

Normally, I see better without my eyes. What is most important lies beneath the surface.

—From her journal

Covered with mud from the curls of her hair to the tips of her toes, Atlanta tramped through the swamp. Thanks to the river god's gift, she could breathe with ease, even in the rancid plumes of vapors. But her legs felt heavier with every step, and she sometimes stumbled on broken branches or tufts of bog grass.

Why am I feeling so weak? she wondered, clambering around the edge of a quicksand pit. *Now that I can breathe so easily, I should feel stronger.*

In the pocket of her gown, the faery rustled his wings vigorously. Though Atlanta barely noticed the trembling against her skin, she could sense that he was trying to communicate with her.

Gently, she pried open the pocket and peered inside. The faery gazed back at her, his tiny eyes gleaming. Without doubt, his wings looked stronger and more luminous than before. Yet this didn't seem to give him any comfort. Instead, the overwhelming feeling he was conveying was fear—not for himself, but for her.

"I'll be careful, little friend," she whispered. "Really, I will."

The vehement shaking of his antennae said clearly that he didn't believe a word of it.

Stepping over a rock, she stubbed her toe—and almost fell into a pit whose banks vibrated with snakes. She grabbed the branch of a dead tree just in time to catch herself. As she stared into the pit, she scolded herself, *Watch your step! You have to get all the way to Grukarr's lair.*

She glanced over her shoulder in the direction she had come from, toward the faraway forest that had long been her home. And Moss Island, the place she was supposed to rendezvous with Promi before Ho Byneri. Would she make it all the way back there in time? Would he?

First, she reminded herself sternly, *I have work to do.*

Onward she trudged, always toward the gleaming summit of Ell Shangro that she glimpsed sometimes through the swirling vapors. The mountain looked closer, its massive ridges towering above the land. Yet this swamp, it seemed, went on and on forever!

She frowned, puzzling over the questions that had troubled her since she began this trek. Why had the swamp expanded so much since her childhood? And was that expansion somehow related to the forest blight? If so, how could the blight be afflicting trees even deep in the interior?

Suddenly, the curtain of vapors ahead shifted—revealing a dark, conical mound that rose out of the bog like a deadly fang. Grukarr's lair!

Atlanta dropped to the ground, hiding behind the rotting carcass of an impala. Through the ribs, she saw that the lair was belching thick black smoke from its peak. Around the base of the mound, within a ring of stones, men were working feverishly, spurred by a dozen or more mistwraiths whose shadowy forms crackled ominously.

This lair isn't a place where Grukarr lives, she realized. *It's where his slaves are forced to make something.*

Staring hard at the mound, she wondered, *What, though? Exactly what is being made here in secret?*

Just beyond the smoking mound, she could see, at the very base of Ell Shangro, the entrance to the tunnel that was, she now knew, the real Passage of Death. Soldiers, loaded down with weapons, continued to pour out of the tunnel. Now the wide plateau above the lair was completely jammed with warriors, stacks of spears and bows and other weapons, wagons bulging with supplies, and hundreds of animals to assist in the invasion—elephants, wildebeests, oxen, and even a few giraffes wearing harnesses to pull carts. She had seen such creatures before, grazing on the meadows west of the forest, but never in such numbers.

Atlanta gasped at the sheer size of this army. Much bigger than what she and Promi had seen in the vision, the invading force now numbered at least ten thousand. It would roll through Ellegandia, as unstoppable as a tidal wave.

No, she remembered. *Surely the pancharm will stop them!*

Atlanta shook her head, spraying clumps of mud. Didn't Grukarr know about the pancharm, placed upon the Great Forest to protect it—and its country—from any invasion? The pancharm was so powerful, she'd been taught, it could stop even an army as massive as this one. So what was Grukarr thinking?

Then, more anxiously, she asked a different question. *What does Grukarr know that I don't?*

Stealthily, she crawled closer, moving like a cloud of vapor across the bog. Just outside the ring of stones, she hid behind a fallen tree whose blackened branches seemed to reach skyward, pleading for help.

Now she could see, in addition to the slaves working, the bodies of many more on the ground. Coughing and tripping on their fallen brethren, the men kept moving only because the mistwraiths constantly shot them with blasts of black sparks that struck like fiery whips. Whenever a man fell over, mistwraiths gathered around and pummeled him with sparks—either to force him back to his feet or to make certain he was really dead.

Out of the doorway at the base of the mound, four slaves emerged, struggling to carry a huge cauldron of some sort of boiling liquid. Lavender in color, the liquid bubbled with poisonous gas that reached upward like a dark, groping hand. Judging by how far the men leaned away from the cauldron, it was clear that this liquid, manufactured deep inside the mound, was powerfully toxic.

What is that horrible stuff? wondered Atlanta, peering closely.

The faery in her pocket beat his wings furiously, whirring with all his strength. A single word formed in Atlanta's mind, a word that made her shudder.

Ultrapoison.

Along with the word came its terrible meaning: a kind of poison deadly to all mortal creatures—especially those with natural magic. She bit her lip, thinking about what that liquid could do to the faery—and to all the magical creatures she loved, as well as the place where they lived. Any forest creature who touched what the cauldron held—whether bird or beast, unicorn or centaur, enchanted seedling or full-grown tree—would die. And judging from its effect on these poor slaves, the liquid would also sicken any human . . . before killing them too.

She scowled. Even immortal beings such as the tree spirits would suffer, especially if their mortal hosts perished. And then where would they go? To find refuge in the spirit realm . . . or to wander aimlessly until at last they withered away completely?

She watched as the slaves set down the cauldron. One of them breathed a little of the gas and fell over, so obviously dead that the mistwraiths wasted no sparks trying to revive him. Other men dragged the body away, while more arrived and placed beside the cauldron a large crate holding a pile of small gray objects.

Snails! They filled the crate, crawling on top of each other, spilling over the sides.

Immediately Atlanta noticed that they looked a lot like the snails she'd seen while crossing the swamp—except that the shells of those snails had glowed with a lovely hue. By contrast, the ones in the crate looked dull.

What, she wondered, *is this all about?*

Just then another man trudged over, bearing heavy iron tongs. Prodded by a blast of sparks from a mistwraith, he grabbed a single snail with the tongs and dipped its shell in the bubbling liquid, careful not to contaminate the living body inside the shell. Then he dropped the snail on the ground. Instantly, the creature started to crawl away, trying to escape to the swamp.

Over and over, the man dipped snails into the cauldron. Most of them managed to get to the ring of stones and slip into the muck beyond, although one was crushed under a man's boot and another was grabbed by a hungry crow flying past. As soon as the crate of snails had been emptied, men replaced it with another full one.

Puzzled, Atlanta risked sitting up higher behind the fallen tree so she could see better. Suddenly she noticed something that froze the blood in her veins. As the snails crawled away, their shells began to change, emitting a lavender glow! With each passing second, the radiance grew stronger, making every snail an alluring lamp that would attract birds and other creatures.

Including me. She glanced down at her hand that had picked up a snail, recalling how the faery had panicked when he sensed what she had touched.

All at once, she realized that her weakness had started soon after that moment. *No!* she cried in silent anguish. *I've been poisoned!*

And then, in a flash, she realized much more. This was why the swamp was steadily expanding! Carried by thousands upon thousands of snails, Grukarr's ultrapoison was contaminating everything on the swamp's borders. On top of that, this same substance was causing the blight—destroying the trees and creatures of the Great Forest! For every time a hungry predator grabbed one of the snails and carried it back to its nest or den in the forest, all the living beings who had touched the toxic shell sickened and died.

Atlanta's mind reeled. *The pancharm. There is a fatal flaw in the pancharm!*

Designed to protect Ellegandia from a massive invasion, whether by mortals or immortals, the pancharm would only survive as long as the Great Forest survived. And the forest could still be destroyed—not by a sweeping invasion, but by a plague that consumed it tree by tree, spreading faster and faster with every hour until it had wiped out everything. A blight.

Atlanta would have screamed in rage, but that would have revealed her presence to the mistwraiths. She clenched both fists and squeezed so hard that her hands ached, then squeezed some more. Nothing could be worse! Everything she loved in this world was going to perish.

Desperately, she thought, *Now I know Grukarr's plan. But I can't do anything to stop it!*

Inside her pocket, the faery trembled, sending out a wave of compassion. But the feeling washed over Atlanta without making her feel any better. For she also knew that her own time was short. Perilously short.

She probably wouldn't have enough strength to get all the way back across the swamp. To warn her beloved forest of the danger. To make the rendezvous at Moss Island.

Or, she thought with a pang of regret, *to see Promi ever again.*

Grinding her teeth, she asked herself, *Is this how it ends for me? Will I just die in this wretched swamp like my parents did?*

Slowly, she shook her head. *No,* she answered grimly. *Not while I can still do something to help.*

CHAPTER 40

Her Last Living Effort

Our last moment can reveal our first priority.

—From her journal

Atlanta stared at the conical mound at the farthest edge of the swamp, knowing the poisonous smoke that poured from its peak was part of Grukarr's terrible plan. A plan that would ultimately kill every tree in the Great Forest, leaving no creature alive—all to clear the way for his invading army.

Peering through the branches of the fallen tree that hid her from view, she watched the shadowy mistwraiths gliding over the ground, ruthlessly shooting black sparks at slaves to make them work harder. Or sometimes, it seemed, simply to make them suffer more pain.

All the while, more and more deadly snails, their shells glowing from the ultrapoison, were released to enter the swamp . . . and the lands beyond.

What can I do to stop this? she cried silently. *I'm just one person, growing weaker all the time.*

She looked at the hand that had held a contaminated snail. *Now I'm dying,* she thought miserably. *Just like the forest.*

Lifting her gaze skyward, she asked again, *What can I do? If not to stop this disaster, at least to slow it down.*

Her eyes focused on something at the base of the mountain Ell Shangro. At the nearest edge of the plateau, which was swarming with soldiers who had come through the Passage of Death, sat a long row of animal pens. Enormous elephants, armored oxen and wildebeests, plus several giraffes jostled for space in those pens. Brought along to assist in the invasion, those beasts had been given little attention—and even less space. As such, they looked angry, uncomfortable, and altogether unhappy.

Maybe . . . , thought Atlanta. Accustomed to reading the moods of other creatures, she knew those animals would leap at any opportunity to escape. She nodded, a desperate plan forming in her mind.

Running a hand through her mud-caked curls, she plotted the best route to the elephants' pen. Spying a large female who was swinging her trunk against the wooden rails that imprisoned her, Atlanta decided to go there first. Luckily, the army hadn't bothered to post any sentries, since no one had expected intruders to find this place.

Atlanta turned back to the lair, knowing she had no time to lose. Mistwraiths kept relentlessly prodding slaves to work until they died. Meanwhile, masses of toxic snails were being released. Every second she delayed, her chances diminished.

Gathering all her strength, she began crawling across the bog, moving as stealthily as a swamp snake. She slipped around the ring of stones at the base of the lair, always alert for the menacing gaze of mistwraiths. Often, she hid behind the dark plumes of vapor that floated over the swamp, using them as cloaks.

Finally, she reached the steep slope that led up to the plateau. Slowly, with great effort, she crept upward, grasping tufts of grass for support. But as she moved higher, she rose above the swamp vapors, making her easy to spot if anyone happened to look her direction.

Heart pounding, she reached the top of the slope. Exhausted from the strain of the climb, she lay facedown to catch her breath. Finally, she lifted her head—and what she saw gave her a surge of hope.

Directly in front of her stood the elephants' pen. Just as she expected, it had been built hastily, with little concern for sturdiness. Much of the wood showed cracks and splits; just a few nails here and there held the structure together. And why not? The soldiers who had built this pen expected to be here for only a short while before launching the invasion.

Right there, watching Atlanta through the rails, stood the female elephant. Both larger and older than she'd seemed from below, the elephant waved her massive, wrinkled trunk as if she was about to bellow a warning to the others in the pen.

Meeting her gaze, Atlanta said quietly, "I'm here to help you, old one."

The elephant studied her for several seconds, then lowered her trunk. Still uncertain, she twisted her huge ears anxiously.

Cautiously, Atlanta crawled over to the pen. Leaning against a post for support, she rose to her feet. Then she went right to work, yanking at the rails that looked the least sturdy. But she was too weak! The rails wouldn't budge.

The elephant joined in, wrapping her powerful trunk around

loose planks and tugging with her enormous weight. At last, a plank pulled free. Then came another. And another.

Suddenly a soldier on the other side of the pen saw Atlanta. He shouted angrily and sprinted toward her, waving his broadsword.

Atlanta peered at the elephant. "Go," she urged. "Go now! Escape while you can!"

But the elephant remained inside the pen. Despite the gap in the rails, she seemed confused, or in any case not willing to break all the way through the fence. As the soldier dashed up to Atlanta, brandishing his sword, the elephant merely watched with her dark eyes rimmed with long lashes.

Pointing his sword at Atlanta's chest, the soldier spat some words in a language she'd never heard before. Beneath his helmet, he glared at her. When she didn't reply, he lifted his sword to strike.

The elephant swung her trunk forcefully, smashing the soldier so hard he flew over backward and tumbled down the slope. For an instant, Atlanta's gaze met the elephant's, and a silent understanding passed between them. Atlanta moved aside, clearing the way.

"Now go," she said, clutching a post for support.

The elephant raised her trunk and bellowed to the other captives. Around the pen, other elephants heard the signal and filled the air with their own bellows. Led by the old female, they crashed through the fence and thundered down the slope. Straight through the area around Grukarr's lair they stampeded, scattering mistwraiths and slaves as they roared through.

All across the plateau, soldiers suddenly turned, shocked to see the elephants escaping. Meanwhile, the other animals realized their time had finally arrived. Oxen burst through their pen, knocking it down, along with the fence containing the giraffes.

Wildebeests joined the stampede, charging across the plateau and smashing through the warriors' encampment. Giraffes shook off their harnesses and kicked over wagons.

Watching the mayhem, Atlanta couldn't help but grin. While she lacked enough strength to walk all the way back to the forest and would eventually die from the toxin, she had at least done her part.

Of course, it would only be a matter of time before this vast army of soldiers regrouped and brought their camp back to order. Just as the mistwraiths would eventually regain control and continue manufacturing the ultrapoison, sending out more snails to spread the blight. *For now, though,* she told herself with satisfaction, *they have a stampede to handle.* And that had been worth her last living effort.

In addition, she took comfort from something else. Many of the animals she'd helped to free would escape. Leaning against the post, she watched elephants and wildebeests running into the swamp. Some would not survive that desolate terrain, of course, but many others would reach the other side safely. Maybe they would even find peaceful places to live, grazing contentedly, far from the invasion that would otherwise have cut short their lives.

Sighing sadly, she whispered, "I'm sorry, Promi. That's the best I could do."

Weakly, she sat on the ground. Soon, she knew, the soldiers would discover her and then kill her. But before she died, she had done something to help her forest home. Though the invasion would still happen, she had slowed it down.

And that, she felt sure, would have made her parents proud.

Just then a warm breeze blew against her face. A large gray shape towered over her—and she realized the breeze had been someone's breath. The female elephant had returned!

Before Atlanta could even start to stand, the elephant's trunk wrapped around her waist and pulled her closer. At the same time, the elephant kneeled down so Atlanta could crawl aboard. Understanding, she pulled herself onto the elephant's massive head.

Atlanta leaned forward, exhausted. The last thing she remembered were the shouts of soldiers, the crackling of mistwraiths, and most surprising, the flutter of long elephant eyelashes against the skin of her forearm.

CHAPTER 41

Better Company

Beautiful things are very hard to create—and far too easy to destroy.

—From her journal

Atlanta awoke to water splashing against her face, drenching her completely. Opening her eyes, she saw the elephant standing above her, spraying water from a stream. Beneath the elephant's trunk, now being used as a hose, an unmistakable grin spread across the creature's broad, wrinkled face.

"All right! That's enough!" Atlanta waved her arms wildly until the spraying stopped. Then she, too, grinned.

Dripping wet, she wiped her face with her sleeve. Her gown was so dirty that she only succeeded in smearing herself with mud. Yet she barely even noticed, for she'd just glimpsed her surroundings.

Trees! No more swamp! She listened, rapt, to the sounds of a blackbird singing and a squirrel scurrying in the branches overhead.

Right away, she recognized where the elephant had brought her—the baobab grove at the eastern edge of the forest, the very spot where she had plucked sprigs of sweetmint before she and Promi had begun their journey across the swamp. All around her, the immense trees lifted their boughs skyward, their smooth gray bark gleaming in the late afternoon light.

Though she still felt weak and a bit dizzy, Atlanta knew well that if the elephant hadn't rescued her, she wouldn't be alive right now. Those soldiers wouldn't have shown her any mercy after what she'd done to disrupt their encampment. And the mistwraiths would have been even more vengeful.

Eagerly, she opened her pocket to check on the faery. "How are you, little friend?"

The faery hopped out and looked at her with bright eyes. Clearly healing well, he perched on top of her wrist. He studied her intently, his luminous blue wings whirring softly by his side. The very sight of him filled her with delight.

Reaching down to the roots by her side, she picked a single wild raspberry. She handed it to him, though the berry was so big it took both his arms to hold it. Instantly, she felt a rush of gratitude.

Very gently, she returned the faery to her pocket. Then she drew a deep breath of air rich with forest aromas. As beautifully as the river god's gift had transformed the rancid air of the bog into something breathable, this was even better. For she was breathing, once again, the good air of home.

She gazed up into the elephant's round eyes. "You saved me, old one. I am grateful."

The elephant's ears, as tattered as ancient leaves, rippled pleasantly. Then, reaching down with her trunk, she helped Atlanta to her feet. For a long moment, they stood there, young woman and old elephant, facing each other. Finally the great creature raised her trunk and lightly stroked Atlanta's cheek.

With a triumphant bob of her head, the elephant turned and strode off toward the west. Her heavy steps shook the ground, making the baobab branches sway in rhythm. Atlanta watched her depart, a huge gray form surrounded by huge gray trees.

All at once, the full seriousness of her situation struck her. *I know Grukarr's plans! And I must warn the forest—as well as Promi!*

Leaning against a tree trunk for support, she raised her arms into the air. "Trees, my old friends! Beware the snails whose shells glow with lavender light. They are poison, I tell you. Grukarr's poison!"

She waited a few seconds, then spoke the same message again, this time in the language of the baobab trees, a language full of deep whooshes punctuated by sharp clacks. But even before she'd finished, their branches stirred, rustling their leaves. Soon the whole grove echoed with intricate whooshing and clattering as the trees tossed and swayed.

Atlanta nodded, certain the message would spread beyond this grove to other trees, and ultimately to the whole forest. *And now,* she thought, *I need to go to Moss Island.*

She pushed off from the trunk and stood on wobbly legs, feeling weaker than before. *Not too weak to walk, though.* She swallowed. *At least . . . not yet.*

Trying not to trip on the wide roots of the baobabs, she trudged through the grove and into the forest beyond. Slowly, she pushed through a field of ferns whose fronds seemed to grab at her legs. Leaning forward, she kept moving, though she felt less steady than ever.

Far above, a dark bird circled in the sky. If Atlanta had noticed it, she would have known by the shape of its wings and its sharp talons that is was some sort of raptor—perhaps the bird most people called a blood falcon, which others chose to call a Royal Huntwing.

Panting from exertion, she entered a dark grove of cedars where the sweet smell of resin helped renew her strength. Even so, she knew that at this rate, she might well get to Moss Island after Ho Byneri—and after Promi had left for somewhere else.

Leaving the cedar grove, she paused to sit on a rock and catch her breath. Absently, she glanced up at the sky—and gasped. For she could see, rising out of the trees ahead, a thick plume of smoke.

Fire!

Must try to put it out! Instantly back on her feet, she lurched toward the source of the smoke. Half running, half stumbling, she pushed herself to the limit, knowing she needed to get there fast to save whatever trees and animals were endangered.

The stench of smoke grew stronger with every stride. She broke through a dense web of acacia branches and crossed a glade where shaggy red mushrooms surrounded a badgers' den. Moments later, she reached a stand of spruce trees by a stream.

Flames rose from one of the spruces, crackling vigorously. Atlanta watched, her lungs heaving, deciding how best to stop the fire.

Then, to her surprise, she saw someone else—an old, white-haired monk in a tattered brown robe. Feverishly, he was darting over to the stream, filling his cook pot with water, dousing the flaming branches, then fetching more water.

She raced over to join him, grabbing his drinking mug for another container. Together, they labored hard for several minutes, continually showering the tree. Though they never said a word to each other, they immediately bonded in the crucial task at hand.

At last, the fire died out. Not even a spark remained, nor a single flaming needle, either in the branches or on the ground.

Atlanta collapsed, exhausted, on the turf laden with spruce cones. The old monk flopped down beside her, breathing almost as hard.

Finally, he turned toward her, regarding her with warm brown eyes. "By the Great Powers, dear child, I'm glad you came when you did!"

"And I'm glad you were here," she replied. "You were already working hard when I arrived."

The old fellow looked at her sheepishly, scratching the white curls atop his head. "As well I should have been. You see, I started the fire myself, by accident, heating up my supper." He waved at the coals from a small cooking fire. "Next time I won't do that so close to a tree."

Atlanta patted his arm. "Lesson learned, then."

"And by the Great Powers, I have plenty more lessons to learn." His face crinkled in a grin. "My name is Honi."

"Atlanta. And I'm still learning, too." Her expression darkened. "Honi, do you know Grukarr?"

Above their heads, branches started creaking angrily in response to the priest's name.

"Certainly," answered the monk, glancing upward. "Can't say I like him, though. I saw too much of his wickedness during my time in the City."

"Well, you were right. He's now started a blight to kill this entire forest! All so he can bring an invading army from the Passage of Death! And meanwhile, he's working with Narkazan in the spirit realm to—"

"Wait now, dear child." Honi waved his hands so she would stop. "You're rushing along faster than a bounding unicorn! I can't follow what you're saying." He peered at her. "On top of that, you look positively ill. Are you feverish?"

She nodded weakly. "I've been poisoned. And . . . it's getting worse."

Quickly, Honi unstrapped his flask. Handing it to her, he said, "Here, my child. Drink this. It's my own special remedy. Never fails to renew my strength."

Taking the flask, she uncapped it and took a sniff. The smell was as sweet as honeysuckle nectar. *Promi,* she thought, *would like this.* Gladly, she took several swallows.

"Thanks," she said, returning the flask. "Now I've got to go to the—"

She halted, puzzled why her tongue suddenly felt numb. Why her dizziness had worsened. Why her eyelids felt so heavy.

Before she could say another word, she crumpled to the ground. Inside her pocket, the faery writhed in distress.

Honi watched her casually, tightening the cap on his flask. With a grin, he said, "You may be brave, my dear. And your forest may be pretty. But the priest is the one who pays me."

Trees all around swished and moaned, swaying angrily. Perched on a low branch, Huntwing looked down at Atlanta's limp body and clacked his beak in approval. Unfolding his rust-colored wings, he lifted off, eager to alert his master.

Meanwhile, the old monk turned to the noisily swaying trees. Looking up at the branches, he said, "If only you really could talk, you'd make much better company."

CHAPTER 42

Predator and Prey

Something must be more painful than the thought of never seeing you again. But I don't know what that is.

—From her journal
(one of the very last entries)

Opening her eyes, Atlanta saw a hazy mesh of leafy branches. She lay on her back on soft soil, and could smell the tangy resins of spruce trees.

I'm still alive, she thought gratefully. And in the forest. *Maybe there's still time to meet Promi—and warn him.*

Weakly, she sat up. Her mind spun, and she felt so dizzy she almost fell back. Then her head started to clear, and through the haze she saw a face gazing down at her. It took a few seconds to realize whose face it was—and when she did, it sent a jolt through every part of her body.

Grukarr!

The priest observed her with a cruel smirk. Reaching up with one hand, he adjusted his white turban, while with the other, he tapped the talons of the blood falcon seated on his shoulder. "Well, well," he said to Huntwing. "Look who has finally woken."

The bird clacked his beak, his savage eyes gleaming.

"How lovely," Grukarr said to Atlanta in a voice dripping with malice. "I knew we would meet again." He paused to stroke the golden beads around his neck. "And you have appeared just in time to help me."

"I will never help you!" Atlanta started to shake her head, but even that slight motion made her mind swim. Planting her hands firmly on the forest floor, she steadied herself until the dizziness departed.

"Oh, poor girl," said the priest with mock sympathy. "Feeling a bit ill, are you?" He whistled the beginning of a pleasant melody. "How unfortunate."

"It's the blight," she snapped. "You poisoned me—just like you're poisoning the forest." Inside her pocket, the faery shook angrily, and she felt a wave of rage that combined with her own. "Just so you can end the pancharm and invade with your army!"

Grukarr raised an eyebrow. "So you know about my plans, do you?" He glanced at the bird on his shoulder. "She is smarter than we thought."

Huntwing ruffled his feathers and glared at the young woman.

"Do you know," asked the priest, "that I can stop the blight at any time?"

Atlanta started.

"Yes, yes," he continued, "with a simple antidote provided by a good friend of mine."

"You mean Narkazan. Your partner in turning the Starstone into a weapon."

This time Grukarr raised both eyebrows. "My, you really have been working hard to understand my plans."

His expression darkened and he snarled, "Then understand this: if you agree to help me, with no more delays, I will stop the blight immediately. I will save your precious forest—and your life, as well." He nodded smugly. "We have not much time left before Ho Byneri—but there is enough for you to tell me where to find the magic I need to gather from those creatures you know so well. Unicorns, dragons, starsisters who shine so bright—and, oh yes, those nasty little things called faeries."

Atlanta felt the faery's wings shaking with rage, so intensely that her whole pocket was vibrating. Not wanting her friend to be discovered by Grukarr, she gently covered the spot with her hand.

"If you help me now," urged the priest, "I will spare you. As well as this forest." Lowering his voice, he added, "And if you don't . . . everything you love in the world will die. *Everything*."

Despite her resolve, Atlanta blanched. Desperate to save the forest, she pleaded, "You don't know what a terrible mistake that would be! If you destroy the forest, you'd also destroy most of this country's resources—good food, clean water—as well as our greatest beauty and magic! And what good will your kingdom be then? You will have killed everything valuable before you gain power."

Grukarr waved his hand dismissively. "You don't really believe that, do you? We can live just fine without your precious forest! All I need to do is tell people to plant some fruit trees, or whatever. Then we'll have food to eat—and none of your magical creatures to cause any trouble. Ellegandia will be a better place."

Huntwing clacked his beak in agreement.

Outraged, Atlanta opened her mouth to reply. But the priest interrupted her.

"Mark my words, Atlanta. You can save this whole forest as well as yourself. Plus, you can spare me the trouble of calling in my army, which would no longer be needed if I get enough magic for our new weapon. Sure, if you help me today, a few of your magical creatures will perish—but the forest will survive. No more blight, no more invasion, no more harm to you and your friends."

He whistled briefly, confident that he had prevailed. "Well, then, what do you say?"

Fixing her gaze on him, she declared, "I say you are a madman! And a scoundrel of the worst kind!"

Grukarr grimaced. "Then I will introduce you to some friends of mine—friends who have ways to persuade you."

He snapped his fingers. Instantly, from the dark grove behind him, emerged six mistwraiths. They floated toward Grukarr, their shadowy folds rippling ominously, leaving a trail of black sparks in their wake.

Seeing them, Huntwing twitched nervously and slid closer to his master's head. But the priest merely bared his teeth in the semblance of a smile.

Atlanta's heart pounded, but she did her best to hide her fear. Deep in the pocket of her gown, though, the faery shivered uncontrollably.

"Welcome," said the priest to the hovering mistwraiths. "I know you have ways to make people scream and writhe with such agony, they will do anything to make you stop. That is what I want you to do to this young woman."

Glancing at Atlanta, he said icily, "Unless she cooperates. I want her help today—yes, to tell you where to go to find all the magic we need for sunrise on Ho Byneri."

The mistwraiths crackled in unison, releasing a fountain of black sparks.

Slowly, Grukarr turned back to Atlanta. "Don't think for a minute that I will show you any mercy. Or that you will be somehow rescued by your friend, that pie thief."

She tensed visibly.

Seeing this, Grukarr chortled. "Too bad about him. He died in great pain, pleading with me to spare his worthless life."

"Liar!" cried Atlanta. Though she hoped with all her heart that what he said wasn't true . . . she feared that Promi had, in fact, been killed.

"Tut-tut, forest girl! You should never have sullied yourself with that vagabond in the first place." He kissed his ruby ring. "But now he won't bother anyone ever again."

Leaning toward her, Grukarr growled, "You have one last chance. Will you help me? Or should I turn you over to these mistwraiths?"

Marshaling her strength, Atlanta rose to her feet. She wobbled unsteadily and grabbed a spruce bough for support. "You," she began slowly, "can count on my . . ."

The priest began to nod expectantly.

"Total refusal," finished Atlanta. "You will never get my help. And you will never win."

Grukarr glared at her and commanded the mistwraiths, "Make her beg for mercy."

Together, the mistwraiths glided toward Atlanta. As they neared their prey, bristling with black sparks, they fanned out and surrounded her. Then, crackling vengefully, they began to advance, tightening their circle as a hangman tightens a noose.

Though barely able to stand, Atlanta held herself upright. Even when she felt the first sensation of fires kindling inside her head, her torso, and her limbs—fires she knew would soon grow much stronger—she remained motionless. All the while, she stared at the priest defiantly.

Suddenly, she noticed a flash of something blue on her gown. The faery! He was bravely climbing out of her pocket, pushing one of his luminous wings into the open. Right away, she guessed what he was doing—hoping to distract the mistwraiths, sacrificing himself so she would gain a little more time.

No! she thought urgently. *Go back, little friend, where you'll be safe.*

The faery ignored her. Now the top of his antennae could be seen, along with most of one wing, poking out of the pocket. While the mistwraiths hadn't noticed him yet, Atlanta knew that would happen in just a few more seconds.

The mistwraiths crackled louder, spouting sparks. At the same time, they started to expand, rising like a mass of shadows around their victim. Meanwhile, Grukarr watched, too fascinated even to whistle.

All at once, the mistwraiths froze. They fell completely silent. And then they shrank back to their normal size, quivered in the air—and vanished.

Stunned, Grukarr gasped. Huntwing shrieked in astonishment and nearly fell off his perch.

Though she was equally surprised, Atlanta took the opportunity to move her hand over to her pocket and stuff her small friend back down inside. *Stay there now,* she told him firmly. *No more heroics.*

"What the . . . ?" asked Grukarr, utterly bewildered. He stared at the spot where the mistwraiths had disappeared, then cursed, "Cut out my enemies' intestines, tie them in knots, and burn them to ashes! They must have been called home by Narkazan."

Rustling his wings, the blood falcon on his shoulder screeched angrily.

"I *know* what that means, you ignorant bird. Something's gone wrong! Trouble in the spirit realm."

Feeling a sudden surge of hope, Atlanta wondered, *Promi? Could he somehow be the cause of Narkazan's troubles?*

Grukarr strode over and grabbed Atlanta by the arm. He gave her a rough shake and declared, "I am changing my plans. Just as any emperor does when he chooses."

"I still won't help you," she vowed.

"Not yet," he replied. "But I have an important meeting with Narkazan, arranged long ago. And I intend to keep it! We will still meet, as planned, on Ho Byneri—and you will be with me."

He scowled at her. "That meeting was supposed to be when I delivered the magic to power the new weapon. But I can't do that now, can I? Not without any mistwraiths. Yet I can still deliver *you*, the key to finding the magic we need."

Again he shook her, so hard her legs nearly buckled. "If you haven't changed your mind by then, Narkazan will make you! Oh, yes. And he won't be nearly as gentle as those mistwraiths. He will take all your knowledge, as well as your life, making you suffer dearly while he does it." Lowering his voice, he added, "And if he leaves you alive, forest girl . . . I will gladly kill you myself."

CHAPTER 43

The Starstone

Many heard your shout, Promi. But I daresay that no one, not even you, understood what it would mean for us all.

—From her journal

Promi flew through the window of Narkazan's cloud palace, knowing this was his only chance to gain the Starstone. And to bring it back to Earth—if it hadn't already been corrupted into the most terrible weapon ever known.

He rolled across the floor of the warlord's private chamber, stopping by a low table draped with a white cloth. Around his neck, he felt a quick squeeze from Kermi's tail—not exactly reassuring, but the closest thing to congratulations he could expect from his sassy companion.

Kneeling behind the table, Promi carefully lifted his head to scan the room. Meanwhile, he reached down with his left hand to check his dagger. It was still in its sheath—yet he knew it wouldn't be any help against immortals. As he thought about what he was up against, his whole chest felt hot with fear.

Carefully, he examined Narkazan's chamber. It was, fortunately, empty of people. Or other creatures . . . at least the sort of creatures who could be seen. Hadn't Theosor warned him that some of Narkazan's warriors were invisible?

The room itself was sparsely furnished. Too sparsely. Whatever treasures the warlord had amassed on his conquests, they weren't here. Aside from the table, the only furniture was a bed with a quilt whose wispy threads seemed like woven clouds, a lamp that glowed mysteriously without any fire, and a regal, high-backed chair with inlaid designs of warriors destroying their enemies. And there weren't any side chambers or closets. The only entrance, other than the window in the wall behind him, was an open doorway.

Puzzled, Promi looked more closely. But the room held no other objects. No works of art. And sadly, no Starstone.

Must move fast, he told himself. *I've got to find that crystal before Narkazan ruins it forever!*

Where should he search, though? The other turrets? The great dome in the center of the cloud palace? A secret storage place where the warlord kept his treasures?

Promi reached inside his pocket and felt the rim of the copper disc he'd stolen from Grukarr. Strangely, just touching its surface made his finger tingle. Maybe the shonsée disc's magic had been aroused by the fact that the Starstone was—or had once been—somewhere in this castle.

Yet . . . even if he could come within sight of the Starstone, what use was this magical magnet if he didn't know how to use it? He frowned, remembering how Grukarr had emphasized that anyone who didn't tap it just the right number of times would surely die. But what number was that?

Worry about that later, he coaxed himself. Right now he needed to concentrate on finding the precious crystal. And fast!

I'll start with the dome. He glanced at Kermi, whose round eyes seemed full of questions. "Don't worry," he whispered, even though the skin of his chest now felt aflame. "I know what I'm doing."

"Harrumph," the little fellow whispered back. "That's what worries me most."

Promi darted to the door and peered down the stairwell. Glad to see that there were, in fact, stairs, he realized that even beings who could fly must occasionally choose to walk. He started down the spiraling stairs made of gleaming white vaporstone. He took the first step—and then, for no particular reason, shot a last glance back at the chamber.

Something about the small table caught his attention. From this lower angle, he saw, under the rim of the white cloth, that the table had no legs. Rather, it had a wide, boxlike base. *That's odd. Why make a table like that?*

"What's the delay, manfool?" demanded Kermi.

Promi didn't respond. For he had just answered his own question. *Because it's not really a table.*

Remembering that the best way to hide something is in plain sight—a principle he'd learned long ago as a thief—he dashed back into the room. He whipped off the cloth. Before him sat a chest, fastened with a hefty lock.

On his shoulder, the kermuncle tensed in surprise. "Can you open it?"

Promi grabbed the lock and pulled. No luck. He wedged his dagger into its opening and twisted. Again, no luck.

Frowning, he knew there was only one possible way. Just as he knew that his next sacrifice would need to be something truly weighty, enough to give him the Starstone. Nothing he'd given up so far would suffice—not his boots, his journal, or even his ability to eat sweets. No, this time the sacrifice would have to be something even bigger. Something much more valuable . . . and also much more painful.

But what?

Voices! Down in the stairwell, he heard deep voices.

"Any time, manfool," groused Kermi. "No hurry."

Desperately, Promi tried to think what to sacrifice. He had very little left!

Kermi's tail squeezed anxiously. "What are you doing? Singing to yourself?"

Suddenly, with heartbreaking certainty, Promi knew what he must sacrifice. The only thing left from his younger days. The last existing link to the parents he couldn't remember. The one source of comfort he could always rely on, even when everything else had been taken away.

The song from his childhood.

More voices echoed in the stairwell, drawing nearer.

He closed his eyes, trying to concentrate. Then he chanted, "Listen one, listen all."

All at once, he heard the familiar rush of wind. He also heard, deep inside his mind, the secret incantation that kept the lock securely closed. Listening carefully, he absorbed the incantation's every sound and rhythm and hint of meaning.

The lock burst apart and clattered to the floor. At the same time, Promi felt a sudden gap, an empty place, in his heart. He knew that he'd sacrificed the song from childhood—but he couldn't remember anything about it. Not a single note.

The voices grew louder by the second.

"Hurry!" hissed Kermi.

Promi threw open the chest. There, all alone, sat the Starstone. Small enough to fit in the palm of his hand, the crystal glowed with pure, pulsing light. And with a mysterious power that suddenly made Promi feel stronger, magnifying his own inner magic.

Not corrupted, he thought with relief. *We got here in time!*

Carefully, he picked up the Starstone. "All right, Kermi. Let's go!"

At that instant Promi was tackled—so hard he lost all the air in his lungs. The Starstone flew into the air. But it never hit the floor, for someone else caught it.

Powerful arms slammed Promi down and pinned him on his back. Eight arms, in fact. They belonged to a pair of shirtless giants who had four arms apiece—along with leathery wings folded against their backs. The warriors' burly bodies, the color of amber, rippled with muscles. Hard as he tried to break free, Promi couldn't budge.

Just then, a new, mist-colored face appeared above him. It looked as sharp as an ax blade, with a long chin and a beaklike nose. A shiny black earring dangled from one ear. And from both sides of the narrow jaw grew large, menacing tusks. Dark red, the tusks curved to sharp points that could easily rip skin apart.

"You dare to enter my chamber!" fumed Narkazan, grasping the glowing crystal. "Who are you?"

Promi glared up at him. "Someone who knows your evil plans."

Narkazan squeezed the Starstone tightly. "Then you know this crystal will make me the most powerful ruler of any realm! I was just about to call forth the magic that will make it my most deadly—"

He stopped abruptly, sniffing the air. "I smell mortal flesh," he declared, clearly surprised.

The warlord's dark gray eyes probed his prisoner, running a finger along one of his tusks. Finally, he announced, "Now I know who you are."

Narkazan turned to his warriors and commanded, "Lift him to his feet."

Instantly, the hulking warriors raised their captive. They might have been picking up a piece of straw, it was so easy. Promi wriggled and tried to twist free, but their many holds on him only tightened.

Narkazan stepped closer. Thoughtfully, he rubbed his narrow

chin. Then he grabbed the collar of Promi's tattered tunic. With a sharp tug, he tore open the cloth on the left side, exposing the mark of the flying bird. With the furious beating of Promi's heart, the bird's wings seemed to be moving through air.

Both of the amber giants started. They stared at the mark, then at their commander, in amazement.

"Yes," declared Narkazan. He nodded, making his earring sway. "I was right. You are the one from the Prophecy." His voice lowered. "I ordered you killed long ago, but you have always eluded me. And now I know why!" His eyes seemed to sizzle with rage. "You are a mere mortal, far beneath my attention."

He glared at his prisoner. "Until now! I shall greatly enjoy driving a stake through your mark—and through your mortal heart." Stroking his pointed chin, he snarled, "On second thought, I won't use a stake. I shall use this knife of yours, so you will know that you died by your own blade."

Unwilling to give the warlord the satisfaction of seeing him struggle, Promi stopped wriggling. Calmly, he said, "You will never succeed."

"Oh?" Narkazan smoothed the front of his cream-colored satin robe. "We shall see about that."

Tilting his angular face toward Promi's sheath, the warlord reached for the dagger. Just as his long fingers were about to touch the hilt—a streak of blue shot from across the room and slammed into his face.

"Aaaakkk!" shrieked Narkazan. He stumbled backward, trying desperately to keep the furry blue creature from scratching out his eyes. "Help me!"

The two brawny warriors released Promi and dashed to their struggling leader. In that same instant, Promi whirled to face Narkazan. The warlord still gripped the Starstone in his fist, so tightly that just the edge of one of the crystal's facets could be seen. Fixing his gaze on that glowing edge, Promi thrust his hand into his pocket and touched the shonsée disc. Clearing his mind, he opened himself to the magic of a Listener.

He heard the prayers of a craftsman laboring to make the disc, the very first vibrations of its magic, and the glad shouts of those who witnessed its power. Then, at last, he heard something else. He tapped the shonsée disc. Twice—one tap each for mortal and immortal beings.

All at once, a brilliant flash of light filled his mind. Miraculously, as the light faded, he felt something new in his pocket. The Starstone!

He waved urgently at Kermi and shouted "Let's go!"

Instantly, Kermi released the warlord. As Narkazan writhed on the floor, groping at his eyes, the agile blue kermuncle evaded the fumbling grasps of the giants. With a single bound, he leaped over their heads and landed on Promi's shoulder. Even as the huge warriors started to pursue them, Promi spun around.

He ran with all his speed to the window and leaped. Sailing into the open air, he heard Narkazan's cry of rage behind him. Silver spears flew past, nearly grazing Promi's head and back. Loud as he could, he shouted, "Theosor!"

Promi fell through the sky, rapidly losing altitude. Suddenly—he heard a familiar roar. The wind lion burst out of the clouds and caught him.

He grasped the wind lion's mane. "We've got it! We've got the Starstone!"

"Excellent, young cub." He roared in triumph. "Now we must escape—if we can."

CHAPTER 44

A Silver Wind

Death is your constant companion, Promi, as close to you as a rider to his steed.

—From her journal

Soaring like a silver wind, Theosor raced away from the cloud palace. He pawed the air constantly, even as his invisible wings vibrated in the mist. Seated on his shoulders, Promi clutched the wind lion's billowing mane.

"Harrumph," said the blue kermuncle clinging to the young man's shoulder. "That was the sloppiest escape I've ever seen."

"It worked," answered Promi. "By the way . . . thanks for your help back there."

Kermi shrugged his little shoulders. "It was either that or die. I just chose the least nasty option."

Digging his fingers into the lionsteed's mane, Promi grinned.

"At least," Kermi went on, "we won't have any more excitement today. All we need to do is escape from this realm without getting caught."

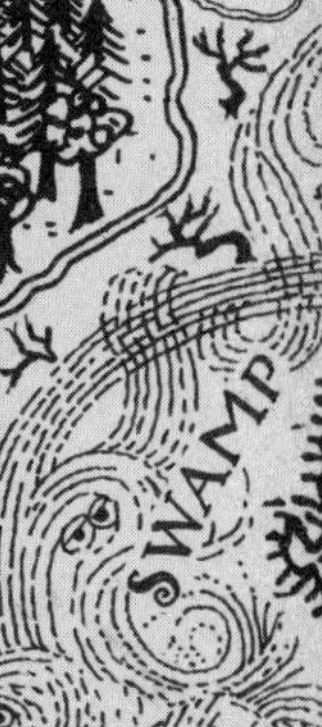

The wind lion shook his great head. "That won't be easy, kermuncle."

"But you're flying so fast," protested Kermi. "How could Narkazan ever—"

His sentence ended as Theosor swerved abruptly to avoid a barrage of black-tipped arrows. One came so close that its fletching brushed against Promi's ear; another one sliced through the torn flap of his tunic.

"Er, Theosor?" Kermi hunched lower, pressing his whiskered face against Promi's shoulder. "You might have a point there."

Casting his gaze to the rear, Promi saw a massive horde of angry immortals in hot pursuit. Hundreds of them! Flying fast—and gaining steadily.

Mistwraiths flew like shadowy comets, crackling with sparks, leaving trails of blackness behind them. With them came a shrieking throng of liquid beasts whose bodies flowed through the air, and whose watery mouths bubbled with dagger-sharp teeth. Yet those teeth seemed gentle compared to those of the huge dragons whose red wings flashed with every stroke. And even more terrifying were the insectlike beasts who had no teeth at all—just multiple eyes and curling, blood-soaked tongues that stretched toward the wind lion.

Among the pursuers came a monster that resembled a winged dinosaur with three separate heads. Worse yet, every few seconds, the heads would dissolve and form again into new ones. Some heads had jaws strong enough to crush boulders, and some had eyes that flashed with black lightning. The only thing the heads had in common was the same deafening roar—and they roared constantly.

Right beside the many-headed dinosaur came a whole troop of amber giants, the same sort of burly, four-armed warriors who had attacked Promi in Narkazan's chamber. Flying faster than Promi would have thought possible, their leathery wings buzzing, they resembled a swarm of enormous bees. And their amber-colored bodies, bulging with muscles, bore weapons of all kinds: gleaming swords, silver-bladed axes, bundles of sharp spears, and bows and arrows slung over their immense shoulders.

At the front of the horde flew scores of warriors in human form. They were the archers who had shot the deadly arrows—and they were now about to release another volley. Exactly how they flew was a mystery of the spirit realm, for they had no wings to carry them aloft. And yet, like Theosor, they could fly with astounding speed.

Though some of the archers were tall and others stout, all had the same mist-colored skin as Narkazan. And they all wore creamy satin robes like their master. Their uniform also included, it seemed, an identical expression, which Promi could recognize even at a distance—intense fury.

Flying at the head of the immortals was the commander himself. If the army was a spear, he was its point. Narkazan's face, thin and sharp as a blade, now bore deep gouges around his eyes from Kermi's assault. And those eyes, as red as his tusks, smoldered like fire coals.

"Shoot!" he ordered, waving angrily at the archers. "And this time, hit the target!"

A huge volley of arrows whizzed through the air, straight at Theosor and his passengers. At that instant, the lion veered sharply and plunged into a windy tunnel of swirling vapors. The howling gusts scattered the arrows, offering a temporary shield from the attack.

Even above the winds, Promi could hear Narkazan's shouts of rage. No shield could hold back his wrath.

Theosor shot out of the swirling tunnel, then flew into a wall of dark, stormy vapors. Bolts of lightning erupted all around, illuminating the darkness, accompanied by deafening booms of thunder. The noise and flashes were constant, as were the buffeting winds, yet somehow he held true to his course. All Promi could do was hold tight to the lion's mane . . . and hope they wouldn't be struck by lightning.

One major blast struck so close that it knocked the wind lion sideways. Promi cried out as he started to slide off. One of his hands lost hold of the wind lion's mane, and the other was slipping fast. Roaring with the strain, Theosor fought to right himself—and did so just in time to stop Promi from falling.

Relieved, Promi hugged the wind lion's neck, smelling the sweat that glistened on the fur. He could feel the powerful muscles tense as they surged forward. "Are you all right, Theosor?"

"No, cub, I am not! And I won't be until we escape."

Promi glanced behind. In the next flash of lightning, he saw dozens of dark shapes through the vapors. Even closer than before! Narkazan's horde was still gaining on them. Now the many-headed dinosaur's roar was so loud it rattled Promi's bones.

They burst out of the stormy vapors into a wide open cloudscape that stretched endlessly before them. Fluffy mounds, too many to count, radiated all the colors of rainbows. These brightly-hued clouds reminded Promi of an enormous field of wildflowers . . . but he knew that each of them was really a world unto itself, with many more worlds hidden within. Looking closely, he glimpsed a colorful array of towers on one, a mass of mottled caverns on another, and what might have been a misty form of fire burning on yet another.

"Get them!" shouted Narkazan to his troops. He wasn't far from his prey now, and his eyes flashed vengefully. "They must not escape!"

Theosor swerved suddenly, plunging straight down into a cloud, a deep blue one that seemed to toss and sway like waves. Instantly, a blue ocean poured over them. Promi coughed and swallowed water, unable to breathe. From somewhere behind, he heard the dinosaur's roar change to a choking, gagging sound.

The wind lion continued to force his way ahead, paddling with his huge paws through this liquid world. While it was almost impossible to see, they heard strange sounds, magnified greatly, echoing all around them. Promi heard Narkazan growling angrily right behind them.

At last, they exploded out of the water—and into a realm of enormous, shifting strings of mist. Rising higher than anyone could see, the vaporous strings twisted and vibrated with majestic slowness. As soon as he'd stopped coughing and could breathe again, Promi realized that the great strings were making rich, deep sounds. Like a gargantuan harp, they produced the most wondrous music he'd ever heard.

No time to savor that music, though. A new volley of arrows whizzed past them—not as many as before, but far too close. Swinging his head around, Promi saw that they had fewer than a hundred pursuers now. Though the army didn't include the dinosaur with the shifting heads or most of the amber giants, the warriors who had stayed with them—including most of the liquid beasts—loomed closer than ever.

Narkazan caught his gaze. "I shall kill you, mortal! You and that blue demon, as well as your lion." Waving his clenched fist, he screamed, "The Starstone is mine!"

"Never!" Promi called back, glancing down at his pocket.

Abruptly, Theosor veered upward, climbing parallel to the misty harp strings. Narkazan and his forces did the same, pressing closer. Then, without warning, the wind lion flipped over backward. He spun a complete circle in the air, so fast that Promi had just shouted that he was falling off when he landed securely again. Only then did he realize that, in the middle of the flip, Theosor had flown directly *into* one of the vaporous strings.

The world around them stretched and contracted, twisting and expanding without end. Everything changed continuously. It was as if they had dived into a constantly bending mirror. Misty shapes emerged and then vanished, stretched to infinite size and then shrank down to nothingness.

No one could follow us here, thought Promi.

They burst out of that surreal realm—and he realized right away he was wrong. Behind them came Narkazan and at least sixty of his warriors. More than half were mistwraiths, crackling with rage. The rest included archers, red-winged dragons, liquid beasts, amber giants, and one insectlike being with hundreds of bright yellow eyes that were all trained on Promi.

Theosor pivoted and plunged into a mass of mist where huge bubbles rose and fell and swirled on all sides. Each bubble, Promi realized with a jolt, held an entirely different world—some brightly lit, others shrouded by darkness, and others metamorphosing from one luminous color to the next.

But Narkazan came as well. Now he flew so close that only a few lengths separated them. His vicious tusks gleamed ominously. Then he raised his arm to give a new command.

Instantly, Theosor dived into one of the darkest bubble worlds. Night surrounded them, a darkness so deep that Promi suddenly wondered whether they had lost not only light but also the ability to see. In that utter blackness, his deepest doubts swelled. Would they survive? Escape Narkazan? Return the Starstone to Earth?

No, he told himself grimly. *We can't possibly get away! There are too many of them. And they're much faster and stronger than we are.*

Even Theosor seemed to feel the oppressive weight of the darkness. His wings' vibrations slowed; his worries grew. He knew well they had entered a voidlike realm that extinguished not only light but also hope, a place where doubts and terrors thrived. Yet he couldn't fight off the growing fear that all his efforts counted for nothing. The wind lion's sturdy neck began to droop lower.

Just then the crystal in Promi's pocket began to glow. Small as it was, it held enormous power to magnify the magic around it—whether from an entire forest or a single wind lion. Slowly, the light swelled. Like a fire coal that brightens steadily until, at last, it bursts into flame, the Starstone became incandescent.

With that magical light, the companions' moods brightened. Promi straightened himself, feeling a surge of hope. Kermi's tail squeezed him with renewed strength. And Theosor released a mighty roar.

They flew out of the darkness into a new realm, one where everything moved in reverse. Backward they zipped through twisting corridors of mist. Alas, flying just in front of them—behind them, really—came Narkazan and a dozen warriors.

Theosor careened sharply into a deep crevasse. Immediately, they entered a realm of such thick mist it seemed almost solid. Any movement—even breathing—was agonizingly difficult. Promi strained to tilt his head, but lacked the strength. With a heroic effort, Theosor turned toward a pulsing circle of light. Muscles straining, he carried them into it—and they could move again.

Light flashed, illuminating a boundless cloudscape. Then the light went out, casting everything into darkness, until it flashed again. This on-off pattern repeated constantly, making every movement seem to jump. Moreover, to Promi's surprise, he had no memory of what had happened between flashes. He guessed that in this realm, time was endlessly fragmented, flowing in disconnected bursts. One instant they were in a fixed position at a certain place, and the next instant all that had changed, with no connection between the two isolated scenes.

When Promi looked back, however, he saw that Narkazan had followed. Only a few mistwraiths now accompanied him, but with every new pulse, the warlord of the spirit realm came closer. Just then, Narkazan reached out to grab Theosor's tail. Promi realized that, with the very next pulse, he would catch them.

In that instant before the next flash of light, the wind lion swerved. They plunged into a shimmering patch of mist. Theosor's move came so abruptly that it caught Narkazan off guard. He, too, veered to follow, but a small gap had opened between them.

"Good work!" cried Promi.

Theosor's head shook. "Not good enough. He's going to catch us, unless . . ."

"Unless what?"

"Unless I do something drastic."

Promi cocked his head, wondering what could be more drastic than what they had already endured. "Do whatever it takes."

The wind lion soared deeper into the mist. He angled sharply right and then left, plunged into new crevasses, and vaulted over luminous archways.

Yet still Narkazan pursued. Though he now flew alone, he drew closer every second.

Theosor flew into vaporous canyons and through nearly invisible holes.

Still Narkazan pursued.

Then the wind lion found the strength somehow to surge with a new burst of speed, moving as fast as silver lightning.

Still Narkazan pursued. Now he was just an arm's length behind, close enough that Promi could hear his snarls.

Theosor veered sharply, diving through the darkest crack in a swirling cloud. Winds gusted over them, making it difficult to fly straight. He turned his head briefly, glancing back at Promi with a great brown eye.

Desperately, Theosor said, "We near the Maelstrom! Those who fall into it never return. Are you willing?"

With no hesitation, Promi replied, "Take us!"

The wind lion roared.

Deeper into the swirling storm they plunged. Narkazan reached toward them—almost touching the lion's tail. "Mine!" he shouted. "You are mine!"

Violent winds howled and screamed as the storm intensified. All the while, darkness deepened around them. Promi glanced over his shoulder to see the warlord's outstretched fingers brush against the tip of Theosor's tail.

The wind lion turned and leaped across a chasm of streaming clouds. Before them, a black hole opened. Darker than even the dark of the void, the hole gaped like a bottomless pit—ever swirling, endlessly deep. *The Maelstrom.*

Theosor flew along the uppermost edge of the hole, teetering on its rim. Winds slammed into them, but somehow he kept his balance. Below, the bottomless hole spun down, down, down.

Seething with rage, Narkazan reached just a little farther. He closed his fist, finally grasping the lion's tail. "Got you!" he shouted triumphantly.

Then Theosor did something totally unexpected.

He stopped. Without warning, in midflight, he came to a sudden halt.

Narkazan smashed into the lion's hind legs, flew into the air, and spun right over Promi's back. His cry of rage turned into a shriek of terror as he plunged, unable to stop himself, into the center of the Maelstrom.

The absolute blackness swallowed him. His voice, like his body, faded into nothingness.

The wind lion, knocked hard by the blow, nearly fell into the Maelstrom, too. But with a powerful lunge, he thrust himself back onto the rim. Seconds later, he leaped through a radiant gap and shot out of the storm.

They sailed into a calmer realm, landing on a flat cloud above a churning river of mist. Promi leaned forward and wrapped his arm around the wind lion's neck. Hugging tight, he said, "You did it, my friend."

The lionsteed shook his immense head, ruffling his mane. "No, young cub. *We* did it."

"Harrumph," said Kermi loudly. "Including me, of course."

Promi nodded. "Yes, you little blue demon. Including you."

"One thing is certain," the kermuncle added. "Your friend Atlanta will be mighty pleased when you return with the Starstone."

Trying to sound more casual than he really felt, Promi replied, "Maybe so."

"Of course, manfool, I'm sure you'll take all the credit for saving it."

"Absolutely." He grinned. "Though I might mention you came along for the ride."

Kermi blew a bubble and popped it in Promi's ear. "How kind of you."

The wind lion roared with laughter, a sound that echoed across the sky.

A new sensation filled Promi—a surge of satisfaction deeper than he'd ever known.

Just then an enormous net dropped over them. Made from the fibrous form of vaporstone, it was impossible to break—though Theosor reared and twisted, doing his very best to try. But the more he fought against the net, the tighter it wrapped around him and his passengers.

Caught! They could not escape.

CHAPTER 45

To See, to Hear, to Touch

When it happened at last, Promi, I didn't know what to say. Which was just fine, since no words could describe how I felt.

—From her journal

On a wide, flat cloud above the surging river of mist, Theosor snarled desperately. He struggled, swiping with his paws and twisting with all his strength against the vaporstone net. But he couldn't break free. The strands only tightened around his wings, his legs, and his passengers.

Promi tore at the net with one hand, but didn't dare let go of the wind lion's mane with the other, lest he fall under the stamping paws. Kermi, meanwhile, didn't even try to escape. He only smacked his long tail against Promi's back.

"Can't you do something, manfool?" the kermuncle demanded. "After all, you're the one in the Prophecy!"

But Promi couldn't do anything. Frustrated, he peered through a hole in the tightening net, scanning the river of mist below them. Like the Deg Boesi rapids that rushed below the bridge where he'd leaped into the spirit realm, this river sped ceaselessly, frothing with white vapors. If only they could somehow get into it . . . the current would carry them away to some other realm.

But how? The net held them fast. And it was secured, somehow, to this cloud.

"What we need now," Kermi grumbled, "is a miracle. Or a quiggleypottle." He shook his head, brushing his whiskers against Promi's cheek. "But they don't just appear whenever you need them, you know."

Promi shot him a glance, making it clear he didn't have any clue what the word meant.

"Harrumph. You *still* don't know the meaning of quiggleypottle? Well then, you should—"

Kermi fell silent. The net was melting away, vanishing into the mist!

Amazed, Promi watched, his eyes almost as wide as Theosor's, as the net simply evaporated. Seconds later, they were completely free. The wind lion pranced across the cloud, shaking his mane jubilantly.

At that instant, human shapes started to materialize all around them: women and men, old and young. Like clouds forming out of clear sky, the people—at least thirty in all—grew increasingly solid. It took only a heartbeat for them to appear fully.

All of them, even the youngest children, had skin that glowed with a silvery sheen. And they all wore long, wispy robes. But unlike the uniforms of Narkazan's warriors, these robes were every color of the rainbow. They had been painted with highly colorful, individual designs of flowers, fruits, poetic phrases, faces, landscapes, creatures, trees, and musical instruments—plus, on the robe of one young woman, a squiggly blue line that looked a lot like the tail of a kermuncle.

"Who are they?" Promi asked the wind lion.

Theosor didn't answer. He merely stopped prancing and stood still except for the slightest tremble of his ears.

"Whoever these people are," said Kermi as he studied the young woman's robe, "they have excellent taste in clothing." He blew a celebratory stream of bubbles which rose, glistening, into the misty sky.

An elder man, with golden eyes and white hair that shimmered like starlight on water, stepped toward them. He walked across the cloud until he stood directly in front of Theosor. As he gazed probingly at the wind lion, Theosor swished his tail. A few seconds passed and then, as if they had been speaking privately, the wind lion bobbed his head for emphasis.

The elder looked at Promi, glancing first at the mark on his chest that showed clearly through his torn tunic, then at his pocket. With a nod of greeting, he declared, "I am Sammelvar. My people and I welcome you at last. We apologize for casting the vapornet over you, but that was the only way we could stop such a powerful wind lion."

Theosor snorted proudly.

Promi caught his breath. For he had just noticed that the design on Sammelvar's robe was a gold-colored replica of his own mark! Like the one over Promi's heart, it was shaped like a mighty bird in flight.

Yes, said Sammelvar telepathically. *We share this mark, you and I.*

Promi drew a sharp breath. Instinctively, he raised his hand to touch the spot on his chest. "You . . . have been waiting for us?"

"For you, Promi," the man answered. Seeing Promi's surprise, he added kindly, "Brave Theosor here told me your name. As well as what you have done to rescue the Starstone—and also to dispose of Narkazan."

As he said those words, many people in his band smiled and traded approving glances. Some of them embraced, while a young girl spun in circles, dancing. One white-haired woman, crying quietly, stepped to Sammelvar's side.

Only one person, the young woman with the kermuncle's tail on her robe, showed no emotion. She stood apart from all the others, seemingly deep in thought. Then Promi noticed something else. Over her eyes, she wore a turquoise band that must have completely blocked her vision. Yet something about the way she was looking at him told him that she could, without doubt, see.

Maybe, he wondered, *she has learned to See as I have learned to Listen.*

At that instant, the young woman nodded.

Intrigued, Promi gazed at her. Had she read his mind?

"We have awaited your arrival," said Sammelvar, "with great hope. That is why the design on my robe is the color of the rising sun that lights your world at the start of a whole new day."

Promi's cheeks flushed. "My friends here did just as much as I did."

Kermi's whiskers bristled. "More, actually." His small blue paw batted the young man's ear. "But he did his part."

As Promi waved away the paw, several people laughed. And for the first time, the young woman broke into a grin.

Putting aside his annoyance, Promi asked Sammelvar, "You have been resisting Narkazan?"

"For a very long time—what would be, in your world, centuries." He ran a hand through his shimmering hair. "While Narkazan wanted only to conquer, to control others, we have stood for the ideal that everyone—mortal and spirit beings alike—deserves to choose his or her own path."

Beside him, the elder woman nodded, her kind eyes sparkling. "As you, Promi, have chosen yours." Then, her tone grave, she added, "But we have lost many brave fighters, vanquished by the warlord's dark magic."

Sammelvar clenched his jaw, remembering someone's loss. "Immortals cannot be killed," he explained. "But Narkazan found ways to make them choose to die, just to end their agony." He scowled. "He also found a way, quite recently, to reverse the power of magical objects. To take something as beautiful as the Starstone, our gift to your world, and turn it into a force of evil—something that would destroy rather than create, kill rather than renew."

"To make it," Promi said disdainfully, "a weapon."

"Right," declared Theosor with a shake of his mane. "But that will not happen now, young cub. He has fallen into the Maelstrom from which no one has ever escaped. At least . . . not yet."

"May he stay there forever!" declared the white-haired woman. "With all his evil magic."

An idea struck Promi. Turning to Sammelvar, he asked, "Is that what the Prophecy means by *the end of all magic*?"

"No," answered the spirit, his golden eyes alight. "Magic is still alive throughout the worlds! And now it can thrive unmolested."

He touched the tips of his fingers together. "Besides, magic in its natural state is neither good nor evil. Only the will of the user, or the craft of the object, makes it so."

"Then what," demanded Promi, "do those words in the Prophecy mean?"

"Those words mean both more and less than they seem." Spoken by the young woman with the turquoise band over her eyes, her comment seemed to swell, echoing across the cloud. Everyone turned toward her.

"That is the way with all prophecies," she explained. "The true meaning will only be known in time, and then only to those with the eyes to see the unseen and the ears to hear the unheard."

To hear the unheard, Promi repeated to himself. The magic of a Listener! *Could she be referring to me?*

As if she'd heard his question, the young woman said to Promi, "In time, you will learn what you need to know, or know what you need to learn."

Bewildered, Promi frowned. "What did you say?"

Taking pity on him, the elder woman explained, "She is a Seer, given to talking in riddles. I am her mother, Escholia, and I can't understand much that she says."

Sammelvar chuckled. "I am her father, and I can't understand *anything* that she says."

The young woman grinned again. "Maybe you will learn when you grow young enough."

Promi furrowed his brow. Trading glances with Sammelvar, he said, "I see what you mean."

The white-haired woman came closer and looked up at Promi, sitting astride the great wind lion. She studied him with her kind eyes, then placed her hand lightly on his ankle. To Promi, her touch felt surprisingly warm. And, in a mysterious way he couldn't begin to explain, it also felt . . . familiar.

But that's impossible, he told himself.

Worry written on her face, Escholia turned to her husband. "He doesn't know, does he?"

Sammelvar shook his head. "In time, my dear, in time."

Promi's back straightened. "Know what?" he demanded.

But the elder man didn't reply. Instead, he asked Promi, "May I see the Starstone?"

Promi reached into his pocket and pulled out the crystal, still attached to the copper disc that had served as a magical magnet. Seeing this, Sammelvar said a simple chant. The shonsée disc sounded a deep, resonant note like a gong—and released the crystal. Gently, Sammelvar took the Starstone.

The instant he touched it, the crystal's facets lit up, blazing with magical light. Beams radiated everywhere, piercing the surrounding clouds and making luminous rainbows in the mist. It was as if he held, in his hand, a glowing star.

"Ah, good crystal," said Sammelvar. "Long has it been since I felt your power."

Raising his eyes to Promi, he smiled. "It lifts my heart to know that soon this will again be on Earth where it belongs."

As he gave it back to Promi, the young man handed him the shonsée disc. "Keep this, Sammelvar. You and your people have given so much to my world. This is a small gift of thanks."

"It is no small gift," he replied. He turned the copper disc slowly, studying its sheen. "Tanalo, the greatest of our magical craftsmen, worked many years to make this. Well do I remember the day he finished—and the joyful expression on his face."

With a thoughtful nod, he added, "It would have pleased him to know how very important it would become. To both our worlds."

Theosor's voice rumbled, "Cub, we must fly! Back in the mortal realm, only a few minutes remain before sunrise on Ho Byneri."

"A few minutes!" Promi exclaimed, surprised. With a pang, he thought, *Atlanta and I were supposed to meet two whole days ago. I hope she's all right.*

Stepping toward him, the young woman with the turquoise band said earnestly, "It is very important that you get back in time for sunrise—*first light Ho Byneri,* in the words of the Prophecy. You must not be late!" Frowning, she added, "And, Promi, I foresee that you will have a different meeting with your friend than you had planned. Very different. There is great danger in the air."

Promi frowned. "Danger for her or for me?"

But the young woman didn't answer.

Escholia took her husband's hand. "Must he go?"

Sammelvar nodded. "He still has important work to do." Facing Promi, he implored, "Do be careful."

"I'll try," the young man replied. Gazing one more time at the cloud, the river of mist, and all the people who had gathered here, he said, "I wish I could stay longer."

"Perhaps," said Sammelvar, "you will someday return."

Theosor gave his mane a mighty shake. "We must fly!"

Replacing the Starstone in his pocket, Promi nodded. "Let's go."

"Even after you get home," cautioned Sammelvar, "you must be vigilant. Do not allow the Starstone to fall into evil hands! Even in your wondrous country, which holds creatures from every other land, there are mortals who would use its power for terrible ends."

Immediately, Promi thought of Grukarr. He knew that Atlanta had hoped to block the priest's plans. But had she succeeded? And more important . . . had she survived?

"Hold tight," commanded the wind lion. As Promi grasped his mane, he reared back and leaped into the air. Promi had barely a chance to glance again at the immortals, and to wonder what had seemed so familiar about the elder woman's touch, before they vanished behind a curtain of vapors.

Through the cloudscapes they flew, fast as the wind. Within Promi's pocket, the Starstone glowed subtly. By his legs, Theosor's magical wings vibrated intensely.

Faster and faster they hurtled, whizzing through tunnels of swirling storms and leaping into luminous gaps between clouds. They flowed with the mist—even, it seemed to Promi at times, *became* the mist. They soared over cloud canyons, through bizarrely different realms, and into waves of vapor that carried them beyond any markings of space or time.

At last, they returned to a world he remembered well. Through the shifting veils of mist, he saw a dilapidated, unfinished bridge. Hundreds of prayer leaves covered with intricate words of blessing snapped and rustled in the breeze. Wooden planks, broken or barely attached, creaked as the bridge swayed. Far below, the river

Deg Boesi, brimming with melted snow, crashed through the gorge.

The Bridge to Nowhere.

Theosor sailed to the end of the bridge and hovered there. Lowering his voice to a tender growl, he said, "We must part, brave cub."

Promi glanced at the eastern horizon. Through the shredding vapors, he could see the first glimmer of light reaching skyward. Sunrise was only seconds away.

The wind lion turned his head, studying him. In the predawn light, his mane shone like liquid silver. Leaning forward, Promi stroked the warm fur of his neck.

"I will miss you, Theosor."

The wind lion's ears trembled. "And I will miss you."

Slowly, Promi slipped off Theosor's broad back and stepped onto the bridge. The planks creaked under his weight. Peering at the wind lion, he said softly, "I bless your eternal qualities."

Theosor roared one last time. Then, with a gust of wind, he vanished into the mist.

CHAPTER 46

Sunrise

Home is not where you find food or rest, but where you find something far more precious. Whatever happens, Promi, I hope you remember that.

—From her journal

Thick vapors shrouded Promi. Though dawn's first light already touched the horizon, very little could penetrate the mist around him.

After the wind lion's departure, he remained at the end of the Bridge to Nowhere, staring into the mist. Prayer leaves, strung from the bridge's collapsing beams, rustled and flapped all around, while the river crashed noisily through the gorge. Yet . . . all he could hear was Theosor's final, echoing roar.

"I'll miss that lion," he muttered to himself.

"Not as much," said Kermi with a thump of his tail against the young man's back, "as you'll miss all the things you've sacrificed. Especially pastries."

Promi shook his head. For while he'd given up many things that were precious indeed, even the song from his childhood—he wasn't thinking about them right now. Instead, he was thinking about an experience he would never have again: soaring through the spirit realm, holding the wind lion's mane.

Feeling the weight of the Starstone in his pocket, Promi's mood brightened. At least he'd managed to rescue it! *Atlanta will be so happy,* he told himself.

And yet . . . even though the Starstone had been saved, the Prophecy hadn't been completely fulfilled. He wondered, once again, about those mysterious words, *the end of all magic.* What did they really mean?

Another phrase from the Prophecy also troubled him: *the ultimate end.* Clearly, that meant something larger, more significant, than Narkazan's demise. But what?

He shrugged, unable to guess. And he certainly wasn't willing to make any more sacrifices to find out. Besides . . . what did he have left to sacrifice?

Suddenly, a single ray of light from the rising sun touched his tunic. Within his pocket, the crystal glowed, magnifying the light of dawn. *The start,* as Sammelvar had said so hopefully, *of a whole new day.*

Sunrise on Ho Byneri! The prophesied time had arrived. And Promi, not anyone else, possessed the Starstone.

He glanced at the mark on his chest—a flying bird, now aglow with new morning light. A feeling of triumph grew inside him, swelling like the sunrise. He allowed himself a satisfied smile. Then he turned and strode across the mist-shrouded bridge.

Time to find Atlanta, he told himself. *And to show her what I've brought back from the spirit realm.*

With a lilt in his step, he crossed the creaky planks. Prayer leaves slapped and waved their words of blessing. Vapors swirled around him, so thick he couldn't see the end of the bridge until he reached it.

Just as he stepped off the rickety structure onto solid ground, he froze.

Grukarr stood directly in front of him! And worse—the priest held a gleaming dagger to Atlanta's throat. His other hand clutched her shoulder.

"You!" exclaimed Grukarr, shaking with fury. "Still alive!"

Huntwing, perched on the priest's shoulder, screeched angrily and slashed at the air with one of his talons.

Atlanta, meanwhile, peered at Promi with such sadness it hurt his heart. Then he noticed she also looked ill—very ill. Her legs wobbled weakly, and her blue-green eyes were dull. On top of that, her skin was strikingly pale, her breathing ragged. What had happened to her?

Instinctively, he started to reach out to her. But he stopped when Grukarr pressed the dagger against her throat. "Come no closer, vagabond! And if you want her to live, do exactly as I command."

Promi locked gazes with Atlanta. "Don't do it," she said hoarsely. "Whatever he asks, don't!"

Grukarr's eyes flashed. "Silence, forest girl! Or I will kill you this instant."

Huntwing clacked his beak and glared at Promi.

"Now," ordered Grukarr, "answer me truthfully. Where is the Starstone? I'm sure that's what you were seeking in the spirit realm—and why Narkazan called back the mistwraiths."

Desperate to keep him from killing Atlanta, but unwilling to tell him the truth, Promi said, "The Starstone was lost. In the Maelstrom. It's gone forever."

Grukarr's eyes narrowed. "You lie." He pressed his blade harder against Atlanta's skin. "One last time," he growled. "Tell me where it is."

"Well . . ." Promi's mind raced. What could he possibly do? He could still hear Sammelvar's warning to keep the Starstone out of evil hands—and no one was more evil than this priest. Yet if he didn't cooperate, Atlanta would die.

"Tell me!"

Promi drew a deep breath, still unsure what to say. Atlanta watched him sorrowfully. He could tell she was silently saying good-bye.

Just then, another ray of light touched his tunic. Within his pocket, the Starstone glowed bright.

Spotting the telltale glow, Grukarr nodded. "Excellent! Your penchant for thievery has proven useful, at last."

For her part, Atlanta groaned, overwhelmed with horror that Grukarr was going to get the precious crystal after all.

"Now," said the priest, "before you hand it over to me, throw your dagger into the gorge. I've seen your throwing skills too many times to forget!" He tilted his head toward the steep cliff beside the bridge. "And do it quickly!"

Frowning, Promi pulled his shimmering blade out of the sheath. With a whip of his arm, he tossed it over the edge. The blade vanished into the vapors and clattered on the rocks. He turned away from it, hoping that, in the sparse light breaking through the mist, the priest couldn't see the slender string that still connected the knife to his wrist.

Grukarr didn't notice the string. But Huntwing did. The bird screeched and flew over to the spot where the string reached over the cliff. A sharp bite with his beak—and he severed it. The blade continued its plunge, falling into the gorge. Satisfied, the bird returned to his master's shoulder.

"Blast you, boy!" fumed Grukarr, his face almost purple with rage. "No more tricks, I warn you!" He shook Atlanta's shoulder. "Do you have any idea what I have endured? What I have sacrificed?"

Promi's glare darkened. *I could tell you something about sacrifice, you monster.*

"Give it to me," commanded the priest. "Now!"

Looking pained, Promi cleared his throat. But just as he finished, in a whisper so quiet it was almost imperceptible, he said, "One more time, Kermi."

The thump of a tail against his shoulder blade told him the message had been received. Kermi, who was clinging to his back, crawled a bit higher.

Slowly, Promi reached into his pocket and pulled out the Starstone. Its glow expanded instantly, illuminating the swirling mist and the bridge beyond.

Grukarr's eyes widened with greed. The Starstone would soon be his! And no one—not even Narkazan—would ever take it away.

Unable to resist, he took his hand off Atlanta's shoulder to reach for the magical crystal. Huntwing rustled his wings in anticipation.

Atlanta, with every bit of strength she had left, elbowed Grukarr in the ribs. The blow made him stumble and drop his dagger. As he cursed wrathfully, she collapsed, utterly spent.

At the same instant, Kermi leaped out of hiding—straight into Huntwing. He smashed into the blood falcon and grabbed hold of the bird's back. Unable to fly, Huntwing shrieked wildly and fell to the ground.

Promi, simultaneously, hurled himself at Grukarr. The priest toppled over, losing his turban. But in that tackle, Promi dropped the Starstone. Terrified he might lose the crystal over the cliff, Promi reached to grab it. Before he could, though, Grukarr knocked him aside. The pair rolled on the ground, slugging and kicking.

Meanwhile, the Starstone rolled to the very edge of the cliff and balanced there. The slightest breeze would be enough to knock it into the raging rapids below.

As Promi wrestled with Grukarr, the fight between Kermi and

Huntwing grew more vicious by the second. Their screeches and snarls filled the air. Feathers flew, as did clumps of blue fur. The blood falcon's beak snapped viciously as he tried to bite his assailant, while his talons raked at anything within reach. Kermi, meanwhile, tightened his tail around the bird's neck.

The two creatures tumbled over each other, a furious tangle of fighting. Perilously close to the canyon's edge, they teetered on top of the cliff. But Huntwing's strength proved superior, and he finally loosened Kermi's grip enough to prepare to bite through the kermuncle's tail. Just as the bird's beak was poised to snap closed, though, Kermi kicked the ground so hard they both tumbled into the gorge.

Swallowed by the vapors rising from the river, Kermi and the blood falcon disappeared.

Grukarr and Promi fought on. With surprising strength, the priest blocked many of Promi's blows and hit back brutally. The young man landed several punches, but his foe showed no sign of relenting.

Finally, Promi landed a kick that sent Grukarr sprawling backward. The priest fell with a thud—then saw, within reach, the Starstone. Eagerly, he grabbed for it, but his groping hand knocked it off its precarious perch.

Grukarr and Promi both froze. They watched, helpless, as the magical crystal teetered for an instant, then plunged over the cliff edge.

A flash of blue wings shot from Atlanta's gown and flew to the spot, disappearing into the gorge. Then, seconds later, the faery rose up again, wings whirring. Balanced in his arms, he held the crystal!

Struggling to hold so much weight, the faery evaded Grukarr's desperate swipes and flew toward Promi. With a final surge, he dropped the Starstone at the young man's feet and landed nearby.

Promi grabbed the crystal, then spun around and picked up

Grukarr's dagger. Panting heavily, bleeding from his lip, he pointed the blade at the priest and said, "Surrender now—or I'll throw this right in your eye."

Grukarr groaned, knowing he was beaten. "All right," he said, painfully rising to his feet.

Although his white robe was streaked with dirt and blood and his turban lay crushed on the ground, he glared at Promi with all the arrogance of an emperor. "Think you have beaten me, do you? Just because you have the Starstone and that knife?"

"Yes," answered Promi, hefting the glowing crystal in his hand. "Your time as ruler of this country has ended before it ever began."

Weakly, Atlanta raised her head. She traded glances with Promi and managed a slight grin before her head fell back to the turf. The faery, having regained his strength, flew to her and landed on her wrist.

"Wrong," declared Grukarr. He stood with regal bearing and snarled, "You may have defeated me in this battle today, vagabond. But it is I who will win the war!"

"How?"

"By my superior cunning!" the priest boasted. "My forces have already been unleashed—forces that will soon destroy your so-called Great Forest. The blight will spread, killing everything. And as the forest declines, so will its magic. And its ability to stop any invasion!" Grukarr beamed. "All I need to do is wait until the right moment, then command my army to smash anyone who dares to oppose my rule."

Promi froze. He'd never realized the fatal flaw in the pancharm and the resulting danger to Ellegandia.

Atlanta released a moan of anguish. And Promi knew that her pain came from more than her illness. It came, as well, from the truth of what Grukarr said.

Growing more confident with every breath, the priest intoned, "I shall yet rule over you, vagabond! And when I am emperor of this land and many others, there will be nowhere you could possibly hide the Starstone that I will not find it."

He thumped his chest. "I will rule all. Anyone who stands in my way will be completely crushed. Nothing you can do will change that!"

That statement plunged deep into Promi's heart as if it were a different kind of dagger. Grukarr was right! The forest would die, the invasion would come, and the Starstone would fall into evil hands. Everything Promi and Atlanta cared about, everything they had fought for, would be forever lost.

"Oh, yes," added Grukarr maliciously, "I should mention one more thing." He chortled, savoring this moment. "Your friend over there, lying on the ground, will soon be dead. For she doesn't have just any illness. She has *the blight*."

The instant he heard those words, Promi knew they were true. All his skill as a Listener told him so. Aghast, he glanced over at Atlanta. Never in his life had he felt so completely powerless.

Enjoying the sudden look of despair on his adversary's face, Grukarr's eyes glittered. "Poetic, isn't it? She will die from the very same plague that will also kill her beloved forest. So she will share the fate of all those trees and creatures she tried to save." The priest nodded. "And she will die very soon—in just a few more seconds, I am certain."

Promi felt ready to burst. In a flash, he knew there was only one thing left to do. And only one sacrifice big enough to have even the slightest chance to do it.

CHAPTER 47

The Last Sacrifice

Whatever we give, we gain. Even if what we gain can be enjoyed only by someone else.

—From her journal

Keeping the dagger pointed at Grukarr, Promi moved to join his fallen friend. He kneeled by Atlanta's side. Though he gazed at her intently, he still glanced frequently at the priest.

Atlanta's breathing, more shallow than ever, sounded like dead leaves rustling in a storm. Her eyes remained closed, her skin as pale as birch bark.

Promi winced. *She is going to die,* he thought desperately. *Unless . . .*

Meanwhile, the faery remained on her wrist, his antennae drooping sadly. Although his wings had fully recovered and now shone radiant blue, he looked even more dejected than when he'd first found Atlanta and Promi in the forest.

Watching with keen interest, Grukarr smirked. *Just what they deserve,* he thought vengefully. *Just what anyone who dares to get in my way deserves.*

Slowly, the priest backed away, edging toward the nearest mud-brick wall across from the dilapidated bridge. Picking a moment when Promi had turned all his attention to Atlanta, Grukarr slipped into a dark alley. He stole into the City, whistling cheerfully.

Although he glimpsed Grukarr's escape and could hear the priest's whistling through the mist, Promi hardly cared. All that mattered now was Atlanta—the young woman who had become someone very special. Who had helped him learn to care for more than his own survival. Who was now about to die.

Looking down at her, he thought, *There is only one way to save you, Atlanta. And only one sacrifice I can make that might be enough.*

He swallowed. *Please forgive me. But . . . I love you that much.*

As if, on some level, she understood what he was going to do, Atlanta moaned painfully.

The faery, too, seemed to understand. He turned toward Promi and shook his head—so hard that his tiny cotton hat, already askew, almost fell off.

I must try, little fellow. Promi clenched his jaw, knowing this was his only chance to save her. And maybe also to stop the blight and end Grukarr's invasion. *It might not work . . . but I have to try.*

Squeezing the Starstone in his hand, he closed his eyes. Then, for the last time, he spoke the chant of a Listener.

"Listen . . ."

Atlanta's whole body shuddered, and she moaned again.

"One . . ."

Promi turned his thoughts toward the enchanted forest that

was Atlanta's home, so rich with life and magical creatures of every kind. And to the marvelous land of Ellegandia, unlike any other place on Earth, a land of wonder and promise and mystery.

"Listen . . ."

Holding tight to the crystal, he stretched his senses to the farthest reaches of the realm. He heard the truest voices of creatures who ran and climbed and hopped and flew. He heard the deepest stirring of the sea, and the songs of whales bigger than islands who peacefully nursed their young. And he heard the endless sweep of the wind, touching trees and stones and brooks all around the world.

With every fiber of his being, Promi called to those sources of magic, summoning their strength to himself. Within his hand, the Starstone glowed brighter and brighter, magnifying all that power.

He concentrated on his deepest desire—to save Atlanta and the world they loved. The value of all that could be saved thrilled him, but at the same time, the knowledge of what he was about to lose broke his heart.

Quietly, he said the final word of the chant.

"All."

The sound of a fierce gust of wind raced across the canyon. It carried the voices of creatures from everywhere, creatures who had heard his call and answered. Together, they joined in a single, sustained roar of magic.

None of the surrounding mist moved, as would have happened with a normal wind. Instead, the mist started to sparkle, shimmering like millions upon millions of rainbows. A brilliant flash of light suddenly burst from the Starstone.

Promi collapsed to the ground. All the magical light faded away . . . along with his life.

CHAPTER 48

The Last True Home

Where do miracles reside? In the places where they appear . . . or in the minds where they are conceived?

—From her journal

Far away from the unfinished bridge at the canyon, in a grove deep in the Great Forest, a withered elm tree quivered. One by one, its shriveled leaves began to tremble. Slowly, they filled with green color that flowed through their veins and across their surfaces, all the way to their outermost edges. The tree straightened, drawing sunlight from above and nutrients from below. For the first time since the blight had struck, it stood healthy and strong.

All around the forest, trees revived. In the dense groves around Moss Island, the ancient stands near the Lakes of Dreams, and the glades below Highmage Hill, trees of all kinds shook off any remnants of disease. And as their strength and color returned, so did the many creatures who had lived in their branches and trunks and roots. Like the trees, those creatures swiftly regained their health.

Even at the forest's easternmost edge, right at the border of the swamp, trees stood straight and tall again. All across the swamp itself, the shells of snails suddenly lost their lavender glow. And at Grukarr's lair, the thick plume of smoke disappeared, along with all the cauldrons where poison had been brewed.

The blight was over.

At the half-finished bridge, Atlanta drew a sharp breath. Feeling stronger, she sat up, astonished by her miraculous recovery. She felt the joyful whirring of the faery's wings on her wrist, but when she turned to look at him, something else caught her attention.

Promi. He lay on the ground beside her, utterly still. The Starstone, glittering subtly, rested in his open hand.

She shrieked and shook him hard. No breath. No sound. No life.

Realizing what he must have done, and what he had sacrificed to save her, she stared at him blankly. She felt numb in a different way from the blight—unable to cry or speak. All she could do was stare at his lifeless body.

Suddenly the ground beneath her shook. Though it was a single tremor that ended immediately, it rattled the gorge, sending rocks tumbling over the edge into the rapids below. In the City, just beyond the nearest wall, a tile broke off someone's roof and clattered on the cobblestones.

The faery, startled, flew up to Atlanta's shoulder and landed on her collar. Gently, he leaned against the skin of her neck. Comforted by his closeness, she reached up and stroked the edge of his wing. Yet she kept her gaze on Promi's motionless form.

Another tremor shook the ground. Stronger than before, this

one cracked several mud-brick walls. Somewhere nearby, a roof collapsed and people screamed for help.

Atlanta looked over her shoulder at the dilapidated bridge. She wouldn't have been surprised if that tremor had been enough to make the whole bridge collapse and tumble into the gorge. But amazingly, the frail-looking structure wasn't even swaying. It stood there, completely undisturbed—as if it was somehow supported by invisible beams anchored in another realm.

Then came another tremor, even stronger. And another after that. Walls toppled, villagers shrieked as their homes crashed down, and the old blue cedar by the bridge rocked with the shaking ground.

But the bridge itself still didn't sway.

In the City, the marketplace erupted in chaos. Carts overturned, animals broke free and stampeded, and people scattered in all directions. Posts holding lines of prayer leaves collapsed, entangling people trying to flee.

"Earthquake!" many shouted.

"The world is ending!"

"Save us, Great Powers!"

Within the Divine Monk's temple, walls crumbled, columns fell, and windows shattered. Roofs collapsed, showering monks and priestesses with broken tiles. Three monks debating on a balcony tumbled to the street, continuing their argument as they fell.

The great bell tower Promi had climbed to escape the temple guard suddenly buckled. It swayed precariously, then fell into a courtyard, smashing gates and arches and an immense prayer drum. The copper dome splintered, and the huge bell crashed to the ground with a deafening *bonnnggg*.

Meanwhile, the Divine Monk, who had been kneeling on his favorite leopard-skin carpet to offer thanks for his breakfast, fell flat on his face. His attending monks screamed in panic and tossed incense everywhere, hoping to dispel the evil forces. But they succeeded only in covering the Divine Monk with powder. So much stuck to his face, which was perspiring even more than usual, that it looked like a lumpy gray mask. Furious, he took a breath to curse the monks—but inhaled the powder and started sneezing uncontrollably.

At the unfinished bridge by the gorge, meanwhile, Atlanta felt the growing power of the tremors. She guessed that all this, too, was the result of Promi's sacrifice. But she couldn't fathom why.

Peering sadly at his body, she wondered what he had hoped to accomplish. Destroy the temple? The City? No, that made no sense. Why would he want to do that?

The army, she realized. *Grukarr's army of invaders!*

Another thought struck her as more tremors rocked the ground beneath her. Maybe he also wanted to destroy the Passage of Death! Without that tunnel, no future army could enter the country. So even if Grukarr or someone else found a new way to stop the pancharm, no invasion could happen. Ellegandia would be safe from outside forces.

But Promi, she thought grimly, *you will never know what you achieved.*

As good as Atlanta's guesses were, however, they caught only part of Promi's goal. Her guesses were bold, to be sure. But his true aspirations had been even bolder.

The epicenter of all the quakes was at the high peaks that bordered Africa, at the very base of the mountain Ell Shangro. Those quakes struck with such force that the tremors shaking the City, far away, were mild by comparison. When the first quake erupted, entire mountain ridges broke apart. Cliffs sheared off, landslides smashed into the valleys below, and the Passage of Death collapsed completely.

Buried under layers of rubble, most of Grukarr's army perished instantly. Those who survived were swallowed by crevasses that opened beneath their feet. Grukarr's lair crumbled and plunged into the deepest crevasse of all.

It was exactly at that moment that, in the City, Grukarr entered the temple's central courtyard. Returning to the place that had become the seat of his power, the place where he had nursed his highest ambitions and developed his greatest plans, he felt a surge of confidence. He would overcome these difficulties just as he'd overcome so many before. He always prevailed in the end.

Brushing some of the soil off his robe, he puffed out his chest regally and strode into the central courtyard. *You,* he told himself, *were born to rule.*

Just then, the first tremors began. Feeling them rock the courtyard, he sat down on the low stone wall that surrounded the temple's well, waiting for them to pass. But they didn't pass. They only grew more severe, shaking the buildings all around him.

This is odd, he thought. *We never have earthquakes in this country.*

He felt a burst of fear. This trouble was caused by his enemies! By that cursed young vagabond and his allies in the spirit realm! But why?

A column supporting a temple balcony collapsed, crashing to the courtyard in an explosion of wood and plaster, crushing several people. Amidst their screams, Grukarr understood. *My army! They want to destroy it—and all my plans!*

He jumped up. Right then, the worst tremor yet struck the temple. Its force knocked the priest off his feet. He pitched over backward, tripped on the wall, and plunged headlong into the well.

Grukarr shrieked. Then, just as abruptly as it had started, his shrieking stopped.

Meanwhile, at the high peaks, the quakes that had destroyed Grukarr's army worsened. Even as those quakes rocked the mountains, powerful storms burst in the sky. Torrential rains fell, pounding the slopes, swelling the country's rivers to their brims and beyond. Before long, those rivers grew into unstoppable blasts of water that tore through canyons, sending up towering clouds of vapor.

On the rugged coasts that bordered three sides of Ellegandia, ocean storms raged with force never known before. Howling winds hurled great waves against the walls of cliffs. Spray shot into the air—so high that, all around the country, rainbows formed, glowing bright as they twined themselves across the sky.

None of this, though, compared with the power of the forces that continued to ravage the high peaks. Whole mountains shifted, lifting upward as their snowy cornices collapsed. Ridges exploded, leaving ever deeper crevasses. Meanwhile, the summit of Ell Shangro spewed smoke and ash.

Ell Shangro quaked violently, down to its roots, ripping apart bedrock that lay unfathomably deep. Suddenly—the whole mountain erupted. Lava blasted from its smoking summit, flowing over the ridges. Molten rivers cut channels that blazed with superheated fire and incinerated anything in their paths. Simultaneously, the Earth itself ruptured, opening a rift that sliced through the volcano and all its neighboring peaks.

Then came the greatest miracle of all.

In a single, violent heave, the entire peninsula of Ellegandia broke off from the rest of the continent. Thunderous explosions echoed everywhere as the lands separated. Then, with astonishing swiftness, the whole country moved out to sea, urged on by gale-force winds that blew with their greatest strength. Like a gigantic boat, it sailed across the watery expanse.

At last, the winds lessened and the waves quieted. Ellegandia came to rest in the middle of the ocean, far beyond the reach of any attackers. At the same time, undersea mountains surged up from the ocean floor, connecting with the country and supporting it firmly.

Seabirds of all kinds wheeled overhead, screeching and whistling in celebration. All around the shores, dolphins leaped joyously, fish swam through the sparkling waters, and whales sang with their deepest harmonies.

For all of them understood that, in this miraculous moment, a new island had been born. Just as Haldor the centaur had foretold that night in the forest. And maybe they understood, as well, that this island was also something more: the last true home of magic on Earth.

The place where nature, in all its richness and glory, could thrive freely.

The place whose people could live in peace with themselves and all their fellow creatures.

The place that Promi had died to save.

Certainly, this new island wasn't perfect. It still held people as wicked as Grukarr. People whose capacity for arrogance and greed, ignorance, and fear could still overwhelm the rest. People who could be taught to hate someone else for following a different spiritual path, or to devour the very wonders that sustained them.

And so, perhaps, this place held the seeds of its own destruction—the possibility that it could someday perish in a terrible cataclysm.

Yet for now, this newly born island was at peace. All alone, radiantly beautiful, it graced the surrounding seas. Much of what it held was a mystery, even to its own inhabitants. And what it might inspire for the future, for unwritten stories and songs, no one could say.

For this was an island of unmatched enchantment.

CHAPTER 49

The End of All Magic

No one, in all the history of the realms, has ever looked more surprised.

—From her journal

At the instant of the new island's birth, just when all the winds and tremors ceased, a much quieter miracle occurred. Promi opened his eyes.

Although he couldn't see much through the clouds of mist that swirled around him, he knew he was alive. Not just because he was breathing the misty air, hearing the rapids that thundered through the gorge, and feeling the thump of his own heartbeat. No, what really convinced him that he was alive was the sight of someone sitting beside him—someone whose face he knew well.

"Atlanta!"

Hesitantly, she nodded, not sure this could

really be true. Then, in a burst of belief, she jumped on him and hugged him hard. He hugged her back, rolling with her on the ground.

For a timeless moment, they laughed and hugged and rolled, then laughed some more. Above them, the faery spun delighted loops in the air, his translucent cloak fluttering behind, his antennae waving jubilantly.

When, at last, the celebration stopped, Atlanta and Promi sat there on the turf, breathless. Suddenly, he noticed the Starstone resting beside them. Drawn by the subtle glow of its facets, he reached to pick it up.

As soon as he closed his hand around the crystal, though, he noticed something new. His skin color had changed! It had a misty, almost silvery sheen. Like the people he'd seen in the spirit realm.

Peering closely at his hand, he tried to understand. Was this just a trick of the morning light shining through the swirling vapors? But no—it looked so real! Atlanta, too, had noticed, and was staring at him, puzzled.

All at once, he realized the truth. "Am I . . . immortal?"

Atlanta shook her head, jostling her curls. "That's not possible."

"Oh, yes it is."

Both of them looked up to see who had spoken. Striding toward them from the mist near the unfinished bridge, a young woman approached. Promi recognized her right away from the turquoise band across her eyes. The Seer!

She wore the same robe he'd seen before, decorated with a squiggly blue line that reminded him of Kermi's tail. Fearing the kermuncle had perished fighting Huntwing, Promi felt a sharp pang that told him, to his own surprise, that he would actually miss the grumpy little fellow who had joined him on so many adventures.

Watching the Seer approach, Promi muttered in disbelief, "It's really her!"

Atlanta nudged him. "You know her?"

"Yes," he replied, as both he and Atlanta bounced to their feet to greet this unexpected visitor. "We met before. In the spirit realm."

Atlanta's eyes widened. "You'll have to fill me in on your travels."

He grinned. "Only if you'll do the same."

"You have a deal," she replied.

Mist curled around the Seer's neck and arms as she joined them. Her face aglow with silver light, she said, "It's against our laws for immortals to come here." She paused, almost blushing, then added, "Although it's been done before." Standing before them, she explained, "This time, Sammelvar and Escholia gave me permission. So I could greet you, Promi, when you awoke." A slight smile touched her face. "You probably have a few questions."

"A few," he replied, glancing down at his silver-skinned hand that held the Starstone.

The young woman from the spirit realm seemed to look right at him, undeterred by the band over her eyes. "You accomplished everything you wanted, Promi. The blight is ended, and your friend here is revived."

Atlanta glanced at him gratefully. Who could have guessed that this young man—whom she'd met just two weeks ago over a lemon pie—would come to mean so much to her world . . . and to her? Sharing her gratitude, the faery, who had settled again on her shoulder, whirred his radiant blue wings.

"You did even more," the spirit continued. "The army of invaders is destroyed, as is their tunnel. And best of all . . . this enchanted country will never be invaded over land again." She leaned closer. "Because this country is now an island, far out to sea."

Atlanta gasped in surprise.

Promi beamed. "I was hoping for that, but wasn't sure it could happen."

"With good reason," said the spirit. "Never before has a Listener been able to call upon so much of nature's power, and to turn that power into action."

"Well," said Promi modestly, "I had this to help." He held up the Starstone, which pulsed with light.

"You did. But you also had something else. Your own unique ability."

"She's right," Atlanta chimed in. "You are unique." She squeezed Promi's hand. "For a pie thief, that is."

He chuckled, then shook his head in amazement. "Can you believe it? An island!"

Atlanta blew a long breath. "Just as Haldor predicted that night."

"That old centaur got it right," said Promi. "And he also deserves credit for giving me the idea. Even though, in his dour way, he also predicted the island would someday be destroyed."

"Let's hope," replied Atlanta, "he's only right about the first part."

"Yes," he agreed. "Creation is much more fun than destruction."

Atlanta nodded. "I'll say."

Turning back to the young woman whose silvery skin was so much like his own, Promi said, "But . . . immortal? Me? How is that—well, er, even . . . well, *possible*?"

"Harrumph," said a cranky voice in the mist by the Seer's feet. "I see you're just as articulate as ever."

"Kermi!" cried both Atlanta and Promi at once.

The furry little creature blew a stream of bubbles that rose, wobbling, toward the sky. Then, blinking his round blue eyes at Promi, he said dryly, "Didn't think I'd miss a chance to make you miserable, did you?"

The young man smiled. "No. Certainly not."

Kermi's whiskers twitched. "Oh, and manfool. I found something you dropped."

Lifting his long tail, the kermuncle produced a gleaming blade. "Yours, I believe."

"My dagger!" Promi reached for it. At the instant his hand touched the hilt, the silver string reached out and wrapped around his wrist, squeezing like the embrace of an old friend. Gratefully, he admired its translucent blade that shimmered like an icicle. As he replaced it in the sheath on his belt, the silver string released its hold. "Thanks, Kermi."

"Well, I figured you need all the help you can get." His oversized ears drooped. "Which is why Jaladay made me promise to stay with you in the first place."

Hearing her name again, Promi thought about Jaladay and her mysterious ways. Her face that seemed to waver between young and old. Her willingness to entrust him with Listener magic. And, above all, her luminous green eyes that glowed like a forest in the light of dawn.

Turning again to the spirit, he asked, "Up there on the cloud, when you spoke to me, you could tell I'm a Listener. Right?"

"That's right."

"How?"

She tapped the turquoise band covering her eyes. "If I shield myself from the distractions of normal sight, I can see in another way. A deeper, truer way."

"You can see the unseen."

"Yes, just as you can hear the unheard."

Something about the way she said that phrase made him catch his breath. Peering at her, he said, "You have a name you haven't told us, don't you?"

The corner of her mouth lifted slightly. "Listen closely. Maybe you can hear it."

He nodded, listening hard, feeling the truth of her identity. "You are . . . Jaladay!"

"Yes." She pulled off the turquoise band, revealing her luminous, deep green eyes.

Puzzled, Atlanta looked at them both. "What haven't you told me?"

"That we met even before the spirit realm," answered Promi. "Just briefly—in the dungeon."

"That's where you're wrong," announced Jaladay. Gazing intently at Promi, she declared, "We have known each other all our lives."

His brow furrowed. "But how? And, well . . . er . . . *how*?"

"So eloquent," observed Kermi. He bounded up Jaladay's leg and perched comfortably on her shoulder. "Some things never change."

Jaladay glanced at the sassy little fellow. "Shall I tell him?"

"Harrumph. Might as well. Though he probably won't understand."

"We have two big things in common," Jaladay explained. "One is we both like to keep a journal." She patted a pocket in her robe. "And the other is . . . we both have the same parents."

His jaw dropped. "You're my *sister*?"

"I warned you," said Kermi grumpily. He blew a big, lopsided bubble that popped on Promi's chin.

"Yes, Promi. We are brother and sister."

The young man turned to Atlanta. "This is even more bizarre than I thought."

"Bizarre is the word," she replied.

"Like me," Jaladay continued, "you were born in the spirit realm."

"Which is why," he realized, "I didn't die from that sacrifice."

"That's right. Your physical, mortal form died, Promi. But you have always been an immortal. So that death returned you to your true life."

He winced. "Try that again. But don't speak like a Seer, all right? Speak to me as you would to—"

"Your idiot brother," finished Kermi.

"All right," Jaladay agreed. "When you were born, Promi, our parents—"

"Wait!" he interrupted, grabbing her arm. "*Our parents.* That means . . . I met them! Sammelvar and Escholia." Biting his lip, he remembered Sammelvar's genuine faith in him, as well as the kindness in Escholia's eyes. And the surprising familiarity of her touch. "That's why they seemed to know me so well."

"Right." Jaladay's green eyes studied him. "But when you were very young, the Prophecy was revealed—first by Famalel, the wind lion, and then by others throughout the spirit world. So our parents were forced to make a choice. The Prophecy was crystal clear, you see, that only one person could possibly restore harmony between the mortal and spirit realms . . . and ensure the free, independent magic of each. And that one person bore a strange mark that nobody could miss."

Instinctively, Promi touched the skin over his heart. He imagined, beneath his fingers, the bird beating its mighty wings.

Jaladay looked at him—or, it seemed, looked *through* him, as if he were no more substantial than the swirling mist from the gorge. "This person, as you can guess, instantly became the archenemy of Narkazan and all who served him. The warlord placed a huge bounty on the prophesied person's head. On *your* head, Promi."

"So they disguised me," he reasoned, "as a mortal. And sent me away to Earth."

"It was the only way to protect you. To give you a chance to live long enough to make whatever choices might affect both worlds." She frowned. "As part of that magical disguise, they needed to erase all your memories of life in the spirit realm. Including your family."

Reaching out to his torn tunic, she touched the skin of his chest. "The only thing no magic was strong enough to disguise was this mark."

Promi traded glances with Atlanta. "For the longest time, when I was small, I thought it was mud or paint or something. I tried to wash it off whenever I bathed in a stream or a fountain."

Kermi erupted with a loud snort. "You actually bathe?"

Promi rolled his eyes. "Wish I could stuff you into my boot again."

With both paws, the kermuncle held his nose. "No, please!"

Atlanta and Jaladay both chuckled.

"When my skill as a Seer told me you'd been thrown into that horrible dungeon," Jaladay confessed, "I couldn't stand the separation any longer. So I decided to look in on you myself." She shot a guilty glance at Kermi. "Yes, yes, I know. That was bending the rules a bit."

The kermuncle shook his head. "More like crashing through the rules, ripping them to shreds, and burning the evidence."

"In any case," she said, turning back to Promi, "I arrived just when you bravely tried to help that poor old woman, to save her from the guard."

Watching him, Atlanta's expression turned to something like admiration.

"Now I see what happened!" Promi slapped his thigh. "That old woman really *did* die. I couldn't save her. And when she did—"

"I entered her body," finished his sister. "It was me you met there, though I had all her physical traits."

He nodded. "Except for your eyes."

She gazed at him affectionately. "Because spirits don't belong in the mortal realm, I could only stay long enough to give you Listener magic."

Promi caught his breath. "Now that I'm no longer mortal, all those sacrifices I made as a Listener—"

"Are ended," she finished. "Which means, Promi, you can eat sweets again."

"Whoo-hoo!" he shouted as the others laughed. "So . . . pastries? Pies? Anything?"

"Anything. As much as you want."

"You'll probably need some practice," Atlanta teased him. "Just to get your eating skills back."

"Right," he agreed with a smack of his lips.

"Of course," Jaladay went on, "the physical things you gave up you'll have to replace." She winked. "Starting with a journal."

"And boots," added Atlanta.

"Maybe not," said Promi, wiggling his toes. "I'm getting used to going barefoot like you."

With a grin, she replied, "What a long way you've come."

"Not long enough," groused Kermi, "to give him any sense."

"That would be asking too much," joshed Promi.

"Harrumph. I'll say."

Suddenly Promi realized something else—this time, about Kermi. Focusing his gaze on the acerbic little fellow, he said, "You're an immortal too! Isn't that right?"

"Took you long enough, manfool."

"That's how you recognized Shirozzz down in his cavern. And why you hid so often." He squinted at the kermuncle. "So why, after we got to the spirit realm, didn't you tell me?"

The blue eyes glittered. "Much more fun to keep you clueless and watch you struggle."

By now, Promi's mind was spinning from all these revelations. *I'm an immortal. She's my sister . . . as well as Jaladay. Who also keeps a journal. Kermi, too, comes from the spirit realm. And oh, by the way—my parents live on a cloud.*

He looked at Jaladay. "This is a lot to absorb."

"It is," she agreed.

"But now," he pressed, "there's one more thing I'd like to understand. It's been bothering me for some time."

"And that is?"

"The meaning of those lines from the Prophecy. First . . . *the end of all magic*. And also . . . *the ultimate end*. What are they really about?"

"What do you think?" asked Jaladay.

He shook his head. "The meaning isn't what I thought, anyway. *The end of all magic* isn't about a person—Narkazan, Sammelvar, or anyone else. And it's not about magic disappearing or being used for evil. No, whatever those words mean, it's something bigger than all that."

"You're on the right track," said Jaladay.

"You're completely hopeless," said Kermi.

"Think about the words," she suggested. "The end . . . of all . . . magic."

Promi closed his eyes, concentrating. In the quietest part of his mind, he Listened. *The end . . . the end . . . the end*. Words echoed in his thoughts; meanings shifted like the wispy clouds of the spirit realm.

He started, understanding at last. Opening his eyes, he said excitedly, "*The end*—that doesn't mean the stop or the finish. No, no! It means *the purpose*. The purpose of all magic!"

Jaladay's green eyes sparkled. "Yes, Promi. The highest purpose. The greatest use. The truest end."

Leaning closer, she asked, "And what do you think is that highest purpose of magic?"

"Love." He felt sure that was right. "The kind of love that's bigger than any one person, the kind you give with all your mind and heart. Love of your friends, your home, your world."

Beaming, she nodded. "So that is the highest purpose—the ultimate end—of magic. And Promi . . . that's exactly what you gave!"

He blinked. “Really? All I did was—”

“You sacrificed your mortal life, the only life you knew, to save your world and the people you love.”

He glanced shyly at Atlanta. “Well . . . I suppose so.”

“And only by sacrificing so much—with the Starstone to magnify your power—could you summon all the magic you needed.” Jaladay studied him, seeing the unseen. “That is why, my brother, what you did is the end of all magic.”

CHAPTER 50

A Quiggleypottle

No way I would have guessed.

—From her journal

The mists swirling around the edge of the canyon began to clear. As the morning sun rose higher, all but the thickest vapors started to shred and melt away. Meanwhile, the onslaught of avalanches that accompanied the new island's break from the mainland had ended, and the rapids returned to their normal levels. The Deg Boesi pounded through its gorge, but no longer with the crashing force of floodwaters.

Now that their surroundings were more visible, Promi looked in amazement at the collapsed walls of the City. He could see smoke rising from the central marketplace. Beyond that, he spied a fallen roof in the Divine

Monk's temple, along with a gap where the great bell tower had stood.

He swallowed. *I did that?*

Turning toward Jaladay, he saw that she was looking wistfully at the Bridge to Nowhere—which now, he knew well, was poorly named. It was, indeed, a bridge to an astonishingly rich and complex world. Staring into the mists that gathered along the broken beams and strings of fluttering prayer leaves, he knew that somewhere out there, beyond what he could see, Theosor was flying with magical wings.

Jaladay gazed at him. Softly, she said, "You did well, brother."

"For a complete imbecile, that is," added Kermi. He curled himself around Jaladay's neck, his long tail hanging down to her elbow.

"Now, now," she scolded. "He did everything we'd hoped, and more."

"Harrumph. With my help, of course."

Playfully, she tugged his tail. "Of course."

Promi wasn't listening. He'd already turned his attention to Atlanta. She was gazing up into the arching branches of the great blue cedar that grew by the canyon's edge. It had, somehow, survived all the tremors. Amidst its dense web of branches, starlike clusters of blue needles oozed resin, spicing the air with a scent both sweet and tart.

It didn't take a Listener to guess what she was thinking. Moving closer, he touched her arm. Gently, he said, "You miss the forest, don't you?"

Without turning from the cedar, she nodded. "I'm so glad that place still lives."

"Here," he said, holding out the Starstone. Its facets radiated light, sending rays between his fingers. "Take this."

Surprised, she peered at him. "For me?"

"For the forest." He placed it in her hand. "But you, of all people, will know the best place to put it."

Squeezing the luminous crystal, she said, "Moss Island. That's the perfect place." Then, a sparkle in her eyes, she asked, "Want to help me bring it there?"

"Was that an invitation?"

"No," she replied. Leaning into him, she gave him a kiss on the lips. As she pulled away, she said, "But that was."

Promi felt almost as if he were flying again, but with no wind lion beneath him. "Well, then . . . I accept."

Atlanta smiled at him. "Good."

Brushing some clumps of mud off her gown of woven vines, she said, "I still can't believe what's happened. No matter how often I think about it, I'm still amazed."

Kermi shook his head. "Don't be too amazed, young woman. After all . . . you do have a quiggleypottle."

Atlanta, Promi, and Jaladay all stared at him, equally confused. "A what?" they asked in unison.

"Do I have to teach you people *everything*?"

"No," answered Jaladay. "Just that. Come on, tell us. What is a quiggleypottle?"

The little fellow sighed. "Are you sure you want to know?"

"Yes!" answered Promi, exasperated.

"Please," begged Atlanta. "Tell us."

Reluctantly, the kermuncle said, "Oh, all right."

He arranged himself comfortably on Jaladay, swinging his tail over the matching design on her robe. "A quiggleypottle, Atlanta, is what you have right now on your shoulder."

She caught her breath. "You mean—"

The faery whirred his wings, brushing the side of her neck ever so gently.

"That's right," said Kermi. "Faeries, as you should know, are almost never found alone. They love to stay together with their colonies in the glens. But on rare occasions . . ." He paused to watch her with his round eyes. "Nothing in the world—in *any* world, actually—is as lucky as a lone faery. Especially one who travels with you as a companion." With a nod, he declared, "And that, my dear, is a quiggleypottle."

Astonished, Atlanta reached up so the faery could hop onto her finger. Bringing him to her face, she gazed in awe at his luminous blue wings, now fully healed. And at his antennae, which stood straight and strong. Though his cotton hat was still askew and he was still missing one of his shoes, he had clearly returned to health.

Studying his minuscule face, she said, "Thank you, little friend. You kept me alive, I'm sure of that."

The faery shrugged his shoulders shyly.

A delightful thought struck Atlanta. "I have a name for you! Something fitting. I'm going to name you Quiggley."

The faery fluttered his wings in approval, and she felt a rush of affection.

Suddenly she frowned. "Now that you're healed . . . I suppose you will want to rejoin your people?"

Sadly, he nodded.

She sighed, then said, "I'll miss you, Quiggley! But I really loved our time together."

He nodded again, more slowly this time.

"So, little friend, you're free to go."

The faery's antennae quivered, and his wings glowed brighter. Then he leaped into the air and started to fly away.

Atlanta and the others watched him depart, his luminous blue wings melting into the mist by the bridge. Then, inexplicably, he turned around. He fluttered back to Atlanta and settled himself on the rim of her pocket.

Looking up at her, he vibrated his antennae vigorously.

"He says," translated Jaladay, "that he wants to return to the

Great Forest. But since his friends are now gone . . . he wonders if *you* would like to be his new best friend."

Delighted, Atlanta grinned at her small companion. "I would love that, Quiggley."

The faery's wings shimmered with light. Then he hopped up to the collar of her purple gown and perched there.

Promi cleared his throat. "Er, Atlanta . . ."

"Yes?"

"When do we leave?"

"Right now," she replied, her smile broadening. "That is . . . if you can keep up."

CHAPTER 51

Things Won, Things Lost

That was when you discovered, Promi, that a heart, unlike a bowl, can be both empty and full at the same time.

—From her journal

Delighted about returning to the forest with Atlanta, Promi drew a deep breath. *So much to do together,* he thought gladly.

He turned to say good-bye to Jaladay—but seeing her, bit his lip. For her expression looked truly somber.

"Brother," she said gently, "you no longer belong in this world."

Her words crashed over his mind like a tidal wave, drowning his hopes. "But—but I . . ."

"Your home, like mine, is in the spirit realm." She gazed at him and through him, her face full of compassion. "You know I'm speaking the truth."

He bristled unhappily. "Well, maybe I do. But it's not fair! It means I saved this world . . . only to lose it."

"No," said Jaladay. Wisps of mist wove through her hair like ribbons. "You really *did* save this world. But, Promi . . . you saved it for others, not for yourself."

Still not willing to agree, he countered, "Can't I just stay? You could make an exception to the rule that keeps immortals from living here."

"Right," chimed in Atlanta. "Like the river god."

Jaladay shook her head. "The river god, like the other immortals in the forest, came long ago, before the great war. No more immortals can stay here." She glanced at the mist rising from the canyon, then added, "Though it is a beautiful place."

Glumly, Promi heaved a sigh. Facing Atlanta, he said, "I guess . . . she's right. But I sure wish it wasn't so."

Atlanta peered at him, dejected. "Is there any other way?"

He didn't answer. Nor did he move, except to twist one of his bare feet into the ground.

"Aw, come on," said Kermi, thumping his tail against Jaladay's shoulder. "Let's just break the law. Why not? Leave him here! Then you and I can go back without him."

She frowned at him. He frowned right back, baring his tiny teeth.

Atlanta, meanwhile, moved closer to Promi. She touched his hand. "Do you think maybe," she asked quietly, "you could still come here to visit sometimes?"

He looked at her, this young woman who had become someone special in his life. And who might, just possibly, have become something more.

"Absolutely," he replied, blinking the mist from his eyes. "Whatever the law says, I need to come back to this realm." He nearly grinned. "Just to have a taste, now and then, of lemon pie."

Atlanta nodded as a tear slid down her cheek. "You can meet some, well, special people over lemon pie."

"That I know," he replied. "Before I go, though . . ." He paused, searching for the right words. "Would you do me a small, um, favor?"

"Sure. What is it?"

"Allow me to choose the name of this new island."

"What?" Disappointed, she asked, "Is that all you can think of at a time like this? A name for the island?"

He looked down at his feet. "It's . . . important."

She shrugged, causing the faery on her collar to flutter his wings. "If you say so."

Promi gazed into her eyes and declared, "I hereby name this place for *you*. From now until the end of time, this magical isle will be known as . . . *Atlantis*."

Jaladay nodded in approval. "A good name."

"Harrumph," griped Kermi. "It will never last."

For her part, Atlanta blushed. She squeezed Promi's hand and whispered, "You really *are* special, you know. And Promi . . . I bless your eternal qualities."

He lingered for another few seconds, watching her. Then he turned away.

Viewing the rickety bridge that hung over the gorge, he watched the mist, noticing how it spiraled so gracefully, how it caressed each and every prayer leaf. He cocked his head, waiting for something. At last, he heard a familiar sound—the distant roar of a lion.

Then, to his delight, he heard something else, a haunting melody that he'd thought he would never hear again. It sounded fresher than ever, as if someone was singing it just for him.

"Come," he said to Jaladay. "Let's go."

She grinned. "There are some people who are waiting to greet you."

Brightening a little, he added, “And there’s also a river of honey somewhere out there I’d like to visit.”

“Let’s go, then. As fast as the wind.”

As he viewed the bridge, Promi saw shafts of morning light pierce the rising mist. And he knew that, for the very first time, day had dawned on the newest island in the sea.

THE MAGICAL ISLE of

Atlantis

LAND of LOST DREAMS,
HOME of CREATURES MOST BIZARRE
& PORTAL to the SPIRIT REALM

Sheer cliffs

Beware the Smelldrude

Beware the crocodiles

MYSTERY BAY

C.o.a.s.t of D.r.a.g.o.n.s

INDRAGRASS MEADOWS

Ancient spirits walk these hills

Vale of Surprises

CITY of GREAT POWERS
(Excellent pastries found here)
Deadly Rapids
Bridge to Nowhere
Wind Horses?
Divine Monk's Temple
Rumors tell of Secret Entrance to Ekh Raku Dungeon
THE GREAT FOREST
Faerie Glens
DEG BOESI RIVER
Waterfall of the Giants
Pathways of Mystery
Moss Island (Home of Mist Maidens)
Woods of Endless Wonders
Highmage Hill
Enchanted Baobab Grove
Lakes of the Stars
(Here light and dark are one)
Wyverns' Lairs
TAB ~ 2012

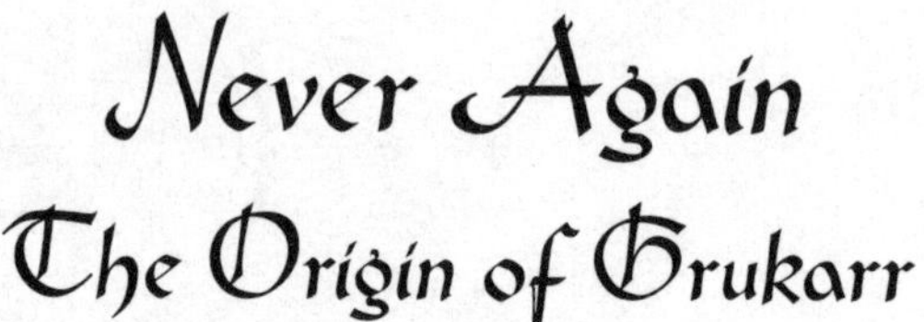

Hello, Readers,

Many of you have wondered about the origins of Grukarr—the ruthless, brutal, power-hungry priest who tries to destroy Promi and Atlanta (and anyone else he can't control) in my novel *Atlantis Rising.*

As the magical isle of Atlantis is finally born, both as a place on the map and a legend in the heart, Grukarr's life seems to end. Not at all prettily. But not so fast! There may still be more of his story to come—as you'll see in the coming books of the Atlantis trilogy.

So for all those who wish to know the secret of Grukarr's origins, here it is. But in this case, alas . . . be careful what you wish for.

—T. A. B.

Copyright © 2014 by Thomas A. Barron

Even as a baby, he loved blueberries.

He loved them fat and round—thoroughly plump. Which pretty much described him at that age, too. He was so plump, in fact, that his crawling looked more like rolling. And when he finally started to walk, it was really a waddle.

Fortunately, Grukarr's mother (who was rather plump herself) enjoyed taking him along as she gathered herbs, roots, bark, and berries for her healing concoctions. Placing him securely on her hip, she hauled him—along with her sack loaded with ceramic jars, assorted tools, a leaf press, and several sizes of knives—out to gather whatever ingredients she needed.

They didn't have far to go. The simple hut they called home sat at the edge of the Great Forest, nearly a day's walk outside the walls of the City of Great Powers (the not-so-humble name recently chosen by the Divine Monk for the town dominated by his temple). Since most of Ellegandia's natural magic could be found in that forest, finding the ingredients for herbal remedies wasn't difficult. Knowing which plant or extract or substance was useful for what ailments—that was the tricky part.

Grukarr's earliest memory came from one of those journeys into the forest with his mother. Though he was only three or four years old at the time, that day never faded in his mind.

"Here you go, my Gru." She placed him on the golden grass of a meadow and tousled his curls. "See if you can find some berries while I fetch silver moss from the stream."

His eyes glowed like candles. "Blue ones, Ma?"

"That's right." Her ruddy cheeks creased in a grin, and she tossed him a wooden bowl from her sack. "Just try to save a few for the bowl, my love."

"Well . . . I'll try."

As she knelt beside the stream, trying to keep her apron out of the water, he turned to the trees bordering the meadow. Though he didn't know any of them by name, he recognized their varied shapes—the tall one with long needles that swished with every breeze, the twisted old one whose branches held round fruit that birds with orange and blue wings loved to eat, the graceful one whose long boughs shaded the stream. Then, lowering his gaze, he spied a familiar patch of blueberry bushes.

Licking his lips, he waddled over. The ripe berries practically fell into his hands as he plucked them. He stuffed them into his mouth, again and again, barely swallowing one handful before taking the next. Soon his lips and tongue were the same deep blue as the berries, and a trickle of blue juice ran down his chin.

He looked over at his mother, bent over the stream. As she tugged on the clump of moss she'd chosen, her ample rump jiggled. The sight made him giggle—with amusement, yes, but even more with affection. He knew that well-padded woman . . . and loved her dearly.

She was his whole world, really. His father, whom Ma called "that vagabond," rarely came home. And when he did, he smelled like the drinking flask he always carried on his belt. Whatever it was didn't smell like any of Ma's healing ingredients that filled the shelves and hung from the rafters of their hut. No, it was more like rotting dandelions at the end of summer—a smell both repulsive and strangely alluring.

"There!" cried Ma, sounding elated. With one last tug, she pulled free the silver moss.

Deftly, she set the moss on a flat slab of wood and started chopping it into tiny flakes. "Come see this, Gru. You'll like what happens next."

Heeding her call, Grukarr waddled as fast as he could to her side, still holding a few berries in his hand. He arrived just in time to see the freshly chopped flakes start to rise up off the cutting board. Like small silver stars, they lifted into the air, glittering and sparkling.

His mouth fell open. He dropped the blueberries, which fell on the cutting board. "Ma . . . that's *magicful.*"

"Indeed it is, my love." She pulled a large bowl from her sack and, holding it upside down over the rising flakes, managed to catch all but a few of them. The ones she missed kept floating skyward, sparkling as they climbed toward the clouds.

Meanwhile, Ma carefully set the bowl facedown on the grass. It trembled from the power of all those flakes that wanted to fly. As they watched the trembling bowl, she placed her hand on her son's chubby neck and stroked his curls. "'Tis the same lovely magic as fills this whole forest," she explained. "Never you forget that."

"I won't, Ma."

Just then, the bowl shook violently—and started rising off the ground!

"More magicful!" he cried, thoroughly entranced.

"Yes, indeed!" She clamped both hands on the bowl and forced it back down to the ground. For good measure, she sat herself right on top of it. For a long moment, she and Grukarr waited in silence, unsure whether she, too, would be carried upward by the moss's powerful magic. But her weight was enough to hold it down.

Finally, she flashed her son a smile. "This is a powerful lot, indeed! It'll make a strong batch of my special potion to spur lovers' desire." Chortling to herself, she whispered, "Maybe I'll slip a little into that handsome woodcutter's ale next time he stops by."

Suddenly her smile vanished. "Blubbering bladders! With all the excitement, I almost forgot the prayer." She shook her head. "But for that I need to kneel—and I don't dare get off this bowl."

"I'll do it, Ma! Let me help."

She hesitated, then said, "All right, my dearest. The voice of an innocent child should mean just as much—or more—to the spirits. Just kneel down on the grass and say what I say."

He flopped down on the meadow—so eagerly that one of his feet smashed the berries on the board. Trying his best to get low to the ground, he stretched out his hands as far as they could. "Ready, Ma," he called, his voice muffled by the grass.

She closed her eyes, concentrating her thoughts. "Thank you, great immortal spirits."

In his small child's voice, made even smaller by the grass, he repeated those words.

"For all the blessings you bring to this forest, your home and ours. . . ."

Obediently he repeated.

"We are grateful with all our life and all our love."

Grukarr did his best to recite. But one mischievous blade of grass tickled his nose, making it very hard to concentrate. As soon as he said the word "love," he sneezed.

He raised his head. "Sorry, Ma! My nose was just too ticklyish."

She burst out laughing. "It's all right, my love."

"Are you sure I didn't spoil the prayer?"

"I'm sure. Why, the spirits themselves have to sneeze sometimes."

He, too, started laughing. She opened her arms wide and he ran to her, burying his blueberry-smeared face in her apron. She hugged him warmly.

"You're a good prayer-giver, my son. There's nothing you need to worry about. Nothing at all."

She stroked his curls—then suddenly stopped with a gasp. He pulled free to see what was wrong. Following her gaze, he saw that the smashed berries on the cutting board made the unmistakable shape of a bird. Yes—a dark bird in flight.

"'Tis a sign," Ma said quietly. "For good or ill, I cannot tell. But it is most certainly a sign."

The years passed, each one much like the last. Grukarr grew taller and stronger. By the age of nine, he could venture into the forest alone to find ingredients for his mother. While he still enjoyed gathering his favorite berries, he now preferred hunting for game with his oaken spear and clever traps.

Sometimes, on his hunts, he forgot to say the required prayer of thanks. But nothing bad happened . . . so he figured it really wasn't necessary after all. He simply stopped doing prayers.

Ever devoted to Ma, he never left her for long. And whenever he returned to the hut, she always gave him a warm welcome (along with a steaming mug of hot apple cider or mushroom soup). The seasons turned, and very little disturbed their daily rhythms.

Apart from his father's sporadic visits to the hut, and the few tradesmen and forest dwellers who came by for help now and then, Grukarr and his mother lived undisturbed. Which was just how he liked it. Sure, he watched with keen interest as she bandaged someone's broken arm, made a fresh poultice for a deep gash, or concocted a potion to banish nightmares. But he always nodded gladly when the door closed behind their visitor. For he had Ma all to himself again.

Sometimes, after a day's outing, Grukarr brought home magical creatures—not to eat but to keep. He captured a pair of color-shifting pigeons, amazed by their constantly changing feathers. Plus a weasel whose claws could freeze water so it could walk across streams even in summer. And a three-tongued toad who could imitate human voices well enough to speak in full sentences.

Alas, Ma never let him keep those creatures for long. And not just because the toad kept talking back to her.

Rather, she knew they belonged in the Great Forest, the source of their wondrous magic. And she knew, as well, that the immortal spirits who lived in the forest and guarded its residents wouldn't take kindly to such behavior. So she commanded her son to set them free.

Grukarr protested loudly. After all, the birds were fun to watch, the weasel's talent was useful for making cold drinks, and the toad scared away overly talkative visitors. Sure, he'd seen some equally magical beings when he and Ma made their annual trip to the city for supplies—creatures caught in the forest and brought to the market for sale. But these creatures he'd collected were different—most of all because they were *his*.

In the end, though, he obeyed his mother's wishes and set them free. But he still couldn't resist capturing more creatures. To avoid Ma's disapproval, he would sometimes hide them in a secret cage in the forest he'd built for just this purpose. There was something about controlling those beasts—something immensely appealing—that he just couldn't resist.

Strangely, after he built the cage, he started to notice a subtle difference in the forest. It could have been just his imagination, but it seemed that sometimes tree branches creaked when he passed beneath them, even when he couldn't feel any wind. Or as he walked, twigs on the ground seemed to snap a bit more loudly than before. More than once, these mishaps startled his prey in time to avoid capture.

Still, Grukarr hardly noticed. After all, random things happened all the time in the forest. Nor did any of this deter him from hunting creatures. If anything, such challenges made the task more enjoyable—and success more sweet.

Then one day he made a new discovery. The most wondrous one he'd ever found.

It was a chilly day near winter's end, with snow still visible among the roots of the trees. Grukarr felt glad for the warm coat and scarf Ma had made for him. All that morning, he'd been pursuing a hare. It was just the right size for Ma's biggest cooking pot . . . and would be just the right taste after several weeks of eating only dried vegetables and roots.

But the canny little beast had eluded him. Bounding speedily through groves of spruce, elm, and acacia, the hare led him on a climb up a steep, rocky hillside. Finally, the creature darted into a cave.

"Good," muttered Grukarr as he stood outside the entrance. He hefted his spear in one hand and his net made from woven rushes in the other. "No escape for you now, master hare."

Cautiously, he entered the cave. He paused after a few steps to allow his eyes to adjust. Yet this cave, somehow, didn't seem all that dark. More like the dim, shadowy time just after sunset.

Just then he noticed a faint yellow glimmer farther down the tunnel. What could it be? A shaft of sunlight through a hole in the rocks? Some sort of creature that had made its home here?

Deeper into the tunnel he walked, spear at the ready. With each step, his boots crunched on pebbles and scattered debris, echoing inside the walls. At last, he rounded a bend—and discovered the source of light.

A crystal embedded in the rock! It glowed with magical fire.

Whooosh. Something raced past his feet, bounding out of the cave. The hare!

But now Grukarr didn't care. He was totally entranced by the glowing yellow crystal.

Slowly, he stepped closer. He stood before the luminous object, captivated by its lustrous beauty. With the butt of his spear, he struck the rock at the crystal's base, hoping to dislodge it. To his surprise, the crystal broke free easily and tumbled to the cave floor.

Retrieving it, he held it carefully in his hands. Every facet glowed with mysterious fire. Yellow rays flooded his palms, shooting beams between his fingers.

"It's almost . . ." he said in amazement, "like holding the sun."

With great care, he wrapped it in his scarf. This would be

something Ma would be delighted to see! And something she'd surely allow him to keep.

He practically pranced home. Every once in a while, he'd stop just to unwrap the crystal and gaze into its fiery facets. Even in full daylight, the yellow beams burst out, wavering across his face.

When he reached the hut, he stowed his spear and net, then hung his coat on the peg. Ma was sitting by the fire, roasting some nuts that she used in a remedy for coughs. Seeing him, she brightened instantly and stood to give him a hug.

"My love!" she exclaimed, and opened her arms wide. "You're home."

"Yes, Ma. And I've brought you something."

A shadow crossed her face. "Not another creature?"

"No, no. Something better."

Eagerly, he unwrapped the crystal and threw the scarf aside. Yellow light poured out of the facets, filling the hut. Grukarr beamed with pride.

Ma gasped—not in astonishment, but in fright. She backed away toward her cabinet of healing ingredients.

"But Ma! It's just a crystal."

"Throw it outside!" she screamed. "It's a—"

Suddenly the crystal sprouted jagged black wings and flew out of his hands—straight at his face. Grukarr shrieked and batted the air wildly. His hand struck the winged beast and knocked it away. Right into Ma's eye!

She fell backward into the cabinet, toppling the shelves and smashing containers. Jars, bowls, and bags full of powders and oils exploded everywhere.

Frozen with shock, Grukarr couldn't move. Yet he saw, with utter clarity, as the beast—which now looked like some sort of poisonous beetle with a dozen crooked legs—started to crawl up his mother's neck.

"No!" he cried, lunging at it.

Too late! The beast climbed up her jaw, onto her chin—then plunged right into her mouth.

Ma gagged, trying to scream. Almost instantly, the color drained from her face. Grukarr rushed to her side and reached inside her mouth, grasping at the evil being. All he got for his efforts was a sharp sting on his fingertip—painful, but not nearly as painful as watching his mother writhe in agony.

Helplessly, he glared at the bulge that now formed in her throat . . . then slithered down into her chest. She moaned with fear, rage, and absolute anguish—a sound he could never, through all his years, forget.

"Ma," he cried, cradling her head. "Ma, I'm sorry! So sorry!"

She peered up at him. Despite everything, she still looked at him lovingly. "My son . . ." she said hoarsely, "you didn't know."

A wave of pain crashed through her, making her shriek and arch her back. "'Tis a skretzno—a crystal shape-shifter. Deadly, always deadly . . . unless . . ."

She grew suddenly paler. Flailing, she wrapped her arms around her chest and wailed.

"*Unless what?*" Fighting back tears, he pressed his gaze into hers. "Ma, tell me! Is there some way to kill this thing? To save you?"

She swallowed painfully. "Y-yes. Tincture of . . . arsenic. Bu-but, my son . . . I don't have it here. Too rare! Maybe—"

Arching her back again, she moaned piteously. The sound hung in the rafters as well as Grukarr's mind. She closed her eyes.

"Maybe what, Ma?" He shook her hard. "Tell me!"

Her eyes fluttered open. "In the city . . . apothecary."

She writhed again, gasped, then fell still.

Grukarr set her head down gently, then dashed out the door. He didn't think to grab his coat or even his mother's purse of coins. With all his strength, he raced to the City of Great Powers.

Six hours later, Grukarr stumbled toward the city gates. Panting hoarsely, his tunic torn by branches and thorns, he looked more like an ancient vagabond than a young man.

The day's last golden light shone on the copper bell tower of the Divine Monk's great temple; a young herder urged his rambunctious goats toward the market square. But Grukarr saw none of that. All he could see was the memory of his mother's agony—agony that he himself had caused.

She gave me life, he silently scolded himself. *She fed me, bathed me, clothed me, held me, taught me . . .*

He ground his teeth. *And what did I give her in thanks*?

Staggering up to the gate keeper, an old fellow with a ragged gray beard and a weather-beaten wool cap, Grukarr managed to say a single word: "Apothecary."

"Go away," grumbled the old fellow. "We've enough beggars here already."

Grukarr grabbed him by the collar and thrust him up against the city's massive oaken gate. "Where," he demanded, "is the apothecary?"

With a gulp, the gate keeper saw the unmistakable desperation in this stranger's eyes. "Er, well . . . down that street. Past the market."

Before the gate keeper even finished, Grukarr hurried off.

He ran down the street, boots clomping on the cobblestones, dodging people constantly. Into the wide market square he burst—and almost crashed into a cart loaded with persimmon fruit. He kept running, swerving past the stalls of wood carvers, rug makers, incense suppliers, tool makers, food merchants, and artisans displaying their handmade jewelry, paintings, and pottery.

Even at day's end, the market thrummed with activity . . . as well as noise. The chimes of the great temple bell were nearly drowned out by hammering blacksmiths, squabbling people, bleating goats, belching camels, and crying babies. Some women arranged in a circle were playing bone flutes and seven-stringed harps. And, as they did everywhere in the city, monks chanted and beat on their blessing drums.

Oblivious to all this, Grukarr pressed on. When a large wagon loaded with crates of pink flamingos blocked his way, he rolled under it and kept running. And when an old monk offered him a wreath of leaves painted with prayers, he just shoved the man aside.

Finally, he reached the far side of the square. He dashed down the widest street, desperately looking at every storefront. He saw a jeweler, a metal worker, and a maker of paper in sheets and scrolls. But no apothecary.

Stumbling from exhaustion, he rounded a bend in the street. Suddenly, on a small, handpainted sign above one door, he saw what he'd been searching for:

BINGLA'S APOTHECARY
Cures for Every Ailment

Throwing open the latch, he slammed his shoulder into the door. It opened onto a steep staircase leading up to the second floor. From somewhere above, he heard a voice humming.

Though his legs ached, he ran up the stairs as fast as he could. At the top, he found himself facing hundreds of shelves crammed with bottles and jars of every size and color, loose bundles of herbs, and numerous bags—all carefully marked with paper labels. Amidst the shelves stood a thin man with a face as sharp as an ax blade. On his head he wore a light-blue turban, the mark of an apothecary.

Ceasing his humming, the apothecary turned around. He peered at this visitor—a wild-eyed boy dressed in rags. "You need help, that's clear."

"Not me," answered Grukarr, panting heavily. "My mother."

"What is it? Infected wound? Fever? The blood sickness?"

Grukarr shook his head. "No. She was attacked."

"By what?"

"By . . . a *skretzno*."

Hearing the word, the apothecary winced. He leaned closer, putting his sharp nose near the boy's. "Are you sure?"

Grukarr nodded.

"How long ago?"

"Hours—half a day."

Somberly, the thin man shook his head. "Then she's gone. Or soon will be."

Grukarr groaned and stepped backward.

"Even if I gave you the cure . . ." The apothecary's eyes darted up to a high shelf near the glass skylight that served as his only window. "Even if I did, she'd be dead by the time you got back to her."

"But—" protested Grukarr. "I must try! Whatever it takes!"

The apothecary shrugged his thin shoulders. "If you insist, boy. But this medicine is very hard to come by—and very expensive."

Grukarr caught his breath, realizing he had no money. "I can pay you back in time. That I promise!"

The man's eyes narrowed. "You mean you came here with no money? You expect me to give you *anything* without payment?"

"But I told you," pleaded Grukarr, nearly tripping over a pile of bound roots as he moved closer, "I will pay you."

Scowling, the apothecary waved his hand. "You're wasting my time, boy."

"But I told you! She's *dying*."

"Get out of here. Now!"

"I won't go without the cure."

"Go away, I said!"

Grukarr lunged at him. But the apothecary spun out of reach

and drew a curved blade from his tunic. It flashed ominously, like the smile of Death itself.

Glaring at Grukarr, the man said, "Go. Or your mother won't be the only one to die today."

Defeated, Grukarr slowly turned away. He slunk down the stairs, his shoulders hunched, feeling so much rage and guilt he was about to explode. He was totally powerless to get the medicine Ma so badly needed!

When he reached the bottom step and turned back for a last glance, he saw the fading light of the end of day, glowing through the skylight at the top of the stairs. And that gave him an idea.

He closed the door behind him, then crossed the street. Not far away he spotted an alley between two mudbrick buildings that faced the apothecary shop. Slipping into the alley, he was swallowed by shadows.

For over an hour he waited . . . though it felt more like a century. How long, he fretted, can Ma hold on? The sky grew darker, and the temple bell chimed several more times. Sounds from the market square diminished, until he heard only the occasional bleat of a goat or squeak of cartwheels.

All the while, he didn't move. When a fly landed on his nose, he didn't brush it off, fearing he might be seen. Even the strange ache he felt in his right hand didn't cause him to stir.

Finally, the shop door opened. The apothecary stepped out, his sharp face peering up and down the street for any sign of that troublesome boy.

Seeing none, he locked the door, adjusted his blue turban, and hurried away down the cobblestones.

Grukarr waited until he felt sure the man had gone. Then he darted across the street, straight to a spindly drainpipe that climbed up the side of the building. Grasping it with both hands, he hoisted himself up and started to climb.

As he neared the roof of the building, the drainpipe suddenly buckled. It was starting to pull away from the wall! Quickly, he worked his way higher, knowing that if he fell, he'd smash into the cobblestones below—and even if he survived the fall, he'd have no other way to get up to the roof.

Just as he reached the top, the drainpipe broke away completely. Grukarr leaped onto the building wall, grasping the edge of the roof with one hand. Below him, the drainpipe slammed into the cobblestones. For an endless moment, he hung there, dangling high above the darkened street.

Desperately, he swung his other hand onto the edge. His fingers barely caught hold. Using all his strength, he pulled himself upward, wriggling higher, until . . .

There! He clambered onto the roof.

Lying on his back on the flat slabs of slate, his lungs heaving, Grukarr knew he had nearly died. But he hadn't—and now he had more work to do. Turning over, he crawled to the skylight.

One kick of his boot shattered the glass, which rained down on the apothecary's shelves. Careful to avoid the jagged pieces around the skylight's rim, he slid himself into the hole feet first. He stretched his legs down to a wooden table. Planting one boot on the table's corner, he lowered himself until the table supported his weight.

Craaash!

The table gave way. Grukarr fell into a wall of shelves, breaking dozens of bottles and covering himself with powders and liquids. Much worse, though, was his right knee. Twisted badly in the fall, it started to ache painfully. He forced himself to stand, but the knee seemed to scream whenever he put weight on it.

Only then did he notice his right hand. It was swollen—badly swollen. And it throbbed like it had been struck with a hammer. Had he hurt it in the fall?

Forcing himself to walk over to the row of shelves where the apothecary had glanced, he peered up at the bottles and jars. Squinting in the dim light, he tried to read the labels. Barely, he discerned the letters "Ars" on one bottle atop the highest shelf. The medicine!

He grabbed a broom that was leaning against the wall. Reaching as high as he could, he tapped the bottle. It tilted, wavering, then began to fall—not toward him, but backward on the shelf.

Grukarr watched helplessly as the bottle slowly tipped over backward. He roared in frustration, sure that now he'd never be able to get it down.

Just then the bottle's cork top struck something behind it. That slight contact made the bottle bounce forward. It teetered on the edge of the shelf . . . and dropped over. Stretching out his good hand, Grukarr caught the bottle before it hit the floor.

Eagerly, he read the label. *Tincture of Arsenic.*

Despite his injured knee and swollen hand, he felt a surge of hope. *I can still save you, Ma*, he called in his mind. *I'm coming!*

He stuffed the bottle into his pocket. Then he took a step toward the stairs. But his knee exploded with pain!

All at once, he realized the truth. He had another long journey ahead—and only one leg that could hold his weight. Grim reality demolished that moment of hope, leaving him aching in body and soul.

Wincing, he made himself move. He hobbled down the stairs, staggered into the street, and limped off. Seconds later, he disappeared into the darkness.

As the first rosy rays of dawn touched the top of the hut, Grukarr crawled slowly toward the doorstep.

All through the night he had limped, stumbled, and finally dragged his broken body through the forest. Sometimes he'd seen golden eyes peering at him through the gloom. More often, though, he'd seen his mother's face, twisted in anguish—and that vision drove him onward.

It took all his strength just to push the door open. His injured knee could hardly bend—and only with extreme pain. The swelling in his right hand had spread into his wrist and then up his arm. The whole arm now dangled useless at his side, like a dead branch still clinging to the tree.

On top of all that, he'd started to tremble with fever. His head throbbed as if a horde of drummers were beating on his brain; his whole body dripped with sweat. And he ached all over—a bone-deep ache that he'd never felt before.

This miserable fever puzzled him. Had he simply stressed his body so much that he'd fallen ill? Did he accidently swallow something poisonous when he crashed into the apothecary's shelves? Or . . .

In a flash, it hit him. *The skretzno.* When it stung his fingertip, it must have given him some of its venom. The same venom that was destroying Ma!

He forced himself to crawl into the hut. Every movement sent waves of pain coursing through his body, and the fever made his mind spin. Yet he struggled onward, bit by bit.

From the doorway, he could see that she lay just where he'd left her, flat on her back, surrounded by the wreckage of her ingredients. But he wasn't close enough yet to tell whether she was still breathing.

"Ma!" he called weakly as he drew nearer. "Ma . . . I'm here."

She didn't respond. Even before he reached her side, he could see that she'd lost almost all the color of her skin. Her cheeks, normally so ruddy, looked as pale as parchment. Worse yet, her whole face was contorted, warped with suffering.

Suffering I caused, he told himself, feeling a pain deeper than anything else.

Finally, he reached her. Placing his ear over her mouth, he listened.

No breath.

"Ma!" He raised himself on his elbow and shook her. "Ma, don't go. . . ."

Still no breath.

He checked for her heartbeat, for any sign of life. But he found none.

Dead.

Grukarr collapsed beside her, his head on her shoulder. And he wept. Tears of loss, guilt, and failure dampened the lifeless form that had once been his mother.

In time, he raised his head. Bitterly, he decided, *Since she has died, so will I.* He rolled over on his back beside the corpse, ready for his own life to end, no matter how long he had to wait. It might take days—but he'd never stir from this spot.

His brow furrowed. That really wasn't the right punishment for what he'd done. No, that was far too easy!

"I want to *suffer*," he told himself. "Just as I deserve! To live in torment for the rest of my days."

Reaching into his pocket, he pulled out the bottle he'd stolen from the apothecary. Nothing on its label told him whether to swallow it or pour it on his hand where he'd been stung. So he chose to do both. With his teeth, he pulled out the cork, then took a swallow.

The liquid scalded his tongue, burning his mouth and throat. Suddenly a new, sharp pain blazed through his entire body. His head started pounding more than ever. His vision darkened; everything spun.

No, he realized, regretting his choice. *I did this wrong . . . like everything else!*

With his last remaining strength, he forced his wobbly hand to pour what remained in the bottle over the hand that had been stung. Then he fell back, slamming his head against the floor. All went dark.

Two days later, Grukarr awoke. At first he wasn't sure where he was—but as soon as he opened his eyes and saw his mother's lifeless body, with so much agony written on her face, the terrible truth came crashing back.

Ma was dead—thanks to his colossal stupidity.

Thirsty, he realized, rubbing his throat. Only then did he notice that he was using his injured hand. The swelling had receded so much that he could use his fingers, while his arm's mobility had returned. And his fever had vanished!

Astonished, he sat up. Though his knee still throbbed and the rest of his body felt beaten and sore, he was clearly alive. Clumsily, he stood up and staggered over to Ma's barrel of fresh water. He drank greedily.

Finally, he took a last swallow and sat on the floor, leaning back against the barrel. Looking grimly at his mother's body, he knew that the first thing he needed to do was to bury her.

Suddenly he caught his breath. That evil beast, the skretzno, might still be inside her! Even now, it could be feeding on her organs. He couldn't let that happen!

Right away, he knew what he needed to do. *Cremation*. Stepping outside the hut, he quickly gathered a pile of broken branches and a few fallen trunks that he could drag over. After carefully placing Ma's body atop the pile, he gave her one last kiss on the cheek.

Then, using her well-worn flint, he started a fire. The wood caught right away and burned avidly, swelling into an inferno. Soon Ma's corpse was engulfed by flames.

Hard though it was, Grukarr made himself watch, absorbing every wrenching detail. Never, never would he forget this! He would always be haunted by the rancid smell of her burning flesh, the sight of her hair catching fire, the sound of her sinews and bones crackling as they oozed blood and marrow.

At last, as the fire faded, he whispered a single sentence. "Goodbye, Ma."

When the heat had died down enough that he could inspect her remains, he used an iron rod from the hut to search for any sign of the skretzno. To his relief, he found nothing—no yellow crystal, no winged beast. He sighed, knowing the deadly shapeshifter had left his mother for good.

What he didn't notice was one jagged black coal that had tumbled to the base of the inferno. Slowly, without any sound, it started crawling out of the funeral pyre back into the forest.

Meanwhile, Grukarr dug a pit and buried what was left of the body. After replacing the soil, he covered everything with a mound of rocks—except for one place right at the top, which he left open. In that spot, he planted something he'd taken from a nearby meadow.

A blueberry bush.

For the rest of that day, he knelt beside the grave. Ignoring his throbbing knee, he spent those hours composing the chant that he would recite every single day for the rest of his life.

Never again will I know her touch, her voice, her love.
Never again will I be powerless.
Never again will I be at the mercy of others.
Never again will I care about someone else.
Never again will I lack control.
Never again will I know her touch, her voice, her love.

As the sun finally set, casting a golden glow on the bush atop the grave, a scholarly monk named Bonlo came out of the forest. He'd seen a tower of smoke rising from this spot and had come to investigate.

The battered, morose boy he found kneeling beside this newly made grave didn't even turn to acknowledge Bonlo. Instead, the boy just continued to stare into the distance, chanting something under his breath.

Always kindhearted, the monk decided immediately to help this lad. To get him food, clothes, and a splint for that swollen knee. And maybe someday to welcome him into the community of monks. Grukarr accepted the help, but not with any gladness.

For while he knew that he would live . . . he also knew that life itself would be his punishment.